Praise for Mary Kubica and *When the Lights Go Out*

"Mary Kubica knows how to do thrillers. [*When the Lights Go Out* is] a mystery that'll keep you turning pages." —*theSkimm*

"Kubica brilliantly unravels the lives of two women in this tense and haunting tale of identity and deceit. [This novel] will keep you questioning everything—and everyone—until the riveting conclusion. A twisty, captivating, edge-of-your-seat read."
—Megan Miranda, *New York Times* bestselling author of *All the Missing Girls*

"Kubica is a helluva storyteller." —*Kirkus Reviews*

"Will keep readers riveted… The ending brings a stunning ironic twist… This intensely moving novel about identity and deceit is strongly recommended." —*Booklist*

"Creepy and oh so clever with a brilliant twist that I did not see coming! Best read with the lights on."
—Alice Feeney, internationally bestselling author of *Sometimes I Lie*

"As fact collided with fiction in Jessie's world, I was on the edge of my seat in real time trying to work out the truth…. And with an ending I never saw coming, I can truly say this book had my adrenaline going and energized me!" —*First for Women*

T0040330

Also by Mary Kubica

The Good Girl
Pretty Baby
Don't You Cry
Every Last Lie
The Other Mrs.
Local Woman Missing

MARY KUBICA

WHEN THE LIGHTS GO OUT

PARK ROW BOOKS

If you purchased this book without a cover you should be aware that this book is stolen property. It was reported as "unsold and destroyed" to the publisher, and neither the author nor the publisher has received any payment for this "stripped book."

PARK
ROW
BOOKS™

Recycling programs
for this product may
not exist in your area.

ISBN-13: 978-0-7783-0775-4

When the Lights Go Out

First published in 2018. This edition published in 2022.

Copyright © 2018 by Mary Kyrychenko

All rights reserved. No part of this book may be used or reproduced in any manner whatsoever without written permission except in the case of brief quotations embodied in critical articles and reviews.

This is a work of fiction. Names, characters, places and incidents are either the product of the author's imagination or are used fictitiously. Any resemblance to actual persons, living or dead, businesses, companies, events or locales is entirely coincidental.

Park Row Books
22 Adelaide St. West, 41st Floor
Toronto, Ontario M5H 4E3, Canada
ParkRowBooks.com
BookClubbish.com

Printed in U.S.A.

For
Dick & Eloise
Rudy & Myrtle

WHEN THE LIGHTS GO OUT

The mind is its own place,
and in itself can make
a heaven of hell,
a hell of heaven.

—John Milton, *Paradise Lost*

prologue

THE CITY SURROUNDS ME. A panorama. With arms outstretched, I can't help but spin, taking it all in. Enjoying the view, knowing fully well this may be the last thing my eyes ever see.

I stare at the four metal steps before me, aware of how frail and broken-down they look. They're orange with rust, paint flaking, some of the slats loose so that when I press my foot to the first step, it buckles beneath me and I fall.

Still, I have no choice but to climb.

I pull myself back up, set my hands on the rails and scale the steps. The sweat bleeds from my palms so that the metal beneath them is slippery, slick. I can't hold tight. I slip from the second step, try again. I call out, voice cracking, a voice that doesn't sound like mine.

As I reach the roof's ledge, my knees give. It takes everything I have not to topple over the edge of the building and onto the street below. Seventeen floors.

I'm so high I could touch the clouds, I think. The sense of

vertigo is overpowering. The ground whooshes up and at me, the skyscrapers, the trees starting to sway until I no longer know what's moving: them or me. Little yellow matchbooks soar up and down the city streets. Cabs.

If I was standing at street level, the ledge would feel plenty wide. But up here it's not. Up here it's a thread and on it, I'm trying to balance my two wobbly feet.

I'm scared. But I've come this far. I can't go back.

There's a moment of calm that comes and goes so quickly I almost don't notice it. For one split second the world is still. I'm at peace. The sun moves higher and higher into the sky, yellow-orange glaring at me through the buildings, making me peaceful and warm. My hands rise beside me as a bird goes soaring by. As if my hands are wings, I think in that moment what it would be like to fly.

And then it comes rushing back to me.

I'm hopelessly alone. Everything hurts. I can no longer think straight; I can no longer see straight; I can no longer speak. I don't know who I am anymore. If I am anyone.

And I know in that moment for certain: I am no one.

I think what it would feel like to fall. The weightlessness of the plunge, of gravity taking over, of relinquishing control. Giving up, surrendering to the universe.

There's a flicker of movement beneath me. A flash of brown, and I know that if I wait any longer, it will be too late. The decision will no longer be mine. I cry out one more time.

And then I go.

JESSIE

I DON'T HAVE TO see myself to know what I look like.

My eyes are fat and bloated, so bloodshot the sclera is bereft of white. The skin around them is red and raw from rubbing. They've been like this for days. Ever since Mom's body began shutting down, her hands and feet cold, blood no longer circulating there. Since she began to drift in and out of consciousness, refusing to eat. Since she became delirious, speaking of things that aren't real.

Over the last few days, her breathing has changed too, becoming noisier and unstable, developing what the doctor called Cheyne-Stokes respiration where, for many seconds at a time, she didn't breathe. Short, shallow breaths followed by no breaths at all. When she didn't breathe, I didn't breathe. Her nails are blue now, the skin of her arms and legs blotchy and gray. "It's a sign of imminent death," the doctor said only yesterday as he set a firm hand on my shoulder and asked if there was someone they could call, someone who could come sit with me until she passed.

"It won't be long now," he'd said.

I had shaken my head, refusing to cry. It wasn't like me to cry. I've sat in the same armchair for nearly a week now, in the same rumpled clothes, leaving only to collect coffee from the hospital cafeteria. "There's no one," I said to the doctor. "It's only Mom and me."

Only Mom and me as it's always been. If I have a father somewhere out there in the world, I don't know a thing about him. Mom didn't want me to know anything about him.

And now this evening, Mom's doctor stands before me again, taking in my bloated eyes, staring at me in concern. This time offering up a pill. He tells me to take it, to go lie down in the empty bed beside Mom's and sleep.

"When's the last time you've slept, Jessie?" he asks, standing there in his starch white smock, tacking on, "I mean, really *slept*," before I can lie. Before I can claim that I slept last night. Because I did, for a whole thirty minutes, at best.

He tells me the longest anyone has gone without sleep. He tells me that people can die without sleep. He says to me, "Sleep deprivation is a serious matter. You need to sleep," though he's not my doctor but Mom's. I don't know why he cares.

But for whatever reason, he goes on to list for me the consequences of not sleeping. Emotional instability. Crying and laughing for no sound reason at all. Behaving erratically. Losing concept of time. Seeing things. Hallucinating. Losing the ability to speak.

And then there are the physical effects of insomnia: heart attack, hypothermia, stroke.

"Sleeping pills don't work for me," I tell him, but he shakes his head, tells me that it's not a sleeping pill. Rather a tranquilizer of some sort, used for anxiety and seizures. "It has a sedative effect," he says. "Calming. It will help you sleep without all the ugly side effects of a sleeping pill."

But I don't need to sleep. What I need instead is to stay awake, to be with Mom until she makes the decision to leave.

I push myself from my chair, strut past the doctor standing in the doorway. "Jessie," he says, a hand falling gently to my arm to try and stop me before I can go. His smile is fake.

"I don't need a pill," I tell him briskly, plucking my arm away. My eyes catch sight of the nurse standing in the hallway beside the nurses' station, her eyes conveying only one thing: pity. "What I need is coffee," I say, not meeting her eye as I slog down the hallway, feet heavy with fatigue.

There's a guy I see in the cafeteria every now and then, a little bit like me. A weak frame lost inside crumpled-up clothes; tired, red eyes but doped up on caffeine. Like me, he's twitchy. On edge. He has a square face; dark, shaggy hair; and thick eyebrows that are sometimes hidden behind a pair of sunglasses so that the rest of us can't see he's been crying. He sits in the cafeteria with his feet perched on a plastic chair, a red sweatshirt hood pulled over his head, sipping his coffee.

I've never talked to him before. I'm not the kind of girl that cute guys talk to.

But tonight, for whatever reason, after I get my cup of coffee, I drop down into the chair beside him, knowing that under any other circumstance, I wouldn't have the nerve to do it. To talk to him. But tonight I do, mostly, I think, to delay going back to Mom's room, to give the doctor his chance to examine her and leave.

"Want to talk about it?" I ask, and at first his look is surprised. Incredulous, even. His gaze rises up from his own coffee cup and he stares at me, his eyes as blue as a blue morpho butterfly's wings.

"The coffee," he says after some time, pushing his cup away. "It tastes like shit," he tells me, as though that's the thing that's bothering him. The only thing. Though I see well enough inside the cup to know that he drank it down to the dregs, so it couldn't have been that bad.

"What's wrong with it?" I ask, sipping from my cup. It's hot and so I peel back the plastic lid and blow on it. Steam rises to greet me as I try again and take another sip. This time, I don't burn my mouth.

There's nothing wrong with the hospital's coffee. It's just the way I like it. Nothing fancy. Just plain old coffee. But still, I dump four packets of Equal in and swirl it around because I don't have a stir stick or spoon.

"It's weak and there are grounds in it," he tells me, giving his abandoned cup the stink eye. "I don't know," he says, shrugging. "Guess I just like my coffee stronger than this."

And yet, he reaches again for the cup before remembering there's nothing left in it.

There's an anger in his demeanor. A sadness. It doesn't have anything to do with the coffee. He just needs something to take his anger out on. I see it in his blue eyes, how he wishes he was somewhere else, anywhere else but here.

I too want to be anywhere else but here.

"My mother's dying," I tell him, looking away because I can't stand to stare into his eyes when I say the words aloud. Instead I gaze toward a window where outside the world has gone black. "She's going to die."

Silence follows. Not an awkward silence, but just silence. He doesn't say he's sorry because he knows, like me, that sorry doesn't mean a thing. Instead, after a minute or two, he says that his brother's been in a motorcycle accident. That a car cut him off and he went flying off the bike, headfirst, into a utility pole.

"There's no saying if he'll make it," he says, talking in euphemisms because it's easier that way than just saying there's a chance he'll die. Kick the bucket. Croak. "Odds are good we'll have to pull the plug sometime soon. The brain damage." He shakes his head, picks at the skin around his fingernails. "It's not looking good," he tells me, and I say, "That sucks," because it does.

I rub at my eyes and he changes topics. "You look tired," he tells me, and I admit that I can't sleep. That I haven't been sleeping. Not for more than thirty minutes at a time, and even that's being generous. "But it's fine," I say, because my lack of sleep is the least of my concerns.

He knows what I'm thinking.

"There's nothing more you can do for your mom," he says. "Now you've got to take care of you. You've got to be ready for what comes next. You ever try melatonin?" he asks, but I shake my head and tell him the same thing I told Mom's doctor.

"Sleeping pills don't work for me."

"It's not a sleeping pill," he says as he reaches into his jeans pocket and pulls out a handful of pills. He slips two tablets into the palm of my hand. "It'll help," he says to me, but any idiot can see that his own eyes are bloodshot and tired. It's obvious this melatonin didn't help him worth shit. But I don't want to be rude. I slip the tablets into the pocket of my own jeans and say thanks.

He stands from the table, chair skidding out from beneath him, and says he'll be right back. I think that it's an excuse and that he's going to take the opportunity to split. "Sure thing," I say, looking the other way as he leaves. Trying not to feel sorry for myself as I'm hit with that sudden sense of being alone. Trying not to think about my future, knowing that when Mom finally dies, I'll be alone forever.

He's gone now and I watch other people in the cafeteria. New grandparents. A group of people sitting at a round table, laughing. Talking about old times, sharing memories. Some sort of hospital technician in blue scrubs eating alone. I reach for my now-empty cup of coffee, thinking that I too should split. Knowing that the doctor is no doubt done with Mom by now, and so I should get back to her.

But then the guy comes back. In his hands are two fresh cups of coffee. He returns to his chair and states the obvious. "Caffeine is the last thing either of us needs," he tells me, saying that it's decaf, and it occurs to me then that this has nothing to do with the coffee, but rather the company.

He digs into his pocket and pulls out four rumpled packets of Equal, dropping them to the table beside my cup. I manage a thanks, flat and mumbled to hide my surprise. He was watching me. He was paying attention. No one ever pays attention to me, aside from Mom.

Beside me he hoists his feet back onto the empty seat across from him, crosses them at the ankles. Drapes the red hood over his head.

I wonder what he'd be doing right now if he wasn't here. If his brother hadn't been in that motorcycle accident. If he wasn't close to dying.

I think that if he had a girlfriend, she'd be here, holding his hand, keeping him company. Wouldn't she?

I tell him things. Things I've never told anyone else. I don't know why. Things about Mom. He doesn't look at me as I talk, but at some imaginary spot on the wall. But I know he's listening.

He tells me things too, about his brother, and for the first time in a while, I think how nice it is to have someone to talk to, or to just share a table with as the conversation in time drifts to quiet and we sit together, drinking our coffees in silence.

Later, after I return to Mom's room, I think about him. The guy from the cafeteria. After the hospital's hallway lights are dimmed and all is quiet—well, mostly quiet save for the ping of the EKG in Mom's room and the rattle of saliva in the back of her throat since she can no longer swallow—I think about him sitting beside his dying brother, also unable to sleep.

In the hospital, Mom sleeps beside me in a drug-induced daze, thanks to the steady drip, drip, drip of lorazepam and morphine into her veins, a solution that keeps her both pain-free and fast asleep at the same time.

Sometime after nine o'clock, the nurse stops by to turn Mom one last time before signing off for the night. She checks her skin for bedsores, running a hand up and down Mom's legs. I've got the TV in the room turned on, anything to drown out that mechanical, metallic sound of Mom's EKG, one that will haunt me for the rest of my life. It's one of those newsmagazine shows—*Dateline*, *60 Minutes*, I don't know which—the one thing that was on when I flipped on the TV. I didn't bother channel surfing; I don't care what I watch. It could be home shopping or cartoons, for all I care. It's just the noise I need to help me forget that Mom is dying. Though, of course, it isn't as easy as that. There isn't a thing in the world that can make me forget. But for a few minutes at least, the news anchors make me feel less alone.

"What are you watching?" the nurse asks, examining Mom's skin, and I say, "I don't even know."

But then we both listen together as the anchors tell the story of some guy who'd assumed the identity of a dead man. He lived for years posing as him, until he got caught.

Leave it to me to watch a show about dead people as a means of forgetting that Mom is dying.

My eyes veer away from the TV and to Mom. I mute the show. Maybe the repetitive ping of the EKG isn't so bad after all. What it says to me is that Mom is still alive. For now.

Ulcers have already formed on her heels and so she lies with feet floating on air, a pillow beneath her calves so they can't touch the bed. "Feeling tired?" the nurse asks, standing in the space between Mom and me. I am, of course, feeling tired. My head hurts, one of those dull headaches that creeps up the nape of the neck. There's a stinging pain behind my eyes too, the kind that makes everything blur. I dig my palms into my sockets to make it go away, but it doesn't quit. My muscles ache, my legs restless. There's the constant urge to move them, to not sit still. It gnaws at me until it's all I can think about: moving my legs. I uncross them, stretch them out before me, recross my legs. For a whole thirty seconds it works. The restlessness stops.

And then it begins again. That prickly urge to move my legs.

If I let it, it'll go on all night until, like last night, when I finally stood and paced the room. All night long. Because it was easier than sitting still.

I think then about what the guy in the cafeteria said. About taking care of myself, about getting ready for what comes next. I think about what comes next, about Mom's and my house, vacant but for me. I wonder if I'll ever sleep again.

"Doc left some clonazepam for you," the nurse says now, as if she knows what I'm thinking. "In case you changed your mind." She says that it could be our little secret, hers and mine. She tells me Mom is in good hands. That I need to take care of myself now, again just like the guy in the cafeteria said.

I relent. If only to make my legs relax. She steps from the room to retrieve the pills. When she returns, I climb onto the empty bed beside Mom and swallow a single clonazepam with a glass of water and sink beneath the covers of the hospital bed. The nurse stays in the room, watching me. She doesn't leave.

"I'm sure you have better things to do than keep me company," I tell her, but she says she doesn't.

"I lost my daughter a long time ago," she says, "and my husband's gone. There's no one at home waiting for me. None other than the cat. If it's all right with you, I'd rather just stay. We can keep each other company, if you don't mind," she says, and I tell her I don't mind.

There's an unearthly quality to her, ghostlike, as if maybe she's one of Mom's friends from her dying delusions, come to visit me. Mom had begun to talk to them the last time she was awake, people in the room who weren't in the room, but who were already dead. It was as if Mom's mind had already crossed over to the other side.

The nurse's smile is kind. Not a pity smile, but authentic. "The waiting is the hardest part," she tells me, and I don't know what she means by it—waiting for the pill to kick in or waiting for Mom to die.

I read something once about something called terminal lucidity. I didn't know if it's real or not, a fact—scientifically proven—or just some superstition a quack thought up. But I'm hoping it's real. Terminal lucidity: a final moment of lucidity before a person dies. A final surge of brainpower and awareness. Where they stir from a coma and speak one last time. Or when an Alzheimer's patient who's so far gone he doesn't know his own wife anymore wakes up suddenly and remembers. People who have been catatonic for decades get up and for a few moments, they're normal. All is good.

Except that it's not.

It doesn't last long, that period of lucidity. Five minutes, maybe more, maybe less. No one knows for sure. It doesn't happen for everyone.

But deep inside I'm hoping for five more lucid moments with Mom.

For her to sit up, for her to speak.

"I'm not tired yet," I confess to the nurse after a few minutes, sure this is a waste of time. I can't sleep. I won't sleep. The restlessness of my legs is persistent, until I have no choice but to dig the melatonin out of my pocket when the nurse turns her back and swallow those too.

The hospital bed is pitted, the blankets abrasive. I'm cold. Beside me, Mom's breathing is dry and uneven, her mouth gaping open like a robin hatchling. Scabs have formed around her lips. She jerks and twitches in her sleep. "What's happening?" I ask the nurse, and she tells me Mom is dreaming.

"Bad dreams?" I ask, worried that nightmares might torment her sleep.

"I can't say for sure," the nurse says. She repositions Mom on her right side, tucking a rolled-up blanket beneath her hip, checking the color of her hands and feet. "No one even knows for sure why we dream," the nurse tells me, adding an extra blanket to my bed in case I catch a draft in my sleep. "Did you know that?" she asks, but I shake my head and tell her no. "Some people think that dreams serve no purpose," she adds, winking. "But I think they do. They're the mind's way of coping, of thinking through a problem. Things we saw, felt, heard. What we're worried about. What we want to achieve. You want to know what I think?" she asks, and without waiting for me to answer, she says, "I think your mom is getting ready to go in that dream of hers. Packing her bags and saying goodbye. Finding her purse and her keys."

I can't remember the last time I'd dreamed.

"It can take up to an hour to kick in," the nurse says, and this time I know she means the medicine.

The nurse catches me staring at Mom. "You can talk to her, you know?" she asks. "She can hear you," she says, but it's awkward then. Talking to Mom while the nurse is in the room. And anyway, I'm not convinced that Mom can really hear me, so I say to the nurse, "I know," but to Mom, I say nothing. I'll say all the things I need to say if we're ever alone. The nurses play Mom's records some of the time because, as they've told me, hearing is the last thing to go. The last of the senses to leave. And because they think it might put her at ease, as if the soulful voice of Gladys Knight & the Pips can penetrate the state of unconsciousness where she's at, and become part of her dreams. The familiar sound of her music, those records I used to hate when I was a kid but now know I'll spend the rest of my life listening to on repeat.

"This must be hard on you," the nurse says, watching me as I stare mournfully at Mom, taking in the shape of her face, her eyes, for what might be the last time. Then she confesses, "I know what it's like to lose someone you love." I don't ask the nurse who, but she tells me anyway, admitting to the little girl she lost nearly two decades ago. Her daughter, only three years old when she died. "We were on vacation," she says. "My husband and me with our little girl." He's her ex-husband now because, as she tells me, their marriage died that day too, same day as their little girl. She tells me how there was nothing Madison loved more than playing in the sand, searching for seashells along the seashore. They'd taken her to the beach that summer. "My last good memories are of the three of us at the beach. I still see her sometimes when I close my eyes. Even after all these years. Bent at the waist in her purple swimsuit, digging fat fingers into the sand for seashells. Funny thing is that I have a hard time remembering her face, but clear as day I see the ruffles of that purple tulle skirt moving in the air."

I don't know what to say. I know I should say something, something empathetic. I should commiserate. But instead I ask, "How did she die?" because I can't help myself. I want to know, and there's a part of me convinced she wants me to ask.

"A hit-and-run," she admits while dropping into an empty armchair in the corner of the room. Same one that I've spent the last few days in. She tells me how the girl wandered into the street when she and her husband weren't paying attention. It was a four-lane road with a speed limit of just twenty-five as it twisted through the small seaside town. The driver rounded a bend at nearly twice that speed, not seeing the little girl before he hit her, before he fled.

"He," she says then. "He." And this time, she laughs, a jaded laugh. "I'll never know one way or the other if the driver was male or female, but to me it's always been *he* because for the life of me I can't see a woman running her car into a child and then fleeing. It goes against our every instinct, to nurture, to protect," she says.

"It's so easy to blame someone else. My husband, the driver of the car. Even Madison herself. But the truth is that it was my fault. I was the one not paying attention. I was the one who let my little girl waddle off into the middle of the street."

And then she shakes her head with the weariness of someone who's replayed the same scene in her life for many years, trying to pinpoint the moment when it all went wrong. When Madison's hand slipped from hers, when she fell from view.

I don't mean for them to, but still, my eyes fill with tears as I picture her little girl in her purple swimsuit, lying in the middle of the road. One minute gathering seashells in the palm of a hand, and the next minute dead. It seems so tragic, so catastrophic, that my own tragedy somehow pales in comparison to hers. Suddenly cancer doesn't seem so bad.

"I'm sorry," I say. "I'm so sorry," but she shoos me off and says no, that she's the one who should be sorry. "I didn't mean to make you sad," she says, seeing my watery eyes. "Just wanted you to know that I can empathize. That I can relate. It's never easy losing someone you love," she says again, and then stands quickly from the armchair, gets back to tending to Mom. She tries to change the subject. "Feeling tired yet?" she asks again, and this time I tell her I don't know. My body feels heavy. That's as much as I knew. But heavy and tired are two different things.

She suggests then, "Why don't I tell you a story while we wait? I tell stories to all my patients to help them sleep."

Mom used to tell me stories. We'd lie together under the covers of my twin-size bed and she'd tell me about her childhood. Her upbringing. Her own mom and dad. But she told it like a fairy tale, like a *once upon a time* kind of story, and it wasn't Mom's story at all, but rather the story of a girl who grew up to marry a prince and become queen.

But then the prince left her. Except she always left that part out. I never knew if he did or if he didn't, or if he was never there to begin with.

"I'm not your patient," I remind the nurse but she says,

"Close enough," while dimming the overhead lights so that I can sleep. She sits down on the edge of my bed, pulling the blanket clear up to my neck with warm, competent hands so that for one second I envy Mom her care.

The nurse's voice is low, her tone flat so she doesn't wake Mom from her deathbed. Her story begins somewhere just outside of Moab, though it doesn't go far.

Almost at once, my eyelids grow heavy; my body becomes numb. My mind fills with fog. I become weightless, sinking into the pitted hospital bed so that I become one with it, the bed and me. The nurse's voice floats away, her words themselves defying gravity and levitating in the air, out of reach but somehow still there, filling my unconscious mind. I close my eyes.

It's there, under the heavy weight of two thermal blankets and at the sound of the woman's hypnotic voice, that I fall asleep. The last thing I remember is hearing about the snarling paths and the sandstone walls of someplace known as the Great Wall.

When I wake up in the morning, Mom is dead.

I slept right through it.

EDEN

May 16, 1996
Egg Harbor

AARON SHOWED ME THE house today. I'm in love with it already—a cornflower blue cottage perched on a forty-five-foot cliff that overlooks the bay. Pine floors and white-washed walls. A screened-in porch. A long wooden staircase that leads down to the dock at the water's edge where the Realtor promised majestic sunsets and fleets of sailboats floating by. *Quaint, charming* and *serene.* Those are the words the Realtor used. Aaron, as always, didn't say much of anything, just stood on the balding lawn with his hands in the pockets of his jeans, staring out at the bay, thinking. He's recently taken a job as a line cook at one of the restaurants in town, a chophouse in Ephraim. The cottage will more than cut his commute time in half. It's also a steal compared to our current mortgage, and set on two acres of waterfront land that spans the heavily wooded backcountry to the rocky shores of Green Bay.

And there's a garden. A ten-by-twenty-or thirty-foot space overrun with brambles and weeds. It's in need of work, but already Aaron has promised raised beds. There is a green-house, a sorry sight if I've ever seen one, set in a sunnier patch of the yard where the grass still grows. Small, shedlike, with aged glass windows and some sort of clear, corrugated roof meant to attract the sun. The door hangs cockeyed, one of its hinges broken. Aaron took a look and said that he can fix it, which comes as no surprise to me. There isn't a thing in this world that Aaron can't fix. Cobwebs cling to the corners of the room like lace. Already I'm imagining rows and rows of peat pots of soil and seed soaking up the sun, waiting to be transported into the garden.

Nearby, a swing hangs from the mighty branch of a burr oak tree. It was the tree that cinched it for me. Or maybe not the tree itself, but the promise of the tree, the notion of children one day causing ruckus and mayhem on the tree's swing, three feet of lumber fastened to the branch with a sturdy rope. I envision them climbing deep into the divots of the tree's trunk and laughing. I can hear them already, Aaron's and my unborn children. Laughing and screaming in delight.

Aaron asked if I loved it as much as him, and I didn't know if he meant whether I loved the cottage as much as I love *him*, or if I loved the cottage as much as he loves the cottage, but either way I told him I did.

Aaron left the Realtor with our bid. It's a buyer's mar-ket, he said, trying to finagle the asking price down a good 10 percent. Me, I would have paid asking price, too afraid to lose the cottage otherwise. Tomorrow we'll know if it's ours.

Tonight I won't sleep. How is it possible to love something so much, to want something so badly, when only hours ago I didn't know it existed?

July 1, 1996
Egg Harbor

The boxes are plentiful. There is no end to the number of cardboard boxes the movers carry through the front door, delivering them to their marked rooms—living room, bedroom, master bath—stomping across our home in dusty work boots. Sixteen hundred square feet of space needing to be filled as Aaron and I divvied up our gender-appropriate tasks, he directing the movers with couches and beds while I unpacked and washed the dishes by hand and placed them in the cabinets. I watched the many laps they took, each man's head beginning to glimmer with sweat. Aaron's too, though he hardly carried a thing, and yet the authority in his voice, the obvious clout as grown men trailed him through our home, heeding his every word, was enough to catch my eye. I watched him round the home time and again, wondering how I was so lucky to have him all to my own.

It wasn't like me to be lucky in love. Not until I met Aaron. The men who came before him were deadbeats and drifters, bottom-feeders. But not Aaron. We dated for a year before he proposed. Tomorrow we celebrate two years. Soon there will be kids, a whole gaggle of little ones spinning circles at our feet. As soon as we're settled, Aaron always said, and now, as my eyes assess the new home, the sprawling landscape, the sixteen hundred square feet of space, three bedrooms—two vacant and left to fill—I realize the time has come and like clockwork, something inside me starts to tick.

When the movers' backs were turned, Aaron kissed me in the kitchen, pinning me against the cabinets, hands gripping my hips. It was unasked for and yet very much wanted as he kissed with his eyes closed, whispering that all of our dreams were finally coming true. Aaron isn't one to be sentimental or romantic, and yet it was true: the cottage, his job, leaving the city. We'd both wanted to get away from Green Bay since the day we were married, his hometown and my hometown, so that two sets of parents couldn't show up at our door on any given day, unsolicited, waging a secret battle as to which in-law could occupy the most of our time. We hadn't gone far, sixty-seven miles to be precise, but enough that visits would be preempted with a simple phone call.

Tonight we made love on the living room floor to the glow of candlelight. The electricity had yet to be turned on and so, other than the dance of candlelight on the whitewashed walls, the house was dark.

Aaron was the first to suggest it, discontinuing my birth control pill, as if he knew what I was thinking, as if he could read my mind. It was as we lay together on the wide wooden floorboards staring out the open windows at the stars, Aaron's prowling hand moving across my thigh, contemplating a second go. That's when he said it. I told him *yes!* that I am ready for a family. That *we* are ready. Aaron is twenty-nine. I am twenty-eight. His paycheck isn't extravagant, and yet it's enough. We aren't spendthrifts; we've been saving for years.

And even though I knew it wasn't possible yet, the pill in my system nipped any possibility of pregnancy in the bud, I still imagined a creature no bigger than a speck starting to take form as Aaron again let himself inside me.

July 9, 1996
Egg Harbor

Our days begin with coffee on the dock, bare feet dangling over the edge, downward toward the bay. The water is cold, and our feet don't reach anyway. But as promised, there are sailboats. Aaron and I spend hours watching them pass by, as well as sandpipers and other shorebirds that come to call, their long legs wading through the shallow water for a meal. We stare at the birds and the sailboats, watching the sun rise higher into the sky, warming our skin, burning off the early-morning fog. Heaven on earth, Aaron says.

As we sit on the dock, Aaron tells me about his nights at the chophouse that steals him from me for ten hours at a time. About the heat of the kitchen, and the persistent noise. The rumble of voices calling out orders in sync. The sputter of boneless rib eye on the grill, the dicing and hashing of vegetables.

His voice is placid. He doesn't complain because Aaron, ever easygoing Aaron, isn't one to complain. Rather he tells me about it, describing it for me so that I can see in my mind's eye what he's doing when he's away from me for half the day. He wears a white chef jacket and black chef pants and a cap, something along the lines of a beanie that is also white. Aaron's been assigned the role of *saucier*, or sauce chef, one that's new to him, but no doubt comes with ease. Because this is the way it is with Aaron. No matter what he tries his hand at, things always come with ease.

Our property is fringed by trees so that as we sit on the deck's edge, Aaron and me, it feels as if we're all alone, partitioned from society by the lake and the trees. If we have neighbors, we've never seen them. Never laid eyes on them. Never spied another home through the canopy of trees. Never are we disturbed by the sound of voices, but only the colloquy of birds as they perch in the trees and yammer back and forth about whatever it is birds talk about. On occasion the helmsmen will wave a hearty hello from behind the steering wheel of their sailboats, but more often than not they're too far away to see Aaron and me at the dock's edge, feet dangling southward, holding hands, sitting in silence, listening to the breeze through the trees.

We're marooned on an island, stranded and shipwrecked, but we don't mind. It's just the way it should be.

Aaron's work shift begins at two in the afternoon and ends when the last customer leaves and the kitchen is clean, most nights stumbling into bed around midnight or after, smelling of sweat and grease.

But the days are ours to do with as we please.

Last week, Aaron repaired the greenhouse door and we stripped it of cobwebs and bugs. We spent days cultivating the garden and Aaron made good on his promise of raised beds, three feet by five feet by ten inches deep, made of white cedar that will one day house cucumbers and zucchini. But not this year. It's far too late in the season to grow produce this year and so for now, we buy it from any number of tatty roadside farm stands. We live two miles from town and even though the population around here expands sevenfold in the summer months thanks to a healthy tourist population, outside town it's still mainly rural, long stretches of open country roads that intersect with nothing but sky.

Instead of planting produce this year, Aaron and I sowed perennial seeds to enjoy next year: baby's breath and lavender and hollyhocks because all the fences and cottages around here, it seems, are flanked with hollyhocks. We placed them in peat pots of gardening soil in the greenhouse and set them in the sunniest spot we could find. In a month or so, we'll transplant them to the garden. They won't bloom for some time, not until next spring. But still, I stand hopeful in the greenhouse, staring at the peat pots, imagining what might be happening beneath the soil's surface, whether the seeds' roots are taking hold, pushing down into the soil to anchor the seedling to this world, or if the seed has merely shriveled up and died in there, a dead embryo in its mother's womb.

As I clear out the last of my birth control pills and run a hand across what I imagine to be my uterus, I wonder what is happening inside there too.

JESSIE

I HAD MOM CREMATED at her request. I carry her around now in a rhubarb-glazed clay urn with a cork in the top, one she bought for herself when the cancer spread. It's cylindrical and inconspicuous, the cork stuck on with an ample amount of Gorilla Glue so I don't lose Mom by chance.

Mom had two wishes when she died, ones she let slip in the last brief moments of consciousness before she drifted off to sleep, a sleep from which she would never wake up. One, that she be cremated and lobbed from the back end of the Washington Island Ferry and into Death's Door. And two, that I find myself and figure out who I am. The second hinged on the esoteric and didn't make obvious sense. I blamed the drugs for it, that and the imminence of death.

I'm nowhere near accomplishing either, though I filled out a college application online. But I have no plans of parting with Mom's remains anytime soon. She's the only thing of value I have left.

I haven't slept in four days, not since some doctor took pity on me and offered me a pill. Three if you count the one where I nearly nodded off at the laundromat waiting for clothes to dry, anesthetized by the sound of sweaters tumbling around a dryer. The effects are obnoxious. I'm tired. I'm grumpy. I can focus on nothing and my reaction time is slow. I've lost the ability to think.

Yesterday, a package arrived from UPS and the driver asked me to sign for it. He stood before me, shoving a pen and a slip of paper up under my nose and I could only stare, unable to put two and two together. He said it again. *Can you sign for it?* He forced the pen into my hand. He pointed at the signature line. For a third time, he asked me to sign.

And even then I scribbled with the cap still on the pen. The man had to snatch it from my hand and uncap it.

I'm pretty sure I've begun to see things too. Things that might not be real, that might not be there. A millipede dashing across the tabletop, an ant on the kitchen floor. Sudden movements, immediate and quick, but the minute I turn, they're gone.

I keep track of the sleepless nights in the notched lines beneath my eyes, like the annual rings of a tree. One wrinkle for each night that I don't sleep. I stare at myself in the mirror each day, counting them all. This morning there were four. The surface effects of insomnia are even worse than what's going on on the inside. My eyes are red and swollen. My eyelids droop. Overnight, wrinkles appear by the masses, while I lie in bed counting sheep. I could go to the clinic and request something else to help me sleep. Some more of the clonazepam. But with the pills in my system, I slept right on through Mom's death. I don't want to think about what else I'd miss.

At McDonald's, I'm asked if I want ketchup with my fries, but I can only stare at the worker dumbly because what I heard was *It's messed up when boats capsize*, and I nod lamely because it is disastrous and sad, and yet so out of left field I can't respond with words.

It's only when he drops a stack of ketchup packets on my tray that my brain makes the translation, too late it seems because I hate ketchup. I dump them on the table when I go, the mother lode for someone who likes it. On the way out the door I trip, because coordination is also affected by a lack of sleep.

Two hours ago I dragged my heavy body from bed after another sleepless night, and now I stand in the center of Mom's and my house, deciding which of our belongings to take and which to leave. I can't stand to stay here much longer, a decision I've come to quickly over the last four days. I've spoken to a Realtor already, figured out next steps. First I'm to pack up what I want to keep, and then everything else will be sold in an estate sale before some junk removal service tosses the rest of our stuff in the trash.

Then some other family will move in to the only home I've ever known.

I'm eyeing the sofa, wondering if I should take it or leave it, when the phone rings. "Hello?" I ask.

A voice on the other end informs me that she's calling from the financial aid office at the college. "There's a problem with your application," she says to me.

"What problem?" I ask the woman on the phone, afraid I'm about to be cited for tax evasion. It's a likely possibility; I'd left blank every question on the FAFSA form that asked about adjusted gross income and tax returns. I might have lied on the application too. There was a question that asked if both of my parents were deceased. I said yes to that, though I don't know if it's true.

Is my father dead?

On the other end of the line, the woman asks me to verify my social security number for her and I do. "That's what I have," she says, and I ask, "Then what's the problem? Has my application been denied?" My heart sinks. How can that be? It's only a community college. It's not like I registered for Yale or Harvard.

"I'm sure it's just a weird mix-up with vital statistics," she says.

"What mix-up?" I ask, feeling relieved for a mix-up as opposed to a denied application. A mix-up can be fixed.

"It's the strangest thing," she says. "There was a death certificate on file for a Jessica Sloane, from seventeen years ago. With your birth date and your social security number. By the looks of this, Ms. Sloane," she says, and I amend *Jessie*, because Ms. Sloane is Mom. "By the looks of this, Jessie," she says, and the words that follow punch me so hard in the gut they make it almost impossible to breathe. "By the looks of this, you're already dead."

And then she laughs as if somehow or other this is funny.

Today I'm looking for a new place to live. Staying in our old home is no longer a viable option because of the residual ghosts of Mom that remain in every corner of the home. The smell of her Crabtree & Evelyn hand cream that fills the bathroom. The feel of the velvet-lined compartments in the mahogany dresser. The chemo caps. The cartons of Ensure on the refrigerator shelf.

I perch in the back seat of a Kia Soul, trying hard not to think too much about the call from the financial aid office. This is easier said than done. Just thinking about it makes my stomach hurt. A mix-up, the woman claimed, but still, it's hard to grapple with the words *you* and *dead* in the same sentence. Though I try to, I can't push them from my mind. The way she and I left things, I'm to provide a copy of my social security card to the college before they'll take another look at my application for a loan, which is a problem because I don't have the first clue where the card is. But it's more than that too. Because the woman also told me about some death index my name was found on. A *death index*. My name on a database maintained by the Social Security Administration of millions of people who have died, nullifying their social security numbers so that no one else can use them, so that I can't use my own social security number. Because, according to the Social Security Administration, I'm dead.

You might want to look into that, she'd suggested before ending our call, and I couldn't help but feel shaken up by it even now, hours later. My name on a death database. Though it's a mistake, of course.

But still I pray this isn't some sort of foresight. A prophecy of what's to come.

I gaze out the window as some woman sits behind the wheel of the Kia, steering us through the streets of Chicago. Her name is Lily and she calls herself an *apartment finder*. The first I'd heard of Lily was days ago, when I'd come home from a cleaning job—hating the feeling of coming home to Mom's and my empty house alone, wishing she was there but knowing she would never be again, making a flip decision to sell the home and leave. I came home, leaving my bike on the sidewalk, and there, hanging on the handle of our front door, was an ad for Lily's efficient and cost-free services. An apartment finder. I'd never heard of such a thing, and yet she was just the thing I needed. The door hanger was in-your-face marketing, the kind I couldn't recycle with the rest of the junk mail. And so I called Lily and we made an appointment to meet.

Lily's parallel parking skills are second to none, though it seems easy enough for someone like me who's never driven a car before. Growing up in an old brick bungalow in Albany Park, there was never a need to drive a car. We didn't have one. The Brown Line or the bus took us everywhere we needed to go. Either that or our own two feet. I also have my Schwinn, Old Faithful, which is surprisingly resilient in even the worst weather, except for, of course, three feet of snow.

I was fifteen when Mom was diagnosed with cancer, which meant that for the time being, my life was on hold, anything that wasn't essential set aside. I went to school. I worked. I helped with the mortgage and saved as much as I could. And I held Mom's hair for her when she puked.

She found the lump herself, slim fingers palpating her own breast because she knew sooner or later this would happen. She didn't tell me about the lump until after she'd been diagnosed with cancer, one mammogram and a biopsy later. She didn't want to worry me. They removed the breast first, followed by months of chemotherapy. But it wasn't long before the cancer returned, in the chest and in the bones this time. The lungs. Back for vengeance.

Jessie, I'm dying. I'm going to die, she had said to me then. We were sitting on the front porch, hand in hand, the day she learned the cancer was back. At that point, her five-year survival rate took a nosedive. She only lived for two more, and none of them great.

The cancer, it's hereditary. Some aberrant gene that runs through our family line, red pegs lined up in my battleship already. Like Mom and her mom before her, it's only a matter of time before I too will sink.

I claimed the back seat of the Kia after Lily dropped her purse into the passenger's chair. She drives with one hand on the horn at all times, so she can scare pedestrians out of the way, those she hollers at from behind safety glass to *shake a leg* and *scoot your boot*. I have no credit history and no bank account, which I've confessed to Lily, and instead carry a pocketful of cash. Her eyes grew wide when I showed her my money, thirty hundred-dollar bills folded in half and stuck inside a wristlet.

"This might be a problem," Lily said, shrugging her shoulders not at the cash but rather the shortage of credit, the absence of a bank account, "but we'll see."

She suggested I offer a landlord more up front to offset the fact that I'm one of those people who keeps all my money in a fireproof safe box beneath my bed. The checks I earn cleaning houses get cashed at Walmart for a three-dollar service fee, and then deposited into my trusty box. I considered signing on with a temp agency once, but thought better of it. There are perks to my job I won't find anywhere else. Because I'm cleaning houses, I don't have to pay taxes to Uncle Sam. I'm an independent contractor. At least that's the way I've always rationalized it in my head, though, for all I know, IRS agents are hot on my heels, planning to nab me for tax evasion.

And still, I load my cleaning supplies into a basket on the back end of Old Faithful each day and pedal off to work, earning as much as two hundred dollars some days by cleaning someone else's home. I do it in peace with my headphones on. I don't have to make small talk. No one supervises me. It's the best job in the world.

"Either that," said Lily as she easily navigated the streets of Chicago, pulling in to an alley behind a high-rise on Sheridan and putting the car in Park, "or you'll need to find someone to cosign on the loan," which isn't an option for me. I have no one to cosign on the loan.

The apartment search is nearly an abject failure.

Lily shows me apartment after apartment. A third-floor unit in a high-rise in Edgewater. A mid-rise on Ashland, newly rehabbed, in my price range though at the high end of it. Unit after unit of boxlike rooms enclosed by four thin gypsum walls, foggy windows that inhibit the light from coming in. The window screens are torn, one stuffed full with an air-conditioning unit, which is supposed to make me happy because, as Lily points out, renters usually have to buy them themselves, those repulsive window units that bar any natural light from entering the room.

The kitchens are tight. The stoves are old and electric. Freckles of mold grow in the showers' grout. The closets smell like urine. Lightbulbs have burned out.

But it isn't the mold or the windows that bother me. It's the noise and the neighbors—strange people just on the other side of drywall, their domestic life partitioned from mine by a paltry combination of plaster and paper. The sense of claustrophobia that settles under my skin as I pretend to listen to Lily as she goes on and on about the two hundred and eighty square feet in the unit. The laundry facilities. The high-speed internet. But all I hear is the noise of someone's hair dryer. Women laughing. Men upstairs screaming at a ball game on TV. A phone conversation streaming through the walls. The ding of a microwave, the smell of someone's lunch.

Four days without sleep. My body is tired, my mind like soup. I lean against the wall, feeling the force of gravity as it threatens to tug my heavy body to the ground.

"What do you think?" Lily asks over the noise of the hair dryer, and I can't help myself.

"I hate it," I say, for the eighth or ninth time in a row, one for as many apartments as we've seen. Insomnia does that too. It keeps us honest because we don't have the energy to manufacture a lie.

"How come?" she asks, and I tell her about the hair dryer next door. How it's loud.

Lily keeps composed, though inside her patience with me must be wearing thin. "Then we keep looking," she says as I follow her out the door. I'd love to believe that she wants me to be happy, that she wants me to find the perfect place to live. But ultimately it comes down to one thing: my signature on a dotted line. What a lease agreement means for Lily is that an afternoon with me isn't a complete waste of time.

"I have one more to show you," she says, promising something different from the last umpteen apartments we've seen. We return to the Kia and I buckle up in the back seat, behind the purse that's already riding shotgun. We drive. Minutes later the car pulls to a sluggish stop before a greystone on Cornelia, gliding easily into a parking spot. The street is residential, lacking completely in communal living structures. No apartments. No condominiums. No high-rises with elevators that overlook crappy convenient marts. No strangers milling around on street corners.

The house is easily a hundred years old, beautiful and yet overwhelming for its grandeur. It's three stories tall and steep, with wide steps that lead to a front porch. A bank of windows lines each floor. There's a flat-as-a-pancake roof. Beneath the first floor there's a garden apartment, peeking up from beneath concrete.

"This is a three flat?" I ask as we step from the car, envisioning stacks of independent units filling the home, all united by a common front door. I expect Lily to say yes.

But instead she laughs at me, saying, "No, this is a private residential home. It's not for sale, not that you could afford it if it was. Easily a million and a half," she says. "Dollars, that is," and I pause beneath a tree to ask what we're doing here. The day is warm, one of those September days that holds autumn at bay. What we want is to climb into sweaters and jeans, sip cocoa, wrap ourselves in blankets and watch the falling leaves. But instead we drip with sweat. The nights grow cold, but the days are hot, thirty-degree variants from morning to night. It won't last long. According to the weatherman, a change is coming, and it's coming soon. But for now, I stand in shorts and a T-shirt, a sweatshirt wrapped around my waist. When the sun goes down, the temperature will too.

"This way," Lily says with a slight nod of the head. I hurry along after her, but before we round the side of the greystone, something catches my eye. A woman walking down the sidewalk in our direction. She's a good thirty feet away, but moving closer to us. I don't see her face at first because of the force of the wind pushing her dark hair forward and into her eyes. But it doesn't matter. It's the posture that does it for me. That and the tiny feet as they shuffle along. It's the unassuming way she holds herself upright, curved at the shoulders just so. It's her shape, the height and width of it. The shade and texture of a periwinkle coat, a parka, midthigh length with a drawstring waist and a hood, though it's much too warm for a coat with a hood.

The coat is the same one as Mom had.

I feel my heart start to beat. My mouth opens and a single word forms there on my lips. *Mom.* Because that's exactly who it is. It's her; it's Mom. She's here, alive, in the flesh, coming to see me. My arm lifts involuntarily and I start to wave, but with the hair in her eyes, she can't see me standing there on the sidewalk six feet away, waving.

Mom doesn't look at me as she passes by. She doesn't see me. She thinks I'm someone else. I call to her, my voice catching as the word comes out, so that it doesn't come out. Instead it gets trapped somewhere in my throat. Tears pool in my eyes and I think that I'm going to lose her, that she's going to keep walking by. And so my hand reaches out and latches on to her arm. A knee-jerk reaction. To stop her from walking past. To prevent her from leaving.

My hand grabs a hold of her forearm, clamping down. But just as it does, the woman frees her face of the hair and casts a glance at me. And I see then what I failed to see before, that this woman is barely thirty years old, much too young to be my mother. And that her face is covered in an enormity of makeup, unlike Mom, who wore her face bare.

Her coat is not periwinkle at all but darker, more like eggplant or wine. And it has no hood. As she nears, I see more clearly. It isn't a coat after all, but a dress.

She looks nothing like Mom.

For a second I feel like I can't breathe, the wind knocked out of me. The woman tugs her arm free. She gives me a dirty look, scooting past me as I slip from the sidewalk, my feet falling on grass.

"I'm sorry," I whisper as she skirts eye contact, avoids my stare. She moves to the far edge of the sidewalk where she'll be two feet away, where I can't reach her. "I thought you were someone else," I breathe as my eyes turn to find Lily with her arms folded, trying to pretend that this didn't just happen.

Of course it's not Mom, I tell myself as I watch the woman in the eggplant dress move on—faster now, no longer shuffling along but now walking at a clipped pace to get away from me.

Of course it's not Mom, because Mom is dead.

"You coming?" Lily asks, and I say yes.

I follow Lily as we sneak along a brick paver patio and into the backyard. My heart still beats hard. My nerves are rattled. The backyard opens up to reveal a patio and a yard, and behind that, a red brick garage with a jade green door. "This is why we're here," says Lily, gesturing to the garage, and I stop where I am and ask, "You want me to live in a garage?"

"It's a carriage house," she says, explaining how there's living space up above, as is apparently evidenced by a window or two on the second and third floors. "These are quite the find. Some people love them. The minute they come on the market, they're usually gone. This listing just came in this morning," she says, telling me how carriage houses used to be just that in the olden days, a place to park a horse and buggy and for the carriage driver to live. Servants' quarters. They're tucked away on an alley, camouflaged behind a far less humble house, living in the shadows of something bigger and better than them.

Which seems to me to be just the thing I need. To be camouflaged, to live hermit-like in seclusion, in the shadows of something grand.

"Can we see?" I ask, meaning the inside, and Lily lets us in through a tall, tapered front door and immediately up a flight of rickety stairs.

It's larger than anything we've yet seen, nearly five hundred square feet of living space that is dilapidated and old, everything painted a hideous brown. The wooden floors have taken a beating. The boards are squeaky and uneven, with square-cut nails that lift right up out of the floorboards to a toe-stubbing height. The kitchen lines a living room wall, if it can even be called a kitchen. An old stove, an old refrigerator and a small bank of cabinets lined in a row beside where a TV should go. The lighting fixtures are archaic, giving off a scant amount of light. The place is minimally furnished; just a couple pieces of furniture that look to be about as decrepit as the home.

The bathroom appears to have had minor renovations. The fixtures, the paint are new, but the floor tile looks to be older than me. "You won't hear a neighbor's hair dryer from here," Lily says. The so-called bedroom is up a second flight of precarious stairs, a loftlike space with an arched ceiling that follows the low roofline.

On the top floor I can't stand upright. I have to hunch.

"This is hardly suitable living space," says Lily, bent at the neck so she doesn't hit her head. Her wedge sandals struggle down the wooden steps, her hand clinging to the banister lest she fall. She doesn't think I will like it, but I do.

Carriage homes like these, Lily says, don't follow the same rules as prescribed in the city's landlord-tenant ordinance. I wouldn't be protected in the same way. They're overlooked when it comes to regular safety inspections. There's only one door, which generally goes against fire codes that require two. Because garbage bins are relegated to the alley that abuts this home, it can be loud. The smell, especially in the summer months, can be sickening, she says.

"Rats are bent on eating from garbage bins, which means..." she begins, but I hold up a hand and stop her there. She doesn't need to tell me. I know exactly what she means.

"What do you think?" Lily asks.

I listen for the sound of women's laughter. For rowdy men screaming at a TV. There are none.

"How do I apply?" I ask.

Lily takes care of the paperwork. The landlord is a woman

by the name of Ms. Geissler, a widow who lives alone in the greystone. We never meet, though Lily provides her with my completed application, a list of references—ladies whose homes I clean—and a letter of recommendation from a former high school guidance counselor. I kiss three grand goodbye, enough to cover first and last months' rent, plus two more for good measure. As they say, money speaks.

At Lily's suggestion, I wait in the car while she goes inside to meet with the landlord. I hold my breath, knowing it's liable the landlord will soon discover the same slipup as the college's financial aid office. That my social security number belongs to a dead girl. And she'll deny my application.

But, to my great relief, she doesn't. It takes less than fifteen minutes for Lily to emerge through the front door of the greystone, a key ring in hand. The keys to the carriage home. I breathe a sigh of relief. As it turns out, Lily let on about my mom and for that reason, Ms. Geissler approved the application without vetting me first. Out of sympathy and pity. Because she felt sorry for me, which is fine by me, so long as I have a place to live. A place that doesn't remind me of Mom.

As we pull away, I stare out the window and toward the imposing home. It's masked in shadows now, the sun slipping down on the opposite side of the street, burying the greystone in shade. The house is dignified but solemn. Sad. The house itself is sad.

From the third story, I watch the window shade slowly peel back, though what's on the other side I can't see because it's shadowy and dim. But I imagine a woman, a widow, standing on the other side, watching until our car disappears from view.

EDEN

July 26, 1996
Egg Harbor

IT JUST SO HAPPENS that we do have neighbors.

They came this afternoon after Aaron had gone off to work, a pregnant Miranda and her two boys, five-year-old Jack and two-year-old Paul. They came trudging down our gravel drive, Miranda pulling both boys in a red Radio Flyer wagon so that by the time they arrived she was sweaty and spent. She'd come to deliver a welcoming gift.

It was the sound of wheels on gravel that caught my attention as I stood on a ladder, painting the living room walls a pale gray, the windows and doors open to expel chemical scents from the air. This is how I now spend my days when Aaron is away. Unpacking boxes of belongings. Cleaning the insides of closets and cabinets. Painting the home.

I saw them through the window first, heard the tired woman growl at the boys to *stop crying* and to *behave*, her cheeks flushed red from the heat and the pregnancy and, I guessed, the desire to impress. Her blond hair blew around her face and into her eyes as she walked. Her body was cemented with a short maternity dress, fastened to her with sweat. On her feet were Birkenstocks. In her eyes, exhaustion and discontent. From the moment I first spied her out the open window I knew one thing: motherhood did not suit her well.

I set down my painting supplies and met them on the porch. Dropping the wagon's handle, Miranda introduced herself first and then the kids, neither of whom said hello, for they were far too busy clawing their way out of the wagon, elbowing one another for room on the porch step. I didn't mind. They had blond hair like their mother, and if it weren't for the apparent age difference could have easily been twins. They fought one another, vying for the right to their mother's free hand. The bigger of the two won out in the end and as he slipped his hand inside Miranda's, the little guy fell to the ground in a puddle of tears. "Get up," Miranda commanded, her sharp voice jabbing through the placid air, apologizing to me for their manners as she tried hard to raise Paul from the ground. But Paul was a deadweight and wouldn't stand, and as she tugged on his underarms he cried out in pain that she'd hurt him. Tears came pouring from his eyes.

"Damn it, Paul," she said, pulling again roughly on those underarms. "Get up."

What she saw were naughty children making a fuss, embarrassing her, making her feel humiliated and ashamed. But not me. I saw something else entirely. I dropped down beside little Paul and held out a hand to him. "There's a tree swing in the backyard. Let's go have a ride on it, and let Mommy rest awhile?" I said. His pale green eyes rose to mine, snot gathering along his nostrils, running downward toward his lips. He wiped at his nose with the back of a dirty hand and nodded his sweet little head.

Miranda had walked far to bring us a blueberry loaf, more

than a block in the heat. The pits of her dress were damp with sweat, the cotton pulled taut across the baby bump. When she spoke, her voice was breathless, exhausted, burned-out from the energy it took to raise two boys on her own, and she confessed to me that this time—while running a hand over that baby—she was hoping for a girl.

She sat on a patio chair, kicking off her Birkenstocks and resting her swollen ankles on another seat as I poured us each a glass of lemonade, conscious of the dried paint on the backs of my hands.

Miranda's husband, she told me, is employed by the Department of Public Works. She stays at home with Jack and Paul, though what she always wanted to be—what she used to be in her life before kids—was a medical malpractice attorney. She asked how long Aaron and I have been married and when I told her, her eyebrows rose up in curiosity and she asked about kids.

Do we have them?

Do we plan to have them?

It seemed an intimate conversation to have with someone I hardly knew, and yet there was a great thrill at saying the words aloud, as if cementing them to reality. I felt my cheeks redden as I thought of that morning before dawn when Aaron rose, dreamlike, above me, lifting my nightgown up over my head. Outside it was dark, just after four o'clock in the morning, and our eyes were still drowsy, heavy with sleep, our minds not yet preoccupied by the thoughts that arrive with daylight. We moved together there on the bed, sinking into the aging mattress. And then later, while grinning at each other over mugs of coffee on the dock, watching as the fleets of sailboats went floating by on the bay, I had to wonder if it happened at all, or if it was only a dream.

When Miranda asked, I told her that we're trying. Trying to have a child, trying to start a family. An odd choice of words for creating a baby, if you ask me. *Trying* is how one learns to ride a bike. To knit, to sew. To write poetry.

And yet it was exactly what we were doing as Aaron and I made love with reckless abandon, and then followed it up a week or two later with a home pregnancy test. The tests were all negative thus far, that lone pink line on the display screen notifying me again and again that I wasn't yet pregnant. I tried not to let it get the best of me, and yet it was hard to do. It wasn't as though Aaron and I minded the time spent *trying*; in fact, we enjoyed it quite a bit, but with every passing month I yearned exponentially more for a baby. For a baby to have, a baby to hold.

I never mentioned to Aaron that I was taking the pregnancy tests.

I took them while he was at work, watching out the cottage window as his car slipped from view and then, when he was out of sight, rushing to the bathroom, where I closed and locked the door in case he mistakenly left something behind and had to return for it.

And then, when the single pink line appeared on the display screen as it always did, I wrapped the negative pregnancy test sticks up in tissue and discarded them discreetly in the garbage bins.

Miranda beamed when I told her that we're trying. "How exciting!" she told me, her smile mirroring the one on my own face.

And then, helping herself to a slice of her own blueberry loaf and running a hand over her bump for a second time, she said that her baby and my baby could one day go to school together.

That they could one day be friends.

And it was a thought that filled me with consummate joy. I grinned.

I'd been a lone wolf for much of my life. An introvert. The kind of woman who never felt comfortable in her own skin. Aaron changed that for me.

The idea thrilled me to bits and, in turn, I instinctively stroked my own empty womb and thought how much I wanted my baby to have a friend.

JESSIE

TONIGHT MAKES FIVE DAYS since I've been asleep. It's my first night in my new place. I spend it not sleeping, but rather imagining myself dead. I think of what it must be like for Mom, being dead. Is there blackness all around her, a pit of nothingness, the blackest of the black holes? Or has time simply stopped for her, and there's no such thing anymore as the living and the dead? Sometimes I wonder if she's not dead at all but rather alive in the clay urn of hers, screaming to get out. I wonder if there's enough oxygen in the urn. Can Mom breathe? But then I remember it doesn't matter anyway.

Mom is dead.

I wonder if it hurts when you die. If it hurt when Mom died. And I think, in frightening detail, what it feels like when you can't breathe. I find myself holding my breath until my lungs begin to hurt, to burn. It's a prickling pain that stretches from my throat to my torso. It's reflexive, automatic when my mouth gapes open, and I suck in all the oxygen I can to soothe the burn.

It hurts, I decide. It hurts to die.

There's a clock on the wall, one that came with the house. *Tick, tock, tick, tock,* it goes all night long, keeping track of the minutes I don't sleep. Keeping count for me. It's loud, a conga drum pounding in my ear, and though I try and remove the batteries, the *tick, tock* doesn't go away. It stays.

I feel out of place in this strange place. The house smells different than what I'm used to, an earthy smell like pine. It's older than Mom's and my old home, where I lived my entire life. One of the windows doesn't close tight so that when the wind whips its way around the house as it does tonight, air sneaks in. I can't feel it but I hear it, the hiss of the wind forcing its way in through a gap.

I lie there in bed, trying hard to catch my breath, to not think about dying, to will myself to do the impossible and sleep. Beside me, on the floor, are four boxes, the only ones I brought from the old home. Some clothes, a few picture frames, and a box of random paperwork Mom kept, just an old white bankers box, kept closed with a string and button. It seemed important enough for Mom to keep, and so I kept it. A thought comes to me now: *Could my social security card be in that box, tucked away with Mom's financial paperwork?*

I climb out of bed and turn on a light, dropping to the floor beside the box. I loosen the string and lift the lid, meeting reams of paper head-on. If there's any sort of method to the madness, I don't see it.

I search through the paperwork for my social security card, to be sure the numbers I dashed off on the FAFSA form weren't incorrect. That I didn't write the wrong ones down by mistake. Because never in my life have I been asked to give my social security number, and so it's conceivable, I think, that I have the numbers mixed-up. I look for the card itself, grabbing stacks of paper by the handful and flipping through them one sheet at a time, hoping the card falls out. But instead I find the deed to our home, an old checkbook ledger. Gas and electric bills. Years' worth of tax returns that gives me pause, because if I know one thing, it's that Uncle Sam isn't about to pay out tax refunds without a social security number.

I set everything else aside except for the tax returns. My eyes go straight to the exemptions, the spot where someone would list their dependents and their dependents' social security numbers, meaning me and my social security number. Except that when I come to it, I find the line blank. Mom didn't list me as a dependent and, though I double-check the year of the form to be sure I was alive at the time, I see that I was. That I was eleven years old at the time the form was completed.

And though I don't know much about income taxes, I do know it would have saved Mom a buck or two if she had thought to use me as a tax deduction. A baby gift from Uncle Sam.

I wonder why Mom, who was frugal to a fault, didn't claim me as a dependent that year.

It was a mistake, I think. An oversight only. I dig through to find another 1040 in the tower of paperwork—this one older, when I was four years old—and search there for my name and social security number, finding it nowhere. Another year that Mom didn't claim me.

I sift through them all, six tax return forms that I can find—my movements becoming faster, more frantic as I dig—and discover that never once did Mom claim me as a dependent. Not one single time.

I turn off the light and get back into bed. I lie there, wondering why Mom didn't claim me as a dependent. What did she know about the IRS that I don't know? Probably a lot, I reason. I don't pay taxes. I've never once been sent a check from them. My only knowledge comes from hearsay, from eavesdropping on clients like Mr. and Mrs. Ricci, discussing whether they could claim Mrs. Ricci's shopping binges as exemptions, all those fancy clothes she toted home in the trunks of cabs.

Mom must've had a good reason for what she did.

I listen to the clock, *tick, tock*. I don't bother closing my eyes except to blink, because I know that I won't sleep. I pull the blanket up clear to my neck because it's cold in the room. Though the thermostat downstairs is set to sixty-eight degrees, I have yet to hear the heat kick on.

Fall is here and winter is coming soon.

I'm rubbing my hands together for friction, to try and create heat. To make myself warm. I rub them together and then press them to my cheeks. Rub and then press, rub and then press. And that's when I hear a noise.

It's sudden, the kind of noise that makes me sit up straighter in bed, that makes me hold my breath to listen.

The only way to describe it is a ping. A ping, and then nothing. Ping, and then nothing. It's a piercing noise when it comes, like some sort of mechanical bleep or chime, the second or two between each ping a welcome reprieve. I rub at my ears, certain at first that the noise originates there, in my own eardrums. That it's merely tinnitus, a ringing in the ears, something only I can hear.

But then I realize it's not coming from my ears.

It's coming from somewhere on the other side of the room.

I stare though the blackness but see nothing. It's too dark to see much of anything, aside from my own hand when it's pressed all the way up to my face. And so I push the blanket from me and rise, following the noise. I move blindly, feet guiding me, my steps small because I don't know what's in front of me. Where the bedroom ends and the stairs begin. I have to be careful so that I don't fall.

I skirt around the edge of the bed, where I find myself on the other side of the room, hunched at the shoulders because the squat ceiling doesn't allow me to stand upright. From there, the noise rises up from the floor to greet me.

I drop to my knees, running my hands over a metal grate by accident. There I discover a floor register, one of those metal contraptions that attaches to the end of an air duct and leads somewhere under the floor, to some other room in the home. That's where the ping is coming from, from some other room in the home. In my imagination, I see a mallet being tapped against the slats of another register in another room, because that's what it sounds like to me. Like metal on metal, rhythmic and fixed.

I lie on the floor, pressing an ear to the grate so I can hear it more clearly. The ping. Which makes me think only of sonar emitting pulses underwater and then waiting for them to return, to see if there's anything out there, anything like whales or submarines. Except the only thing here is me.

I'm overcome with the strangest thought then. An irrational thought but one that somehow makes sense.

Someone is trying to speak to me. To communicate with me.

I press my lips again to the cold metal grate and call out, "Hello?"

At first there's no reply. The ping disappears, and as I sit there, waiting foolishly for someone to respond to me through the floor register, I realize this is ridiculous. Of course there's no one at the other end of the floor register speaking to me.

Because if there was, that would mean they're in the carriage home with me.

A chill rises up my spine, one vertebra at a time.

Is there someone in the carriage home with me?

I rise to my feet and scurry across the room—quicker this time, forgetting altogether about falling down stairs. I reach out to flip on the bedroom light. A yellow glare spreads over the room, obliterating the darkness. I stand at the top of the steps, staring down over the rest of the carriage home, listening for sounds, watching for movement. But there are none.

"Is anyone there?" I call over the stairwell, my voice timid and afraid. My heart beats hard; my hands begin to sweat. For three or four minutes, no one appears and in time, logic begins to watch over me. I shake my head, feeling stupid.

Of course no one is here.

It's the newness of the home that's to blame. That's what has me on edge. Because for the first time in my entire life, I'm alone and somewhere new. I feel lost without Mom, not knowing who I am or where I belong. If I belong anywhere.

I turn off the bedroom light, and the room is once again plunged into darkness. It's darker now than it was before because my eyes have adjusted to the light. I creep across the room and back toward the bed, reminding myself that this house is old. Old homes come with all sorts of strange but innocuous noises. Rats living in the insulation, the settling of the home, water moving through the pipes. That's all that it is.

As I reach for the bed, I almost have myself convinced.

Until seconds later when the voices come. Female voices by the pitch of it, higher than that of a man. I suck in a gulp of air and hold it in, not believing my own ears.

Someone is there.

The voices are hard to hear, as if they're a million miles

away, the sound dampened by distance and the network of aluminum tubes that make up the ductwork. At first it's only sounds, the cadence of women speaking, but no words that I can make out.

Until I do.

"It won't be long now," I hear, and at first I'm scared. My knees buckle. My throat constricts. My hands go to my throat without meaning to, pressing hard against my vocal cords. My tongue turns to sandpaper and though I'm cold, sweat breeds on my skin.

I see women in some sort of insulated room, by the sound of it. Patients in a psych ward, the walls covered with plastic and foam; a door, padded on the inside, but reinforced with steel. No knob on the door. No way to leave. That's where I imagine the women are.

I stagger back to the floor register, setting myself down over it. I press my ear to the grate, willing the voices to return again, but at the same time hoping they won't. Because I pray that no one is here.

I call into the floor register, my voice mousy at first, scared, "What? What won't be long now?" Though my words are a whisper only, and if they were standing in the very same room as me, two feet away, they wouldn't hear.

I cup my hands around my lips, pressing them flush to the floor register this time, so close I taste the bitter metal in my mouth. I call out, voice louder and more emphatic than it was before, "Can you hear me? Is anyone there?"

The only words I hear are low and plaintive. "She's dead to the world." But to my question there is no reply. Whoever is there can't hear me.

The voices are hollow at first before they go silent. They disappear completely as I sit there, pressing my ear to the floor register in vain. But the only sound that I hear now is the *tick, tock* of the wall clock.

My pulse is going at a breakneck speed. It pounds hard through my temple, my wrist. Wind rattles the carriage home, hissing its way in through the window's gap.

A noise returns from the floor just then and I think that they are back. The women, the voices. The ping. I press my ear to the metal grate and listen.

But this time the only thing that comes is a rush of luke-warm air blasting into me.

The heat. The heat has finally kicked on.

I think of the maze of tubes that work their way through the home and into this room from the furnace. The pipes and fittings and ducts. The ductwork, which, for a home this old, whimpers at every bend like the high pitch of female voices speaking, a whimper that my tired mind only doctored into words. There were never any women there.

It was the furnace's burners igniting, starting to produce heat. The furnace spurting air into the home. It comes out with a whine this time, and I press my hands to the grate to thaw them out.

I'm aware suddenly of just how much my entire body aches.

The insomnia has taken my sleep from me, and now it's taking my mind. Turning the gray matter to sludge. How long can I go on, I wonder, without sleep?

I return to bed and lie down on the mattress, staring out the open window at the sky. It's turned black now, though before I can sleep, dawn will be here. Not in the blink of an eye because that's not the way it is with insomnia.

Time is as slow as the three-toed sloth when you can't sleep.

EDEN

THE DAYS HAVE GROWN longer now that the task of getting settled into the cottage is through. The walls are painted; the unpacking is done. The garden has become a waiting game, staring at the soil, waiting for something to appear. Always waiting.

Every day, once Aaron has gone off to work, the next ten hours last a lifetime to me. Ten hours with nothing to do but wait until Aaron comes home to keep me company. Afternoons alone are lonely; dinners alone are lonely. I can't fall asleep until Aaron, completely tuckered out from another work shift, drops into bed beside me, nor can I bring myself to admit to him that I am lonely and bored.

Before leaving Green Bay I worked reception for a local pediatrician. It wasn't anything glamorous or ambitious, answering phones, greeting customers, coding medical records, tallying up bills, but it was *something*. But now Aaron has suggested that I not work, that I stay home, that soon enough we'll have a baby to raise and then I'll have something to do.

On occasion Miranda and her boys stop by for a visit, their afternoons long and lonely as well. We sit in the backyard, watching Jack and Paul wreak havoc on the tree swing, and as we do, I listen to Miranda depreciate parenthood, complain about her husband and her kids, knock the tedium of her everyday routine: the frozen waffles, the syrup in the hair, the messy bath times and all the books that she and her children are meant to read but never do because it's far too easy to just let them watch TV. Her husband—Joe—wants her to limit TV time to an hour a day, and Miranda laughed at this, saying Joe didn't have the first clue what it was like to be pregnant, what it was like to raise rough-and-tumble boys like Jack and Paul. She'd take any quiet time she could get, even if it meant they sat perched in front of the TV for five hours at a time, so close they were liable to go deaf and blind. She didn't care. Anything so long as they were quiet.

These were the words Miranda used and I stared at her openmouthed; I could hardly believe my ears. I agreed with Joe, treading carefully, delicately, saying how I'd read that too much TV can lead to obesity in children, to aggressiveness among other things, and she made light of this, saying I didn't know the first thing about being a mother.

"Just wait until you're a mother," she said. "Then you'll see," while hoisting her bare feet onto my patio chair and drinking her lemonade.

And then when adorable little Paul ran over and made every attempt to scamper onto her lap, hot and sweating, Miranda shirked away, saying, "Come on, buddy, it's too hot for laps today," while pushing him off as if he was some sort of bug who'd landed on her legs.

In that moment, what I wanted to do—what I ought to have done—was pull him up onto my own lap. Let him rest his tiny head on my shoulder for a while. He was tired too, in addition to hot and sweating, his eyes begging for a cool bath and his afternoon nap, though Miranda was too busy whining about the drudgery of motherhood and wasn't yet ready to leave.

Suddenly I wanted to feel the weight of him on my own two legs; I craved the heat of his skin on mine. I wanted to press those blond curls away from his eyes.

I've started noticing kids with more frequency lately. Little kids, big kids. Babies. Kids at the park. Kids at the market. Kids walking down the streets of town, holding hands with their fathers and mothers. It seems everyone in the world suddenly had kids, everyone but Aaron and me.

Had they been there all along and I failed to notice?

Or did they arrive just then and there the moment Aaron and I decided to conceive?

I didn't welcome Paul onto my lap as I wanted to do, but watched instead as he pouted and walked away, forced off Miranda's lap with her own two hands. His eyes were downcast, his bottom lip thrust out. He cried, not big crocodile tears but rather quiet and ashamed tears, the tears of someone who'd been told one too many times not to cry.

And, as he disappeared to a corner of the yard to be sad, Miranda released a massive sigh of relief, grateful Paul was gone and she could once again breathe.

August 14, 1996
Egg Harbor

It's starting to become apparent that sex alone doesn't lead to a baby.

When I woke this morning with blood dotting the inside of my underwear, my belly seized by a cramp, I knew another month had come and gone without a child. After the second month of trying, that blood in my underwear came as a startling blow, and there in the bathroom, hunched over the toilet seat, staring at the candy-apple red flecks on the lining of my favorite lace underwear, I began to sob. I kept it quiet and stifled, so that Aaron, in the kitchen brewing our morning coffee, couldn't hear. I didn't want him to know that I was upset. For whatever reason, I'd convinced myself over the last few days that every single twitch and prick I felt were the earliest signs of pregnancy. The tenderness in my chest, the desire to lay waste to almost everything I could find in the pantry, especially that which was high calorie, high fat.

These weren't signs of pregnancy after all, but rather signs of my period. The same ones I'd felt every single month for the last fifteen years of my life, since the middle of seventh grade when I started my period in science class, red blood seeping through a pair of white jean shorts. And now my biological clock had only convinced me I was pregnant. I'd been sure I was nauseated, morning sickness *already*, when what it was was a change in hormones, my uterus clearing the decks, paving the way, getting ready to welcome a life that wouldn't be.

I feel empty now, robbed of something that was mine, but why?

How can I grieve for something I never had?

After Aaron left for work, I scrubbed my underwear clean with detergent and bleach and headed into town. I couldn't bring myself to tell him about the blood. Of course we don't much talk about babies and pregnancy or use words like *ovulation* or *conceive*. Ostensibly, we just have sex, though inwardly what I'm thinking about, what we're *both* thinking about, as we lie together in the moments afterward, my head draped across his chest, his warm hands massaging me, moving yo-

yo-like up and down my back, is the end product, our handi-work, our creation, Aaron and me coming together, the best of him and the best of me fusing to create a baby.

I know he wants this as much as I do.

Only one time did Aaron whisper to me as we lay there in the darkness of the bedroom, still trying hard to catch our breaths after we were through, that he wondered what she would look like and when I asked, "Who?" he said, "Our baby girl. Our baby girl." I beamed there from ear to ear and when I told him I didn't know, he said, "I bet she'll look like you."

And then he kissed me slowly and deeply, the kind of kiss I felt all the way to my every extremity, and though he didn't say it, I knew that in Aaron's eyes if our baby girl looked like me, that she'd be the most beautiful girl in the world.

In all my life no one has ever made me feel as special as Aaron makes me feel.

I've watched him garden, watched the way he carefully carries the peat pots from greenhouse to garden, his every move screaming of paternal instinct; the way he digs the perfect holes, assessing their dimensions twice for accuracy; the way he lays the tiny biodegradable contraptions inside as if setting an infant in a crib, scattering soil over the top as gently as drawing a blanket to a sleeping child's chin. He waters and watches and waits, and as he does, I watch him, this solid figure who, by his stature alone should be anything but gentle and soft-spoken, and yet he is. He wears his chestnut hair short these days, easier to hide behind the chef's cap so there can be no false claims of hair in food, at least not from him, his hands and forearms marked with a selection of scratches and burns. For as long as I remember, he's had them, those scratches and burns: badges of honor, war wounds dating back to his culinary school years.

There are times I find that I can't take my eyes off those scars.

Each time he steps carefully through the garden, tending the seeds, careful not to step on our seedlings, it strikes me what a good father Aaron will one day be, so patient, so protective, so loving, the way he is with me.

And so, to say the words aloud now, to tell him I've started my period, would be to confess to Aaron that though we *tried* again this month, *tried* to conceive a baby, we failed.

After I wiped my eyes, I joined him on the dock for coffee and together we watched the boats pass by and shortly before two o'clock, as always, he left for work and again I was alone.

JESSIE

EVERYTHING CHANGES WITH THE break of day.

As the sun rises, gliding over the horizon, the world turns bright. The oppressive burden of night disappears. For the first time in eight long hours, I can breathe.

In daylight, I find myself standing above the floor register on the bedroom floor, feet straddling it. I stare down at the black rectangle between my legs. There's nothing ominous about it; it's just an ordinary metal grate, cold now, the furnace no longer producing heat. I rub at my arms in an effort to warm them up.

I shower and dress and head out into the day. Outside it's a cold start, no more than forty degrees that will rise up to sixty-five by midday. The sky is blue for now, though there's rain in the forecast. The grass is wet with dew. My fingers are cold as I lock the door.

From where I stand, I catch a glimpse of my landlord through the window of her own kitchen. It's the back of her, just a pouf of hair and the ribs of a blue sweater before they meet with the wooden slats of a chair. It is a distorted image at best, muddled by the reflection of the outside world on glass. She doesn't see me.

I could knock on the door, make an introduction, but that really isn't my thing.

I round the side of the carriage home, gathering Old Faithful from the alleyway where I left her, leaned up against the side of the home. Ivy grows up the brick of the garage, the leaves starting to turn red. The alley is abandoned. There is nothing more than garage doors and Dumpsters here. City of Chicago garbage bins. No people. No rats. No feral cats. No signs of life anywhere. I settle Mom and her urn into the basket on back, nothing more than a metal milk crate that I keep secure with bungee cords. We set off down the street.

It's no secret that Chicago is the alley capital of the country, with over a thousand miles of shadowy backstreets. The kind of darkened corridors where people like to hide their trash and vermin, and nobodies like me.

Morning traffic, as always, is a mess. Millions of people move this way and that like cattle in a cattle drive. My first stop is the same as always: coffee. I take it to go with a sugar twist from the bakery, where the donuts are fresh and the coffee is hot and cheap. I don't have six bucks a day to spend on coffee, and the owner knows me, sort of. She always says hello and calls me Jenny, and I don't have the heart to tell her that, after all these years, she's got it wrong. I set my coffee in the cup holder, pedaling away, making my way toward the Loop. I take my time, moving in wide circles around cars and trucks illegally parked in the bike lines, careful to avoid the city's sewage grates. I stay away from potholes.

Having no luck finding my social security card in the box of Mom's paperwork, I started the day with an idea in mind:

getting a new one. That and figuring out how to get my name removed from this inauspicious death index it's on. I head toward the Social Security Office and there, wait in line for a mind-numbing hour, only to learn that in order to get a new social security card, I need to prove who I am. Something more legitimate than just my word. I need to provide some sort of official identifying documentation like a driver's license or a birth certificate that says I'm Jessica Sloane, neither of which I have.

On the advice of an employee at the Social Security Office, I head next to the Cook County Clerk's Office in the Richard J. Daley Center—the Bureau of Vital Records—in the hopes of tracking my birth certificate down.

When I arrive at the Daley Center, the plaza is teeming with people. I tie Old Faithful up to the bike rack outside, watching as men and women in business suits take wide strides across the plaza. I rush past the Picasso and into the imposing lobby, where I wait in line to pass through security, looking on as others empty their pockets with the speed of a snail. I make it through the X-ray machine and the contents of my bag are searched. When I'm deemed harmless, the guard sends me on my way to the clerk's office, which is in the lower level of the building.

A surge of people wait before the elevator doors and so I take the stairs alone, heading down where I take my place in a long line, sighing in solidarity with those who also wait, avoiding eye contact, losing patience.

When it's my turn, an employee beckons, "Next," with a hand held up in the air so that I see her there, hunched over a computer screen, shoulders sagging. I go to her, telling her what I need.

Suddenly it dawns on me all the information I'm liable to

find when the woman locates my birth certificate. Not only the documentation I need to prove I'm Jessica Sloane, but the place where I was born. The exact time I slipped from Mom's womb. The name of the obstetrician who stood below, waiting to catch me as I fell.

My father's name.

In just a few short minutes, I'll know once and for all who he is. Not only will I have proof of my own identity, but of my father's as well.

I would never have done something as flagrant as seek out my birth certificate from vital records if Mom were still alive. That would have broken her heart, my having access to all these things she never wanted me to have. Searching our home seemed innocent enough, but tracking down my birth certificate feels like a really egregious act were she still here.

But Mom told me to *find myself*, and that's what I'm trying to do. To get into college, to make something of myself. To do something that would make Mom proud, all of which I can't do without a social security card.

"I need to get a copy of my birth certificate," I say to the employee. My heart quickens as she slides a request form across the counter. She tells me to fill it out. I reach for a pen, completing as much of the form as I can. It isn't much. I can't answer the question that pertains to place of birth or anything having to do with my dad—what his name is, where he was born.

It's only as I pause in my writing that the worker takes pity on me. Her eyes soften ever so slightly and she says, "You don't have to fill it all in," while staring uncomfortably at the urn in the crook of my arm, seeing the way the pen in my hand hovers above the words *father's name*. "Just as much as you know," she adds, telling me she can try and look it up with what little

I know. I slide the form back to her, half-complete, and she says she'll just need the payment and to see a photo ID.

A photo ID.

It's easy to explain why I don't have a photo ID. Because by this point in most people's lives, they have a driver's license, which is something I also don't have. Because the cancer came the year I turned fifteen, the year I was meant to enroll in my high school's after-school drivers' education program. Because after we learned that Mom had an invasive tumor in her left breast, knowing how to drive a car—in a city where we didn't need or own a car—didn't take top priority. Because my afternoons were tied up with Mom from then on, riding the bus with her to bajillions of doctor appointments or working to help pay for our home and her care. Because once I knew there was a good chance Mom would die, I wanted to spend every minute I could with her.

And yet I'm loath to tell the worker the bind I'm in because I know how it will sound. And so instead of coming clean, I root around in the pockets of my jeans, extracting the lining. I dive a hand deep into the depths of my bag searching for something I know isn't there. I pluck thirty dollars out of my wallet—the cost of the birth certificate is only fifteen—and try handing it to the woman. "Keep the change, please," I say, bemoaning in a low voice how my license was in my bag just this morning. How it must have fallen from my wallet on the way in. How it was there, but now it's gone.

I press the urn to my chest, hoping the woman's mercy will prevail and she'll pocket the extra fifteen bucks and get me what I need. She stares at the money for a minute and then asks whether I have any other form of ID. An insurance card or voter registration, but I shake my head and tell her no. I don't have either of these things. Mom had health insurance.

A rock-bottom plan that helped pay for cancer treatment, though I'm still in the hole more than I care to think about. But Mom never added me to her insurance plan because she said it wasn't something I needed. I was young and healthy and the rare trip to the clinic could be paid for with cash. Those required school vaccines I got at the Department of Public Health because they were cheap.

"Got any mail with your name on it?" the woman wants to know, but I shrug my shoulders and tell her no. She gives me a look. Disbelief, I think. I'm as much of a skeptic as the next guy; I know how this sounds.

"Please, ma'am," I beg. I'm tired and I don't know what else to do. My eyes feel heavy, threatening to close. There's the greatest desire to lie down on the floor and sleep. Except that it's only a tease, my body playing tricks on me. Even if I lie outstretched on the linoleum tiles, I still wouldn't sleep.

"I really need that birth certificate, ma'am," I say, shuffling in place, and it must be something about the way my voice cracks or the tears that well in my eyes that makes her lean forward and snatch the money from the countertop. She gathers the bills into her hand, counting them one at a time. Her eyes take a quick poll of the room to see if anyone else is watching, listening, before she whispers, "How about this. How about I see if I can find anything first. Then we'll figure out what to do about the ID."

I say okay.

She takes the form and begins typing information onto the rows of keys.

My heart pounds inside my chest. My hands sweat. In just a few short minutes, I'll know who my father is. I start thinking about his name. Whether he's still alive. And if he is, if he thinks about me the way I think about him.

By now, there are at least twenty people in line behind me. The room isn't large by any means. It's stodgy and drab, and everyone is looking at everyone else like they're a common criminal. Ladies clutch their purses to their sides. A kid in line screams that he has to pee. As he yells, I glance over my shoulder to see this poor kid, maybe four years old, hand pressed to his groin, eyes wide and ready to burst, his mother reading him the riot act for nature's call.

"There were no records found," the woman says to me then. Not at all the words I expected to hear. My face falls flat; my mouth parts. For a second I'm confused, unable to produce coherent thoughts or words.

I fight to find my voice, asking, "Are you sure you spelled it correctly?" imagining her hunting and pecking for the letters, clipping the corner edge of some surplus letter by mistake, misspelling my name.

But her face remains motionless. She doesn't attempt another search, as I'd hoped she'd do. She doesn't glance down at the computer or check her work.

"I'm sure," she says, raising a hand into the air to beckon for the next customer.

"But wait," I say, stopping her. Not willing to give up just yet.

"There were no records found, miss," she tells me again, and I ask, feeling incredulous, "What does that mean then, *no records found*?" because what I'm suddenly realizing is that, instead of being *dead*, the crux of the matter is that there is no birth record on file for me.

I can't be dead because I haven't yet been born.

The Bureau of Vital Records doesn't even know I exist.

"Of course you must have found something," I argue, not

waiting for a reply. My voice elevates. "How can there be no birth certificate for me when clearly I'm alive?"

And then I pinch a fold of skin on my arm, watching as it swells and turns red before shriveling back down to size. I do it so that she and I can both see I'm alive.

"Ma'am," she says, and there's a shift in posture, her empathy quickly giving way to aggravation. I've become a pest. "You left half this form blank," she says.

I argue that she told me I could. That she was the one who said I didn't have to fill it all out. She ignores me, continues to speak. "Who's to say you were even born in Illinois? Were you born in Illinois?" she asks, challenging me, calling my bluff, and I realize that I don't know. I don't know where I was born. All my life, I only assumed. Because Mom never told me otherwise and I never thought to ask.

"No records found means that I couldn't locate a birth certificate based on the information you gave me. You want to find your birth certificate, you need to fill in the rest of these blanks," she tells me, slipping the request form back to me as I stare down helplessly at all the missing information, *name of father*, *place of birth*, wondering if what I filled in was even correct to begin with.

Was Mom always a Sloane like me? That I'd also assumed. But if she was married when I was born, then maybe she had a different last name, one she ditched at some point over the last twenty years for some reason I don't know?

"And next time," the employee tacks on as I back dismally away, losing hope, running blindly into another woman in line, "be sure and bring your ID."

I make my way out the door, climbing back up to the first floor two steps at a time. The building's stairwell is industrial and dark, a flash of gray that comes at me quickly. It spirals upward in circles for thirty floors or more. When I arrive on the first floor, slipping through the stairwell door, crowds flood the lobby of the Daley Center. I'm grateful for this, for the anonymity of it all. I camouflage myself among the wayward teens who've been summoned here for court, those with purple-dyed hair and heads hidden beneath sweatshirt hoods. I make my way back outside, nowhere closer to finding my father or proving my identity.

As far as the world is concerned, I'm still dead.

EDEN

September 14, 1996
Egg Harbor

THE TOWN WAS MOBBED with people today as it always is on Saturdays, vacationers trying hard to take advantage of the last few warm days before fall arrives. It's September now, days shy of the equinox, and as September eventually bleeds into October, the seas of people will finally leave. They come for the hundreds of miles of shorelines, the extensive gift shops, the food. But by December, this far north into Wisconsin, the temperatures will hurtle to twenty or thirty degrees, mounds of snow will obstruct the streets, and the skies will be endlessly gray. And then no one will want to be here, least of all me. Aaron and I will spend the Midwest winter as we always do, imagining the warm places in the world we hope to one day go, places where cold and snow don't exist. St. Lucia, Fiji, Belize.

Places we will never go.

I spent the day while Aaron was at work wandering the town's streets, simulating a tourist. I visited gift shops; I bought a T-shirt and ice cream, a book on sailing. I rode the Washington Island Ferry through Death's Door, spending the late-afternoon hours exploring the crystal clear waters and the polished white stones of Schoolhouse Beach, trying to skip rocks out over the lake, and like getting pregnant, failing at that too.

Back in town I watched families wander from store to store, mothers with buggies, fathers with toddlers perched on their backs. I stared at them as afternoon blended into evening, seated on a bench at Beach View Park, watching as families laid out blankets, staking their claim to a patch of land for the night's sunset display.

The children were everywhere, and I started to wonder why something in so much abundance could ever be hard to achieve.

October 8, 1996
Egg Harbor

Each time Miranda and her boys stop by, she has a new suggestion for me, some tip on how to hasten conception. No subject is too personal or too taboo to discuss, from the style of Aaron's underwear to various positions that supposedly aid in fertilization as she lounges on my back patio or living room sofa, weather depending, and cites for me the reasons she believes Aaron and I are not yet pregnant—though never once did I ask.

As she talks, Jack and Paul loiter before us, performing for me a song they learned, a magic trick, how they can make their eyes go crossed. They stand before me as Miranda spells out the effects of tight underpants on the male genitalia, saying over and over again, "Look at me, Miss Eden. Look what I can do," while folding their tongues in half, or trying to make them stretch clear to the ends of their noses, and, as Miranda talks louder to counter their escalating tones, it hits me how attention-starved they are, how they would give anything for her to watch them for a minute, to praise their talents. Every day, there is dirt wedged beneath their nails and some sort of food on their cheeks and chins. Their outfits are cobbled together with clothing that doesn't match and hardly fits.

I clap my hands for Jack and Paul, but Miranda tells them to go away. To go play.

Every day.

As her baby bump swells more and more, I'm pestered by Miranda to *hurry up*, to get knocked up, so that her baby and my baby can still go to school together as I've promised her they would.

If I wait much longer they'll be in different grades.

That's what Miranda has told me.

"September is the cutoff, don't you know?"

According to Miranda's timeline, I have until September of next year to have a baby. Twelve months, which leaves only three to get pregnant.

"It's not that we're not trying," I've tried to explain, and she counters with a flip of the hand and a slapdash "I know, I know," and then it's back to the underwear we go. To help with Aaron's and my fertility issues, she suggested a pillow beneath my hips to help steer sperm in the right direction. "It's all about gravity," she says.

At every visit I watch the size of her own baby bump swell, her maternity shirts no longer able to cover its overwhelming girth. I tell myself that her suggestions are only old wives' tales, not rooted in truth, but how am I to know if that's true?

But today when she lounged on my sofa, peering at me with that same expression on her face—mouth parted, eyebrows raised—and asked if I was keeping track of my ovulation, I realized how stupid it was of me, how naive.

This was Aaron's and my first foray into babymaking. I was sure it was something that just *happened*, that there was no need to time or plan. In the moment, I told her yes, of course I was keeping track of my dates, because I couldn't bring myself to say otherwise, to admit to her that it never occurred to me to figure out when I was and when I wasn't ovulating. Aaron and I both come from large families, and the number of grandchildren our parents have been blessed with is in no way in short supply. It seemed a given that after ample time, after many months of waking up in the morning to Aaron's soft fingers tracing my bare skin, thumbs hooking through the lacy edges of my underpants, gliding them proficiently over my thighs, sooner or later we'd succeed. We'd make a baby as we intended to do.

But for the first time I've come to realize that this is going to take more than time.

After Miranda left I drove to the library and sought out a guidebook on pregnancy and there, in the stacks of books, plotted out my approximate menstrual cycle. I figured out the first date of my last period. I counted backward; I did the math. It wouldn't be perfect, that I knew—my periods had never been perfect—but it would be close. And close to perfect was better than nothing for me.

And now, knowing that in just two days' time I will be ovulating fills me with an abundant amount of hope. Aaron and I were doing it wrong all along, missing out on the best times to get pregnant, likely omitting my most fertile days, those negligible hours when conception can occur. On the way home I stopped at the market and picked up a pocket-size calendar and, at home, with a red pen, circled my most fertile days for the next three months, through the end of the year.

This time we'll get it right.

JESSIE

I PUSH MY WAY through the turnstile doors and step outside, making my way across the plaza. Beside the Eternal Flame, I pause, overcome with the sudden urge to scale the fence and lie down beside the puny little fire in the fetal position. To fall to my side on the cold concrete, beside the memorial for fallen soldiers. To pull my knees up to my chest in the middle of all those pigeons who huddle around it, trying to keep warm. The land around the flame is thick with birds, the concrete white from their waste. That's where I want to lie. Because I'm so tired I can no longer stand upright.

People breeze past me. No one bothers to look. A passing shoulder slams into mine. The man never apologizes and I wonder, *Can he see me? Am I here?*

I head to the bike rack, finding Old Faithful ensnared beneath the pedals and handlebars of a dozen or more poorly placed bikes. I have to tug with all my might to get her out and still I can't do it. The frustration over my identity boils inside me until I feel myself begin to lose it. All this red tape preventing me from getting what I need, from proving who I am. I'm starting to question it myself. *Am I still me?*

The debilitating effects of insomnia return to me then, suddenly and without warning. General aches and pains plague every muscle in my body because I can't sleep. Because I haven't been sleeping. My feet hurt. My legs threaten to give. I shift my weight from one leg to the next, needing to sit. It's all I can think about for the next few seconds.

Sitting down.

Pins and needles stab my legs. I wrench on the bike, yanking as hard as I can, but still she doesn't budge. "Need a hand?" I hear, and though clearly I need a hand, there's a part of me feeling so suddenly indignant that I turn with every intent of telling the person that *I've got it.* Words clipped. Expression flat.

But when I turn, I see a pair of blue eyes staring back at me. Royal blue eyes like the big round gum balls that drop down the chute of a gum-ball machine. And my words get lost inside my throat somewhere as I rub at my bleary eyes to be sure I'm seeing what I think I'm seeing. Because I know these eyes. Because I've seen these eyes before.

"It's you," I say, the surprise in my voice clear-cut.

"It's me," he says. And then he reaches over and hoists Old Faithful inches above the other bikes, those that have held her prisoner all this time. It's effortless to him, like nothing.

He looks different than the last time I saw him. Because the last time I saw him he was folded over the cafeteria table, drinking coffee in a sweatshirt and jeans. Now he's dressed to the nines in black slacks, a dress shirt and tie, and I know what it means. It means that his brother has died. His brother, who was hurt in a motorcycle accident after a car cut him off and he went flying off the bike, soaring headfirst through the air and into a utility pole without a helmet to protect his head.

He held vigil beside his brother's hospital bed while I held vigil beside Mom's. And now, six days later, his eyes still look tired and sad. When he smiles, it's strained and unconvincing. He's gotten a haircut. The dark, messy hair has been given a trim and though it's not prim or tidy—not by a long shot— it looks clean. Combed back. Much different than the hair I saw those days and nights in the hospital cafeteria, his head stuffed under the hood of a red sweatshirt. We only spoke the one night, him fussing about the coffee, telling me how he'd rather be anywhere but there. But still, there's the innate sense that I know him. That we shared something intimate. Something much more personal than coffee. That we're bound by a similar sense of loss, united by grief. Both collateral damage in his brother's and my mother's demise.

He sets Old Faithful down on the ground and passes the handlebar to me. I take her in my hand, seeing the way his nails are bitten to the quick, the skin torn along the edges. A row of rubber bands rests on his wrist, the last one tucked halfway beneath the cuff of the dress shirt. A single word is written on the back of the hand with blue ink. I can't read what it is.

He runs his hands through his hair and only then do I think what I must look like.

It can't be good.

"What are you doing here?" I ask, as if I have any more right being here than him.

He speaks in incomplete sentences, and still I get the gist. "The wake," he says. "St. Peter's. I needed some air."

He points in the direction of some church just a couple of blocks from here, one that's too far to see from where we stand. Though still I look, seeing that the sun has slipped from the sky and is hidden now behind a cloud. While I was inside the building, the clouds rolled into the city, one by one. They changed the morning's blue sky to one that is plush and white, filling the sky like cotton balls, making the day ambiguous and gray.

I don't ask when or how his brother died and he doesn't ask about Mom. He doesn't need to because he knows. He can see it in my eyes that she has died. Neither of us offer our condolences.

He rams his hands into the pockets of his slacks. "You never told me your name," he says. If I was the kind of girl that felt comfortable in situations like these, I'd say something snarky like *Well, you never asked*.

But I don't because it's not that type of conversation, and I'm not that girl.

"Jessie," I say, sticking my hand out by means of introduction. His handshake is firm, his hand warm as he presses it to mine.

"Liam," he says, eyes straying, and I take it as my cue to leave. Because there isn't anything more to say. The one and only conversation we had in the hospital, words were sparse, but unlike in the hospital we're no longer killing time, just waiting for people to die. That night, before the conversation drifted to quiet and we sat in silence for over an hour, sipping our coffees, we talked about private things, nonpublic things, things we weren't apt to tell the rest of the world. He told me about his brother beating him up when they were kids. About how he would lock him out of the house in the rain and shove his head in the toilet, giving him a swirly when their folks weren't home. *Such a bastard*, he said, though I got the sense that that was then and this was now. That over the years, things changed. But he didn't say when or how.

I told him about Mom's hair and fingernails, both of which she lost thanks to chemotherapy. Her eyelashes too. I told him about the clumps of hair that fell out, and how I watched on in horror as Mom held fistfuls of it in her hands. How there were whole clods of it on her pillowcase when she awoke in the morning, masses of it filling the shower drain. I said that Mom never cried, that only I cried. It grew back, after the cancer was in remission for the first time, soft fuzz that grew a little thicker than it was before chemotherapy. A little more brown. It never reached her shoulders before the cancer returned.

"You should get back to the wake," I tell him now as we stand there in the middle of Daley Plaza. But he only shrugs his shoulders and tells me that the wake is through. That everyone split.

"The funeral's tomorrow," he says as I wrap my fingers around Old Faithful's handlebars. I don't know what to say to that. There isn't anything to say to that.

Turns out, I don't need to say anything. "You never said what you're doing here," he says then, but as I'm about to explain I realize that there's no easy answer for it, because the reason I'm standing outside Daley Center is far more convoluted than his. And so instead of answering, I sigh and say, "Long story," thinking that he'll just say okay and walk away because chances are good he didn't want to know in the first place. He was probably only being polite because I asked what he was doing here, and so he thought he should too, that he should reciprocate out of courtesy.

But as he shifts in place and tells me, "I have time," I realize that he wants me to stay.

There's a sadness in his eyes, the likeness to mine uncanny. We walk. Out of the plaza, down Washington and toward

Clark Street, me towing Old Faithful by the handlebar. We walk in the street because it's illegal to ride a bike on the sidewalk in the city. I don't know what time it is, but what I can say is that the haste of rush hour is past, the clog of morning traffic like hair in a shower drain. Impossible to get through. It's gone, as if some plumber stopped by and dropped a gallon of Drano on the street, ameliorating the clog. People move slowly now. They take their time. Without the blockage we easily slip through, weaving in and out of pedestrians and cars.

"I stopped by vital records," I say. "I needed to get my birth certificate. Except that didn't go as planned," I explain as we turn a right on Clark, which is a one-way street around here. All the cars come directly at us. They miss us by a hair's breadth at times because there are no bike lanes. Not that it matters because half of the time when there are, cars and trucks illegally park and I have to veer around them and into traffic. The number of bike-related deaths in the city is staggering; I just hope that one day one of them isn't me.

Liam asks why getting my birth certificate didn't go as planned. He's a good ten inches taller than me, broad in the shoulders but narrow around the hips. At just over five feet, I've always been on the short side. My whole life, for as long as I can remember, I've been short. Kids in school used to make fun of me. They'd call me names like shrimp, peanut. Squirt.

He towers over me, his body slim but in the tailored clothes, he doesn't look too thin. I remember him in the hospital— oversize sweatshirt and jeans, getting swallowed up by fabric. Then he looked thin.

I start at the beginning and tell Liam the whole story. Otherwise it won't make sense. And even then it doesn't make much sense because I'm having a hard time wrapping my head around it myself. I tell him about applying to college, the phone call from the financial aid office. The woman's cheery voice on the other end of the line, laughing, telling me I'm dead. I tell him about the wasted time spent trying to find my social security card, the worthless trip to the Social Security Office. The one that led me here, to the Daley Center in search of my birth certificate, though that too was a waste.

"I don't have a birth certificate," I close with. "At least not one in the state of Illinois. And without a birth certificate or a social security number, there's no way to prove who I am or that I even exist. But what freaks me out even more," I admit, "is this implication that—"

But before I can get the words out, birds swarm around me, moving in from all directions. Pigeons with beady eyes and little bobbing heads, pecking at something on the street. They fight over it, their squawks loud and angry. I try to side-step them, but their movements are arbitrary, aimless; there's no predicting where they'll go. I step on the tail feathers of one by chance and it scurries, wings slapping together to get away from me.

As I go to take another step, I see what the skirmish is all about. It's another pigeon, dead, lying on the street where my foot should go. The other birds move in on it, pecking at it, trying to eat it, and just like that, there's nowhere for me to put my foot. It throws off my stride, makes me lose balance. The dead pigeon lies on its back, spread-eagle-like. Its wings are fanned on either side of its body, white belly exposed, its neck turned too far in one direction, broken I think. I see only one beady eye, the other somehow missing. Its beak is tucked into the crook of a neck, and on the street beside it are flecks of blood.

I nearly step on the carcass as my body lurches forward, stumbling, and I'm sure I'll fall. My heartbeat kicks up a notch or two, hands sweaty, and like that I'm at the mercy of the bird and the street.

I let go of Old Faithful's handlebars by accident. I watch as she topples onto the street, certain I'm about to go with her. People turn to see what the racket is, the clang of the bike on the street, the sound of my scream. My hands reach for something to latch on to, coming up empty until Liam grabs me by the wrist, steadying me.

"Jessie?" he asks, and I have to fight for a minute to catch my breath. I'm breathing hard, seeing only pigeons nipping the bloody flesh of a dead bird. And I'm thinking about that bird, wondering what happened to kill the bird. How did it die? If it was killed by a car or a bike, or a run-in with a building window maybe. Maybe it flew headfirst into the Thompson Center before sliding down, down, down to the ground.

"Jessie?" Liam asks again because I still haven't replied. His eyes watch me, uneasy, as he makes sure I'm steady on my feet before leaning down to reclaim Old Faithful from the street.

"Are you okay?" he asks, and, "What happened?" and I shake my head and say, "The damn bird. Those pigeons."

"What bird?" he asks. "What pigeons?"

I turn to point them out to him. But when I look back on to the street behind me, there's no bird. No pigeons. The only thing there is a squandered hot dog that lies on the asphalt. Half-eaten, gravel stuck to what remains of it. Chunky green relish spilling from the bun, red ketchup splattered here and there like blood.

There's no dead bird.

There was never a dead bird.

The world loses balance all of a sudden, the street beneath my feet unpredictable and insecure. I think of sinkholes, when the earth suddenly decides to give, roadways collapsing like Play-Doh, sucking people in and swallowing them whole.

I shake my head. "Just tripped over my own feet," I say, but I can see in Liam's eyes: he doesn't believe me.

We move on.

Liam waits for me to finish whatever it is I was saying before I saw the bird, but now my train of thought is gone. I can think only of the bird, the pigeons, the flecks of blood. And so he reminds me. And then I remember.

What freaks me out the most, I tell him, is the implication that I'm already dead.

He asks about the death database. What it is and what it's called, and so I tell him what the woman from the financial aid office told me.

"The Death Master File," I say, which in and of itself sounds like something the grim reaper must carry along with him, a listing of all the souls he's sent to collect. Liam looks it up on his smartphone, and soon finds out that access to the file is restricted. That not just anybody can look at it. He tells me what I already know. That it's a listing of millions of people who have died, them and their social security numbers. It's used as a means to prevent fraud and identity theft. To stop living people from opening credit cards and getting mortgages in the name of someone who's already dead.

"So somehow I got placed on this list, and now my social security number is good for nothing until I clean up this mess. Because on paper, I'm dead. And I can't find my social security card or figure out how to get a new card because I don't have the other documentation I need to do it."

"Listen to this," Liam says as a disclaimer pops up on his phone and he reads, quoting verbatim, "'In rare instances it is possible for the records of a person who is not deceased to be included erroneously in the DMF.'"

I ask him how that can happen. "A clerical error," he says, meaning with the stroke of one wrong computer key someone who's alive and well is suddenly dead. Or not dead but undocumented, which is almost as good as being dead, I'm quickly learning.

The only reason my own death went unnoticed for all this time, I think, is because I haven't once been asked to give my social security number. But sooner or later it was bound to happen. When I sought out a driver's license, made an attempt to open a credit card. An attempt that would have been denied.

As we scoot onto the pedestrian side of the Clark Street Bridge and cross over the Chicago River, I think of people in the same situation as me, unable to access their own bank accounts and going broke. Those who don't have the money for food or shelter, though they *do* have the money; it's just that it's tied up in some bank account they can't access because the bank is certain they're dead.

"People get locked out of their own lives, interrogated by police for suspected identity theft when the person whose identity they've supposedly stolen is themselves," Liam says as he drops his phone into the back pocket of his pants, and I utter under my breath, "What a mess."

I stare down below, beneath the metal grates of the bridge, where a tour is underway, tourists exploring the polluted grayish-green waters of the Chicago River. The tour guide steers passengers' attention to the bridge—built in 1929, a bascule bridge, she says—and all eyes move to Liam and me, taking photos, pointing upward some twenty feet or more to the bridge on which we stand.

"You really are Jessie, aren't you?" His words are dry, meant to be funny, though they're not. His tone is deadpan, his face expressionless.

And though I know it's in jest, it's a question that nags at me.

I am Jessie, aren't I? Am I Jessica Sloane?

We continue to walk. Down Clark and left on Superior, my feet following Liam's lead. We're quiet. We don't speak much. He asks if I've been sleeping. He says that I look tired and I pause, looking at my own reflection in the glass facade of a building. I see what he sees. The sunken eyes surrounded by puffy red skin, the tip of my nose red.

I make light of the insomnia. I say that sleep is a waste of time. That there are so many more productive things I could be doing instead of sleeping.

"It's not good for you, Jessie," he tells me. "You need to sleep. The melatonin," he says, same as he did in the hospital when he slipped those pills into the palm of my hand. "Give it a try." *I did give it a try*, I think. I tried the melatonin—that and the clonazepam—and slept right on through Mom's death. Never again.

I tell him that I will but I won't.

And then he stops beside a mid-rise, saying, "This is me. This is where I live."

This building beside us is five or six stories tall, flanked with floor-to-ceiling windows. A sign out front offers spacious open-plan lofts for sale. A doorman patrols the revolving front door and there's something very moneyed about it that makes me feel out of place and ill at ease. The Liam before me is suddenly at odds with the Liam I remember from the hospital, the one who was bedraggled, a bit dog-eared like me.

A look of confusion must pass on my face. "My brother and I lived here together," he explains. His voice is deep and there's no rise or fall to his intonation as he speaks, telling me, "He was a software engineer."

I fill in the missing pieces. His brother made the money. He paid for the condo. And now he's gone.

"You'll be okay?" I ask, and his reply is detached.

"What's that they say?" he asks, plucking at the row of rubber bands on his wrist so that I see now what it says on his hand in the blue ink. *Adam.* His brother's name, I think. "About death and taxes?"

That nothing is certain but death and taxes. That's what they say. But he's not looking for an answer. What he's saying is that he may or may not be okay, but there's no way to know right now. Same as me.

We say our goodbyes. I watch as he slips through the doors of the apartment building, disappearing behind a wall of glass.

EDEN

November 14, 1996
Egg Harbor

IT'S NOVEMBER NOW.

The gray skies have descended, everything perpetually overcast and sad. The boats have been pulled from the bay, leaving it barren and empty, like my womb. The seasonal shops are closed. The tourists took their cue to leave.

Two weeks ago, on the first of November, Miranda had that baby of hers, a seven pound, three ounce beautiful baby boy who she and Joe named Carter. I visited in the hospital the day after he was born, her only visitor aside from Joe. I saw it in her eyes as soon as I entered the postpartum room, Miranda swaddling baby Carter with a look of arrant dissatisfaction on her face. Her lips were pursed, her eyebrows creased, crow's-feet forming around the eyes.

As I walked in—swapping places with Joe, who went to the cafeteria for coffee—her disillusioned eyes rose to mine and she confessed aloud so that baby Carter could hear, not bothering to lower her voice or to press her hands to his ears to muffle the rotten words, "All I wanted was a baby girl. Is it too much to ask for one little girl? But instead it's another goddamn boy."

Her words knocked the wind out of my lungs. They made it hard to breathe. They were so ugly and vile, and I saw a look in Miranda's eyes as she spoke of him, eyes dropping to his. A look that made my heart hurt. Only a day old and already she abhorred her baby boy.

I asked if I could hold him and she said yes, handing him off with too much inclination, too much ease, as if grateful to be rid of him. I took baby Carter to a chair in the corner of the room and peered at his inappreciable wisps of blond hair and his heavy, tired eyes, thinking to myself, *What difference does it make if he's a boy or girl, only that he's happy and healthy?*

And I felt angry for the first time at Miranda. Not just annoyed but truly angry. Angry that she had three beautiful baby boys and I had none. Angry that she didn't love her babies or value her babies, that she couldn't understand another woman—one like me—would give life and limb for a child.

Oh, what I wouldn't give for a child.

I had a thought then.

Would Miranda care if I rose to my feet and carried baby Carter from the room?

Would she even notice?

The hospital experience, for Miranda, was a welcomed furlough from motherhood. From what I'd been told, Carter spent his time in the nursery, being cared for by nurses round the clock except when he needed to eat, and only then did nurses carry him, crying and discontent, to his mother, and she welcomed him grudgingly, embittered to her chest. And then as soon as he was full, his eyes drifting lazily to sleep, she asked the nurses to take him away so that she could sleep.

Spread out on her hospital bed in an indiscreet polka-dot

gown, I watched Miranda sleep. Or pretend to sleep at least, so that she didn't have to tend to her child. She was exhausted, yes, from many hours of labor and delivery, from the every-other-hour feedings, and yet I wondered if her eyes were merely closed so that she could remain insensible to her baby boy, who lay limply in my arms, head misshapen, skin wrinkly and pink as a newborn's should be. Miranda's hair was brushed away from her face, pulled taut into a ponytail that lay flat against the bed. Her arms and hands were stretched out by her sides. She breathed with her mouth open, nostrils flaring with each inhalation and exhalation of air.

I whispered her name. There was no reply.

It was almost as if she was asking me, begging me, daring me to take her child.

And so I did.

I stood from the inflexible armchair, slowly, gradually, piecemeal-like so that the chair wouldn't make a sound. So that the floor wouldn't cheep. So that my own two feet wouldn't betray me. I flexed one muscle and then the next until I was standing upright, holding my breath.

I crossed the room, creeping by degrees so my shoes wouldn't squeak on the floors. Miranda's eyes were closed, enjoying the peace and serenity of having someone else care for her child.

It didn't occur to her for one instant that someone might try and take her baby.

I slipped into the hallway without a peep. Two left turns and there Carter and I were, standing before the nursery, staring through glass at a half dozen sleeping babies. They lay bundled like burritos in their pink and blue blankets, with knitted hats atop their near-bald heads. They were sleeping, every last one of them, completely tuckered out. The newborns slept in rolling bassinets all arranged on display so that grandmas and grandpas could see. If it wasn't for the slip of paper in each bassinet with the baby's name and date of birth in blue ink, there was no telling them apart aside from the obvious distinction of pink and blue.

How easy it would be for two to be swapped, or for one to up and disappear.

One nurse stood guard of them all, a shepherd in the pasture keeping watch over her sheep. What I wouldn't give to be that nurse, to be tasked with caring for the infinite number of newborn babies that rotated in and out of the nursery each day.

I wondered if she ever had a weakness for any one of these babies. A fondness. Was there ever one colicky child who caught her eye, the runt of a litter of multiples she wanted to bring home as her own?

From down the hallway a door opened and I saw the main hospital on the other side, areas other than the labor and delivery ward. A common hallway. The hospital's information booth. The doorway was twenty steps away at best, and there was nothing but two unlocked doors to prevent Carter and me from leaving. There was no alarm, at least none that I could see. There was no system to buzz people in and out. It was an open door, an invitation.

How easily Carter and I could just leave.

I looked around; the nursery nurse had her back in my direction, attention now focused on one little baby who was trying to wake up. Behind me, there was only a single woman at the nurses' station, a middle-aged lady on the phone. Other than that, the ward was quiet and still, all patient doors pulled closed, mothers on the other side in the throes of labor or fast asleep.

I peered to the doorway again, those swinging double doors

just twenty steps away from where I stood. I didn't think about the rest, about what I would tell Aaron or what Miranda might do when she awoke and realized Carter was gone. My heart beat quickly as desire and instinct told me to do it and to do it quickly, to move with purpose, to not draw attention to myself. In my arms, I held the very thing Aaron and I had been trying for for months. A baby.

Miranda didn't want him anyway. I was doing her a favor, I reasoned.

How easily this baby could be mine.

I thought of only one thing in that moment as I stood frozen, staring through glass at the plentiful sleeping babies.

How easy it would be to just go.

I didn't do it, of course, but it would be remiss to say the idea never crossed my mind.

JESSIE

I PEDAL TOWARD ROSCOE Village. As I do, I stare over my shoulder, back into the Loop at the peaks of skyscrapers that rise into the sky like distant mountain summits. I watch as the urban streets become residential.

Once in Roscoe Village, I duck into a burger joint on Addison. My stomach is empty by now, the morning's sugar high having given way to a glucose crash, one which makes me irritable and edgy. I've had nothing to eat but a donut all day—a donut and coffee—though since Mom's death, my hip bones protrude from my waistline and the bones of my rib cage are startlingly transparent.

I'm not *not* eating on purpose. I've just had no desire to eat.

I order a hamburger and take it to the counter to eat. There, I stare out the window at the world as it passes by without me. A bus goes by, the 152 heading east. A plastic bag floats through the air, surfing the airstream. Middle school kids amble by in private school uniforms—starchy plaid split-neck jumpers; burgundy sweater-vests; pressed pants—with backpacks so heavy they nearly tip over from the weight of them. An older woman stands beside the bus stop. The 152 gathers her up and goes, disappearing in a puff of smoke.

I eat part of my burger, wrapping the rest up for the trash. As I'm about to go, a voice stops me. I turn to see a woman standing beside me in jeans and a cardigan, a pair of white gym shoes on her feet. Her graying hair is wound back into a bun.

"Jessie? Jessie Sloane? Is that you?"

But before I can say one way or another if it's me, she decides for me. "It *is* you," she declares as she tells me that she remembers me when I was yea high, her hand pegged at about thirty-seven inches in the air. And then she embraces me, this strange woman wrapping her thickset arms around my neck and declaring again, "It is you."

Except that I don't know who she is. Not until she tells me. And even then, I still don't know.

"It's me," she says. "Mrs. Zulpo. Eleanor Zulpo. Your mother used to clean my home when you were a girl. In Lincoln Park," she tells me, tacking on details as if it might help me remember. "Tree-lined street, beautiful box beam ceilings, rooms flooded with natural light," she says, though she and her husband don't live there anymore, not since the housing market crash when she had to give up her home. When they had to downsize. That's what she tells me.

I draw a blank. I don't remember.

Like me, Mom used to clean homes. Mostly upscale places that we could never afford. She taught me everything I know. My first foray into the family business came when I was about twelve years old and would get down on my hands and knees beside her and scrub floors.

But before that, when I was too young to clean, Mom would lug me along on assignments and there I'd spend my days playing pretend in strangers' homes. Cooking imaginary meals in their palatial kitchens, tucking my imaginary children into their mammoth beds before Mom scooched me out of the way so she could wash the sheets.

"You don't remember me," Eleanor Zulpo decides, realizing that it must have been sixteen or seventeen years ago or so, when I was three or four. "Of course you don't remember," she says, loosening her hold on my neck, telling me that I look just the same as I did back then. "It's those dimples," she says, pointing at them. "Those adorable dimples. I'd know these dimples anywhere.

"I read about your mother in the paper," she says then, sitting beside me on her own stool, unwrapping a hot dog. The sight of it alone, that hot dog, lying out on a foil wrapper, slathered in ketchup and relish—that and the smell— reminds me of the dead bird. The pigeon. And instead of a hot dog, I suddenly see blood, guts, gore, and I gag, vomit inching its way up my esophagus. I reach for my drink and force it back down, gargling, trying to get the taste of vomit from my mouth.

Mrs. Zulpo—*Eleanor*, she says to call her—doesn't notice. She keeps going. "I saw her obituary," she's saying. "It was a great write-up, a lovely tribute for a lovely woman," she says. I tell her that it was.

I submitted the death notice to the newspaper. I covered the cost of the obituary. I found an old photo of Mom to use, one that was a good six years old at least, taken back before she got sick.

We'd lived our entire lives in private, but for whatever reason I felt the whole world should know that she was dead.

"There have been other cleaning women since your mother. But never anyone as good as she was, as conscientious, as thorough. She was one of a kind, Jessie," she says, and I tell her I know. Eleanor tells me stories. Things I didn't know, or maybe I did. Memories that have been lost to time, erased clear from my brain's hard drive. About the time I helped myself to her Wedgwood china when Mom was cleaning. How I snatched it right from her hutch and set the dining room table to have a tea party with. "Wedgwood china," she tells me, grinning. "A single cup and saucer go for about a hundred dollars each. They had been my own mother's, given to me when she died. Heirlooms. Your poor mother," she laughs. "She nearly had a heart attack when she found you. I told her it was fine, that it wasn't like anything had gotten hurt. And besides, it was nice to see the dishes being put to use for a change."

And then she tells me that, at her suggestion, the three of us sat down at the dining room table and drank lemonade from the Wedgwood china.

It fills me with a sudden sense of nostalgia. A yearning for the past.

"What else do you remember?" I ask, needing more. Needing someone to fill in the gaps for me, all those details I can no longer remember.

Eleanor tells me how her children were grown by the time I arrived, and so it was nice to have a child in the house again. She didn't work outside of the home. When Mom and I came, she was grateful for the company. She used to look forward to the days we'd come. Usually she'd play with me while Mom cleaned, hide-and-go-seek in her home, or build forts from the newly washed sheets.

"You were a funny girl, Jessie," she tells me. "Silly and strong willed, a great sense of humor to boot," she says. "A bit ornery too. But those dimples," she adds as she takes a bite of the hot dog, speaking through a full mouth, "with those dimples you could get away with murder, Jessie." She laughs.

She says that anything Mom wanted done, she had to ask me twice. That the lunch Mom brought along for me, I refused to eat. That I was a far cry from shy, and would spend half of my days in her home creating a show to perform for her and Mom before we'd leave.

"You used to march around, insisting like the dickens that your name wasn't Jessie. Because you didn't like it back then, I think," she says then, saying I was adamant about it, insistent that my name wasn't Jessie. That my name was something else, but she doesn't remember what. "You would pout your face and stomp your foot and insist that people stop calling you Jessie. *Stop calling me that*, you'd cry, face turning red. Your mother would go along with it for a while, trying to ignore your antics. Because she knew you were doing it for attention and, if she didn't give in to you, sooner or later you'd quit. Though rarely did you quit," she smiles, telling me I was a headstrong little girl.

"You knew what you wanted," she says.

Eventually Mom would have enough of it, Eleanor tells me, and she'd get down to eye level and say, *That's enough, Jessie. We talked about this, remember?*

But I have no memory of this at all.

Why would I go around masquerading as something other than Jessie? I don't have time to come up with an answer because soon Eleanor is telling me how I used to carry an animal everywhere I went—a stuffed dog or a bear or a rabbit—but I couldn't care less about that because what I'm wondering is why in the world I would be so unrelenting about that name. About the name Jessie. Why I would insist it wasn't mine.

"And then there was your mother's name," Eleanor says

before I have a chance to think it through, and I ask, "What about it?"

Her eyebrows crease. She removes a pair of glasses and sets them on the countertop, rubbing at her eyes. "It's just that most little girls call their mother *Mom* or *Mommy*."

She leaves it at that and so I ask, "And I didn't?" thinking suddenly that Eleanor is mistaken. That she's wrong. Time has altered these memories of hers, or she's mistaken Mom and me for some other cleaning lady and child. Another child with dimples like mine. Because in all my life, she's only ever been one thing to me—Mom—or so I think.

Eleanor shakes her head and at the same time I see my hands before me, gripping the edges of the countertop, also shaking.

"You didn't," she says. "You called her by her given name."

Eleanor tells me that Mom would put up with it to a certain extent but then every now and again she'd get down and whisper in my ear, *We've talked about this, Jessie. Remember?* Same as she said about my own name. *You're to call me Mom.*

"For a short while, you'd remember. You'd remember to call your mother *Mom*. But before too long, you'd forget and go back to calling her by her Christian name. Eden."

I don't remember doing that.

EDEN

I drove the speed limit the entire way, not wanting to draw attention to myself. It snowed much of the time and the roads were slick, though being a Midwesterner, I'm quite accustomed to driving on slick roads. This wasn't my first time with snow. And yet it was my first getaway, my first flight. My first vanishing act of what I hoped wouldn't be many, because I prayed that the world would let me disappear, that he would let me go.

I found myself staring in the rearview mirror nearly the entire time, all along Highway 42 and to the interstate, knuckles turning white from their grip on the steering wheel, though I knew there was no logical way he knew where I was, or that he watched me leave. But still.

He might just be there.

When I arrived, the first thing I did was find an apartment that I could afford, which wasn't easy considering I have so little in the way of money, nearly nothing at all, quite literally ten dollars more than was the rent payment, which means that for the immediate future, we'll be eating bread and cheese. I purchased a paper at a newsstand and, on a snow-covered park bench, scanned the for-rent ads, settling on a studio apartment in Hyde Park. The building is all wrapped up in a creamy yellow brick facade that's gone to rack and ruin; it looks abandoned, uncared for and unloved, like me. The ad trumpeted a French Renaissance charm but if it's there, I can't see it.

On the way into the building, I watched a drug deal transpire on the street. It happened right there, right before my eyes, two shadowy figures lurking beside the building, where the tall structure obstructs the sun's rays, making the men harder to see. They were men, of course, because I find it hard to believe that two women would stand on the street corner trading money for drugs, a wad of folded-up cash for the clear plastic bag of pills that passed from one hand to the next. I never saw their faces or their eyes, for their heads were cloaked in the hoods of sweatshirts like headscarves. And yet the men were tall, lanky, flat. Undeniably men.

We passed by quickly, my eyes tethered to the broken concrete of the street, feet kicking up pebbles as I went, certain I could feel their eyes on me. I inserted my key and ducked into the foyer of the apartment complex, grateful to be separated by a wall of glass.

We can't stay here forever. It isn't safe, I don't think.

And now, inside the apartment, I bolt the door behind me and stare out the peephole for a minute or two, to be certain no one followed me in. Not the drug dealer or his buyer, and not anyone else. I move to the window next, parting the dusty, broken mini-blinds with my fingertips, peering out, my fingers turning gray with dust. I survey the street below to be sure we haven't been followed, that no one knows we are here.

The last tenant had been recently evicted, her belongings never reclaimed. Because of this, I've been endowed with a foul-smelling sofa, a banged-up table, a mattress with worrisome stains. That and a carton of eggs that expired last week. I don't think we'll eat them.

I open the newspaper and again turn to the classified ads. But this time, instead of searching the apartment listing, I go to the wanted ads, searching for a job as a house cleaner because really, that's the extent of my qualifications, and after the stunt I pulled at the hospital, references are out of the question. *Must be courteous, conscientious, previous experience preferred*, I read. *Must speak English. Have good communication skills, a great work ethic.* The wages are noted; I tally the number of hours I will need to work to pay another month's worth of rent in this shoddy complex. Sixty hours—that's what I'd need to work. Though we also need to eat.

This is no longer just about me.

I try to relax but she's kicking and upset now, thrashing about, and I find that I can't relax. I tell her it's okay, that she doesn't need to worry, that she's safe here with me, though even I don't know if that's true because I have yet to decipher if we're safe here, if I'm safe. I stroke her, running my hand along the flushed skin, and for a moment—only a moment—she stops fighting. She gives in.

I try on a name for size.

"Jessie," I say, taking her stillness as consent.

I'll call her Jessie.

I'm not a bad person, I remind myself, though in that moment as I sit—watching a roach as it scurries across the worn carpeting, reaching a wall, shimmying along the baseboards to where the rest of its family no doubt lies waiting—reflecting on the last twenty-four hours of my life, the last twenty-four days and weeks, I'm not entirely certain that's true. All sorts of emotions get churned up inside me, everything from sadness to regret and shame, and I think of him standing unsuspectingly at the cottage, knocking on the door in vain.

"You're not a bad person," I incant, believing that if I think on it long enough, if I say it enough times, a thousand times over, it might somehow turn true.

I didn't set out to do the things I did. There was never any willful intent, any malice, only a pining for something I didn't have, something I so desperately needed. You wouldn't condemn a famished child for stealing a loaf of bread, now would you? A homeowner for shooting an armed intruder to protect his family?

I'm not a bad person, I decide, far more resolute this time. I only did what I had to do.

JESSIE

WHEN I FINALLY MAKE my way back to Cornelia Avenue, it's evening. The colors of the sky have begun to change. Shadows fall across the street. The sun is thinking about going down.

I walk along Cornelia beside Old Faithful, staring at the million-dollar homes that fringe the street. They're mostly newly gutted homes with small tracts of grass. For each home lies a single tree on the road verge, fully grown. Its leaves form a canopy over the street where it joins with the tree on the other side. Conjoined twins.

The temperatures have fallen. It's no more than fifty-some degrees outside, a cold that creeps under my clothing, chilling me to the bone. The heat in the carriage home is stingy at best, when it runs. Though I toyed with the thermostat this morning, setting the temperature to seventy-two degrees, the furnace never kicked on before I left. When I arrive, it will be cold inside.

As I make my way along the street, the dread of nighttime

creeps in. The fear of eight long hours of darkness with nothing to do and only morbid thoughts to keep me company.

The front door of the greystone is open as I approach, though Ms. Geissler is nowhere to be seen. I stop on the sidewalk, wondering if I should let her know or if I should keep going. What I want to do is keep going, but my conscience says otherwise.

There's a garden on the front lawn of the greystone, one I didn't notice before, but now I do. It's not huge because city living doesn't allow for things to be huge. But it's magical. A blanket of yellows and oranges and reds that warms the earth. Tiny white butterflies hover above the blooms, levitating midair.

I blink once and they're gone because most likely they were never really there.

I make my way down the walkway, climbing the steps toward the front door. The home is large; three stories tall with a garden apartment to boot, one that peeks at me from beneath street level, hidden behind a black metal fence.

As I knock on the door, it pushes open more than it was before. My eyes take in the foyer, a carpeted runner, an unlit chandelier that dangles from the ceiling. "Hello?" I call out into the empty space, but if my landlord is here, she doesn't hear me.

My fingers press the doorbell and I hear the chime of it from inside, but still, there's no reply. "Hello?" I call again, laying a hand flat against the door and pressing it the rest of the way open. My feet cross the threshold as I step into the home.

I reach for a light switch and toggle it up and down, but nothing happens. The chandelier above me remains dark. It's not black in the home because the sun has yet to go all the way down. There's still some light outside, but it's fading fast. Soon it will be gone.

"Ms. Geissler?" I call out, explaining who I am and why I'm here. "It's Jessie," I say. "Jessie Sloane. Your new tenant. I just moved in to the carriage home," I call out, and at first I think the worst, that she's here somewhere, but that she's hurt. That she's had a nasty fall. That she can't answer me because she's lying on the ground just waiting to be found. That she's dead.

I don't think the obvious. That Ms. Geissler's in the shower and can't hear me. That she forgot to close the door on the way out rather than the way in. That she's not here.

"Ms. Geissler?" I call again, with an urgency to my voice this time. "Hello? Are you here?"

And it's only then that I hear the sound of a piano playing from upstairs. Classical music, I think. The kind you've heard before because it's famous. Mozart. Beethoven. I don't know which. The piano is quieted down from the distance, diluted, but still I hear it, the music staccato-like, sharp and disconnected.

And I breathe a sigh of relief because she's here. Because she's fine.

I could go home now.

I *should* go home now.

I should pull the door fully closed behind me and leave.

But instead I find myself hesitating at the base of the stairs. My hand grips the baluster as I stare up the flight of stairs, into the dark, cavernous second floor of the home. Because now the classical music has turned into some sort of ballad, and I find that it's haunting and beautiful.

That it's calling me, summoning me up the stairs.

Begging me to come and listen, to come and see.

And instead of leaving, my feet carry me up the stairs before I can think this through. I hold my breath as I go, listening only to the sound of the piano. Climbing upward, one step at a time.

The house is large, each room sprawling and grand, though they're hard to see for the scarcity of light, which becomes even more dim with each minute that passes by. Upstairs, my legs carry me to the bedroom from which the music comes. The only room that, as far as I can see, boasts light. The door is pulled to and so there's only a sliver of it. Only a sliver of light peeking from beneath the door slab.

I go to it.

Standing before the closed door, I listen to the sound of the piano play. My hand drops to the door's handle and it's unintentional when I turn the knob. I can't help myself; it just happens. I press a hand flat against the door and push it open, so slowly so that it doesn't squeak. I see her there on the piano's bench, her back to me. Her fingers move nimbly over the piano keys, foot pressing against the pedal with obvious expertise. I find myself entranced by her song, by the rhythmic motion of her hands and feet.

And then she stops playing.

And it strikes me suddenly, an awareness.

She knows that I am here.

I shouldn't be here.

All at once I feel like a trespasser. Like I've gone too far. This is not my home and I have no business being here.

She doesn't turn. "Something I can help you with?" she asks and I gasp first before I laugh. A nervous laugh. An exhausted laugh. One I can't make stop though I try. And only then does she turn and look at me as I press my hands to my mouth to smother the laugh.

Ms. Geissler looks to me to be about sixty years old. Her

hair is short, a dyed blond that's feathered around the edges. She wears glasses, dark, plastic frames that sit on the bridge of her nose. There's a frailty about her, her body gaunt, cloaked in a cotton dress. She rises to her feet and only then do I see that she's petite. There are lines on her face, laugh lines, frown lines, crow's-feet. And yet they look more regal than old. She's a beautiful woman.

"Jessie, isn't it?" she asks, and though it takes a minute to find my voice, I say that it is. She says that it's nice to meet me. She steps toward me, slipping her hand into mine. My hand shakes as it did this afternoon, a quiver that won't quit.

"I'm sorry," I stammer. "I didn't mean to interrupt," I say. Though I've done far worse than interrupt. "I rang the doorbell. I knocked. The front door was open," I explain, voice as doddery as my hands, just barely managing to scrape the memories together and remember why I'm here. "You left your front door open," I say again, for lack of anything better to say.

"Oh," she says, chastising the door latch. How it's old. How it doesn't work properly. How she needs to get it fixed, as she needs to get many things in this old home fixed.

"How is everything with the carriage home?" she asks instead, and I tell her fine. I say how much I like it. I compliment the hardwood floors because I can think of nothing else to say. I say that they are pretty. I thank her for letting me stay there. She says it's no bother.

It's awkward and uncomfortable, all the conversation forced. I think then that I should leave. I've overstayed my welcome because I was never welcome in the first place.

But just as I'm about to say my goodbyes and go, a noise comes from somewhere upstairs. From the third floor of the home. What it sounds like to me is the thud of a textbook falling. Something heavy and dense. I glance upward, finding a hatch there, a pulldown ladder that when folded up and stowed away becomes one with the ceiling, as it is now.

"What's that?" I ask, but Ms. Geissler's face goes suddenly blank, and she shakes her head, asking, "What's what?"

"The noise," I say. "Is someone there?" as I point up toward the ceiling.

"I didn't hear anything," she replies.

I hold my breath and listen in vain for more noises coming from up above. But they don't come. The house is silent, and I know then: I made it up.

My eyes burn. I rub at them, making them more red than they were before, still aware of my shaking hands.

"I must be mistaken," I say, holding my hands out before me so that I can see the way they tremble. They're cold. But that's not the reason for the trembling. It's something far worse than that, I think. Something neurological. I have my brain to thank for this. Because after all these nights without sleep, my brain functions are out of whack.

I try and convince myself that the shaky hands aren't degenerative. That they aren't getting worse. And yet there's no denying the fact.

My hands are shaking far more than they were this afternoon.

It's as if she can read my mind.

"You've been having trouble sleeping," she says, more of a statement than a question. She's not asking me because she knows. Behind the glasses, her eyes are a soft gray, staring at me in pity. I wonder how it is she knows I haven't been sleeping. Does it have something to do with the dark circles under my eyes, the bags, the red pools of blood that flood my sclera?

"I saw your light on late last night," she says by means of

explanation, and I think of myself last night. Hearing the strange pinging sound through the floor register, the voices, and turning the light on to investigate. It was nothing, of course, though still I spent the rest of the night lying in bed unable to sleep, forever indebted to the sun when it finally decided to rise and I headed off in search of caffeine, my magical potion, which becomes far less potent with each passing day that I don't sleep.

What makes not sleeping even worse than the crippling fatigue is the boredom that infiltrates those nighttime hours. The misery. The morbid thoughts that keep me company all night long. Last night I found myself thinking about ashes and bone fragments. That's what remains after a body has been incinerated. When Mom came back to me from the crematorium, I expected something soft, like the ashes left behind in Mom's and my fireplace. On cold nights, she and I used to toss in a few logs, sit on the floor beneath the same blanket, trying to stay warm. When the fire burned out, the ashes that remained were soft. Delicate. I didn't know that Mom's ashes would be coarse like sand, like cat litter, and not soft like ashes. Or that there would be bone fragments.

After Mom's 130 pounds were reduced to just 4, I didn't have the wherewithal to bring the urn to the crematorium with me so that they could place her inside. And so instead she came to me in a little baggie in a sturdy box. I was tasked with making the transfer to the rhubarb urn, this straight, canister-like contraption that's anything but the round body, narrow neck of your classic urn. You wouldn't even know it was an urn except for Mom's name impressed in the clay along with the years of her birth and death. Her stint on earth. Forty-nine years.

I made the transfer at the kitchen table, the day after I

brought her remains home from the crematorium. The same table where we used to eat. I used a funnel. Same funnel we used to use when transferring sugar cookie icing to the piping bags. When I was done, a fine mist of Mom covered the tabletop. I wiped her away with the palm of a hand. Then Mom was stuck to me, and it wasn't like I could just wash her off with soap and water. Because it was Mom. I couldn't just wash Mom down the kitchen sink.

These are the things you don't think about when someone has died. You don't want to think about them.

And yet these are the thoughts that keep me up all night. A fine mist of Mom on the palm of my hand.

"I couldn't sleep," I say, leaving it at that, pretending it was a one-time thing, not letting on to the fact that I haven't slept in all these nights.

"Try a glass of warm milk," she offers. "It always helps me sleep like a baby," she says, and I tell her I will. But I won't. I've tried that already and besides, I hate the taste of warm milk.

But then it comes again. The noise, one I'm certain I didn't imagine this time. Another dull thud.

And it's unintentional when my shaky hand lifts up to tug down the ladder and see for myself what's inside.

"You don't want to do that," Ms. Geissler snaps, her words brusque.

I freeze in place, insisting, "There's something there," and only then does she reconsider.

"I didn't want to scare you," she explains, and I breathe a sigh of relief. I didn't imagine the noise. It was there.

"It's squirrels," she tells me. "They've taken over the place," she laments. "I haven't stepped foot up there for a while." She says that she's been working with a pest control service to have them removed, but she's quite sure the service is more adept at bringing squirrels into her home then getting them out. The space is uninhabitable for now, until the problem gets sorted out. She can't bring herself to go up there, not until the squirrels are gone and her contractor repairs the damage.

"The squirrels," she complains, "have chewed holes in the walls. They've gnawed their way through electrical wires. They've ruined a perfectly good lamp. I've switched services, mind you. But getting rid of squirrels is no easy task. I need a roofer to come and replace the tiles and block the squirrels' way in, but the roofer won't come until all the squirrels are out. The darn things have it in for me," she says, sighing exasperatedly, and it doesn't once occur to me not to believe her.

I say to her, "Sounds like a mess."

Out the window, I see that the sun has finished setting. Darkness has arrived, anchoring itself to the earth for the night. Ending another day.

"It's getting late," I say, excusing myself, saying my goodbyes, and leaving.

I make my way around the periphery of the house, cutting across the patio and onto the lawn. There I pause midstride, hands on hips, and look skyward to see that the stars are lost somewhere behind the clouds. That there isn't a star in sight. The moon is there, but only a sliver of it. A crescent moon that doesn't do anything to light up the night. The fall air is cool; goose bumps appear on my arms. I rub at them, hoping the friction will make them go away. For now it does, though I'm dreading another night in the freezing cold carriage home.

The home is enveloped in blackness as I arrive. I have to fight to get the key into its hole. Twice I drop it, scrabbling around on the stoop to hunt it down.

The sound of a siren in the distance startles me. As I glance backward, over my shoulder to see the red and blue emergency lights whirling through the sky, I find Ms. Geissler standing in the back doorway of her home. She's illuminated by kitchen lights, easier to see than me, who stands in total darkness.

And yet her eyes are unmistakably on mine as if she's been watching me the entire time.

I find the keyhole and open the door. I hurry inside.

As I climb the lopsided steps, I feel the weight of fatigue bearing down on me. Fatigue from physical exertion and fatigue from lack of sleep. I lie down on the mattress, staring at my shaky hands before my eyes. There's an anemic quality to them. Blanched and mealy, the skin at their edges disappearing somehow, evanescing, like a loose thread being tugged from the hem of a shirt, the whole thing unraveling, coming apart at the seams. That's me. Coming apart at the seams. Little by little, I'm disappearing.

I look again at my hands, and this time they are fine. Intact. But still shaking.

I close my eyes and even though sleep is there within reach and I stretch my hand out to grab it, it's unattainable. Elusive and shifty. It moves away, mocking me. Laughing in my face.

For as tired as I am, I still cannot sleep.

EDEN

December 21, 1996
Egg Harbor

FOR MONTHS NOW, AARON and I have become slaves
to the red circles on my pocket-size calendar, our intima-
cies slated out in advance. During my most fertile days we
make love two, sometimes three times a day, though there's
something inorganic about it now, something mechanical and
forced. Our entire world, it seems, has become about making
a baby, and I struggle to remember what our lives were like
before we made the decision to start a family.

Two nights ago I stayed up until he was home from work,
in bed, reading my book. Twice I rose from bed to look outside, searching through the bare trees for signs of headlights
in the distance—a shock of blinding yellow against the blackness of night—rambling down the long, winding drive. But
there were none. The night was pitch-black, no moon anywhere, not a star to be seen. It seemed to take forever for him
to be home.

The bedroom lamp was dimmed, a candle burning on
the dresser for ambience, though when he finally did arrive,

Aaron took one look at that candle and blew it out, thinking I'd gotten tired and plumb forgot about the burning candle. The small room filled with the noxious smell of smoke as he pulled his chef getup from his body, dropping it to the floor. He climbed into bed beside me, saying how he was so tired, how his feet hurt. His words were slurred with simple lethargy and fatigue. He didn't bother to turn off the light. I smelled the chophouse on him, the garlic, the Worcestershire sauce, the flesh of chops and steaks.

And yet there it was, another red-circled date on the calendar.

Beneath the blankets I wore a satin robe and beneath the robe nothing, though in it I didn't feel nearly as sexy as I'd thought I would, as I'd *hoped* I would, a feeling that was only exacerbated when I untied the ribbon from around my waist, revealing myself to him, and in Aaron's eyes spied a moment of hesitation, an excuse ready to form on his lips.

"Remember?" I asked, childlike hope in my eyes. "I'm ovulating," I reminded him, and before he could speak, before he could tell me why it wasn't a good night, I lowered myself beneath the sheets and easily changed his mind.

I don't think he minded that I did. In fact, I think he was quite pleased.

When we were through, Aaron pulled away and moved to his side of the bed, leaving me and my elevated hips alone in the hopes that this time, gravity might work its magic.

For three days in a row now it's gone like this, though tonight Aaron did object and it was much harder to make him acquiesce, and even when he did there was little satisfaction in it, little pleasure, but rather the knowledge that he was doing this for me. Because I wanted him to. Because I was making him do it. There was resentment in it, disgruntlement in his every move. When we were done I offered a pitiful *thank you*, which felt entirely wrong, as we each drifted to our own side of the bed, an ocean of space spread between us.

It's become apparent that these days we do it because we have to, not because either of us wants to have sex. We skip any sort of foreplay and get straight to the grunt work, finding sex as pleasurable as brushing teeth or washing dishes. Our movements have become as repetitive and predictable as cleaning laundry.

Just like any other of our daily chores, we've begun to grudgingly make love for three days out of the month, finding the other twenty-seven to be a blissful reprieve.

January 9, 1997
Egg Harbor

It took nearly thirty minutes to get to the obstetrician appointment, and all along the way, all I could hear was the grinding of snow beneath the tires' tread. Outside it was cold, a frosty thirty-two degrees, and the plump clouds looked like they might burst apart at the seams at any moment, burying us with three more inches of snow. Aaron was torn, worried we wouldn't be home in time for his shift, but feeling the need to go too. To be at the appointment. He vacillated about it for a good five or ten minutes, standing in the open doorway, letting the cold air into our home.

In the end, he decided to go so that as we drove south on Highway 42, both of us quiet, I felt a great guilt about it, knowing that if he was late to work, it would be my fault.

The obstetrician was in Sturgeon Bay, a seventeen-mile drive. He was the closest I could find and also came with a recommendation, one from Miranda, the only woman in town I knew well enough to ask. Miranda, who drove her three boys to my home last week in her Dodge Caravan—windshield caked with ice crystals still, so that it was near impossible to see through the rimy glass—because it was far too cold to walk.

Miranda, who sat sprawled on my sofa, feet raised to the coffee table, while I rocked her crying two-month-old baby, Carter, to sleep.

Miranda, who was so overwhelmed with motherhood that she couldn't stand to be alone with her own three kids.

Miranda, who revealed to me that she was pregnant again, that it was a mistake this time, that they hadn't been trying. "Because who in their right mind tries for more when they already have three kids?" she asked, staring at me sadly as if I should take pity on her for this obvious misfortune, but what I felt instead was infuriated and sick, anger and bile rising quickly inside me.

Miranda confessed to me that though she and Joe had waited the recommended six weeks after Carter was born to fool around, sure enough, Joe managed to knock her up on the first try, and already the morning sickness had set in so that her boys were forced to watch even more TV than ever before because Miranda didn't have the stamina to entertain them all day, let alone feed them. "The nerve of that bastard," she said of Joe and his evident virility, and then she asked what in the world was taking Aaron and me so long to conceive.

"You don't think," she asked, eyes wide, "that you're infertile, do you? That that handsome husband of yours is shooting blanks?"

As I sat beside him in the car, driving to the obstetrician appointment, listening to the pulverization of snow beneath the wheels, staring at the clouds, I couldn't help but wonder if that was the case. Was Aaron shooting blanks? Was Aaron *infertile*?

Aaron, who could do anything, who could fix anything, could not create a child?

Aaron, to whom everything came so easily, had difficulty making a baby?

The thought alone made me angry and annoyed. Angry at Aaron because why, for all the things he was so capable of doing, was he incapable of doing *this*?

Why couldn't he fix this? Why couldn't he make this right?

Assigning fault seemed to be the name of the game these days, pointing fingers, attaching blame. Whose fault was it that we didn't yet have a baby?

March 11, 1997
Egg Harbor

What I've come to learn after being referred to a fertility specialist is that even though I get my period each month with moderate regularity, my body isn't ovulating correctly, isn't always ovulating. *Anovulation*, it's called, a word I've never heard of before but now think about at every waking hour and when I should be asleep. If I'm being honest, this comes as little surprise to me. My body is simply going through the motions, the preparations of the endometrium—the lining of my uterus readying itself to welcome a fertilized egg—and then sloughing off when no egg moves in. It's not that the egg wasn't fertilized by Aaron's sperm. It's that it simply wasn't there to begin with.

Today I began my third cycle of Clomid. After months of this, I have no sense of humility left, no modesty. I've paraded my private parts for every doctor, nurse and technician in the fertility clinic to see, while all Aaron ever had to do was drop off a sperm sample and endure a simple blood draw. It hardly seems fair. The first month I didn't ovulate. Last month we upped the dosage and, though Dr. Landry spied two follicles when he performed his ultrasound—forcing the transvaginal ultrasound probe between my legs so that I should rightfully have felt violated and ashamed, but no longer did, sending Aaron and me home with strict orders to have sex—we didn't get pregnant.

The pills make me weepy all the time, for no apparent reason at all, though having seen the inventory of potential side effects, I consider it a blessing that the only one I'm doomed to endure is the predisposition for crying. I cry at the market; I cry in the car. I cry at home while mopping floors and folding laundry and standing in the doorway to one of the spare bedrooms, wondering if it will ever hold a child, steeling myself for another cycle of Clomid that will likely end again with my monthly flow.

To counter Aaron's low sperm motility, as it's called, he's switched to wearing loose-fitting underpants (I don't tell Miranda this), and is tasked with finding ways to reduce stress in his life, stress which neither of us knew he had. He now sleeps until after ten o'clock every morning so that we no longer share our day's coffee on the dock, which is fine anyway seeing as the eternal winter has trapped us indoors and there are no sailboats to be seen on the bay, none until spring. He takes herbal supplements and when the temperatures aren't too abysmal will go for a walk or a run, so that our days together are mere hours at best. This too is fine, seeing as we don't have much to talk about anymore, nothing that doesn't involve the many things the world is reluctant to let us have: strong, capable sperm; regular ovulation; a positive pregnancy test; a baby.

It isn't that Aaron doesn't have enough sperm—he does—it's that what he has doesn't swim properly and isn't able to travel the four inches or so to where my egg may or may not be waiting.

In short, we're both to blame, though there isn't a moment that I don't wonder which of us is to blame more and even though I think it's me, I *know* it's me, there is a part of me aggrieved that I'm the only one forced to record my body temperature, to take ovulation tests, to cry in public for no sound reason at all, to travel to the fertility clinic again and again, to be probed so that some doctor or technician can gaze inside me and at my ovaries, while all Aaron has to do is take an herbal supplement from time to time and exercise on occasion.

It doesn't seem fair. It doesn't seem right.

I've come to resent Aaron for this, as I've come to resent him for many things.

March 13, 1997
Egg Harbor

I field questions nearly every day about when Aaron and I are going to have a baby, often from my stepmother or Aaron's mother, calling on the phone when he's at work, asking not-so-subtly for grandchildren.

When can they expect them? When will there be good news to share?

It's not that grandchildren are in short supply because they aren't. Instead it's that Aaron and I have been married for over two years, and society doesn't take well to that: two nearly thirty-years-olds, married for over two years without kids, as if there's something unthinkable about it, something taboo.

Is there something wrong with that?

It feels as if there is.

A married woman of my age without a child is quite the anomaly these days.

I can't bring myself to say aloud that we're trying, *trying and failing* to make a baby because I don't want pity and I don't want advice. And so instead I tell Aaron's mother and my stepmother *soon*, wishing that my own mother were still alive because hers is the only advice I want and need.

I spend my days waiting. Waiting for Aaron to wake up, waiting for Aaron to leave, waiting for Aaron to get home so I can again close my eyes and sleep. Waiting for a new cycle of Clomid to begin, to ovulate, to make love to Aaron like robots would do, hasty and unfeeling, and then waiting for the negative pregnancy test results, the loyal, trusty blood.

It's the only thing I can depend on anymore. That sooner or later, my period will come.

March 14, 1997
Egg Harbor

Spring looms on the horizon.

It's weeks away still, but every now and then a day blooms before me, fifty or sixty degrees and full of sun, so that it's easier to get through than the endlessly gray winter days.

These rare springlike days I leave the cottage when Aaron is away and head into town. I've discovered a dance studio there, completely by chance—I didn't seek it out—a small single-story cottage on Church Street that tiny ballerinas move in and out of all day.

The first day I spotted the studio, I saw an empty park bench nearby, which was warm and welcoming, set directly in a shaft of sunlight so that even though it was no more than fifty-two degrees outside, I felt snug, my skin warm from the sun's generous beams.

For nearly an hour I watched the ballerinas, toddlers mainly in leotards with their hair pinned neatly back in buns. Their little voices were happy and high-pitched, like birds, as they clung to their mothers' hands, coming and going like clockwork, nearly every hour on the hour.

There was one group in particular that caught my eye. A group of sixteen—eight mothers and their daughters—who arrived en masse around noon, a whole bundle of giggly girls with women trailing behind, women who sipped lattes and gossiped while I sat alone on a park bench, feeling sorry for myself, isolated from society because I didn't fit in. Because I didn't have a child.

The women were beautiful, every last one of them, which for whatever reason made me feel dirty, self-conscious and ashamed. I smiled as they walked by, but not one looked at me and no one smiled in reply. They wore peasant tops and floaty skirts; cowboy boots; big, baggy sweaters; hobo bags; while me, on the other hand, I sat wrapped up in a sweatshirt of Aaron's that had faded and shrunk in the wash, feeling alone, bloated, desperate, wanting for a child.

How different I am from those mothers.

I could never be one of them, one of those women who travel in a pack, whispering secrets about their husbands, their children's nighttime habits, which little ones still wet the bed. All because I didn't have a child. Because without a child, I had nothing to offer them.

Because I'm nothing, I easily reasoned then, if not a mother.

There's no other justification for my life.

I watched them as they walked by, as they closed in on the dance studio. And then, after the women had passed and I assumed the parade was through, I noticed one little girl straggling behind, nearly stagnant on the sidewalk. Struggling to keep up. Too busy examining the buds on the trees. Smaller than the rest, which made me think of the piglet in Charlotte's Web. Wilbur, saved from slaughter by little Fern. I was captivated by her, holding my breath as she passed by, joining the others in the studio. Only when she was gone did I allow myself to breathe.

And now twice, sometimes three times a week I find myself sitting there on that bench, watching the dancers come and go, wishing one of them, any single one of them—but especially the littlest one, a head shorter than the rest, straw-colored hair and a collection of freckles, whose tiny feet always lag behind so that one day I worry she'll be forgotten—was mine.

I've become an addict really, and the only thing that eases the symptoms of withdrawal is seeing children, is being in the company of children. They are my fix, an antidote for the restlessness, the irritability, the tremor of my hands that is only exacerbated with each passing month that I don't get pregnant.

The little girl can't be more than three years old, pudgy arms, legs and cheeks still padded with baby fat that will one day wear away, no doubt, so that she'll look like any one of the ladies she tags along after, with their long limbs and their long hair and their coffee.

I don't like the way I feel sitting there on that park bench, eyeing children who are not mine. But I have nothing better to do with my time, and I don't think I could stop if I tried.

I suggested to Aaron that I look for a job, for some diversion from the long, lonely afternoons while he is away. Aaron isn't game. He'd rather I *not* work, which makes no sense to me. The financial burden of fertility treatments is steep; we could use the additional income. We've begun to argue about things like the cost of ground beef, the cost of electricity.

Aaron and I are monitoring the Clomid cycles, which means for each failed attempt we are quite literally throwing away hundreds of dollars for the medication, blood work and ultrasounds to see whether my body is releasing eggs, and when. Insurance won't cover these costs because, of course, some high-and-mighty insurance company doesn't give a darn whether Aaron and I ever have a baby, and so the procedure is considered *elective*. We are electing to waste thousands of dollars to try and conceive a baby, while other parents, far less capable or worthy parents, are given one for free.

"You're under so much stress already," Aaron said when I suggested applying for a job, and "Why not just focus on this?" meaning making a baby, as if somehow I'd been unfocused, and as if that lack of focus was the reason we were still without a child. I'd been too cavalier about it, too casual, too devil-may-care. He didn't use those words, not a single one of them, and yet that's exactly what I heard when he came home from work after midnight that night and, though I lamented about being bored all day, about being alone, he suggested I not apply for a job, but rather focus on *this*, with a sweeping gesture toward my vacuous womb.

I screamed at him then. I slammed a door. I locked him out of the bedroom so he slept on the sofa for the night.

Never before have I screamed at him. Never before have I raised my voice.

He didn't object to sleeping on the sofa. It was one in the morning. He was tired, he told me. "Eden, that's enough," he said with a sigh while gathering his pillow from the head of our bed. "I need to sleep."

I sat there in the bedroom that night, in the dark, propped up against pillows and not lying down. My hands still shook even hours after my fit was through. A headache slunk up the base of my neck and consumed my skull so that every part of my head hurt. My eyes burned from crying and though I tried to blame the medication for this—after all, mood swings and a propensity for crying were both common side effects of the Clomid—I didn't know whether or not they were to blame this time.

Maybe it was just me.

I felt sorry come morning.

But I didn't apologize and neither did Aaron. Instead he left for work earlier than ever before and I returned to the dance studio, an addict in need of a fix.

March 19, 1997
Egg Harbor

When Clomid alone failed to work, Dr. Landry suggested IUI. Intrauterine insemination. Placing Aaron's sluggish sperm directly into my uterus so that they don't have to paddle through those four inches of mucousy space all on their own, so that they will have an easier time finding and fertilizing my egg without getting lost, swimming in circles in my vaginal canal as they are apt to do. Each month, Aaron and I have quite literally thrown away money, frittered away follicles and eggs, doled out hundreds of dollars on medication and ultrasounds for nothing. My trips to see Dr. Landry have been a waste. It's time to try something new. Intrauterine insemination will add a couple hundred dollars to our monthly expenditure, but will also increase the likelihood of conception, especially in cases like ours where low sperm motility is to blame.

There it was again, that word: *blame.*

There is also the added benefit that with IUI Aaron and I won't have to have sex, which is a blessing in and of itself. Aaron is capable of collecting his sample all on his own in the comfort of a private room at the clinic, complete with pornographic videos and magazines, where sexy, buxom women far more appealing to the eye than me will help us create a child. It mortified him to have to do this, and yet after months of invasive ultrasounds and repeated blood draws, after digesting medication that made me moody, that made me cry, after poking myself in the gut with shots of hormones for months on end, this seemed only fair. This seemed right. The nurse tendered my assistance, saying I could keep Aaron company if I'd like, but with a sideways glance, he went in without me and closed the door, and there was a spasm of jealousy, a shooting pain searing through my head as though someone had momentarily lodged an ice pick into my skull.

I envisioned Aaron on the other side of that door, aroused by some strumpet on the television screen and not me.

And then hours later, after the sperm had been collected and cleaned, it was my turn to be put to work, to lie on the exam table, completely undressed from the waist down with only a drape sheet to provide that false sense of privacy, while Dr. Landry placed first a catheter and then Aaron's sperm inside me.

And then sent us home to wait.

Aaron, as always, went to work, leaving me alone and bored, and so I drove into town and sought out that small dance studio on Church Street and sat on the park bench, watching the little ballerinas come and go, searching for the smallest one with the straw-like hair and freckles, a head shorter than the rest, who always struggled to keep up with her mother and friends.

I had to wait awhile, but eventually she came and my heart skipped a beat. My hands went numb. I held my breath.

I saw her ambling first through the double blue doors of the studio, already lagging behind before she'd ever stepped foot outside, grappling with the weight of the door because there was no one around to hold it for her. Her tiny head barely surpassed the door's crash bar. The others were already a good five or ten paces ahead, moving down the concrete sidewalk in the direction of town, little girls gabbing merrily about an afternoon playdate while their mothers followed behind, paper cups of coffee in hand. Only once did a mother turn around to see where she was, calling out, "Snap to it, Olivia, or you'll get left behind," and then she turned again, facing forward, never again checking on Olivia, who brought up the rear, the caboose on some sort of high-speed train that had somehow gotten off track.

She had a name now. *Olivia.*

But Olivia's mother was fully immersed in a conversation with the ladies, listening to one of the other mothers complain about her husband's long hours and relentless travel schedule. He was in Tampa Bay this week on business, and that new admin assistant from the office had gone along too, the one her husband talked about at the dinner table, so that she couldn't help but be concerned.

"You don't think?" asked one of the other ladies, and Olivia's mother piped in with "Oh, you poor thing."

And it was decided then. This woman's husband was having an affair.

Through all this, no one paid attention to Olivia, who had fallen even farther behind.

I had no intent of rising from the park bench as she passed by. None at all. The thought didn't cross my mind until a single bobby pin fell from her hair, a silver sprung hairpin that dropped to the ground at such a frequency only I could hear. Little Olivia kept walking, leaving the hairpin behind. Her mother kept walking, now nearly twenty or thirty paces ahead. Only I paused to retrieve the hairpin, falling in line behind Olivia and the rest of her troupe, six steps behind and struck dumb.

I couldn't speak.

I could have called her by name; I could have tapped her on the shoulder and handed her the bobby pin. But I didn't. Instead I shadowed her by a mere three feet, eyes gaping at the lavender leotard and tutu, the sheer white tights, the hair done up in a bun, starting to lose its hold as strands of brown and yellow drifted through the springlike air. Beside our feet, the snow had melted, leaving puddles that returning birds paused to drink from. On the trees there were buds, tiny shamrock-green buds about to burst forth with leaves.

I never once thought about taking her, about grabbing a hold of her with my hand pressed to her mouth so that she wouldn't scream. I didn't think of luring her away, bewitching her with the promise of a puppy or ice cream. I only wanted to watch for a while, to walk a breath behind and pretend for just this one moment in time that she was mine.

As I followed Olivia down the sidewalk, a conversation played out in my mind.

Slow down, baby girl, I thought to myself, whispering the words in my head. *Come hold Mama's hand*, I urged, and in my imaginings I held out my hand as little Olivia slackened a bit, slowing down, turning to me so I could see the color of her eyes, the wealth of freckles she'd no doubt one day either outgrow or grow to hate. She slipped her hand inside mine and I squeezed tight, careful not to let go as we passed through an intersection while the traffic on either side paused to let us through. Olivia's hand was easy to hold. Her steps fell into sync with mine.

It was the raucous laughter of the other girls that broke my trance, bringing me back to the earth, back to my physical existence. To reality. They had all turned at once, calling Olivia a snail, a slowpoke, waiting for her to catch up so they could go get ice-cream cones, and even though I knew it was all in jest—Olivia's piping laughter was proof of this, no?—my heart ached for her for being called names, for being the poky little puppy, always lagging behind.

And then my heart ached for me when she skipped off with her friends, leaving me behind, standing alone on the sidewalk with her bobby pin in my hand.

I hoped that just once she would turn and see me and know that I was there.

I kept Olivia's bobby pin as a token of luck.

Ten days later, my period arrived.

And now another month has come and gone without a baby.

JESSIE

MY NIGHTTIME THOUGHTS CAN be grouped into four categories. They follow the same pattern, the same predictable rotation each night. Wash, rinse, dry, repeat.

It all begins with the morbid thoughts where I obsess over death and dying, of being dead, trapped inside an urn, unable to breathe. They settle in around twilight, when the sun sinks beneath the horizon, slipping away to play with kids on the other side of the world. It's then that I start to wonder how much time I have left on earth. I think about how and when I will die. Will it hurt when I die? Did it hurt when Mom died?

These morbid thoughts soon mutate into grieving, sinking ones where I miss Mom so much it hurts. By this point in the night, the world has turned black and I lie on my mattress in a black room, confined by blackness. A prisoner of the night. In all my life, it was always Mom and me, like Batman and Robin, Lucy and Ethel. Shaggy and Scooby-Doo. We were a team. Without her I don't know what to do. I spend half the night pleading for her back. Because I don't know who I am without her. Because, without her, I am nothing.

I don't cry about it because my eyes are done crying. They've dried up. And so instead I think things like, if Mom isn't here, then I don't want to be here either. It's grim, and yet it's true.

My thoughts go on like this for what feels like hours because it probably is. Eventually they turn into a guilt trip, where I loathe myself for sleeping through Mom's death. For getting testy with her when she puked for the sixth time in a row, missing the toilet by a mile. For not speaking to her for weeks when she wouldn't come clean to me about my dad. For not holding her hand the time she chaperoned my fifth grade field trip to the planetarium, or bothering to thank her for the embroidery thread she got me in middle school—a half dozen colors to make friendship bracelets with. I'd only huffed and stomped off to another room, thinking how stupid could she be. Didn't she know I didn't have any friends? These memories haunt me now.

In truth, Mom and I hardly fought. The only arguments she and I ever had were mostly over my father. Mom never wanted to talk about him—she refused to talk about him—and so I snuck around her back to try and learn more.

I was six years old when I first realized I didn't have a father. Until then I was too oblivious to see that other kids did and I didn't. Mom and I lived alone. We kept to ourselves much of the time. I didn't go to preschool and I didn't have friends. I didn't know much of anything outside of my world with Mom, not until school began, and then my world grew exponentially larger, though still, in comparison to everyone else's, it was small.

It was my first day of kindergarten when I realized that all of the kids in the class, aside from me, had both a mom and a dad. I remember that day, organizing our belongings inside the bulky metal cubbyholes, while our moms hovered in the classroom, talking to the teacher, talking to other moms. Everyone except for my mom, because she stood there alone, talking to no one. This confused me. Why didn't Mom talk to the other women?

But what confused me even more was the huddle of men in the classroom. A whole busload of them. Not just moms, but moms *and* men. Who were these men, and what were they doing here?

I asked one little girl. I pointed at the giant of a man standing by her side. *Who is that?* I asked, eyes wide, looking skyward. She said it was her dad, and though I'd heard that word before, it wasn't one that was readily in my vocabulary.

I tallied up the men in the room, realizing that every single child had one but me.

The mention of my father didn't come up again until later in the school year, when some kid asked where he was. We'd had a music performance and, while everyone else had a mom and dad in tow—grandma and grandpa too—I only had Mom. And things like that, when you're six, are big news. How Jessie Sloane doesn't have a dad.

Where's your dad? the kid asked, all dressed up in a sweater-vest and pants.

I don't have one, I said, thinking that was the end of it. But he came back with some comment about how *everyone has a dad*, and others started to laugh.

I asked Mom about it that night at home. I had to know. *Where's my dad?* I asked, standing in her bedroom doorway while she lay on the bed, bare feet crossed at the ankles, reading a book. Even at six years old, I could see that she was tired from a day spent cleaning someone else's home.

I didn't wait for her reply. *Joey Malone said everyone has a dad,* I told Mom as she uncrossed her ankles and set her bookmark between the pages of her book. *So where's mine?* I asked, feeling aggrieved all of a sudden. As aggrieved as a little kid can be.

Mom was keeping something from me.

Mom had a secret that she wouldn't share with me.

Mom's face turned as red as hot coal. *Joey had no right to say that,* she told me. *Not everyone has a dad. Not you.*

But her answer came with no explanation.

Maybe he was dead. Maybe they were divorced. Maybe they were never married in the first place. Or maybe I never really had a dad.

Still, I started snooping around the house to be sure, in case there was something hiding there that I might find. Evidence. A clue.

A few years later I became more tenacious about it, more annoying. I asked Mom again where my father was. What had happened to him. *Is he dead?* I wanted to know. I said that word with the testiness of a preteen. The exasperation. *Dead.*

But she wouldn't say. Time and again, she changed the subject; she pretended not to hear me ask. She had a brilliant way of mincing words, of making me forget what I had asked. Of clamming up and saying nothing.

And yet, again and again, I asked. A hundred times after that. But never did she tell me.

I became ruthless about it.

When I was twelve I set a place at the dinner table for him. Whoever he might be. Just in case he decided to show. Mom swiped his silverware from the table post-haste. Flung it back in the drawer.

Let's not do this, Jessie, she said.

I searched city streets for his face. Never sure what I was looking for, but always looking. I wondered if he had blondish hair and dimples like me. Or if he was a brunette, a redhead, maybe even some other ethnicity.

Maybe we looked nothing alike.

Or maybe we were the kind that could pass for twins.

I learned that dimples are inherited. A dominant trait. Meaning only one parent would have to have them for me to have them. And seeing as Mom had none, I easily reasoned that they came from *him*. From *Dad*. That, barring some sort of genetic mutation, I'd inherited them from my father.

What a dimple really is is a birth defect. A short facial muscle that pulls on your skin when you smile, causing indentations in the cheek. My father and I are, therefore, both defected.

I made up names for him. Occupations. I sized up men with dimples at random, wondering if any of them were him.

I imagined him with a different wife and kids. Me with half brothers and sisters, a family. In my delusion, every last one of them had dimples.

Before bed, I'd leave the porch light on, so that he could find our home if ever he came to visit. So that he'd know which one was ours. Which bungalow in a sea of bungalows belonged to me.

When I was fourteen, I attempted a crop top for school. It wasn't my thing, bearing my belly button for all to see. But it was a camouflage T, soft and green, and I was fourteen. Feeling rebellious. Trying to fit in with the crowd but failing. Instead I stood out like a sore thumb, always light-years behind the latest fad.

Mom's mouth dropped. She shook her head. She said no to

the crop top, told me to march upstairs and change. To *march*. I put up a fight, standing with my hands on my hips, pouting. Sputtering the nonsense of a fourteen-year-old girl.

But Mom would have none of it. It wasn't up for discussion, she told me, saying for a third time to *march*. Pointing at the stairs.

My words were brisk. *I bet that if my dad were here, he'd let me,* I said. She looked hurt, visibly wounded. I'd hurt her and I was glad I did.

Are you ever going to tell me about him? I asked. It was a fair question. I deserved to know, or so my fourteen-year-old self believed I did. I didn't once consider the reasons she kept him from me, or the ramifications of knowing who he was. But Mom did.

Qui vivra verra, Mom replied, holding her hands up in the air. Her favorite saying, one that rolled eloquently off her tongue. *Only time will tell* is in essence what it means, but this time what it was was a way to be evasive. To avoid my question yet again.

I stormed out of the room. Marched up the stairs and slammed a bedroom door. I put on a sweatshirt that covered every square inch of me.

Not a year later, the cancer came.

And then I started wishing I'd never asked about my dad.

I dwell on those memories now, hating myself for what I put Mom through.

But every night around 3:00 a.m., when I've exhausted all the thoughts of death and grief and guilt for a single night, my imagination begins to take flight. My imagination or my memories, though some nights I have a hard time determining which is which. Tonight it's a memory, I think, one so far-flung that my brain has to cobble pieces of it together, adding to the gaps so that it makes sense. Filling in the blanks. I see that kindergarten classroom, a poster of the golden rule taped to the cinder block walls. A big bookcase, a rectangular rug with the alphabet depicted on it—the alphabet plus simple pictures, an apple for *A*, a bird for *B*—the American flag. A chalkboard with the teacher's name written on it in perfect penmanship. I see Mom standing there before the teacher, making an introduction, saying to the teacher that she is Eden and I am Jessie, and then the teacher squats just so and reaches out a hand to me and I shake it. Her smile is warm and sincere as she rises back up to Mom.

Mrs. Roberts stands with the clipboard in hand, making sure each child's paperwork is complete and that they've brought their supplies. Mom hovers self-consciously before her, hands behind her back, fingers laced. Mom and Mrs. Roberts talk and as they do, words reach my ears—*birth certificate*, I think I hear—and Mom stiffens at Mrs. Roberts's request.

"Pardon me?" Mom asks, and Mrs. Roberts explains how there's a note from the school office that she's yet to provide a copy of my birth certificate with the other registration materials. A certified copy, with the raised seal.

Mom doesn't miss a beat. She says something about a house fire. "We lost everything," she says, and Mrs. Roberts's face turns sad.

"How awful," Mrs. Roberts says consolingly as I, six-year-old me, asks unsuspectingly, "What fire?" Because there was never a fire. Not in our home. We didn't lose a thing.

Mom shushes me. Mrs. Roberts lays a hand on Mom's arm and says just as soon as she can get a replacement, that would be fine.

But then, like that, the memory disappears, and I have to wonder if it was a memory at all or only my imagination.

Tonight as I lie on the mattress in a misplaced belief that if I lie here long enough, eventually I will sleep, I think of a dead three-year-old Jessica Sloane, having to remind myself that it's a typographical error only, that she doesn't exist.

The room is quiet as I lie in bed wondering what she looked like. For three years old, I picture chubby wrists and knees, innocent eyes, an endless smile. I wonder if that's what she looked like. But then again I remember. There is no other Jessica Sloane. She *is* me.

A heavy silence flattens me in bed, filling every crevice in the room like a poisonous gas. I think that maybe it could kill me, that silence. Displacing all the oxygen in the room with a smothering quiet. The only thing I hear is the *tick, tock, tick, tock* of the wall clock, keeping time.

I rise to my knees and gaze out the window into the yard, seeing only the back of Ms. Geissler's home from here. It's tall and imposing, three floors of limestone and brick. Such a big home for one woman alone.

There's a balcony in the back of the home, a basic, rudimentary sort of thing. Wooden scaffolding that soars up three floors, a wooden slab to stand upon. It looks unsafe to me. Unsound. Not up to code.

As I kneel before the window, I rest my elbows on the sill. Foolishly believing that I blend into the blackness of the room, that no one can see me from here. The house is dark, except for a single light that's turned on. A yellow hue fills the margins of a window. The rest of it is blocked by a drawn window shade. I can't see into the room, just that frame of light around the window shade.

Ms. Geissler must have forgotten to turn the light off before she went to bed, I rationalize, because it's the middle of the night, and no one should be awake but me.

But as I stare, I see that the frame of light behind the window shade is moving, because the window shade inside it is also moving. It's a gentle back and forth motion, as if a person had been standing just seconds ago behind it, lifting the edges of the shade to peer out.

I imagine her at the window, gazing out, seeing me lying on the mattress, pretending to sleep. I think of her own admission—*I saw your light on late last night*—and imagine that last night, like this, she stood at the window, staring at me. Me, who naively obliged, leaving the shades open wide, basic white roller shades that I didn't once think necessary to pull down.

But now suddenly I do.

I watch the motion of the window shade as it slows and then stops.

And then, like that, the light flicks off.

The yellow edges of the window disappear. The greystone is engulfed in total darkness. I'd think nothing of it, but then it occurs to me that the light was coming from the third floor of the home. The place with the squirrels. The place where Ms. Geissler doesn't go.

She was lying to me.

Why would she lie to me?

I crawl back into bed. I throw the covers over my head.

I make poor attempts to placate myself, to convince myself that the light is on a timer. That it's automated. That it goes on and off of its own free will. That a heat vent was spewing warm air directly at the window shade, making it move.

But it's not so easy to believe.

EDEN

May 14, 2001
Chicago

I watch as, beside me, Jessie sleeps. She's out for the count now—finally, after a long, feverish night—spread out on a blanket on the floor, arms splayed in opposite directions like the wings of a jetliner. Her pale face is placid and calm, unlike last night when it was a fiery red, the fever and the fury creeping up her neckline, inflaming her forehead and cheeks. She'd cried out all night in discomfort, wailing, unable to get a hold of her own breath. Her fever capped at 103 degrees and I was grateful for this, for the fact that it wasn't high enough to necessitate a visit to the emergency room. I don't know if I'd have had it in me to go to the hospital had we needed to. I find that the very notion of hospitals—the antiseptic smells, the insipid hallways, the vigilant eyes—still gets under my skin sometimes, like some form of PTSD, I think, because just thinking about being in one rattles my nerves, makes me dizzy, makes my chest hurt. I don't know that I could ever go back to one, not after what I've done. I'm certain they'd see clear through me, that—even with all these miles spread between us—they, the doctors, the nurses, the ladies at the reception desk, would know just exactly who I am, as if I have my own scarlet *A* forever etched into my shirt as a reminder of my guilt.

I stare at Jessie, sound asleep on the quilted blanket beside me. Her hair fans out around her face. Her arms, both of them, are thrust upward and over her head now like goalposts. There isn't a single line on her skin anywhere, and though I don't want to wake her, I stroke the back of a finger across her tranquil ivory cheek, grateful she still sleeps.

It takes my breath away sometimes, the way that she looks absolutely nothing like me, but is instead all blond hair and blue-eyed. And then there are those dimples—those dimples!— the most telling of all, so that I've tried sucking my cheeks in from time to time in the hopes of replicating them on my own skin. It doesn't work, of course, and instead of dimples I'm left with a fish face that makes Jessie laugh. There are times I find that I have to remind myself that I am a mother, that I am her mother, and I wonder if others see the hesitation in me, the doubt, or if it's only in my mind.

Yesterday as we were walking from the French bakery, the one with the luscious petits fours for which I had a sudden craving, the woman behind the counter wished me a happy Mother's Day, and there was something querying about it that I didn't like. It rubbed me the wrong way. What started as a polite greeting turned into a question instead, as if she doubted at that last moment—words already out of her mouth, too late to pluck them back—whether she should be wishing me a happy Mother's Day.

Was I the child's mother? Was I a mother? After all, we looked nothing alike, and of course the lack of a wedding ring raised a red flag. Perhaps I was only the child's babysitter, her nanny, the au pair.

As I thanked the woman I saw her turn red with shame, believing she'd misspoken. But I grabbed for Jessie and said,

"Come along, my darling girl," as if that might validate it for both her and me. As if it might make my maternity more real.

All afternoon I found myself overthinking, wondering what exactly that woman saw that made her question whether I was Jessie's mother. Was it the manner in which I carried myself, the way I spoke, the lack of a physical resemblance? I thought about it all day and night, wanting to know, needing to know, so that whatever it was, I could next time disguise it better.

JESSIE

THE DAY BEGINS WITH a cleaning assignment, the first in two weeks. It's a good thing for more reasons than one. These days, cash is in short supply, and I need something to do with my time. Something better than to obsess over my social security number or lack thereof, Ms. Geissler staring out her window, watching me—which, even by the light of day, still rattles me. So much so that before I leave, I eye the window shades in the carriage home, fully intent on pulling each and every one down so that no one can see inside while I'm gone.

I slip out of the carriage home quietly, setting the door closed.

I make my way down the alleyway in back, avoiding Ms. Geissler.

At 7:30 a.m., I arrive at the home on Paulina, a typical workers cottage. I have to ring the doorbell twice before Mrs. Pugh comes to the door and even then, when she draws it open, there's a deliberateness about it. It's not the breezy way she typically throws open the door and welcomes me in. Her voice is out of joint, uncharacteristic of her typical chirpiness. "Jessie," she says at seeing me standing there. The word falls flat, her eyes dropping to the mop and bucket in my hands, the cleaning caddy stuffed up under my arm. It's far more than my two arms can carry, so that I feel clumsy though I haven't dropped anything. Not yet.

As the sun rises, it lands on the nape of my neck, making it warm, which is a relief from the near-hypothermic way I spent the night in the carriage home. Cold enough to freeze. My teeth chattered all night, body wrapped up in the one blanket I could find. Three pairs of socks on my feet.

It isn't so much a welcome. "Jessie?" is what Mrs. Pugh really means, a question more than anything, as if she's surprised to see me, as if she's asking why I'm here. She stands before me in a robe and slippers, shielded by the door. There's no workout attire as expected. No yoga mat and no gym shoes. She must not be feeling well, I guess, because at eight in the morning Mrs. Pugh has yoga, so that by seven thirty, she's always dressed, hair done up in a ponytail with strands that hang loose and frame her face. But not today.

"Am I early?" I ask, looking at my watch, which tells me it's seven thirty. I'm not early because I'm right on time. I hear Mr. Pugh call from the distance, "Who's there?" he asks.

"It's Jessie," she says.

"Jessie?" he asks, the tone of his voice equally confused. As if he doesn't know who I am, which of course he does. I've been cleaning their home for years. Every Tuesday.

"It's Wednesday," Mrs. Pugh tells me. "You're not early, Jessie," she says. And I can't make out that expression on her face, but I can see that she's not happy. "You're a day *late*. You were supposed to be here yesterday," she tells me, and it startles me, this sudden revelation that today is Wednesday. That it's not Tuesday after all, in which case my whole week's been mixed-up. I wonder what else I missed. I feel groundless all of a sudden, standing high on a ledge with nothing to hang on to.

My apology is effusive. "I'm sorry," I sputter. "I'm so, so sorry," as I try and make my way past Mrs. Pugh and into their home to clean it now, but she stands in my way and says not to bother. "We had friends over last night, Jessie. Parents from the preschool. We needed the home cleaned," she says as she tugs tighter on the cord of the robe to keep whatever's inside concealed.

"I had to find someone else to clean it," she says as she stares at me, not into my eyes, but somewhere beneath. She raises a finger, points at my chest so that I look down but see nothing. She says, "Jessie, your..." but then her voice drifts off. She reconsiders. Puts her hand down and says instead, "I tried calling you. You didn't answer."

"I'm so sorry," I say again. "I could rake the leaves," I suggest, though the number of leaves on their lawn is negligible. It's too early in the season for many leaves to be falling. But I say it so that I'll have something, anything to do. "Mow the lawn?" I ask, hearing how desperate I sound, but she shakes her head and tells me, "We have a service. They take care of the yard work."

"Of course," I say, feeling stupid. I back away, not bothering to turn and look where I'm going, missing the one concrete step that separates the front stoop from the walkway. One step, a ten-inch rise. I drop straight down, landing gracelessly somehow or other on the balls of my feet, whacking my teeth together in the process. I don't fall, but the mop slips from my hands, its clang echoing up and down the street.

I turn to leave, tripping over the mop as I do, and only then does Mrs. Pugh take pity on me. "Our company," she begins, "last night. Six kids and twelve adults can make quite the mess."

She opens the door wider and invites me inside. My thanks is as over-the-top as my apology. It has nothing to do with money, but everything to do with time. Everything to do with keeping myself occupied.

I wipe down the kitchen countertops and cabinets; I wash the floors. In the bathroom, I scrub like the devil, taking out all my anxiety on the subway tiles. It doesn't help.

As I move from the bathroom to Mr. and Mrs. Pugh's bedroom, I catch sight of a computer sitting on a writing desk and it gives me an idea. The desk is minimalist, as is the computer. A sleek silver laptop that prompts me for a password as I lift it open and press the return key, holding my breath to listen for the sound of footsteps sweeping down the hall. It doesn't take a genius to figure this one out. Taped there to the desk is the password, as well as the password for every one of Mr. and Mrs. Pugh's financial accounts. Their credit cards, their bank accounts. Their Vanguard funds. I type the code and easily get in. I could probably appropriate a few hundred thousand from them if I wanted to. But that's not what I'm here to do.

Mr. Pugh has gone off to work and so for now it's only Mrs. Pugh and me. Mrs. Pugh, who sat in the sunroom drinking her coffee and reading a book when I excused myself to clean. I pray she stays put, that she doesn't come wandering into her bedroom and catch me meddling with her things.

I pull up a search engine and type my own name into it. Jessica Sloane. I'm not sure what I expect to find. Or rather what I expect to find is nothing. But instead I find an interior designer with my name, one that takes up the first two pages of results. Around page three I find a doctor named

Jessica Sloane. Even farther down the page, a Pilates instructor. A Tumblr account for a fourth woman of the same name.

But me specifically, I'm nowhere there. Though it's not like I'd have a reason to be on the internet. I've done nothing noteworthy with my life; I don't have social media; I've never been on the news. For the last twenty years, Mom and I have lived as sequestered a life as we could. Like nuns, except that we didn't pray. We just kept to ourselves.

I click on the tab for images. Hundreds of photographs load before my eyes. Hundreds of photographs of rooms the interior designer Jessica Sloane has designed. They're dramatic and fussy and not at all my style. There are photographs of her too. Her and Jessica Sloane, MD, all decked out in a white lab coat with a stethoscope slung around her neck, smiling. Trying hard to look empathetic and intelligent all at the same time. I click the news tab at the top of the page, finding articles about them too.

I pause then, hands frozen above the keyboard, hearing a noise from down the hall. The house is long and narrow, each of the rooms small. I listen, hearing water streaming from the kitchen faucet, the coffee maker warming up to brew another pot. Mrs. Pugh is making herself more coffee.

Only when Mrs. Pugh's gentle footfalls drift away do I return to the screen.

On a whim, I insert my middle name, certain the search will come back empty. But instead it narrows the results down to a manageable thirty-two, which is not at all what I was expecting, and at first I think the computer is wrong.

It's the top hit on the page that catches my eye, a newspaper clipping dated seventeen years ago. The headline reads Hit-and-Run Driver Kills Girl, Age Three.

It takes my breath away. My eyes can't believe what they

see. The words. The picture. The caption beneath the image that reads, in italics, Jessica Jane Sloane.

That's me.

My hands clutch the edge of the desktop, squeezing hard, white-knuckled from the grip.

I go on to read an article that describes a child walking into traffic and being struck by a car. The car sped on, it says, leaving the girl for dead in the street. According to witness accounts, the car was going too fast, driving erratically. Assumptions were made that the driver was drunk, though no one got a good look at him or her, nor did anyone catch a glimpse of the license plate number. There were discrepancies as to the color of the car, which went to prove the unreliability of eyewitness accounts. They couldn't be trusted. The girl, Jessica Jane Sloane, was carted to the local hospital via ambulance, and there she died.

I click back on the images tab and spy a photograph of little Jessica Sloane in a purple bathing suit. In it, she's happy. She's three years old.

My head spins. My fingers go numb. They lose feeling completely as I stare at the little girl's face and think, *Who is this girl and what's she got to do with me?*

EDEN

THEY SAY THAT VODKA has no smell to it, and yet it was clear as day to me, the smell of it on Aaron's breath as he dropped into bed beside me tonight, the clock trumpeting 1:13 in the morning. Over the last few weeks, I'd noticed a gradual shift in his work schedule, each night him coming home later than ever before.

At first he said nothing, just stared blankly at me when I asked if he'd had something to drink. He didn't say yes, but he didn't say no either, and it seemed reasonable enough to assume he *had* been drinking, though he need not say one way or the other because I could smell it on his breath.

It just so happened that Aaron and a couple of coworkers had stuck around for a nightcap after their shift was through. It had been a bad night, *shitty* was the word Aaron used, Aaron who didn't ever used to complain. Damien was a no-show and Aaron was in the weeds all night, struggling to keep up on the line.

"It was just one for the road," he said. "It's not like I'm

drunk, Eden. It was one drink. One stupid drink," he said as he set the pillow over his head.

I didn't need to remind him of the effects of alcohol on male fertility. He knew. He knew because Dr. Landry had told us all those many months before when we discussed ways to better improve Aaron's low sperm motility.

I didn't need to tell him how I had been alone all day, for eleven hours this time. Nearly twelve. He knew this too. He knew that I didn't like to go to sleep until he was here, in bed beside me. He knew that most days the boredom and loneliness consumed me, and what else was there to do for those eleven or twelve hours besides think about how much I craved a baby?

I rolled over onto my side of the bed, taking the blanket with me.

"So now you're mad?" Aaron asked as he sat there, exposed. I didn't say yes or no but I didn't need to say one way or the other because Aaron could see my posture, could sense me tense up in fury and rage. He tried to reach out for me, but I pulled away. He sighed. "I needed to unwind for a bit. To have a little fun," he said by means of explanation, but it only made things worse, imagining him with coworkers, drinking vodka and having fun.

"What's so wrong with that?" he asked. "Do you have any idea how stressful it is for me at work?" but I had a different thought then, one that went back to money. Not only was Aaron coming home later each night, drinking after work with friends—*female friends?* I wanted to ask, but couldn't do it quite yet, too afraid to know the truth, that Aaron was throwing back shots of vodka with the pretty cooks and waitresses while I sat, a prisoner in my own home—he was blowing our money on booze. Money that could otherwise be saved for fertility treatments. For a baby.

"You don't need to be wasting our money like that," I said. "We hardly have enough as it is."

And then I did ask him who he was drinking with and he rattled off names. Casey. Riley. Pat. Names that were all conveniently unisex. Names that kept me up half the night wondering if they were male or female.

"Who's Casey?" I asked, censoriously, and when he didn't reply I created her in my mind's eye: tall and svelte with long butterscotch hair and pecan eyes. Flirtatious and tactile, predisposed to standing too close and touching so that I envisioned her, this make-believe woman, with her nimble hand on Aaron's arm.

Perfect teeth.

A flawless complexion.

An effortless laugh.

I've gained ten pounds now due to the many months of fertility treatments. I'm bloated all the time, in addition to moody and upset. The water retention has made my fingers grow fat. Most days my wedding ring barely fits with the water weight and stays hidden at home in a dresser drawer.

And then Aaron asked, "What happened to you, Eden? You used to be so much fun," while pulling the blanket from me. His final hurrah.

I lay there in the dark, completely exposed.

There was a part of me that remembered that Eden, the fun Eden, but in the moment she seemed so far gone, she was hard to remember anymore.

April 14, 1997
Egg Harbor

Today I watched a mourning dove in the gutter of our home get pelted with hail. She was female, a mother-to-be, beautiful with delicate beige plumage, perched on three oval eggs in the aluminum gutter. She'd spent days with her man friend, methodically assembling the nest of twigs and grass blades—while I watched on from the second-story window as they scurried back and forth from tree to trough, collecting materials and sticking them flimsily together—not thinking once of the rainwater that would soon stream past her shanty or the pellets of frozen ice that would one day take her life.

It was golf ball–size hail, a fusillade of machine-gun fire streaming down from the pale green sky. I've never felt so helpless, watching as she sat there, hunkered down over her eggs, protecting them until the bitter end. It went on for six and a half calamitous minutes, and when it was through she lay there, unmoving, folded lifeless over the eggs like a hooded cloak and I didn't know what to do. There was no blood. I would have expected there to be blood, and yet the internal damage was no doubt worse than that which I could see from the outside, evidence of the great lengths some mothers will go to protect their children. She could have flown away, sought shelter beneath the elm or cottonwood trees that crowded the yard, diminishing our view of the lake.

But she didn't. She stayed.

The storm passed. The clouds drifted away and the sun began to shine. A rainbow appeared in the sky. The hail melted. Rainwater evaporated. The only sign of the storm was the dead bird.

Aaron watched on as I schlepped the old wooden ladder to the back of the cottage and began to climb. He asked what I was doing as I shimmied up those steps in bare feet, the shaky ladder teetering on the lawn. At the top rung I saw her, splayed sideways, head lolling over the edge of the gutter. I pressed a single finger to her chest, feeling for a heartbeat and, at finding none, removed her body from the trench. Beneath her corpse, the eggs were still intact.

She died a martyr.

I buried her beneath the trellis, which the snowdrift clematis had overtaken at this time of year, white flowers powdering the wood.

They say that mourning doves mate for life. As far as I could tell, her man friend never returned to grieve his loss or to check on the eggs.

Sometimes this is the way it is with men.

April 24, 1997
Egg Harbor

I can't trust myself to stay at home all day anymore.

All too often, I drive into town and park outside the dance studio, watching the little ballerinas come and go. It rains many days now, this time of year, and so they come toting umbrellas, skipping over puddles, walking faster than ever before, though always, *always*, does little Olivia lag behind, and on the most inclement of days, when no one else wants to be outside, I am sure that she will be forgotten. It makes me sick to my stomach to do so, to watch the ballerinas in their leotards and tutus and tights, a Peeping Tom by my own right; it isn't perverse, there's nothing depraved about the thoughts that run through my mind, and yet I know in my heart of hearts that it's unhealthy, pining this way for someone else's child.

And so, against Aaron's will, I found a job. Some useful way to spend my days other than keeping vigil of the ballet studio, watching the ballerinas come and go.

We rarely talk these days anymore, other than that time spent in limbo each month, while they wash Aaron's sperm before injecting it inside me. Then we talk. About what, I don't know. About nothing. When I ask him questions, I'm astounded by the brevity of his replies, one-or two-word responses that leave no room for dialogue. He doesn't make eye contact. He asks me nothing. We kill time in the lobby of the fertility clinic before my name is called and only then am I granted amnesty, a pardon, a reason not to have to sit in the lobby and speak to my husband.

The job is at the hospital. The position is in billing as a medical coder, one I have ample experience in after all those years working for a pediatrician in Green Bay. And so now, I spend eight hours a day reading through patient files to figure out what they're to be billed for; I enter data; I submit to insurance companies; I mail invoices to patients. It feels good to be doing something with my days, to be earning an income.

And yet the position comes with its fair share of downsides too.

Yesterday as I sifted through patient files, I came across a little girl, a toddler killed in an auto-ped accident. In other words, she wandered into the street when her mother wasn't looking and was hit by a passing car on the roadway, a four-lane highway that cut right through town. The little girl (and though I, myself, never laid eyes on her, I conjured her up in my mind anyway, her tiny, broken frame still clad in a pair of denim overalls with blood-stained pigtails in her light brown hair) was transported to our hospital by ambulance, and there, received a multitude of treatments, from a CT scan to assess brain damage, to an operation to control internal bleeding and swelling in the brain. A decompressive craniectomy, as was noted in the extensive patient chart. There were blood transfusions. She was on narcotics for pain. An anesthesiologist was called to deliver a local anesthetic to put her to sleep for the surgery. The surgery itself lasted six hours, and each of these items came with an exorbitant price tag, one the family's shoddy insurance company was loath to pay. For six tortuous hours while the little girl's mother, I can only imagine, sat on a chair in the waiting room, biting her nails to the quick, a neurosurgeon, along with a team of doctors and nurses and scrub techs, removed part of the girl's brain to allow room for the swelling inside.

Still, she died.

By the time the paperwork made it to me in coding and billing, it had been days since the angels carried her away. Her mother no longer stood within the hospitals' walls, sobbing for her child. Her body had been removed from the morgue, transported to the funeral home, buried in the ground.

And yet for me, it's a fresh wound. One that will stay with me for a long time to come. As I typed the billing codes into the system, I cried for a little girl I've never met, tears snaking down my eyes and onto the computer keys, knowing that she will never truly be anything more than a name and a social security number to me, but still it makes me cry, grieving for someone I don't know, consumed with the unwanted knowledge that healthy little girls—like the sick and the elderly—die too.

But there are perquisites to the job too.

I wear a name badge that gains me access to every nook and cranny in the whole entire hospital, including the birthing center, where I can watch newborn babies being tended to in the nursery, lying immobile in their rolling bassinets, bundled like burritos with knitted hats on their perfectly pink and misshapen heads. I didn't seek them out—in fact, I swore to myself that I would abstain from visiting the newborn babies—but I saw them anyway when a pair of grandparents-to-be stopped me in the hall and asked the way to labor and delivery. I had no choice but to lead them there, to steer them through the mazelike hospital halls, through the double doors and into the unit where the newborn babies caught my eye.

And now I stand there for what feels like hours, staring through glass, coming to terms with my fait accompli. No workday passes without at least one visit to the nursery room and as I sit at my desk coding patient files, it's all I can think about, seeing those babies. Getting my fix. I've come to know the nurses now—thanks to the frequency of my visits. They address me by name, sometimes holding up the newest infants so I can see their puffy, half-closed eyes, their still-bowed legs from being cramped inside a warm, cozy uterus, their cone-shaped heads from being suctioned through their mother's vaginal canal and into the world.

When they ask, I tell them I'm training to be a nursery room nurse myself, that I'm in the process of earning my associates' degree in nursing and, that as soon as I do, I'm going to apply for a job here, in our hospital's nursery room. I tell them I come to watch and learn, to see how the experts do it. I flatter the nurses so they don't think it odd that I spend every free second away from billing and coding staring at babies who are not mine. They smile and say how fantastic that is and sometimes, if I'm really lucky, they sneak me inside so I can stroke the soft skin of a tiny babe.

Though that, of course, isn't the real reason I come.

JESSIE

IT'S NOT YET TEN in the morning when I leave the Pughs' home. The day stretches out before me like the Sahara, massive and deserted and dry. And now I'm even more agitated than I was before, all nervous energy with nothing to do. Nowhere to go. No one to talk to.

I carry with me in my bag a printout of the newspaper article I found on the Pughs' laptop, grateful when Mrs. Pugh called down the hall that she was stepping out for a bit, and I was able to send it to the printer without her hearing me. Because if I knew one thing, it was that I needed to take the article with me.

I hop on Old Faithful and ride. I turn aimlessly, unplanned at each intersection, my head lost in the clouds. I move in circles so that three times I pass by the very same delicatessen without meaning to. I speak to Mom. I ask her questions about my lack of a birth certificate, my missing social security card, the girl in the article. Who is she, and what does she have to do with me? Does she have anything to do with me? *Tell me, Mom*, I scream in my head. *Tell me!*

It isn't until a woman standing on a street corner stares at me like I'm crazy that I realize I've been speaking out loud.

In time I find my way into the Loop. It isn't intentional. I don't go there on purpose. It's something far more subliminal than that, that makes my legs pedal hard, steering me to the Art Institute on Michigan Avenue, where I park Old Faithful just steps from the bronze lions and walk.

I don't go to the museum.

Rather I head to the south end of the building where, just off Michigan Avenue, I slip into this secret world of raised flower beds and a grove of hawthorn trees. I'd never have known what kind of tree they were, but Mom knew, Mom who found this spot by accident one day when I was young and we were exploring. It was fall and the trees were angular and uneven, a brassy shade of copper that peeked through the green of nearby trees as they do now.

Let's see what this place is, Mom had said that day, grabbing a hold of my hand and drawing me in. That first day, I didn't want to go. Rather I wanted to climb on the lions' backs and ride. But Mom had said no. The lions were to look at. They weren't for riding, though she let me pet them as we passed by.

The entrance to the garden is guarded by honey locust trees, which keep the rest of it hidden from the urban world on the other side. I slip in. I walk down a handful of steps that dip inches below street level. I move between the trees, lost in an enclave beneath an awning of leaves. Transported somewhere hundreds of miles from a city street.

There are people here. It's not as if I'm the only one who knows about this place. And yet those that are here are placid. Quiet. Drinking coffee and smoothies, reading books, staring into space. A woman picks at the edges of a muffin wrapper, offering scraps to a nearby bird.

This was one of Mom's favorite spots in the city. We'd come here and she'd spend hours sitting on the edge of the raised beds. She'd watch as I scaled them with my arms extended, imagining myself as a tightrope walker. They're large—a good twenty feet by twenty feet or more—so it was always quite the feat when I could get around without falling.

Mom let me do it for hours. She never got bored.

There was one place in the garden Mom liked more than the rest because it was secluded, set back from the street entrance, the water fountain and the pool. Even in the most secluded of places, she found the most covert place to hide.

I make my way there now because I think that somehow I might feel closer to Mom if I sit there. That somehow we'll be able to commune.

But when I get there, that spot is already occupied. A man sits there, reading the newspaper. Truth be told, it makes me crabby, thinking what nerve he has to sit in Mom's favorite spot. And so I sit opposite him on another bed, twenty feet away or more, watching him, waiting for him to leave. I stare at him, thinking it'll make him uncomfortable and he'll go.

But he's not uncomfortable because he doesn't even see me staring. He's too preoccupied by the newspaper in his hands.

I can't say one way or the other if he's tall or short because he's sitting. He's got his legs crossed, ankle to knee, and his clothes are all sorts of nondescript. Pants, shirt, shoes. Nothing noteworthy about them. They're clothes. The sleeves of his shirt are thrust to the elbows. There, on his left arm beneath the cuff of the shirt, is a scar. It peeks out from beneath the sleeve, a six-inch gash that's healed poorly. The skin around it is puckered and pink.

His face looks sad. That's the first thought I have. That the expression on his face—that and his body language—is one of sadness. The way his mouth pulls down at the corners, a slight tug there at the edges of his lips. The way his shoulders slouch. I should know because each time I look in the mirror, I see the very same thing. On his face is a patch of hair, a tight beard, trimmed and tidy. It gives off an aura of mystery and regality. His skin is tanned like the hide of a moose, stretched and dried in the sun before being smoked over a fire. Like he's spent too much time outside in the sun.

He isn't thumbing through the newspaper, but instead he's got his eyes peeled to some story on the top page, the paper folded so that he can hone in on it. Something bad has happened in the world, I think. Something bad always happens. I wonder what it is this time. Terrorist attack. Women and children being slaughtered by their own leaders. A shooting in an elementary school. Children murdered by their own moms and dads.

I watch his eyes, the movement of them as he scans the story. Moving left to right. Dropping down to read the next line. But his eyes are lowered, gazing down on the newspaper and so I can't see much, none other than the lashes and the lids. He bites a lip. He bites hard so that the pain of the lip overrides whatever it is he's feeling on the inside. I do that too.

He reaches for a cup of coffee set on the marble edge of the raised bed. I read the corrugated sleeve on the cup. A coffee bar on Dearborn. I've never been there before, but I know the place. I've seen it before.

And then he gets up to go, and I ready myself to make a move for his seat. He slips an orange baseball cap over the brown hair, though as he goes, he leaves his newspaper behind. Because he's sad. Because he's distracted.

He walks away and I notice a shoe is untied, the cuff of a pant leg stuck in the shoe's tongue. He leaves it there. For a second or two I watch him go.

But then, standing and making my way to the raised bed, I call to him, "Sir," while grabbing the newspaper so that the wind doesn't have a chance to scatter it around the garden. "Sir," I call again, "your newspaper."

But he's walking away and before I can run to him, something leaps off the page at me. It grabs me by the throat so that I can't speak and I can't move. I'm frozen in place, a bronze statue like the lions who stand before the Art Institute, guarding its entrance.

There on the top of the newspaper is Mom's beautiful face. Her beautiful brown eyes and brown hair, both watered down by the black-and-white newsprint.

Her obituary. The one I put in the paper because I needed the world to know she was dead. To solidify it. To make it real. Because only then, when it was written in print for all of the world to see, would I believe it.

This man. The sad man sitting in Mom's and my spot in the garden. He was reading her obituary.

He had the newspaper folded so that Mom's face was on top, and it was these words his eyes spanned as he bit his lip so that he wouldn't cry.

Mom's obituary is what made this man sad.

I read over the words. Mom's death notice, which was brief because there wasn't a whole lot of information to provide. No memorial service. No one to send flowers to.

The final line reads "Eden Sloane is survived by her daughter, Jessica."

My legs lose feeling. I go slack jawed. Because there's one word on the newsprint that the man has circled and it's my name. Jessica.

EDEN

July 12, 2003
Chicago

The park is named after some poet, I've come to learn. Though no one pays attention to things like that because, to most people, it's just a park where kids romp around on the playground and, on the other side of a chain-link fence, boys play basketball, the repeated *thump, thump, thump* of the ball on concrete a steady refrain. They're older boys mostly, teenagers, and they spout from their mouths a flurry of curse words at regular intervals, and I feel grateful Jessie is still too young to know what any of it means, though she pauses from time to time to watch them. To just stand on the playground and stare.

There are baseball fields off in the distance, and on the other side of a bridge, a path that snakes along the river where she and I sometimes walk, but not today. Today she played on the playground, and for the first time ever, found a friend. Not the kind of friend we'd keep in touch with after today or invite over for a playdate. No, Jessie and I don't have those types of friends.

Rather she's the kind of friend who, for fifteen or twenty minutes at best, is a bosom body. A soul mate.

I watched as Jessie and the little girl chased each other in dizzying circles, up the stairs and down the slide. Again and again and again. As far as I knew, they never exchanged names. Because that's the way it is with kids. Uncomplicated. Straightforward. Easy.

There was no one else on the playground but the two of them, and the only ones sitting on the periphery of it were the little girl's mother, pushing a newborn in an old-fashioned buggy, and me. It took some time, a few awkward glances my way, before she rose from her own park bench and came to mine, standing before me, offering a hello. I too said hello, staring down into the buggy at the infant sound asleep beneath a yellow blanket.

"How sweet," I said.

The baby, Piper, she told me, was twelve days old, born on the first of July. The woman moved guardedly, as if in pain, and I didn't ask before she told me, "Piper was breech," telling me how her baby was fully intent on entering the world feetfirst. "The doctors did everything they could to change that. But no such luck," she explained, sitting softly beside me on the park bench and describing in too much detail what a C-section is like. The incision. The surgical staples. The scar she'd no doubt have. She lifted the hem of her shirt then so that I could see it myself, and I blushed at the sight of her still-pregnant belly, at the bloated butterfly tattoo that sat just inches from the healing incision, at the canvas of fair skin. She was oversharing and I blamed the newness of childbirth for it, the fact that to her it was still fresh. The only thing these days that occupied her mind.

"With Amelia it was different," she admitted, and I made the easy assumption that Amelia was the older of the two, the little girl, maybe five years old, who Jessie made a train with at the top of the slide—wrapping her skinny legs around the midsection of a girl she hardly knew—and together they catapulted down to the wood chips below, landing on their rear ends, laughing. "Twenty-some hours of labor, three hours of pushing," she said, going on far too long about the gush of water when her membranes ruptured, like the pop of a water balloon. Her, worried only that she might poop on the bed, as one of her girlfriends had done. The broken blood vessels left behind on her face from hours of pushing, thin, red veins that snaked this way and that across her skin. Some doctor she didn't know delivering her baby. Her breasts engorged, her unable to produce milk following childbirth. Having to relent to formula, which her mommy's groups abhorred.

I felt uncomfortable, if I was being honest, about this sudden revelation of information from a woman I didn't know. But it dawned on me then that this is the type of thing women do, this is the type of thing *mothers* do: share their experiences, swap stories, foster camaraderie.

She looked at me expectantly, as if it was my turn to share. She was quiet, watching me, and when I didn't respond, she prompted, "And your girl?" and I knew then that I must tell her something, that I must offer up some version of the truth. I pictured those wide hospital halls, the glaring lights. "She was a vaginal birth?" she asked, that word alone—*vaginal*—making me turn redder than I was before. Because these were the kinds of conversations I didn't have. Intimate. Friendly.

Most of my conversations ended at hello.

I felt my head nod without my permission, and I knew I must say more, that a nod of the head alone wouldn't suffice.

And so I told her about the hospital room. I told her about the huddle of people who gathered around me, the nurses clinging to either of my legs, encouraging me to push. Incanting it in my ear—push, push—as I gathered handfuls of bedding in my hands and bore down with all of my might. The epidural had worn off by then, or maybe it was never there to begin with. All I felt was pain, a pain so intense it was as if my insides were on fire, about to rupture. I was certain I would soon explode. A hand stroked the sweaty hair from my face, whispering words of encouragement into an ear as I screamed, this crude, ugly scream, but I didn't care how crude or ugly it was. The nurses wrenched on either of my legs, stretching me apart, making me wide. *Push*, they said again and again, and I did, I pushed for dear life, watching as that flash of black spilled from inside of me and into the doctor's gentle hands.

But then I remembered.

That wasn't me.

JESSIE

BEFORE I CAN TEAR my eyes from Mom's face on the newspaper's obituaries page, from my own circled name, the man has slipped from the garden and disappeared from sight. I attempt to run after him, barreling through the rows of hawthorn trees as quickly as my legs can carry me. But still, when I come rushing out onto Michigan Avenue, chest heaving, breathing hard, he's gone. The sidewalk is inundated with people, with kids, a middle school field trip to the Art Institute, and they're all lined up in two parallel rows before the museum's concrete steps. Clogging the sidewalk. I push past bubbly preteens who are incognizant of my desperation, who don't care. By the time I reach the other side, there's no sign of the man anywhere. The man with the sad eyes and the untied shoe.

I stare up and down the street, completely aghast. A muscle in my eyelid twitches, a spasm. Something involuntary, something I can't make go away though I try. It's extremely annoying. The street is a wide six-lane divided street jam-packed with people and cars, a median strip in the center that's plugged with flowers and trees, making it even harder to see the other side. But still I walk, searching the streets for the man.

I hurry down Michigan with a heavy, desperate tread. The wind is a wall by now, and I lean into it to walk. It's exhausting. All the while, my eyelid twitches. I turn left at Randolph, a temporary reprieve from the militant headwind, which now comes at me from the side so that I slope laterally, a perfect seventy-five-degree angle. At Clark, I turn right, not quite knowing where I'm going, but trying desperately to find the man. I climb northward, gazing into storefronts to see if he's there. I stare down alleyways, out of breath by the time I come to a six-story building on Superior Street, one that's flanked with floor-to-ceiling windows and looks oddly familiar to me.

I spin in a circle, taking it in, the doorman in uniform, the sign outside that reads Spacious, Open-plan Lofts for Sale. Inquire Inside. I know where I am. I've been here before.

Just like that, I'm standing at Liam's front door.

I didn't know I was coming here. I didn't come here on purpose. But here I am, and now that I'm here, I make an attempt to scoot past the doorman and into the building. Because maybe Liam can help me think this through. The little girl in the car accident, the man in the garden. He'll make me see that there's nothing sordid going on. That it's only a coincidence.

The doorman stands on the curb, hailing a cab for a resident. "Can I help you, miss?" he asks, catching sight of me out of the corner of his eye, as he steers the resident into the back seat of the cab and closes the door for her.

He steps closer to me. "I'm here to see Liam," I say.

His smile is mocking. Wary. "Liam who?" he asks, playing dumb, and I freeze, realizing only then that I don't have a last name. That to me he's just Liam. That until yesterday he wasn't even that, because before yesterday he didn't have a name. He was only the guy from the hospital, the one with the blue eyes.

But I also realize that the doorman knows fully well what Liam's last name is. He isn't curious. He's testing me, checking to see how well I know Liam before he lets me in.

"I don't know his last name," I admit, feeling uncomfortable as my feet shift in place. At first he's hesitant, not sure he wants to phone Liam or not. For all he knows, I'm someone Liam is avoiding, someone he doesn't want to see. And that's his job, to keep unwanted visitors at bay, unwanted visitors like me.

He sizes me up and down. He asks twice what my name is. Both times I say Jessie, though for the first time I start to doubt that it is. I feel disheveled, disoriented, and though I have no idea what I look like, I can see it in the doorman's eyes. It's not good. I run my hands through my hair; I rub at my twitching eyes.

"Is Liam expecting you?" he asks, and I'm not quick enough on my feet to lie. I tell him no.

"Can you call him for me, please?" I plead, the desperation in my voice palpable to both him and me.

The doorman reluctantly phones Liam for me, but Liam doesn't answer his call. "He's not home," he tells me, setting the phone down. I feel the skeptic in me start to take hold. He's lying. He didn't call him. He only pretended he did, but he didn't. I think that maybe the number he dialed wasn't Liam at all, or maybe he didn't push enough digits for the call to go through. Or he hung up before Liam had a chance to answer.

I'm about to get angry, but then I remember. The funeral. Liam's brother's funeral is today. He's at the funeral. He's not home.

I excuse myself, walking from the building, feeling mud-dled. There's a convenient mart next door to the apartment building. I slip inside and buy a Coke, hoping the caffeine will make me feel less mixed-up. Or, at minimum, curtail the throbbing in my head from the day's lack of caffeine.

Back outside, I drop down onto the curb to catch my breath. I need to think things through, but my mind can focus on only one thing. What if Jessica Sloane with my social security number did die when she was three? She wasn't erroneously classified as dead because she was really dead. Then I've been living with a mistaken social security number all this time, with a mistaken identity.

Is it possible that the other Jessica Sloane and I have social security numbers so close they're off by only a single digit, or have two numbers that are interchanged? Maybe she died and someone unwittingly typed my social security number into the death database. The names matched, so they didn't think twice. An oversight only.

Doubtful.

And then my mind gravitates to the man in the garden. Who is he, and what was he doing there? What does he want with me?

"Jessie?" I hear, and when I look up from the street, I see Liam making his way toward me. All dressed up in a black suit and tie. Looking undeniably sleek but also tired like me.

I rise from the curb and bridge the gap, and, as we close in on one another, his face darkens. "Your shirt," he says as he points to it, to my shirt, and tells me that I've got it on inside out. Which wouldn't be so obvious were it not for the label sitting smack-dab beneath my chin, a blaring thing. I pluck it from my skin for a better look.

Not only do I have my shirt on inside out, but it's backward. And now that Liam has pointed it out for me, I feel the high neckline, the cotton taut in places it isn't meant to be taut. In that moment I have no memory of ever grabbing the shirt from the closet, slipping it from its hanger, of ever putting it on.

It's a blessing that I'm even dressed.

"Come inside," he says, his eyes hanging on a little longer than they ordinarily would. "You can fix it there."

But I say, "No," shooing him off, feeling suddenly asinine. "It's just a stupid shirt anyway; it's not like anyone noticed." And then I sigh, feeling completely exasperated. Exasperated and exhausted. He hears it in my voice.

"Jessie," he says, his voice far more resolute this time. "Come inside. Keep me company."

We step inside the building and wait for the elevator to come. "Did you sleep last night?" he asks. I don't say yes or no, but my silence gives it away. In my head, I tally the days up. I lose track at number four and have to start again, counting on my fingers this time, reaching seven.

It's been seven days since I've slept.

"I looked it up," Liam tells me as the elevator comes for us. Though it doesn't align with the lobby floor—a fact that I realize all too late—and so I trip on the way in, stumbling over that one-inch rise. Liam latches on to my arm, steadying me. He doesn't let go. Not until I draw my arm away, stepping closer to the wall so that I can use it for leverage if need be.

"Looked what up?" I ask as the elevator sweeps us up to the sixth floor. I feel suddenly rocky on my feet. Nauseous.

"The longest a person has ever gone without sleep," Liam says.

He tells me how people die from lack of sleep. About lab rats who died from lack of sleep. "How long?" I ask.

"Eleven days," he says. "Eleven, Jessie," he repeats to drive the point home, I think. "You need to sleep."

"I will," I say, but chances are good that I won't.

I ask how the funeral went because I don't want to talk about my lack of sleep or the fact that in four more days I'm liable to die because of it. The funeral, he says, went as well as to be expected for a funeral. His shoulders shrug and his expression is flat. He doesn't say more.

The elevator arrives at the sixth floor. He leads us to his apartment, walking a half step ahead of me. At the door, I stop a few feet back, waiting as he opens it. Inside, the space is big and roomy with ceilings that are extraordinarily high, track lighting, exposed brick. Sunlight pours in through floor-to-ceiling windows. "You coming?" he asks.

I walk past him and into the apartment as behind me he closes the door.

He offers me something to drink. I say no because I have my Coke, which I uncap and take a swig of. But as I raise the bottle up to my lips, there's that tremor to my hand again, the one I can't make stop.

Liam tugs the tie from his neck and slips the suit jacket off. Throws it over the arm of a chair. Unbuttons his shirt. Rolls the cuffs of it to his elbows. Finds himself a water in the refrigerator and sinks into a low-slung chair. He never asks what I'm doing here.

I give the article to Liam, my hand still shaking as I do. I sit on a chair opposite him. I don't bother fixing my shirt.

"What's this?" he asks, but it's one of those questions that isn't really a question because already he's reading the story of Jessica Sloane, who was killed by a hit-and-run driver at the age of three. When he comes to the end of it he tells me what I already know. He says that this is strange.

I assert, "I mean, it's just a coincidence, right? A mistake?"

His face is impassive. He doesn't say an emphatic *yes* as I'd hoped he would; he doesn't put my mind at ease. This time, there are too many holes that don't line up.

"I don't know," he admits, saying, "It's just that it's strange, Jessie. I mean, yesterday it was a coincidence. Yesterday it was a mistake. Yesterday someone screwed up. But now it's like it isn't so much an accident as it is someone intentionally trying to keep you off the radar. You have no birth certificate, you can't find your social security card and the social security number you think is yours matches up with that of a dead girl. One who might just have the same name as you."

The expression on his face says it all. Something sordid is going on here. Something bad.

"It's just hard to believe that she's not you," he says while motioning to the photograph in the article, but when I look at the child's face, I see nothing but a stranger looking back at me. I've never seen this girl before.

"But it's not me," I argue, voice trembling. "She doesn't look a thing like me. Look at the shape of her eyes, her nose. It's all different," I allege, rising to my feet. "It's all wrong."

"I didn't mean that," he says, his voice gentle. "That's not what I meant, Jessie. I just mean," he says. "I just mean that I think it's possible there's something going on here, some sort of identity theft."

"What do you mean, identity theft?" I ask, except I know what he means. What he's suggesting is not that my identity has been stolen, but that I've stolen the identity of someone else—unpremeditated on my part, but still identity theft.

"Jessie," he starts, but I shake my head and he stops.

At first there's nothing but silence. I drop back down into my chair. I think it through. "You think my mother changed my name, gave me a phony identity and passed me off as a dead girl?" I ask, the words themselves unthinkable. Not something that could possibly be real. For a second I feel like I might vomit. The Coke gathers in my stomach, burning the lining of it. There's hardly any food inside me, which, when coupled with everything else, doesn't sit well. The pain starts somewhere around my navel and creeps up my chest. An agonizing lump that plunks itself behind the breastbone.

"But no," I say decisively, rising to my feet again and beginning to pace. Why would Mom do that? Why in the world would Mom steal the identity of a girl who had died and give it to me? "Why?" I ask out loud, though the answer slowly dawns on me, that if Mom went around passing me off as a dead girl, then no one would know she had stolen another child's identity. Because that child was dead.

I watch as Liam grabs for a laptop on the coffee table and types quick, harried words into it. He moves from his chair and comes to me and together we stare at the words on the screen. There's a whole word for it, he tells me. "Ghosting. Thieves open bank accounts and credit cards using a dead person's social security number," he says. "They pore over obituaries to see who's died, and then rack up thousands of dollars of debt in some stiff's name."

"But why?" I ask dumbly, though I'm not that dumb. I just can't wrap my head around it. People do this kind of thing for financial gain, but Mom and I were never rich. We weren't living a life of riches. We lived paycheck to paycheck.

Besides, Mom would never do anything to harm someone; she would never steal.

There has to be more to it than that.

If—and that's a big *if*—she took the identity of a dead child and gave it to me, then it was for some other reason than financial gain. But what? I can't even begin to guess.

I swallow the last of my Coke. It's like rubbing salt in an open wound. The pain in my chest gets worse so that I cough and, as I do, all I can think of is corroded pipes, the lining of my esophagus plugged up and rusty.

I let an idea dwell for a short time, and then quickly expunge it from my mind.

Find yourself, Mom told me. One of two wishes she had for me before she died.

Maybe she didn't mean for me to apply to college. Maybe it was far less esoteric than that. Maybe it was quite literal.

Find yourself, she said, because Jessie Sloane isn't you.

EDEN

May 28, 1997
Egg Harbor

AS SPRING RIPENS INTO summer, tourists reappear. The town comes to life with a certain vivacity that was missing during the dismal days of winter. Trees burgeon, flowers bloom.

Miranda and her three boys appear like magic at my front door each day that I'm not working—and often, I'd venture to guess, when I am—toting blueberry loaves and apple pies.

As the boys play in the tree swing (that by now was meant to hold my own child, the two of us nestled snugly together, he or she on the seat of my lap, weightless and grinning as we lift off from the ground and take flight), Miranda and I sip lemonade. As always she sells short the joys of marriage and motherhood, while little Carter crawls on the lawn before us on all fours, eating dirt. She complains about everything from what a jerk her husband, Joe, can be—coming home late from work, missing dinner, not helping with the boys' bedtime routine—to the monotony of her days, to the amount of food three growing boys consume. She can never keep the cabinets fully stocked, she tells me, because the minute she buys it they eat it all, which leads into an onslaught on the difficulties of grocery shopping with three boys, and she describes it for me: the poking and the prodding of each other, the name-calling—birdbrain, imbecile, idiot—the running off headlong down the market's aisles, bumping into strangers, begging and crying for things that Miranda has already said no to, trying to sneak it past her and into the basket, screaming and calling her names when she snatches it out of their dirty hands and returns it to the store shelf.

"That must be so difficult," I say, trying my hardest to sound empathetic, but when Miranda replies with "You have no idea, Eden. Can you even grasp how lucky you are, getting to grocery shop alone?" it's all I can do not to scream.

I would give life and limb to grocery shop with a child.

Miranda doesn't bother asking how the fertility treatments are going, though just last night Aaron and I made the decision to give in vitro fertilization a try. Or rather, I should say, *I* made the decision to give in vitro a try. The cost of it is extortionate, thousands of dollars for a single cycle, for Dr. Landry to go inside one time and pluck an egg or two from my ovaries to combine with Aaron's sperm, making an embryo, a *baby*, in a culture dish. As one grows bacteria. It seems scientific, synthetic, and yet there isn't anything I wouldn't do for a child.

I know this now.

But Aaron isn't so sure. As we stood in the kitchen last night, both of us speaking in acerbic tones, he calculated the costs we've paid over the year, all the pelvic ultrasounds and semen analyses, the Clomid cycles, the trigger shots, intrauterine insemination. The grand total tallied up to some ten thousand dollars already spent trying to create a child, an expenditure that will nearly double with one single cycle of IVF. Aaron and I don't have this kind of money. He reminds me of this relentlessly, as he reminds me how happy we used to be before we ever made the decision to start a family, and I have this vague recollection of a couple, a man and a woman—as if in another life—sitting on a dock, holding hands, watching sailboats float by on a bay.

"I think we should stop, Eden," he said, trying hard to reach out to me but I pulled away. "I think we should be happy with what we have."

"And what's that?" I asked, up in arms. What did we possibly have without a baby?

"Us," he said, looking sad. "You and me. That's what we have."

I wouldn't be deterred.

"We will do this," I told him of the in vitro fertilization. Hands on hips, my expression flat. An imperial fiat.

I left the room so it couldn't be further discussed.

I've taken out three credit cards in my own name, and charge each appointment with Dr. Landry to them in sequence. Never are we able to pay more than the minimum payment for each. The interest fees soar monthly as the cottage degenerates bit by bit. The furnace went out; we need to replace the plumbing throughout the entire home before the decades-old steel pipes wear out for good. The windows are drafty; they too need to be replaced before another winter comes or we'll spend an arm and a leg to heat the home, watching our money quite literally go out the window.

But each of these plays second fiddle to making a baby.

Aaron and I argue daily about money. The cost of groceries, the cost of clothes.

What concessions can we make so that we can save more for a baby?

Do we really need two cars, cable TV, a new pair of shoes?

"This is ridiculous," Aaron says as he holds up a shoe, the outsole flapping loose like a hangnail. "I can't go to work like this." And yet I argue with him, claiming he's being extravagant by not making do with the shoe. "Surely you can get another month out of those shoes," I say, suggesting he use some glue, though it isn't about the shoe, but rather what the hundred dollars for another pair of shoes will buy. An appointment with Dr. Landry, a hormone shot, a month's worth of Clomid.

But Aaron swears he needs the shoe, which inside makes me fume.

How selfish can he be? Where are his priorities?

At each unwelcome visit, when Miranda and her boys appear at my door without invitation, her belly continues to swell, another baby on the way, "Hopefully a girl this time," she says, fingers laced together in the air.

If Aaron and I hurry up, she reminds me for the umpteenth time, joining me in the backyard for another glass of lemonade, her baby and my baby can one day go to school together. They can be friends.

I smile.

And though I don't say it aloud, I think to myself that I'd rather die than have my baby and Miranda's baby be friends.

June 13, 1997
Egg Harbor

The hollyhocks are in bloom. Just the sight of them lined up defiantly against the weathered picket fence stabs me in the chest. They stand high above the rest of the flowers in the garden, six feet tall or more. Their bold bell-shaped flowers burn red against the greenery.

It's been a year then since Aaron and I planted the seedlings in the lawn against the fence where they'd be sheltered from the rain and the wind. And now here they are, exhibitionists in my flower bed, outshining the roses and lilies.

Reminding me of all the wasted time Aaron and I have spent trying to have a baby.

When Aaron was at work, I took a pair of scissors to them, cutting hard through the thick stem. I seethed as I did it, crying, taking out a year's worth of rage on the flowers. I screamed like a maniac, grateful that, thanks to the deep rim of trees surrounding our yard, no one was around to see or hear my outburst. I grabbed handfuls of stems and tugged with all my might, wresting the roots from the ground where I stomped on them like a child. I tore the flowers from their stems, shredding them into a million pieces until my hands were yellow with pollen and I was out of breath from the outburst.

When I was finished, I threw them away, beneath the garbage where all the negative pregnancy tests go.

The deer, I'll blame, when Aaron asks what happened to the flowers. I'll say that the deer have had their way with the hollyhocks, eating them to the quick.

And he'll be more upset about this than he is our lack of a baby.

After all our hard work.

"Such a shame," he'll say, before waging a war against the innocent deer.

JESSIE

I TAKE THE BROWN Line back to the carriage home, walking the last couple of blocks from the station at Paulina. I feel lost without my bike. I don't have my bike, Old Faithful, because I left it outside the Art Institute, tethered to some sort of loopy bike rack, when I walked to Liam's, chasing after the mystery man.

It's dark inside by the time I arrive, night falling quickly. I close the door behind me and jiggle the handle a couple of times to be sure it's closed tight. I'm in a trance, thinking about little else but the dead Jessica Sloane. The one who is three years old. The one who is me but not me all at the same time. Lines from the newspaper article run through my mind, committed to memory already.

A four-lane highway with a speed limit of just twenty-five.

The road twisted through the small seaside town.

The driver rounded a bend at nearly twice that speed.

Every time I close my eyes I see her face.

I have only a vague recollection of riding the elevator

downstairs; of pushing my way through the turnstile doors of Liam's apartment building; of walking to the Merchandise Mart to catch the train with him at my side. He'd offered to cover the cost of a cab for me but I said no.

Still, he walked me there, to the Merchandise Mart, and paid to stand on the platform beside me, waiting until the Brown Line came. And now that I look, I see his jacket draped over me, keeping me warm. He must've put it there, but that I don't remember.

I turn and walk up the carriage house's stairway, a rickety old thing with steps that are a bit concave, the edges worn away. The steps sink at their center. They squeak. The tread pitches downward from a century's worth of weight, and I cling to the railing so I don't fall.

When I get to the top I have to fight for breath. The steepness of the steps isn't to blame, nor for once my overwhelming fatigue.

What knocks the wind from my lungs is something else entirely.

Because as my feet hit the wooden floorboards and my eyes size up the open rooms, I see that the white window curtains I'd pulled shut before I left, so that no one could see inside while I was gone—every single one of them is open wide.

It's instinctive, the way the blood coagulates inside me. It becomes thick and gooey so that I can't move.

Someone was here.

My gut feeling is to hide. There's a closet nearby, a catch-all for coats and shoes. My eyes go to it. I could hide. I could bury myself in a dark nothingness and cower on the floor in fear. Because whoever opened the blinds might still be here. Inside the old home.

I listen for strange noises. For calculated footfalls coming for me. For the sound of restrained breaths, slow, repressed and controlled unlike mine. I listen for the groan of floorboards, but the only sound I hear is that of my own heartbeat.

I don't hide.

I've never been a particularly courageous person. Mom always said to face my fears, to take matters into my own hands, to fight for what was mine. And so I make my way slowly through the home, searching for signs of life.

Much of the carriage house is easy to see from where I stand. But then there are those places I can't see. An upstairs closet, the bathroom, under the eaves of the pitched roof where shadows make it hard to see. All of that is up another set of stairs, on the third floor of the home.

I ascend those steps on tiptoes, the arches of my feet beginning to burn. Convinced that if I walk on tiptoes, the intruder won't hear me, that he or she won't know that I am here.

Upstairs, I see a figure hunkered down beneath the sloped ceiling and my breath leaves me. It's hidden to the side of the mattress, trying to hold still and yet moving in a gentle rhythm.

What I see is a man on bent knee, crouched down, waiting to lunge at me as I reach the top of the staircase.

I gasp aloud, attempting to brace for impact. But instead I lose balance, slipping backward on the top step and sliding downward the eight-or nine-inch rise to the step below. I catch myself there, gripping tightly to the stairwell banister before I plunge down an entire flight of stairs, head over heels over head. Breaking my neck.

My heart pounds hard.

I cling to the banister and realize that no one has lunged at me.

And this time, when I look again, there's no one there.

It's just the shadow of a tree streaming in through an open window. The leaves are hair, the branches arms and legs. The gentle rhythm, the movement of wind. No one is there.

I turn to make my way to the bathroom. It's a small room, but as I come to it, I take note: the door isn't pressed flush against the wall as it should be. Behind the open door, there is enough space for a body to hide.

I have to muster every ounce of courage I have to go on. It isn't easy. My feet don't want to move, but they do. It's slow, deliberate.

When I reach the bathroom door, I don't step inside. I don't look behind the door.

Rather my movements are sudden and abrupt, an impulse. I kick the door as hard as I can, where it ricochets off the wall, the rubber stopper running headfirst into the baseboard, not bumping into a person first. Because there's nobody there to slow it down. There's nobody there at all.

As I make my way inside the bathroom, I find the shower curtain pulled tight, stretched from wall to wall. It billows slightly. Heat spews from a nearby vent, though that's not the reason for the movement. Instead what I envision is a figure standing on the other side of the curtain, the breath from his or her lungs making the curtain move.

Someone is there, hiding behind the shower curtain.

I tread delicately. On tiptoes. Two steps, and then three.

I reach out a hand, aware that the blood throughout my entire body has stopped flowing. That I'm holding my breath. That my heart has ceased beating.

I feel the cotton of the shower curtain in my shaking hand, the plastic of its liner. I grab a fistful of it and pull hard, finding myself face-to-face with the white tiles of the shower wall.

There's no one there. It's only me.

The carriage home is empty. Whoever was here has gone for now.

I do only one thing then, and that's check the fire safe box where I keep my money, to be sure someone hasn't swiped every last penny from me. Because why else would someone break into the carriage home except to steal from me? I keep the box in the closet these days, hidden in the corner beneath the hem of a long winter coat where, God willing, no one will ever find it. I open the closet door, drop to my knees and gather the box in my hands. The box is locked. When I slip the key inside, I find every dollar accounted for. Whoever was here didn't steal money from me.

I try not to let my imagination get the best of me, but to force logic to prevail. I tell myself that I never closed the shades in the first place. That I only thought about doing it, but never did. I think long and hard, trying to remember the smooth, woven feel of the white roller shade in my hand as I drew it southward and let go, watching it hold.

Did that happen, or did I only imagine it did?

Or maybe whatever springlike mechanism that makes the shades open failed to keep them closed. The ratchet and pin that hold them in place didn't work. Simple human error or mechanical failure.

Or maybe someone *was* there, lifting the roller shades one by one so that when I returned, they could see me. I tell myself no. That the front door was locked. And that, as far as I know, only one person but me has a key. My landlord.

I step from the closet and make my way to a nearby window where I stare out and toward Ms. Geissler's home. The room turns warm all of a sudden. Beneath my arms, I sweat.

There's no one there, no one that I can see.

And yet, as it was last night, there's a light on in the third-story window of the greystone home. The window shades are lowered, but not pulled all the way down. They don't lie flush against the window sill. There's a gap. Albeit a small one, only a couple of inches at best.

But still, a gap.

And as I stare at that gap for half the night, sometime around midnight I see a shadow pass by. Just a shadow, but nothing more.

EDEN

July 2, 1997
Egg Harbor

BE STILL MY BEATING heart, it worked! We're going to have a baby!

One single cycle of IVF and, as I sat on the toilet today after Aaron had gone off to work, the all-familiar pregnancy test cradled between my fingers, I spied not one single line this time, but two. Two! Two pink lines running parallel on the display screen.

My heart hammered quickly inside my chest. It was all I could do not to scream.

And still I had my doubts—after months of seeing only one line, it was easy to convince myself that I was imagining the second one there, that I had quite simply fashioned it in my mind. The one line was bright pink like bubble gum, the same dependable line that greeted me each month, bringing stinging tears to my eyes.

But the other, this new line, was a light pink, the lightest of light, the mere suggestion of pink, a whisper that something might be there.

I pray that it's not a deception of my mind.

I went to the market wearing mismatching shoes. I drove above the speed limit with the window open, though outside it poured down rain. I ran into the store without an umbrella, saturating my hair. If anyone noticed my shoes, they didn't point it out.

I purchased three additional pregnancy tests of assorted brands in case one had a tendency toward being inaccurate. I took them home and urinated on them all, every last one of them, and in the end, there were six lines.

Three additional pregnancy tests.

Six pink lines.

Aaron and I are going to have a baby.

July 5, 1997
Egg Harbor

For days we've been living in a constant state of euphoria.

I walk around the home, floating on air. I dream up baby names for boys and girls. I go to the hardware store and get samples of paint for the nursery room walls.

At home alone, I find myself dancing. Spinning in graceful circles around the living room floors. In all my life, I've never danced before. But I can't help myself. I can't stop my feet from swaying, my arms wrapped around myself, holding on to the life within. Dancing with my unborn child. I find an old record and set it on the turntable. I carefully place the needle on it, and move in tune to the music as Gladys Knight sings a song for me.

The day I discovered the positive pregnancy tests, I phoned Aaron at work to deliver the news. He was euphoric in a way I'd rarely seen him before. He left work at once and came home earlier than ever before, pulling his car in to the drive minutes before eight o'clock.

He brought me ice cream in bed; he fed it to me with a bent-out-of-shape spoon. He lay in bed beside me and rubbed my back. He massaged my feet. He stroked my hair. He told me how amazing I was, how gorgeous, and how already I had that beautiful pregnancy glow.

He stared at me then, just stared, and inside my heart began to cantor, a kaleidoscope of butterflies flitting inside me. I knew what would come next and it was then that my body began to want him, to need him like it hadn't for so long before. I soughed at his touch, my skin breaking out in goose-flesh as he ran a hand across my arm, lacing his fingers through mine. As he stared, he said again that if our baby girl looked anything like me, that she would be the prettiest thing around. And then he tucked a strand of hair behind my ear and I knew that in that moment, I was the most beautiful girl in the world to him.

Our baby girl.

He held me tightly and kissed me like he hadn't in months, slowly and deeply at first, growing ravenous, a starved man who hadn't been fed in years, and it was then that I realized I too was empty and famished.

My breath quickened as he slid a steady hand up the skirt of my nightgown.

"You think it's okay?" I gasped as Aaron withdrew my underpants and set them aside, though there was nothing more that I wanted in that moment than a fresh start for Aaron and me and our baby, to be able to erase all the animosity in a single moment, with a single deed.

"You think it's safe?" I begged, and Aaron assured me that everything was okay, and, as we moved together there on the bed, I believed him. For the first time in a long time, I believed him.

July 14, 1997
Egg Harbor

An ultrasound with Dr. Landry confirmed the pregnancy, though there was no need for Dr. Landry's attestation because I, for one, already knew that it was true, that the manifold of pregnancy tests didn't lie. The battle with morning sickness had begun already, a misnomer if I'd ever heard one for it was morning, noon and night sickness. Not once did I complain, but rather welcomed the nausea and the fatigue as a gift.

Dr. Landry told Aaron and me that our tiny embryo is currently measuring one-half of a centimeter from crown to rump. As I lay on the examination table, feet in stirrups, for once not put off by the wand inside me, the complete invasion of privacy that I've come to accept as par for the course, Dr. Landry pointed out the gestational sac and the yolk sac, but I couldn't take my eyes off that pint-size nub that would one day be a baby.

Aaron held my hand the entire time. He stroked my hair. He kissed my lips when the image appeared, dark and grainy and impossible to see were it not for Dr. Landry's informative voice and thin finger telling us what was the gestational sac and what was the yolk sac, and where our baby was growing, and then, once I found it, the embryo—a half centimeter long with paddle-like arms and legs and webbing between its toes and fingers, none of which I could see for myself though Dr. Landry told us were there—the one thing in the world I loved more than anything else, I couldn't divert my eyes.

There was a heartbeat. We couldn't hear it yet, but we could *see* it. It was there, the movements of it on the ultrasound screen. Our baby had a heart and a heartbeat, and blood that coursed through his or her tiny body. Its heart had chambers—four of them Dr. Landry said!—and beat like a racehorse, a heartbeat that easily trumped mine, though it too was going at a steady gallop.

I'm six weeks along. And we have a due date now.

By May, Aaron and I will finally have a baby. We'll be parents!

How will I possibly be able to wait that long to hold my baby in my arms?

July 16, 1997
Egg Harbor

I told my stepmother about the baby today. I didn't mean to; it just happened. We were on the phone when she asked—as she had so many times in the past—"How much longer are we going to have to wait for you and Aaron to have a baby?" and it wasn't so much that I told her, because I didn't, but it was the lack of a response that gave it away, the silence, because I was too busy beaming behind the handset, trying to no avail to manufacture a lie.

If Nora could have seen me, she would have noticed the way my skin turned pink; she, like Aaron, would have seen the way I glowed. She would have seen me run a delicate hand across the cotton of my blouse—a link to the life inside—and triumphantly smile.

She said nothing at first, nothing in response to my nothing.

"When were you thinking you'd tell us?" she asked then with the slightest hint of malice—Nora, of course, needs to be the first to know everything—followed immediately by "Does Aaron's mother already know?" and there was jealousy and skepticism in her voice long before she offered her congratulations and said how happy she is for Aaron and me.

I called Aaron's mother next before Nora had a chance to call for herself, boasting that she knew a whole thirty seconds before Aaron's mother did.

It was like a wildfire then, that instant burst of pregnancy news that caught quickly, spreading through the family from phone call to phone call like a raging inferno. By the end of the day, nearly everyone would know our news.

Miranda arrived as Aaron's mother and I were saying good-bye, and catching a glimpse of my hand still situated on the cotton of my blouse, she said to me, "It's about goddamn time, Eden."

And then she hugged me, a quick, careless hug, sending her boys into the backyard to play alone so she could lie on my sofa and rest. Little Carter didn't want to go; he, himself, was still a baby, and so she picked him up and plopped him in Jack's arms and said again to *go* and we stood there, watching them walk away, listening as Carter cried. She was massive again, still months away from giving birth to baby number four, and the evidence of it was everywhere: in her tired eyes, her unwashed hair, her inflated legs.

Pregnancy did not suit Miranda well.

Her maternity shirts no longer fit correctly, leaving a fraction of her stomach exposed, ashy skin drawn tightly around her baby, a black, vertical line etched on her body from belly button down. Miranda herself didn't have a pregnancy glow, but rather was covered in blotchy brown spots all over her skin; the hormones were not working in her favor.

"Just wait until you're as fat as me," she said, seeing the way I watched her drop onto the sofa, a giraffe making an ungainly attempt to sit.

"Well I have news too," she said then, as if she couldn't stand me being happy, as if she couldn't take a back seat to my glad tidings for once. "We're going to have a girl!" she screeched, clapping her own hands, going on to say how—though Joe didn't know it yet—she'd had a peek at her medical file when the obstetrician was out of the room during her last appointment, and there, in the margins of the paperwork, saw the Venus symbol written with black ink.

"Finally," she said, frowning out the window at her three boys, fifty-pound Jack lugging twenty-pound Carter around, Carter who still cried. "After everything I've been through," she said, and I wanted to be happy for her, I really did.

But I couldn't bring myself to be.

She didn't deserve another baby any more than a murderer deserves clemency.

I was grateful when, an hour later, Paul wet himself and they had to leave.

Aaron had wanted to keep the news of our pregnancy a secret for a while longer, but I couldn't help myself. I wanted to shout it from the rooftops, to let everyone in the whole entire universe know that I was going to be a mother. "Why wait?" I asked later that afternoon as he prepared for work. I frowned at him, feeling punctured that he would want to keep our baby a secret. We'd spent a year trying to achieve this, watched our lives and our marriage flounder to make a baby, drained our savings and accrued mass amounts of debt on our credit cards.

And yet I couldn't be happier. I couldn't be more thrilled.

This was the one thing that I wanted more than anything. More than *anything*.

I wanted everyone to know about it.

"Just in case," Aaron replied when I asked why we should keep our baby a secret, why we should wait to share the news.

"In case what?" I asked, provoking him, but he wouldn't say the words out loud. He was being cautiously optimistic, I knew, but what I wanted was for him to be jubilant like me. He stood before me in the kitchen, slipping his feet into a pair of new shoes, waterproof, slip-proof black loafers that cost us an arm and a leg. But none of that mattered now, not trivial things like the cost of groceries, the cost of shoes.

We were going to have a baby.

He stood and came to me, wrapping his arms around the small of my back, and I breathed him in, the scent of his aftershave and soap because Aaron, of course, didn't wear cologne. His hands were rough from years of hard work, the scrubbing of dishes, the scalding sauces that bubbled over onto his hands, burning them. The many near misses with a utility knife. The gashes and lacerations, healed now but always there. Aaron's hands were rough and worn, but also the softest things in the world to me as they slipped under the hemline of my blouse and stroked my bare skin.

He wouldn't say the words out loud, but he didn't have to. I knew exactly what he was thinking.

"We saw our baby," I told him, whispering the words into his ear. "We saw the heartbeat. Everything is fine."

JESSIE

I'M OUT THE DOOR early, hurrying to the side of the carriage home to collect my bike, but when I arrive, I see that she's gone. That she's not there. That the spot where I left her last night is completely empty.

There's a moment of panic.

Someone has stolen Old Faithful from me.

My heart picks up speed, my face warming with frustration and anger and fear. I look up and down the alleyway as my heart sinks. For a minute, tears well in my eyes. I could cry.

But then I remember leaving Old Faithful tethered to the bike rack outside the Art Institute. No one has taken her from me. I left her there.

I take the Brown Line out to Albany Park, getting off at Kimball. From there it's a walk to Mom's and my old home, a classic Chicago-style bungalow that's boxy and brick with a low-pitched roof on a street where every single home is a replica of the next. The desperation has gotten under my skin now, a do-or-die need to find my birth certificate, to find my social security card, to figure out who the hell I am. I need to make a final sweep of the home to see if there's anything there, anything I may have missed. Because the estate sale will kick off soon, and then it will be too late. Everything that was once mine will be gone.

I've only been gone a couple of days. But as I make my way down the sidewalk, I feel homesick. I miss Mom more than ever. I miss my home. The sight of the for-sale sign plunged into the green grass makes my stomach churn, my Realtor's pretty face smeared across the corner of it. I'd picked her, this Realtor, because I saw her face and name on a similar sign somewhere down the street. There was a number to call and so I called it. And like that, the house is on the market and soon, any evidence of my time with Mom will be gone.

The house looks different than it did before. The only thing still here are the ghosts we've left behind. Aside from our house, the rest of the block looks annoyingly the same, as if no one noticed that I'd left or that Mom died, which most likely they didn't. The only person I see outside is our neighbor Mr. Henderson from next door. There he stands on his own front porch, thinning hair standing vertical, a cigar in hand. Smoke billowing around his head. Mr. Henderson wears corduroy pants, slippers, a fisherman cardigan. Though as far as I know, he doesn't fish. Instead he teaches English lit at a local college and is pretentious as all get-out. Mr. Henderson couldn't be bothered to help after Mom's cancer spread to the bones, leaving her far more susceptible to fracture. She fell one morning when I was at school, shattering a hip, lying there on her back, calling out an open window for help.

He heard her cries as he sat there in his own front room, sucking away on his cigar. No doubt he heard her cries, though later, as the ambulance carried her away and he stood watching from his porch steps—merely a snoop and not a Samaritan—he claimed he did not.

I pay extra attention to the sidewalk as I walk along, taking care not to step on the cracks. Not that it matters because Mom wouldn't feel it anyway if my footfalls broke her back. *Step on a crack, break your mother's back.*

I cross the street, refusing to say hello to Mr. Henderson, refusing to meet his curious eye. I dig into my bag for the keys, climbing up the stairs and to the front door.

This neighborhood has been around for near forever. Most of the homes are circa 1920-something, during some sort of housing boom when thousands of bungalows sprung up overnight, fulfilling dreams of homeownership for that exploding middle class. Because the homes were practical and affordable. And because there were a ton of them. Up and down the street, all I see is nothing but trees and brick, trees and brick. Trees and brick as far as the eye can see. I have no doubt Mom chose Albany Park to live because it's relatively affordable, a good place to raise kids. Money was a luxury Mom and I didn't have. Not that I can say I grew up poor, because I didn't. But Mom was frugal and we weren't rich.

We planned a big dinner out for when the cancer was finally in remission for the second time around. Gibsons Steakhouse. Mom was going to buy a new dress to wear because she never spent money on herself. Any time there was a little extra to spare, she spent it on me.

Needless to say, Gibsons Steakhouse never happened.

The day Mom found out the cancer was back, she was sitting outside on the front stoop when I got home from school. She'd been to the doctor for back pain, the kind that no amount of ibuprofen could fix. Pain she hadn't told me about until that afternoon. She thought it was a herniated disc, back strain, sciatica. Effects of the job.

As it turned out, it was the breast cancer, back for vengeance. Metastasized to the bones, the lungs.

She told me to sit. She held my hand, caressed each finger one at a time while I committed to memory the length and shape of her fingers, the asymmetry of the knucklebones, the blue rivers of veins that swept across the thinning skin.

She said to me that day on the stoop, *Jessie, I'm dying. I'm going to die.*

I cried. But she said it was all right. She wasn't afraid to die. She was stoic. *When?* I asked, like some stupid child. Like Mom had any way of knowing exactly when it would happen.

What she said was *Sooner or later we all die, Jessie. It's only a matter of time. And this is mine.*

I unlock the door and step inside. I'm inundated with the smell almost immediately. The smell of Mom. Her hand lotion, Crabtree & Evelyn's Summer Hill. It nearly knocks me from my feet. It's diffused through the rooms and if I didn't know any better, I'd think that Mom was still here with me. Heart still ticking, not yet dead. I hear that death rattle, the saliva pooling there in the back of her throat. The nurses' gentle footfalls, close enough to touch. As if they're still there, still walking in orbits around me. Lathering lotion on Mom's hands and feet, turning her every few hours to keep bedsores from forming on her skin.

The smell of the lotion is overpowering. It binds to the millions of tiny little hairs in my nose, bringing me to my knees every time I breathe. *Mom.*

And I find that I'm looking for her, half-certain that when I turn she'll be standing there in the arched doorway of the kitchen, sagging body leaning against the doorway because she doesn't have the energy to hold it upright anymore, a soft cotton hat covering her bald head. Asking how I got along at school today in that way that she does, teeth gritted through the pain that managed to breeze in and past the narcotics sometimes.

How'd you get along at school today, Jessie?

But it's not real, I remind myself.

The nurses are not here.

Mom is dead.

And only then am I aware of the silence. Of the earsplitting silence that now worms its way through the cracks of our home.

I don't know where to begin. I searched the entire home already, but I look anyway, starting in my bedroom, planning to work my way down in search of the social security card. I pluck desk and dresser drawers from their tracks. I dig beneath clothes I've intentionally left in the dresser drawers, those I no longer need. I lift rugs from the floor and check beneath. I canvass my closet. No luck.

I make my way to Mom's bedroom, where I see that the liquidator has begun to tag items for sale. Mom's clothes now hang from a rolling rack beside her bed. I run my hands over a knit cardigan, her favorite. If I'd had my wits about me at the time, I would have had Mom cremated in the cardigan so she could spend all of eternity in it. But instead she wore a hospital gown, white and wrinkled with snowflakes, a single tie on the otherwise open back. The funeral home gathered her body from the hospital within hours after she died. But there was a mandatory waiting period before the cremation could begin. Twenty-four hours, in case I changed my mind.

I spent those twenty-four hours parked outside the funeral home's doors, sitting on the curb because they didn't have a bench. And because I couldn't bring myself to go home without Mom.

The liquidator will take some 40 percent of all sales, which is fine by me. Anything so that I don't have to be involved in the process, so that I don't have to watch our possessions walk out the door in the arms of someone new.

I pull open the closet door to reveal a large walk-in. It's empty now, all of Mom's clothes moved to the rack beside the bed. Only hooks and a mirror remain—a silver-framed oval mirror that Mom and I used to make silly faces in front of when I was a girl. I'd stand on a chair so that I could see inside, and there we'd stare at our reflections side by side in the glass.

The mirror hangs on the closet wall, an oversight only, for it won't be long before the liquidator pulls that too from the wall and sticks a price tag on it, snatching memories right along with it, memories of my crossed eyeballs, Mom's fish face.

I run a hand along the glass, remembering how sometimes we didn't make silly faces at all. How sometimes I'd just sit on the floor beside her feet and watch as Mom stared at herself, her dark hair and eyes so unlike the dishwater-blond hair that sat on my head, the tufts of eyebrow hair that stuck straight up, same as they do now. Unlike me, Mom didn't have dimples. My dimples are much more than simple holes in the cheeks, but more like deep comma-shaped gorges. I didn't get those from Mom. There isn't one feature on my face that came from her.

Even as a kid, I saw the way Mom looked when she stared at her reflection in the mirror. She looked sad. I wondered what she saw. For some reason I don't think it was the same pretty face that I saw.

I'm about to leave when I spot something out of the corner of my eye, something I've never noticed in Mom's closet before. Something that would have otherwise been hidden behind the hems of clothes, except that now there are no clothes to taint the view.

I have to look twice to be sure that it's there, that I'm not only imagining it's there. What it is is black, metal, covered in louvers. A door. A boxy little door that hovers less than a foot above the hardwood floors.

I drop to my hands and knees and pull on the door's knob, finding a crawl space on the other side. A *crawl space*. I never knew we had a crawl space before.

The space is dark and dingy, the ceiling low. The floor is dirt, covered only by a thick sheet of plastic. I can't believe I never found this place before. How many times did I dig my way through Mom's closet for clues as to who my father could be? But as it so happened, I never dug far enough. Instead I gave up when I got to the clothes, taking for granted that there was nothing on the other side but a wall.

Only one time did Mom bring my father up all on her own, without my begging. I was twelve years old. Mom had had a glass of wine before bed. She said to me that night, seconds before she fell asleep, head draped over the rock-hard sofa arm, *A long time ago, I did something I'm not proud of, Jessie. Something that shames me. And that's how I got you.*

The next thing I heard was the sound of her half-drunk snore, but by morning I couldn't bring myself to ask what she'd meant by it.

I reach inside the crawl space and drag something out. What it is, I don't know. Not until I get it into the closet's light do I see that it's a plastic storage bin, and the adrenaline kicks in at the prospect of what I might find inside. My social security card, for one, but more likely, something having to do with my father, which suddenly, in this moment, takes precedence. Something Mom kept tucked away so that I wouldn't find it.

I tear the lid off, finding photo albums inside. I find myself feeling hopeful, wondering what I'll find in them. Photos of Mom, photos of my father, photos of Mom and her own mom and dad.

But of course not. Instead it's me. All me.

I set the album aside to take back to the carriage home with me.

I crawl toward the crawl space, feeling blindly inside for another box. I can't reach far enough in to grab it, and so I have to crawl in through the door. Inside, the space is only about thirty-six-inches tall. I'm not fully in before claustrophobia settles in. The dirty floors and wooden beams close in around me. The darkness is smothering. The only light comes from behind. I find another storage bin and drag it out backward, through the access panel and onto the closet floor, grateful for a little elbow room.

I open the lid and have a look, hoping that this is the mother lode I've been in search of. The answer to all the questions I have. But it's not. It's nothing, just a bunch of inconsequential items in a plastic storage bin, which makes me realize this isn't a secret crawl space at all, but just a *crawl space*. For storage. For stuff Mom had no other place to put.

She didn't intentionally keep this a secret from me. I just never knew it was here.

I sigh, feeling uncomfortable and glum. I rise to my feet, stretching my hands above my head, arching my back. But my movements are quick and careless. The blood flees my brain as I stand up, leaving me light-headed and dizzy. All of these nights without sleep are taking their toll on me. I reach for the wall to steady myself, crashing into the mirror as I do. I watch on helplessly as the mirror loses its hold on the wall and I can't catch it in time. I'm too slow to stop it from falling.

It slips from its nail and slams to the ground, scratching the wall as it does, leaving a four-foot scrape in the paint. The entire mirror shatters before my eyes. Broken glass spreads like spiderwebs, chunks falling to the hardwood floors. And all I can think about is bad luck. Seven entire years of bad luck that await me now.

I curse out loud, wondering if there's any hope of salvaging the mirror. I start to gather the biggest chunks in my hand, careful that I don't step on the tiny shards of glass.

My eyes are so caught up in what's happening on the floor that at first I don't see the small compartment dug into the wall. A little recess carved there into the drywall, hidden behind where the mirror should go. A hole that's been fitted with a sturdy box.

And I think for a moment that my eyes deceive me. That I'm only imagining the compartment is there. Because why in the world would there be a secret storage compartment on Mom's closet wall? I rub at my eyes, certain it will disappear as I do. But sure enough, it's still here.

For at least twenty seconds I stare at that box without moving.

Mom had a stash of personal stuff she kept hidden from me.

I think of all the times Mom and I looked together in the mirror when I was a girl. All I ever saw was a mirror—our own silly expressions looking back at us through the glass— but for Mom it was a portal to her private world, a gateway to the things she didn't want me to see.

It feels an enormous invasion of privacy for me to snoop but I can't help myself. I reach my hand inside Mom's secret box. There's only one item there. It's a scrap of glossy white paper pressed into the corner of the box. My chest clenches. I hold my breath.

This could be something.

Or, like the plastic storage bins hidden in the crawl space, this could be nothing.

I have to use a fingernail to emancipate the scrap. When I do, I turn it over in my hands to see. It's a photograph that some part of my memory reminds me I've seen before.

But with the memory of the photograph comes the memory of Mom's face. Openmouthed and afraid. She knew I'd seen it. But what happened next has been wiped clean from my brain's hard drive. Either that or entombed beneath a gazillion other memories, harder than others to dig up.

Mom hid this photograph from me.

It's the kind of photograph that looks a little dated, a little old. Not crazy old, like archaic. But older than me. The colors are faded, the blues a little less blue, and the greens a little less green than they used to be. It's a picture of a lake. A long seashore of blue. Tan sand, darker where the water hits it. White ripples of waves. Evergreen trees line the edges of the lake. There is a pier suspended over the water, one that looks unsound, unsafe. Like at any moment it could sink into the lake and get carried away with the waves. If I squint my eyes up tight, there's a boat out there on the water. A sailboat, just a simple sloop with a single white mast. That's what I see.

Mom knew a whole lot about sailboats, which she relayed to me when we used to walk past DuSable Harbor on occasion, hand in hand. *See that one over there, Jessie?* she'd ask, slipping her hand away long enough to point at it. I'd pretend to look. Pretend to look because I didn't really care, her words falling on deaf ears. *That's a cutter,* or, *that's a catamaran,* she'd tell me. She had a book on them, a heavy coffee-table book called *Sailing*. Though as far as I knew, Mom had never once stepped foot on a sailboat in her entire life. At least not since I've been alive. I forget sometimes that Mom had a life that preceded mine.

But the lake and the sailboat are only an afterthought to the image I see, because there's also a man in the photograph, one with brown hair and a large stature. He's tall and husky with thick wrists exposed by a flannel shirt that's rolled up to the elbows. There's a watch on a right wrist, a hat in his hand. He stands with his back to the camera, blurred at the edges because he wasn't standing still when the shutter button was pressed. He's not centered on the photo paper, as if he was moving away when the picture was snapped.

The photograph wasn't meant to be of him.

The central object is the sailboat. The picture is of the boat. And the man only got in the way. By today's terms, a photobomb.

The man stands with his hands on his hips, left knee bent a bit. His head is pitched to the right. He has blue jeans on—saggy ones, not formfitting. The ends are fraying, turning white. One of his gym shoes is untied. Strands of hair move in the wind.

I wish that he would turn and look at me, so that I could see his eyes, the shape of his nose. Whether we look anything alike.

Is this man my father?

Why did Mom hide this photo from me?

Why did she not want me to know anything about this lake or this boat or this man?

I think of all those times I sat cross-legged on the closet floor beside her feet, watching as she stared sullenly at her own reflection in the mirror. What I thought was that she didn't like what she saw. A modest, unpretentious face, a bit earthy with dark hair and dark eyes.

And then, years later when the cancer settled in, that same face became cadaverous. She lost more weight than she had to spare, face thinning, cheekbones hollowed out—an image she despised. That's what I thought she was looking at when she stared in the mirror.

But now I think that maybe she wasn't looking at herself as much as she was looking through the glass, reflecting on the life she left behind, the one she kept hidden from me behind that mirror.

EDEN

WHAT AARON TOLD THE emergency room physician was that there was blood, "Some blood," he said, "spotting," which to me equated to a teaspoon or two, enough to dirty a single pad, but the amount of blood I saw was measured in liters and gallons.

It came gushing out of me, a deluge of blood pouring down from the sky, rivers and streams overflowing their banks, dousing the earth, sweeping homes from their foundations. Everywhere I looked there was blood.

The day was hot and I wore shorts, and the blood, it saturated my underpants first before snaking down the inside of my bare leg, a thin, red zigzag emblazoned against my fair white skin.

"I have my period," I told Aaron as we were there in the backyard—he staring openmouthed at me, on his knees, installing chicken wire around the flower bed so the deer couldn't poach from us again, making off with our beautiful hollyhock blooms.

In retrospect there were warning signs, maybe: the suggestion of a cramp, some lower back pain, tokens of pregnancy as well as menstruation and miscarriage. The fact that the nausea had abated during the last twenty-four hours was, to me, a welcome blessing and not once a sign of catastrophe.

"You're pregnant," Aaron said lightly, rising to his feet and coming to me, but I couldn't process his words, couldn't make sense of what was happening. It was my period again, come to me like it does every month without fail. There was dirt on his forehead, and his hands were red, etched with the impression of chicken wire. "You don't have your period, Eden," he said, dropping the wire cutters to the ground and taking my hands into his.

He wiped the blood from my leg with his own sweaty T-shirt.

In the car I sat on a kitchen towel.

We didn't speak on the way to the emergency room.

He told the attending physician that there was *some blood*, that I was *spotting*.

An ultrasound was performed. This time, there was no heartbeat.

The baby's heartbeat had disappeared.

Both Aaron's and the doctor's eyes wandered to mine, though I wouldn't meet theirs, too busy staring at the black gestational sac on the monitor, at the stillness of the screen, the lack of movement. The absence of sound.

Aaron reached out a hand to mine but I couldn't feel it. I only saw that it was there.

I was insensible. I was stone-cold.

"What now?" Aaron asked the physician who'd been sent down from obstetrics to perform the ultrasound, a woman who would soon return to labor and delivery to deliver someone else's healthy newborn.

"We'll perform a dilation and curettage," she said, "to eliminate any remaining tissue from the womb."

Tissue. As if only a few hours ago that tissue hadn't been a child.

In that moment, I couldn't speak. I couldn't even bring myself to cry.

They put me to sleep for the procedure.

I prayed I'd never wake up again.

JESSIE

I LEAVE ALBANY PARK, taking the train into the Loop, where I make my way to the Art Institute to collect my bike. From there, I pedal to the coffee bar on Dearborn, the one where the man at the garden had purchased his coffee, the name I'd read on the paper sleeve of his coffee cup. People are religious about their coffee and their routines, and so it seems logical enough to think that if he was here yesterday, he'll come again today. I need to find him. I need to ask him why he was in the garden—*Mom's and my* special garden—sitting there, reading her obituary. I need to hear why Mom's obituary made him sad. How does he know Mom?

I bring the photograph of the man with me. I carry it in the front pocket of my bag.

The man who I think might be my father.

At random stoplights I slip my hand into the pocket of my bag and pull it out. I try to spot some nicety I haven't yet seen, some minor detail in the image I've managed to overlook, like the swollen clouds or the gangly-looking bird that perches on a rock at the water's edge.

The sleeves of the man's flannel shirt are shoved to his elbows in the picture. A raised red line bridges a lower arm. Scar tissue, I think, or maybe just an anomaly in the photograph, a streak of light or a reflection. I wonder what any of it means. If it means anything. If the clouds or the birds or the scar can provide details about the man or the land on which he stands.

Where was this picture taken?

And more importantly, who is he?

I search in vain for the smoking gun to tell me who he is. How I know him. What this man has to do with me. I wonder if the answer is there, staring me in the face, and I simply can't see it.

And then the light turns green and I carefully shove the picture back into my bag and pedal on toward the coffee shop.

When I arrive, I press in through the door, past people who are coming out. The coffee bar is eclectic, cluttered with mismatching tables and chairs. There are stacks of magazines and books.

Between the grinding and gurgling of the espresso machine, the roar of people talking, the coffee shop is loud. I order a coffee and carry it to the kiosk to douse it with sugar. A blue velvet sofa lines a wall, and I help myself to it, sinking into the wilted center, watching as caffeine-deprived customers come and go. The line grows long enough that the last person stands in the doorway because he doesn't clear the doorframe. Instead he props it open with his body, letting the fall air in. Napkins blow from a table and litter the floor.

As I sit there waiting for the man from the garden to magically appear, I pull the photograph from my pocket one more time, taking in the man's stature, the color of his hair. Imagining his eyes. In the image, they're looking out toward the sailboat, away from the camera lens, and so I can't see them. I can't see what they look like, but I can imagine.

They're blue like mine, and he has dimples too.

I sip from my coffee, place the photograph back in my bag.

My mind drifts and I find myself thinking about the other Jessica Sloane. The one who is not me. And I know with a sudden translucence that I am not Jessica Sloane, but that I'm somebody else. That Jessica Sloane died when she was three and for whatever reason, Mom stole her social security number and gave it to me. This is no longer a hypothetical. I know.

But there are ways of finding out who you are, aside from a birth certificate, social security number or name. Because if I'm not Jessica Sloane, then I need to know who I really am. I think of forensic identification, stuff like fingerprints, DNA, handwriting analysis, dentistry. Ways to prove one's identity aside from birth certificates and social security numbers. Everyone in the whole wide world is supposedly unique, like the stripes of a zebra or the spots of a giraffe. Snowflakes. It's near mathematically and scientifically impossible that any two could be the same. Even the creases of our feet are distinct, which is one of the reasons babies' footprints are taken after birth. For identification purposes. Because no two footprints are alike. So hospitals know which baby is which if ever they get separated from their moms or dads. In case the ID bands slip from their ankles or wrists. I stare at my fingerprints, thinking the answer to who I am is sitting there, in all those miniscule lines that make me unique, a single snowflake, one in twenty trillion falling in a snowstorm, drifting aimlessly and alone.

I don't know who I am, but I'm not Jessica Sloane.

It's hours later when I catch a smidge of orange pass by the storefront window, and I know right away: it's him. It's the orange baseball cap that he wore, slipping it over his hair before he left the garden. He's here, come and gone for coffee and somehow, in a daze, I all but missed him.

I rise too quickly from the blue velvet sofa, spilling a lukewarm coffee, my third of the day, down the front of me, staining my shirt a translucent brown. I don't bother blotting it with napkins before I go scurrying for the door, knocking into a stanchion post along the way. I knock it over with a clang, leaving it on the floor as people stare. "What's the hurry?" I hear breathed through the air. "What's her problem?" followed by a giggle, a snort.

I press my way out onto the city street, following the pinprick of orange in the distance, a beacon of light as it slaloms this way and that down the street. I run, pushing my way past people walking too slowly, trying desperately to bridge the gap from him to me.

As I narrow in on him, I reach out and tug on something, my hand bearing down hard. A little boy cries out, and, as they turn to me, I see. A little boy in a superhero costume. The Flash. He's perched on his father's shoulders, making him tall. The costume is red and yellow with a mask that covers his face. It's the type of mask that covers everything, leaving only slits for the mouth, nose and eyes. Like the costume, it's also red and yellow. Not orange, though my mind mutated them for me, mixing the red and yellow, turning them into orange.

Once again, my eyes have deceived me.

He isn't the man from the garden after all.

EDEN

June 17, 2005
Chicago

It's been a couple of hours since it happened, and still I can't get my heart rhythm to slow. I feel off, a dull headache in the back of my neck that simply won't quit, my handwriting like chicken scratch from the shaking hands. Jessie is quiet now, tucked into bed with her lights turned off. I'd read her a story before bed, hoping it might help her forget. Hoping it might replace the photograph she saw with the fun of leading imaginary beasts on a wild rumpus around her bedroom. She was laughing by the time she went to bed, and I can only pray that she dreams tonight of Emile and Bernard, and not of Aaron.

I, however, will dream only of Aaron.

I think I covered my tracks quite well, but I won't ever know. There's no telling what goes on inside a little girl's mind, which details of our lives are committed to memory and which we forget.

For the first time tonight, past and present collided, and it made me realize one thing: that I have to be more wary of where I hide my things. Jessie is older now and more inquisitive. She's liable to have questions for me that I can't answer because I don't want to answer them. I have to be more careful if I'm going to keep my past from her.

It's not that I don't love her. It's that I do.

We'd just finished up dinner when it happened. I was in the kitchen, wiping down the countertops, and she'd disappeared down the hall to, presumably, go play. She was in her room, or so I thought at the time, quiet as a church mouse. That should have been my warning, because for as fiery and high-spirited as she is, Jessie is rarely quiet.

I don't know how much time passed—ten minutes, an hour while I was stupidly relishing in the quiet and didn't once think to check on her—when she appeared there in the doorway to the kitchen with an item in her hand, asking of me, "Who's this?"

Her eyes, when I turned to her, were doe-eyed, her hair falling into her forehead like it hadn't seen a brush in weeks. There were dust bunnies clinging to the fabric of her pants and I knew right away that she'd been somewhere she shouldn't have been, on her hands and knees, digging through things.

"Where'd you find this?" I asked, taking it from her hand. I heard my voice crack as I said it, and though I couldn't see it, I was certain my face was masked in fear. My voice wasn't angry. It was scared.

Jessie had found it under my bed, of course, where she'd been snooping. The photograph had been stashed inside an envelope, inside a box, and under the bed, the kind of thing one didn't just happen to stumble upon. She went searching for it. Or rather she went searching for something and she found it, because up until a few minutes before, she didn't know this photograph existed, the photograph I'd snatched all those years ago in the yard of our cottage, a photograph of our glorious view—the lake with a sailboat out at sea—meant to be only of the lake and the sailboat, though Aaron stepped into the frame just as I took the picture. He'd apologized and later, after the pictures were developed, we'd laughed over it. Aaron thought he'd ruined my photograph, but what he'd done was the opposite of that. He'd made it perfect. He'd made it complete.

Up until a few minutes ago, Jessie didn't know Aaron existed because those *Who's my father?* questions have only just begun to surface, and so far I've been able to quell them all with the suggestion of milk and cookies or ice cream.

"Who is it, Mommy?" she asked again when I didn't respond.

"Just an old friend," I said, trying to settle my jittery voice as I opened a kitchen drawer—the closest thing to me—and slid it inside. I'd find a better hiding spot later after she'd gone to sleep. I could feel my cheeks inflame, my hands start to shake.

"Are you mad at me?" Jessie asked then, eyes swelling with tears, mistaking what I was feeling for anger when what it was was sadness and regret and shame.

"No, baby," I said, dropping down to my knees and drawing her into me. "Mommy could never be mad at you," I told her, and then I smiled as widely as I could and grabbed a hold of her hand. "How about some ice cream before we get ready for bed?" I proposed, and of course there was no hesitation, no wavering. Jessie screamed an easy *yes!* while jumping up and down, and so we carried bowls of chocolate ice cream onto the front porch to eat, watching as the sun made its final descent beneath the horizon. I helped her with a bath and we read about the wild rumpus. I tucked her into bed. She asked me to lie with her as she always does these days, and so I curled under the covers beside her, and she pressed her body into mine, a lean arm flung across my chest, pinning me down.

This was everything I ever wanted and more.

I lay there until her breaths became flat and slow, and then I returned to my own room. There I sat on the bed, clutching the photograph of Aaron in my hand, still trying to catch my breath. This photograph had been hidden beneath the bed for years. I've known it was there, of course, but couldn't bear the idea of looking at it, not until it was forced quite literally into my hand. It was the only keepsake I kept of him, just the one single photograph—not our wedding photographs, not my engagement ring—because in it, he's looking away. He's not looking at me, and so I can't see that love and adoration in his eye.

I can't see the anger.

I stare at the photograph, wondering what Aaron must look like now. Is he graying slowly like me, or is his hair still a chestnut brown? Is he fuller around the middle, or maybe he's more slim? And then I start to wonder if he's eating okay, if he's sleeping okay, if some other woman now spends her nights beside him in bed. My mind gets stuck there, a skipping record. I can't unsee this image, imaginary as it may be, of a woman lying beside Aaron, peacefully asleep—her head tucked into the crook of his arm, his hand on the small of her back—where I used to be.

I won't let myself dwell on the past.

I move quickly, having to get rid of the evidence before Jessie wakes up and goes snooping again. I put the photograph where she'll never find it, and then, when it's done, I tiptoe back into Jessie's room and stand there at the edge of the bed, forcing the past to some locked chamber in my mind, the same spot where that woman's voice is buried, the high-pitched squeal as she chased me down on the street.

Get your hands off my child.

I slip back under the covers beside Jessie so that when she awakes in the morning, she'll never know I was gone. A simple sleight of hand.

JESSIE

THAT NIGHT, I CLIMB into bed with my clothes still on. I don't bother changing them. I just want to get into bed, to be in bed. The bed used to be my safe place. But after all these nights not sleeping—eight of them, eight days and nights without sleeping now—the bed is my torture chamber too.

I read once about a man who died because he couldn't sleep. Fatal familial insomnia, it was called. Within twelve months from the time symptoms appeared, he was dead.

I think this is what's happening to me.

It started with a single bad night of sleep. For whatever reason, his mind wouldn't shut off. Wouldn't let him rest. One night turned into two, and before long he'd gone weeks without a decent night of sleep. *Relaxed wakefulness* is what it was called, though it was anything but relaxed. He never made it past stage 1 of non-REM sleep, the stage between wakefulness and sleep. He never dreamed. It was a light sleep at best when he was lucky, lasting less than ten minutes at a time, the kind of sleep interrupted by a hypnic jerk, by an overwhelming sense of falling.

I have it worse, I think. Because a light sleep, to me, would be a dream come true.

He walked the earth in a stupor, asleep but awake. Awake but asleep. He spent his days in a hallucination of sorts, not sure if he was alive or dead. He heard buzzing noises all the time. People calling out his name though no one was there. A voice whispering odd decrees on repeat. *Just do it already. Just jump.* A hand touching his arm and he'd whirl around, agitated and afraid, to find himself alone. The panic attacks were infinite. His brain was on overdrive all the time. There was no way to hit the switch and shut it down.

As a result, his brain's tasks were all out of whack. His muscles twitched. His heart raced. His blood pressure soared. Coordination was lost. He could no longer function properly. It went on like this until he died.

The most gruesome part? Though the body goes to pot, the mind does not. Thought processes remain relatively intact. They're clued in completely to their own demise.

The ill sweat profusely.

They stop eating, speaking.

They shrivel to nothing but a glassy-eyed stare, eyes shrunken to mere pinpricks, like mine. And then they die. Because, after those long, agonizing nights lying in bed, failing to truly sleep, fatal familial insomnia is nothing but a death sentence for them. The grim reaper coming to steal their life.

I'm waiting for my time.

I sit up in bed. I don't delude myself into lying down because I know I won't sleep. And so I sit, engulfed in blackness, legs pulled up to my chest. The blanket is kicked to the end of the bed because, though it's cold in the carriage home,

I've begun to sweat. The sweat, it gathers under my arms and in my hairline. My palms are damp with it. The soles of my feet. The skin between my fingers and toes.

My heart beats rapidly.

My head spins.

I stare into blackness, seeing things that I hope are not there. I go through the motions. The typical night, thinking the morbid thoughts, followed by the grieving ones where I miss Mom so much it hurts. It's a pain in my sternum this time, like heartburn or indigestion. Except that it's grief.

And then when I'm done grieving, the self-loathing comes, where I despise myself for all of that which I *would've, could've, should've* done differently. Said I love you while she could still hear me. Hugged her longer and with more frequency. Run a hand over the dark chocolate fuzz that had started to regrow on her scalp after her last round of chemo was through.

I bullet point them all in my mind. All the things I should've done.

The silence and the blackness of the room become suddenly suffocating and I feel like I can't breathe. I'm drowning in silence. Being asphyxiated by it.

I turn to my knees and peel the shade back, gazing outside. The world tonight is dark, a carbon gray. Not quite black, but close enough. Little by little, my eyes adapt to it, and though it's dark outside, I can see. Not perfectly, but I can see something. A halo of light from a streetlamp, a half a block away. Orion the hunter, brightening the sky. His shield is aimed at me as he hovers, light-years above the greystone, club hoisted above his head with a dog at his feet. For whatever reason, the light makes me feel less alone and less scared.

And then, as the moonlight slips out from behind a cloud, it settles on the greystone. As my eyes adjust to it, the house begins to slowly take shape. My eyes rise up from ground level, grazing over the kitchen's sliding glass door, an enclosed porch, up the home's rear facade, and there they make out an amorphous shape standing in the open window of the third floor. The very same window, which, for the last two nights, radiated light.

Except that tonight it's dark. There is no light, but rather a pair of eyes.

The bile in my stomach begins to rise. I feel like I could be sick. I press a hand to my mouth to silence my own scream.

The moonlight reflects off the eyes, making them glint in the darkness of night. They're undeniable. They're *there*. I'm not just making them up.

But beyond the eyes I see little else. Just a formless, shadowy shape to let me know that someone is standing in the window, watching me.

I let the shade go and it falls closed.

I grab Mom and her urn from a bedside table and slip to the floor, thinking that I don't want to be here in this carriage home, that I want to leave. That I'd rather be anywhere else in the world but here. But also realizing that I have nowhere to go. I press Mom to me and hold her tight because with her in my arms, I feel less alone. I scoot to a wall and press my back to it, heart beating hard. I try to defuse my fears, to make myself feel better, by telling myself that it's only Ms. Geissler. That it's only Ms. Geissler watching me.

And yet it doesn't make me feel better. Because Ms. Geissler is a stranger to me. We've hardly met. I don't know a single thing about her, other than she lied about the squirrels inside her home, but for what reason, I don't know.

My heart pounds. My hands are moist. They sweat and again I'm sure that I am dying. That the perspiration is a symptom of fatal familial insomnia, which has stolen my sleep from me and is now coming to take my life.

I want to get out of here. I want to leave. And yet I paid nearly everything I have to be here. I can't get out of here, I can't leave. I have nowhere to go.

I pull my knees into my chest. I drop my head to them and close my eyes. I pray to sleep, over and over I say it. *Please just let me sleep. Please just let me sleep. Please just let me sleep.* I beg for morning to come, for the sun to rise higher and higher in the sky, chasing the nighttime away.

For eight days now it's gone like this. Eight nights.

How many more days and nights can I go on without sleep?

And then I hear something. Just a murmur, faint at first like the sound of a piano playing from some other room. A gentle melody. But, of course, that can't be because there's no piano in the next room, and no one here to play it but me. And I'm not playing a piano.

My ears stand at attention. My head tips. I listen, and though I want to stay, firmly anchored to the wall where I can see through the darkness to know what's coming for me, I lift my body from the floor, carrying Mom's ashes with me. It's unintentional when I press a single palm down on the ground to hoist myself up. The other clutches tightly to Mom, pressing her to my chest like a newborn baby. I stand to an almost-upright position, bent at the shoulders so I don't hit my head on the low ceiling. And still I do hit my head, crashing into a low-lying wooden beam, so hard that when I press my fingers to it I feel the undeniably sticky texture of blood.

I tiptoe down the steps, one tread at a time, so slowly that it's almost as if I'm not moving at all. As I descend, voices surface. Not just one, but two or three or four. One lead and a host of background singers to accompany the piano. It makes me gasp for breath. My legs become weak, incapacitated; they start to give as I clutch the stair railing for support, squeezing so tightly the muscles of my hands cramp.

I can't go on. I don't want to go on. But I do because I have to. Because there's nothing there, because there's some reasonable explanation for the sound. A car stereo playing outside the carriage home, maybe, the tune getting carried in through an open window.

But I won't know what it is unless I go see.

I force myself to creep down the steps. I edge across the floorboards, willing myself forward, creeping, one step at a time. Following the sound, which comes from a wall and not the window at all because the window is closed tight.

The song isn't coming from the stereo of a car parked somewhere outside.

It's coming from inside the carriage home.

I go after the sound, and it leads me to an old vintage pie safe pressed flush against a wall, a petite bookshelf with a couple of shelves and a door. It's one of the few pieces of furniture that came with the carriage home.

I grab a hold of the knob and pull the door open swiftly, dropping to my knees. As I gaze inside, I find that it's empty, which makes no sense because the song is in there. It's coming from the pie safe. I feel blindly with my hands, moving them up and down the edges of the shelves, feeling for something, though what I don't know.

And then a thought comes to me.

What if the sound isn't coming from the pie safe? What if it's coming from somewhere behind?

I don't think twice. I shove the pie safe out of the way. It isn't heavy, but it isn't light either. I press a shoulder into it. It takes some jostling as it skids across the floor.

And there, on the wall behind where the pie safe was placed, I discover a cast-iron air return grille. One of those wall-mounted vents that leads into the duct system. It's an air return, one that sucks stale air from the room and cycles it back through the home's ductwork, leading, I have to assume, to the floor register upstairs where I heard the undeniable ping the other night. Ping, and then nothing. Ping, and then nothing.

Except that nothing is getting sucked up in here. Instead it's getting forced out.

And it's not air at all, but music. Gladys Knight & the Pips, "Midnight Train to Georgia."

How can this be?

I press my whole body against the grille to listen to the song. Mom's favorite. One she used to play over and over again until I got sick of it. Until I pouted and told her to turn it off because it was old people music. Those were the words I used. *Old people music.*

I'm stricken with the most impossible of thoughts, one that makes the hairs on my arms stand on end.

Mom is there. Inside the home's ductwork.

I set the urn down on the floor and, at first, try to jerk the whole thing off the wall with both of my hands. It won't budge. I grip the edges of the grille and pull, but I don't have a good grip on it and it slips easily from my grasp. I tumble backward, falling to the floor. The air return grille is wedged on too tight, held to the wall with four screws, one in each corner. I make an attempt to unscrew each with a bare hand, pinching and twisting the jagged screws until the skin splits, catching a sharp edge of it, one that's been whet over time. My finger starts to drip with blood.

But the screws don't move. Not even a little bit.

I grit my teeth and pinch and twist harder, but still nothing. They don't budge the slightest bit.

And so I wedge a fingernail into the slotted screw and turn. But all that happens is my nail breaks, getting ripped in two, leaving my nails in tatters. I curse out loud from the pain of it before hoisting myself from the floor and hurrying to the kitchen for a knife. I shuffle through a cutlery drawer—tossing forks and spoons out of the way, spilling them one by one to the floor—and find a butter knife.

I run back to the air return. I fall again to my knees.

I stick the knife into the screw head, turning counterclockwise as hard as I can. Bearing down on that knife with my whole body weight.

This time, it turns.

I spin and I spin that knife, desperate, gasping, as if I might just find Mom inside the air return. Because for this moment that's exactly what I'm thinking. That that's where she is. Inside the air return. I don't know how or why, but she is. She's *there*. I'm just sure of it.

I pluck one screw from the wall and move on to the next one. And the next one. And the next. All four screws tumble to the ground.

The grille loses its grip on the wall and falls. The sound is clamorous. I shove it out of the way and look inside. It's some sort of stainless steel box set there behind the air return grille, one that changes course about a foot of the way in. I can't see far enough inside to see where it goes and so I reach in a hand, grasping, sweating, but come up empty, thinking that behind that curve there are miles and miles of pipes and tubes which somehow or other lead to Mom. Mom is at the end of those tubes, listening to her music, speaking to me.

I try going in headfirst and then feetfirst. But I don't fit and in time give up, because I don't know what else to do.

I spend the rest of the night lying on the floor beside the air return in the fetal position, listening to Gladys Knight sing to me.

EDEN

We bought our first computer today, at Jessie's insistence. I'd been saving for some time for it, hoping to surprise her because, as Jessie says, we're the last two people in the world without a computer, which may or may not be true.

We had to take a cab to the store for it, so that we could tote the boxes home in the trunk of the cab, while the driver waited impatiently for us to load and unload, meter running the whole time, never once offering to help. And then, at home, after Jessie and I lugged the boxes to the office, we sat on the floor, methodically reading instructions and trying our best to decipher which cords went where. The directions might as well have been written in Japanese, the illustrations done up for a four-year-old.

When all was said and done, I was shocked to find that, when we turned it on, the thing came to life, some sort of revolving image—*a screen saver*, Jessie told me—moving about on the screen.

Jessie went straight for the internet. "Look yourself up," she encouraged me, and I asked what she meant by that, thinking she'd just use this computer to type up papers for school. I hadn't thought much of her fiddling around on the internet, but I saw quickly that it was the one thing on her mind, the reason she wanted this computer. To look stuff up on the internet.

"Go ahead," she said again with an enthusiastic nod of the head, dishwater hair falling into her eyes. "Type in your name," she told me, "and see what you find."

But I laughed only, telling her we wouldn't find anything, because certainly I'm not on the internet. That's the kind of thing reserved for celebrities and politicians. Not everyday, ordinary people like me. But Jessie was certain.

"The internet knows everything," she told me, emphasizing that word *everything*, and I filled instantly with dread, trying to assure myself that it was only the ramblings of an eager preteen, that certainly the internet couldn't know *everything*, like some sort of omniscient god.

But Jessie's hands breezed past mine, and with nimble fingers, she typed *Eden Sloane* onto the keyboard and pressed the return key.

It didn't happen right away.

No, there was a moment of naive disbelief while the computer did its thing. In that moment, I assured myself that we'd find nothing. Nothing at all. Of course the internet didn't know anything about me because why would it? What reason did I have to be on the internet?

But then an image popped onto the screen before us. And there was my name, highlighted any number of times. My stomach dropped at the sight of them, all these results the computer had gathered for Eden Sloane. Some of them, I saw—as my eyes sailed past the results one at a time, trying to decipher which secrets of mine Jessie would soon find—were not me. There was a split second of relief.

It's another Eden Sloane. It's not *me*.

But then one listing caught my eye, rattling me to the core. Because there, on the internet, for anyone to see, was my name and, beside it, the address of Jessie's and my home, our little bungalow on the northwest side of Chicago, where I thought no one could find us, where I stupidly believed there was no way to know where we were.

I was wrong.

Because now I see that any and everyone is privy to that information, that anyone who's looking for me can find out just exactly where I am.

It was unconscious then, the way that I rose to my feet quickly and moved to the window, pulling the curtains closed post-haste. When Jessie gave me a look, I blamed the glare of sunlight on the computer screen—a glare that wasn't ever there—and she believed me.

I haven't disappeared after all.

All this time, I've been out in the open, living right under everyone's noses.

My throat constricted and went dry. I choked on my own saliva. I coughed, a desperate, panicked cough, unable for a moment to breathe past the saliva that was lodged in my throat.

"You okay?" Jessie asked, patting my back, and I nodded my head yes, though even I didn't know if that was true or not. Was I okay?

When I could speak, I asked her to run down the hall and fetch me a glass of water.

As she did, I snatched the electrical cord from the socket, watching as the screen turned blissfully black. I started packing the computer back in its box the moment Jessie left and, that very same afternoon, planned to hail another cab and return it to the store.

When Jessie returned with the glass of water and asked what I was doing—as I sat there on my haunches, wrapping foam paper around the computer parts—I told her that the computer was broken. That there was something wrong with it, which of course there was. There was something very wrong with it.

I told her that it would have to go back. I avoided Jessie's eyes as, there in the doorway, her face quickly fell. "Can we get a new one?" she asked, and though I said yes, I didn't for one second mean it.

Because there would be something wrong with that computer too.

As Jessie and I stood on the drive, waiting for a cab to appear, I couldn't help but wonder, *What other secrets of mine did the internet hold?*

JESSIE

THE MUSIC GETS CHASED away with morning's first light, and now the house is silent and still. It startles me, the way the music suddenly stops, and now that it's gone, I have to wonder if it was ever really there. I sit up with a start, sticking to the wooden floor. I've been sweating. I say my own name aloud to be sure I can still speak, that fatal familial insomnia hasn't stolen my voice from me already. "Jessica Sloane," I say, my words slurred.

I find myself on my hands and knees searching for Mom's urn, knowing I left her here beside me last night. I comb through the planks of the hardwood floors, as if somehow or other she's slipped through the millimeter gap between boards.

It's a sinking feeling. A spreading, sinking feeling that comes to me at once.

I've lost Mom.

I don't know who I am anymore. I can't go on, I won't go on without her here. I hold my breath and refuse to breathe. And just when I think I'm about to die, I see her. Just two feet away, on the other side of me, right where I left her. My panic comes to a halt.

Mom is still here. She's not yet gone. I release my breath and, at the same time, somehow hear the labored sound of Mom breathing through the air return. Short, shallow breaths followed by no breaths at all.

Only in daylight do I give up my perch. I rise to my feet, arching my back from the stiff muscles that come with three or four hours of lying on the hardwood floors. I creep across the room slowly, deliberately, one step at a time, my legs half-asleep. And I'm jealous of them because at least some small part of me still knows how to sleep.

In the shower, I shampoo my hair. I reach for the conditioner and end up dumping another handful of shampoo on my scalp. I wash my body and then, because I can't remember if I did, I wash it again. Though later, when my skin starts to secrete a sour smell, I wonder if I washed at all.

I head off for a cleaning assignment. As I scrub away on the homeowner's porcelain floors, I notice that my fingernails are still intact. Not a single nail is torn. There's no dried blood clinging to my fingertips because they haven't been bleeding. Even now I feel the sharp edges of the screw head burrowing into my fingertips, and I'm not sure if that happened or if I only imagined it did.

I lock up before I leave. I load my paraphernalia onto the back end of Old Faithful. Mop, bucket, rubber gloves. The September day is sunny and warm. I ride in the street, on tapered one-way streets, which narrow with parked cars like the thickening of arteries with deposits of fat.

I stop for coffee and a donut, taking them to go. "Have a good one, Jenny," the owner of the bakery says to me as I leave, and I think maybe she doesn't have it wrong after all.

Maybe she knows something I don't know. Maybe I really am a Jenny, since I'm no longer Jessica Sloane.

I pedal past a police station. On the sidewalk before the brick building, I pause. I think about stepping inside, asking them to fingerprint me. Maybe they can look my prints up in their system and tell me who I am. But I'm not sure that's how it works. I'm sure they'd need a reason to fingerprint me, and I'm not sure I have one to give. Not a good one anyway. Not one that wouldn't raise red flags.

But then my mind drifts to the notion of DNA, one of those in-home kits that you mail away. Those that claim, with a simple swab of the cheek, to help you figure out your family tree, find distant relatives, discover unknown ethnicities. It's just what I need. To figure out who I am.

I return to the coffee bar on Dearborn and sit there on the blue velvet sofa, waiting for the man from the garden. Hoping he'll come today. I see orange everywhere I look. On a shirt, a shoelace, a flyer taped to a store window, in a flower bed. But none are the man.

I go to the garden, slipping back in between the honey locust trees and finding my way to Mom's favorite spot. It's empty, except for a bird, a little brown thing, a sparrow, pecking away in the dirt for food. I scare it away as I make my way to the edge of the raised bed, sitting on the marbled edge, my eyes circumspect but also tired. The twitch in my eye has yet to go away. If anything, it's gotten worse. It twitches incessantly, only stopping when I dig the heels of my hands into it and press hard.

After an hour or two, I give up. I take the long way back to the carriage home because I'm in no hurry to return. I bike past the elementary school at the corner of Cornelia and Hoyne, a stately structure made almost entirely of red brick, four floors that are tall and thin and deep. Kids play outside, on a parking lot playground beside the school building. The flag is at half-staff; someone has died. The kids are rowdy, unruly, loud, like howler monkeys defending their territory. They scurry to the top of the jungle gym, laying claim to the swings and slides.

I round the corner at Cornelia. A bell rings, calling the kids inside from play. They'll go home soon; it's midafternoon. Once they're gone, the world is suddenly silent. The trees stand tall and proud, the sun's light getting scattered at random through their leaves, dusting the sidewalk.

As I near in on the greystone, I watch as, across the street from it, a little boy schlepps a bucket, waddling down to the sidewalk with his mother on his heels. He flips the bucket upside down and a stack of chalk falls to the concrete. It makes a racket. A single blue piece nearly rolls into the street but he stops it in time, running awkwardly after it. His mother asks him what he's going to draw, waving her hand at me, calling out hello. He's going to draw a hippopotamus.

Ms. Geissler is also outside. She's bent at the waist, picking weeds from her flower bed, plucking and gathering them in her hands. She wears gaudy gardening gloves and, on her head, a wide-brimmed straw hat that keeps the sun from her skin.

I see her and feel a rush of anger well inside me. A rush of anger and unease, among other things. I think of Ms. Geissler there in the third-story window watching me at night. The third story, which is overrun with squirrels. The third story, where she claims she hasn't been in months. I think of the eyes, of *her* eyes, pressed to the window like the eyes of an owl, big enough and bright enough to catch prey on even the darkest of nights.

But it's more than that too, because I'm certain that someone has been in the carriage home when I wasn't there. Only two people should have a key to that home, and it's Ms. Geissler and me.

The carriage home is technically hers, but as far as I'm concerned, she shouldn't be allowed to come and go without reasonable notice. Without letting me know in advance, twenty-four hours in my opinion. It's one thing if the pipes had burst or sewage was overflowing from the toilet, but so far, that's not the case.

I think of what Lily the apartment finder said about carriage homes not abiding by the same rules as prescribed in the city's landlord-tenant ordinance. Living here, I wouldn't be protected in the same way, she'd told me.

Did she mean I'd have a complete lack of privacy? That Ms. Geissler could enter my home without permission? Open and close my window shades? Stare in through the glass at me?

For some reason, I don't think so.

At first I think I should keep going, that I should pedal right on by. But then I have second thoughts. I want to speak to her, because there's something nefarious going on here— many nefarious things—and I want to know what it is.

I force down the kickstand of Old Faithful and stand, hands on my hips behind Ms. Geissler. As I do, words emerge. I don't think them through.

"Why have you been watching me?" I ask.

Her smile is warm. "Jessie," she says kindly, as if she didn't hear my question or the tone of my voice at all. Instead she says that it's nice to see me today. "How about this weather?" she asks, hands elevated, praising the sun and the sky for this glorious day.

And I'm thrown easily off track, thinking then only about the weather. Forgetting about the pair of eyes watching me at night. Forgetting the fear I felt at stepping inside the carriage home and finding the shades open wide.

I snap to. "Why have you been watching me?" I ask, and her face clouds over in confusion. Her eyebrows crease.

"I don't know what you mean," she declares.

"I saw you," I assert, pointing a finger at the windows up above. The windows that are dark now, not a light on inside. They're obscure, shadows only. The only thing that I can see is the outside world getting cast back at me. A reflection. "Standing up there," I say. "Three nights in a row now," I say, though the truth is that I've lost count. It could be three. It could be four or more. "You've been staring into the house, watching me. Spying on me. Why?" I demand. "Why are you watching me?"

The smile slips from her face. Or rather gets replaced with one that's more pitying. Ruts form between her eyes, deep trenches in the skin. She pulls the hat from her head and a great big cluster of hair falls from her head, getting trapped in the straw brim. Like Mom's used to do before she bit the bullet and shaved it all off. I see her and me standing together in the shower basin. Starting with an electric shaver first, and then a cheap, plastic disposable razor. Rubbing gobs of aloe vera on it when we were through.

"Well, aren't you going to say something?" I ask when Ms. Geissler doesn't say anything. I can't stand to see her looking at me piteously, saying nothing. "You have no right," I say, my eyes lost on the clump of hair that has fallen out of her scalp. She grabs a hold of it, plucks it from the hat and releases it to the wind. "No right," I tell her, "to be spying on me."

"Jessie," Ms. Geissler says. Her voice bleeds of sympathy, empathy. Or darn good theatrics. I don't know which, but whatever it is, I don't like it one bit. "Jessie, dear," she says again. "You're still not sleeping, no?" she asks. I feel my knees become liquid. They soften. I want to say no, that I haven't been sleeping. I want her to tell me to try warm milk. A spoonful of honey. To listen to music before I go to bed. Calming music. Lullabies. Not because I trust her; I don't. But because I want someone to tell me about the music and the voices that come to life in the ductwork at night. About Jessica Sloane.

In that moment I see her, Jessica Sloane, in her purple bathing suit, lying dead on the street. Pigeons circle around her, staring at her with their beady eyes.

Ms. Geissler stands before me, staring. "Jessie, are you all right?" she asks, and only then do I realize that she's been speaking to me. That she's been speaking to me and I didn't hear a word. "You don't look all right," she decides, empathy in her eyes, but I won't let her divert me from my track. I look around, remembering where I am. Remembering what I was going to say.

"Slept like a baby," I lie.

I look to the ground for the clump of hair that fell from Ms. Geissler's head, but it's not there. All there is is a cluster of leaves, a mixture of yellows and browns that shrivel on the lawn. As my eyes rise to Ms. Geissler, she replaces the hat on her head. And there I see it. A single wilted yellow leaf, folded like a moth in its cocoon, clinging to the straw of the hat.

There was never a clump of hair. I'd only imagined it was hair. It was just leaves. Leaves falling from a nearby tree, getting snagged on the hat as she hunched over the lawn, tending garden.

"I see you there in the window. Every single night. I know you see me. You were in my home," I snap, my tone turning vitriolic. "That's trespassing, you know?" I say. "An invasion of privacy. I could call the police. I should call the police."

She's quiet at first. "Jessie, honey," she says, the look on her face one of concern. Condolence. Shame. "Oh, Jessie. Poor, poor, Jessie," she says instead, pitying me, ignoring my threat to call the police. She takes a step toward me, makes an attempt to stroke my arm with her gaudy gardening gloves. But I pull back. "You must be mistaken, dear," she says. "The third floor, I told you already," she says, making a sweeping gesture of the greystone behind her. "I don't go up there anymore. I haven't been up there in months."

It's a lie. I know that's not true. I know because she was there.

"I saw the light on in the attic. I saw you standing there in the window looking out. Watching me."

"No," she says to me, shaking her head, looking concerned and confused. "There are no lights up there in the attic. I'd had a lamp once, just an old floor lamp, nothing special, but the squirrels chewed their way right through the cord. Can you imagine?" she says then, tsking her tongue and shaking her head. "Pesky little things. It's a wonder they didn't electrocute themselves." And for the briefest of moments it sounds so genuine, so real, that I almost see the squirrels' overgrown teeth gnawing their way through the cord, cutting power to the floor lamp.

But not quite.

"I know what I saw," I insist.

But somewhere deep inside me, I also wonder if I do.

"You must be mistaken, Jessie," she says. "Maybe it was a dream. You've lost your mother. Grief can be a terrible thing. The isolation, the desperation—" But I stop her before she can cite for me the stages of grief. Her eyes now are chock-full of condolence. Sorrow. They mock me. I know what she's doing. With her pitiful eyes and her compassion, she's trying to make me question my own sanity, to make me think I'm crazy. A by-product of the insomnia and the grief.

But I know what I saw. There was a light on in the third floor. There were eyes in the window, watching me.

"Then let me see," I insist. My words are assertive. I attempt to call her bluff. "Let me go to the attic. Let me see for myself that there is no light there."

Her lips curve upward. She grins. Not a happy smile, not a mocking smile, but an appeasing one. She's placating me. "Oh, I don't think so. It's quite the mess, Jessie. I don't even think it's safe to go up there," she says. Not until she can get her contractor out to clean it up, which she says she really needs to do. It's been too long and the attic, for now, is just a waste of space. And then she says that she must go. Rain is on its way, she says, staring skyward. Until now I didn't notice the storm clouds rolling in. It was all blue sky and sun, but now it's not. Now there are clouds. "The weeds are calling me," Ms. Geissler says, turning, stepping closer to the thistle and away from me.

And then, in that moment, from up above, the clouds burst apart at the seams. Rainwater comes pouring down. Just like that, the sun-dappled sidewalks are gone, getting replaced with puddles. I take my eyes off Ms. Geissler, looking down, to see my feet submerged in a puddle of water. Across the street, the little boy's chalk hippopotamus gets washed away, rallying his tears. He begins to cry. But not before first throwing his chalk so that it breaks in two, screaming, "It's ruined," and then stomping off and heading inside, hot on his mother's heels.

I look back toward Ms. Geissler, but already she's gone.

In the distance, a screen door slams and there I am.

Hair matted down, wet clothes binding to me. All alone.

★ ★ ★

The rain, only a cloudburst, is through. Over and done with. No sooner had I fled the lawn for the cover of indoors than it stopped. The sun forced its way through the clouds again like a baby chick breaking free from an eggshell. The world turned yellow, golden.

Drop by drop the rain disappeared, going back up the way it came down. And then the sun set, turning the world to pink and then purple and then black, welcoming another sleepless night.

I stare out the window and into the third story of Ms. Geissler's home. I stare until my eyes get tired from it, so tired that my retinas begin to burn, the lid continuing to twitch. And yet I can't bring myself to blink because in those milliseconds, I might miss something, a flicker of light, eyes in the window staring back at me. The house itself blurs, softening at the edges because I've been staring too long.

But still, I don't blink.

The shades on the third-story window are drawn. All three of them pulled taut. Like the world outside, the room is dark. For hours on end, there's no one there. Evidence that I'm mistaken. Evidence that I am wrong. That Ms. Geissler hasn't been standing in the window watching me at night, and that my imagination only made it up. It couldn't have been a dream because when you don't sleep you don't dream. And so instead it was my mind playing games with me.

All night long, the window remains empty and black. It's cold in the carriage home because I've turned the heat completely off in an effort to prevent noises from sneaking in through the ductwork. So far, it's working. There are no voices; there are no pings. No music. But as a result, the temperature in the carriage home hurtles to fifty degrees. My fingers and toes go numb.

As I lie there in bed listening to the *tick, tock* of the wall clock, it dawns on me. Mom is not my biological mom. It seems so transparent, so *glaring* there in the witching hour. As if it's been staring me in the face all this time and I just failed to see. I look nothing like her, for starters, which doesn't necessarily matter because for all I know I'm a dead ringer of my dad. But still, it's cause for doubt.

If Mom is not my biological mother, then how did I come to be with her? How did I come to think of her as my mom?

Maybe it was something innocuous, like she adopted me as a child. And in an effort to keep me from my birth mom—who, for all she knew, would try and track me down in an attempt to regain custody—she stole a dead child's identity and gave it to me so that I'd be impossible to find. Maybe my birth mother was abusive, neglectful. Or maybe she was thirteen years old, a victim of rape, not ready to be a mother. A teenager who'd gotten loaded at a party and went too far with some guy. Mom was saving me from a life of abuse and neglect at the hands of a reluctant mother.

Or maybe it's not so innocuous after all.

Maybe it's more toxic than that. Maybe I wasn't adopted, but rather taken. Kidnapped. It's a thought I go to only because it's the middle of the night, the time my imagination most often takes flight.

Did Mom *kidnap* me?

I feel an overwhelming sense of guilt for thinking these things about Mom. That she took me. That I'm not hers. That she did something illicit, that she did something wrong. I think of myself, twelve years old, Mom, woozy on a glass of wine, confessing, *A long time ago, I did something I'm not proud of, Jessie. Something that shames me.*

And that's how I got you.

I know now what she means.

Eleanor Zulpo, the woman Mom used to work for when I was a girl, told me that as a child, I insisted my name was something other than Jessie. She remembered that I'd pout my face and stomp my foot and demand that Mom stop calling me Jessie.

Jessie isn't my real name. That much I already know. It's a name Mom forced on me, one I accepted with resistance, because even a three-or four-year-old knows their name and isn't quick to change it.

But not only did I call myself by a different name, but I called Mom *Eden.* Did I call her Eden because she wasn't my mom? Because she'd *kidnapped* me? Because my mom was someone else, and if so, then who?

In the back of my mind I tell myself that if, *if*, Mom kidnapped me—that word itself lumbering through my brain, clumsy and awkward, finding it hard to travel from neuron to neuron because the very idea of it is so incompatible with *Mom*, who was always so loving, so kind—she had a good reason to do it. She wasn't just some run-of-the-mill child abductor.

But something doesn't add up, like a puzzle with interlocking pieces, the rounded tabs and the carved-out openings that are all supposed to connect. They don't.

Because there's the photograph of the man. The one I hold so tightly in my grip that the edges of it begin to disintegrate with sweat. I spend the night holding the photograph of the man with the lake and the trees, knowing he meant something to Mom, that she intentionally kept this photograph and this man from me.

Who is he? I have to find him. I have to find him so that I can know who he is, if he's my father. Then I'll know how and when and why I came to be with Mom. Mom who is not my mom.

I look hard for something, for some clue that I've failed to see. The cut of his hair, the color of the lake, the type of trees in the backdrop. The way he stands, the brand of his jeans—the tag far too small to read, but still I try—that sailboat in the distance. Is it really white like I believed it to be, or is it more of a pale yellow, or white with pale yellow stripes? None of which matter.

And then I see it. It's a small thing, but significant enough to me. Because suddenly every detail is significant to me.

This man is left-handed. I know this, or convince myself I know it, because he's wearing his watch on his right wrist. It isn't one of those hard-and-fast rules, and yet it's common enough to be true. People tend to wear their watches on their nondominant wrists.

I think that there are only a handful of lefties in the world, which narrows down my search exponentially, though still the field is huge. Instead of being one in seven billion, the odds that I'll find this man are now more like one in seven hundred million.

And I know it then; I'll never find this man.

He could be anywhere. He could be anyone. Even if I found myself staring right at him, I'd never know it because I've never seen his face before.

I set the photograph aside. I'm so cold that my skin turns mottled and gray. It's got a purplish tint to it and looks like it's covered in lace, a white overlay to the purple skin. I sit there on the floor, staring at my hands, my legs. All that exposed skin, which is as cold and as mottled as Mom's was before she died.

And I come to one conclusion: like Mom, I'm also dying.

At first, everything around me is black. I can't bring myself to move. I'm too cold, too tired, too scared to move. I can't bring myself to throw the covers over my arms and legs. Night goes by with the speed of a sloth. Painfully slow.

But then it begins. Sunrise. Daylight. Morning comes. Out the window, I watch it happen.

It starts as a single pixel of light. The sun still tucked safely below the horizon, scattering its light into the atmosphere. A semidarkness. A soft glow of yellow and blue. The clouds thicken around it, getting drawn in, like nuts and bolts to a magnet. They flush at their edges, turning shades of pink and red. As if the clouds themselves are embarrassed.

The sun rises higher and higher into the sky.

And just like that, day has arrived.

The air in the room starts to warm thanks to the sun's rays pouring in the open window. My mottled, purple skin disappears, getting replaced with a healthy pink. I'm not dying after all. I'm still very much alive, it seems. For now at least.

EDEN

IT'S BEEN TWO WEEKS since they took my baby from me.

Today, Aaron and I sat in Dr. Landry's office.

"The good news," Dr. Landry said, face firm, undeviating, with no hint of a smile, "is that we now know you can get pregnant. Your body is capable of that. But maintaining the pregnancy is proving to be another matter."

We had only been there a couple of minutes. Aaron and I sat beside each other on matching tufted armchairs, Dr. Landry on a swivel chair behind his desk. In my hand I clenched a tissue, dabbing at my cheeks as Dr. Landry stared at me.

I asked him, "How long until we can try again?" meaning all of us, another round of IVF at the cost of another ten thousand dollars, money that Aaron and I most certainly didn't have because we didn't have it the first time around. I now had three credit cards in my name and each were nearly maxed out. The minimum payment alone was more than I could pay. I'd never been in debt before; I'd never been behind on payments; I'd never been in the red. I'd never been bankrupt. It made me anxious, and yet I easily reasoned that it was money well spent.

I'd sell my own organs—a spare kidney or the lobe of a lung—before giving up on a baby.

He was dressed down today, no lab coat as usual, and, as Aaron attempted to cling to my hand, I pulled away, folding my hands in my lap. The numbness, the narcosis, it stuck around me like a cold that wouldn't quit. When I wasn't in bed crying, then I was numb. I felt nothing. I had only two modes these days: sad and numb.

Dr. Landry replied with "There's really no definitive answer to that; we can try again whenever you're ready," but his words were blighted by Aaron's incredulous sigh because Aaron, as he'd already told me, didn't want to try again. He wanted to be through.

The reason was simple.

The reason was me.

For the last two weeks, I couldn't bring myself to get out of bed. Morning, noon and night, I cried for my lost child, wondering how it was possible to grieve for something that was never truly mine.

Man plans, and God laughs. Isn't that what they say?

Aaron didn't want me to make another appointment with Dr. Landry. He had other suggestions for whom I should call instead: a therapist, a support group. Maybe all I needed was some time away, he foolishly believed. A trip by myself to one of those places I've forever longed to go. St. Lucia, Fiji, Belize. As if lying by the seashore and drinking a cocktail might help me forget the fact that I'd just lost a child, might annihilate that desire to ever have a child, so that when I returned I'd feel fresh, revived, happy.

"I don't want a goddamn vacation!" I screamed at him then, lying in bed, blankets over my head, coming up from under the covers only for air. "I want a baby. Why don't you get that, Aaron? What's so difficult to understand?"

And it was only then in broad daylight, when I dared to poke my head out of my own dark cavern, that I could see Aaron's eyes were red and swollen, his heart visibly broken like mine. His shirt was wrinkled, the buttons lined up incorrectly, his hair standing on end. His facial hair had grown threefold, proof to me that he, like me, wasn't leaving the house, that he too couldn't bring himself to go to work.

But I didn't acknowledge this.

"I know what you're feeling," he said quietly, compassionately, his voice losing control as he wiped at his eyes with the back of a shirtsleeve.

"Trust me," he said. "I get it."

A better person would have realized that Aaron had lost something too. A better person would have consoled him, would have let him console and be consoled. But not me.

This was my loss, not his.

"Go away," I barked then, and I heard it in my own voice, heard it and hated it but said it nonetheless. "You have no idea what I'm feeling. Don't stand there and pretend you know what it's like to lose a child."

I returned to my cave, throwing the blankets back over my head where I could scarcely breathe.

"This baby. This pregnancy. This need to get pregnant," Aaron lamented as he stood in the doorway, urging me to eat, to get out of bed, to go for a walk, to get some fresh air. "They've gotten the best of you, Eden. They've turned you into someone I don't recognize anymore. Someone I don't know."

And then he reminded me of who I was before that day we decided to start a family.

Fun loving. Benevolent and genuine. Carefree.

"I'd give anything to go back to being Aaron and Eden. Just us. Just you and me," he said, and for a bat of an eye I remembered us on our wedding day, riding in on horseback on Aaron's family farm in a regal ball gown, exchanging nuptials beneath the nighttime sky. A celebration worthy of a fairy tale. I had found my everything. I had married my prince.

But suddenly my everything wasn't good enough.

I needed more.

"I want to try right away. As soon as we can," I told Dr. Landry today as we sat in his office, and it was then that Aaron stood up from his tufted armchair and left the room.

September 8, 1997
Egg Harbor

Aaron didn't show up at the fertility clinic for today's appointment.

For weeks I've gone through the whole rigmarole, the process of developing follicles, of returning to Dr. Landry's office every few days to have my blood drawn and an ultrasound performed to see if there were any viable candidates for the procedure. I've been injected with a legion of hormones, each which leave blood blisters along my skin and a gamut of side effects, from headaches to hot flashes to moodiness and pain.

Already, Dr. Landry has forewarned me that, should implantation occur, Aaron and I will need to administer shots of progesterone into my backside to not only make a baby this time, but to help maintain the pregnancy. We'll do it daily, for ten weeks or more. "It's not for the faint of heart," he assured me, but I told him I'm ready. "I'll do anything, *anything*," I swore to Dr. Landry as he listed the side effects of the progesterone shots—the weight gain, the facial hair, the unbearable pain—to have a baby.

And then, when a mature follicle was ready, spotted on Dr. Landry's ultrasound monitor where not so long ago sat the image of a baby with a heartbeat and webbed hands and feet, we scheduled an appointment for the egg retrieval, where Dr. Landry planned to insert a needle deep inside me to remove the eggs from my womb.

Today was that day.

Except it wasn't.

I sat for hours waiting for Aaron to come and deliver his sperm.

Three hours and fourteen minutes to be precise, watching as other couples—six, eight, ten of them—came and went through the glass doors.

I read each of the magazines in the waiting room two times.

I made an attempt to phone Aaron, but he didn't answer my call.

I told the receptionist, who stared at me with shame and regret, that Aaron was only running late, that he would be here soon.

That he was caught up in traffic.

And then, after another hour of waiting, I asked to speak to a nurse and one was fetched for me, and, standing closer to her than appropriate so that she had to take a half step back to regain her personal space, I wondered whether they had any of Aaron's sperm remaining from the analysis or our first round of IVF. Certainly they had some remaining in storage, a few drops even, a single sperm, half-dead, clinging to the edges of a petri dish.

But she shook her head remorsefully, apologized and said no.

"I'm sorry," she said. "There is no sperm."

The nurse took a step away, but before she could go I laid a hand on her arm and asked whether my eggs could be removed now, if they could simply be stored somewhere, held on to until Aaron came to make his deposit. It seemed completely possible, like layaway, but I was reminded then of the little life span an egg has after ovulation. "There isn't time," she said, and it was then and only then that I inquired about donor sperm, an idea that settled in my mind slowly, one morsel at a time, while I spent hours in the fertility reception room, reading pregnancy magazine after pregnancy magazine, waiting for Aaron to come.

Donor sperm.

Two words I thought I'd never have to use in my entire life.

The desperation in my voice was tangible to every single person in the room, but none more than me. "Can we use donor sperm?" I begged, latching on to her arm now, fingernails leaving crescent-shape indentations in her skin.

"Where is your husband, Eden?" the nurse asked, stepping away, pretending altogether that I had never uttered those words, *donor sperm*. She was speaking down to me, that I knew. That I could clearly hear, as she riffled through a patient file in her hands, another patient's file, obviously distracted and needing to be somewhere other than in the reception area with me.

"Where's Aaron?"

It was then that I told her how he must have gotten caught up at work, except that was a lie because it was Monday, the one day in which Aaron never worked.

I inquired again about donor sperm—certainly they had vials and vials of male sperm stored somewhere in this facility that I could use—but the nurse assured me that they would need consent from me and Aaron—from the both of us—to use someone else's sperm.

In other words, Aaron would need to be present to give his consent, he would need to be here, and Aaron wasn't here.

Aaron wasn't running late and he wouldn't be there soon.

He had no intention of coming at all.

He just didn't tell me.

Not until I came home from the fertility clinic to find him at the kitchen table, drinking a beer. A beer! Suffice to say I lost it completely, feeling enraged. I screamed at him then like I'd never done before, uttering words I could never take back. Coming at him with fists raised, thinking for a minute that I could hit him. That I *would* hit him. I'd never done a thing like that before, and my fists stopped just shy of him as I turned on myself instead, pulling my own hair, screaming like a maniac. Aaron didn't flinch. I'd scarcely ever raised my voice to Aaron before, and it left me feeling rattled long after he left the room, walking out on me midsentence. It was the medication doing it, I convinced myself as I stood there in the empty kitchen in silence, strands of my own hair in my hands, watching as outside the sun went down—an arc of pinks and blues setting over our share of the bay, heaven on earth as we once so foolishly believed—the myriad fertility drugs affecting my judgment. They were the reason why I screamed and yelled, and yet I had every reason in the world to be angry.

Aaron never showed for the appointment.

He never came to deliver his sperm.

My eggs were ready and waiting, but where was he?

"Where were you?" I demanded as I lifted his empty beer bottle from the kitchen table and hurled it against the wall, longing and hoping for the release of a thousand minuscule shards of glass when all it was was two. Two large chunks of amber glass falling to the floor with a dull thud, leaving me far from satisfied. I reached for a collection of mail then, set there on the table's edge, and hurled that every which way too, bills and late notices drifting to the ground like fallen leaves.

"I told you," he said after I'd followed him into the living room—voice remarkably composed because he had likely sat there half the day rehearsing what he was going to say—"that I was through. We've been at this for a year," he said. "Over a year. We're broke, Eden. Everything we've worked for is gone. We have no more money to invest in this," he said, holding out a bill for me, one that arrived in today's mail, a credit card statement with a seventeen-thousand-dollar debt. "Look what this has done to us. To our marriage. To you.

"I can't keep doing this," he told me.

"I meant it, Eden. I'm through.

"It's time for you to choose."

And then he reached for a packed bag that sat on the hallway floor.

The front door opened and then closed again, and I wondered if that was it then.

If that was the last time I'd ever lay eyes on Aaron.

JESSIE

I SIT ON THE sofa beside Liam, in his apartment. His laptop is on my thighs. I find my way to the website for the National Center for Missing & Exploited Children, thinking that if Mom stole me, for whatever reason, if I had a family before her, then maybe someone once reported me as missing. Maybe my real family is missing me.

On the website, I discover countless babies stolen from their cribs. Kids who got on the bus, but never made it home from school. Pregnant women last seen on the gritty footage of parking lot surveillance cameras. Infant twins missing after a parent was found dead. Babies lifted from hospital nurseries.

One by one, I become absorbed in the sad stories. The stories of the missing. Thumbnail image by thumbnail image, I open them all. I read about a toddler who was last seen playing on his own front porch in some small town in Georgia, where he lived with his father and stepmother in Jeffersonville, Georgia. He was last seen at approximately ten fifteen on a Tuesday morning, way back in 1995. His hair is sandy and his eyes are green. An age-progressed photo shows what he might look like today, if he's even still alive. He was taken by his mother in a custody battle. There's a picture of her too. In it, she looks a little agrarian, a little unsophisticated, a little mean. Her hair is sparse and thin, her skin weathered and blotchy.

I think that it's possible that, like the little boy from Jeffersonville, Georgia, I am a child stolen from my front porch or from my crib, a child that climbed aboard the school bus one morning and never came home that afternoon.

"What did you find?" Liam asks as I scroll through the website, finding a search form.

"Nothing yet," I tell him. But I hope I will soon.

I fill in as much as I think I know and leave the rest blank. I am child. I am female. These are things I know. I make up the dates I may or may not have gone missing. I fill them in, this three-year gap that stretches clear from the day Jessica Sloane was born until the day she died. Three years. Three momentary years. Shorter than a presidential term, than the span between Olympic Games, between leap years.

I watch as over one hundred cases load. One hundred little girls missing in a three-plus-year time span. One hundred little girls missing in a three-year time span that now, seventeen years later, still haven't been found. It makes me sad. I think of their parents, of their real moms and dads.

One by one I click on the images and they tell me everything I need: when and where the child went missing; the color of their eyes, their hair, how old they would be. There are age-progressed photos, though how accurate they are, I don't know. Ivy Marsh went missing at the age of two. She was last seen in Lawton, Oklahoma, a little girl with blue eyes, blond hair, dimples like me. Kristin Tate went missing on her third birthday, last seen in Wimberly, Texas. She too has dimples.

I scroll down the page and click the arrow, move to the second page, and then the third. The fourth. "What are you looking for?" Liam asks, glancing over my shoulder to see what I see.

"I don't know," I say, but then I take it back, telling him that what I'm looking for is me. I take in the age-progressed photos of children who went missing nearly twenty years ago, wondering if any of them might look like me. Though I tell myself that an age-progressed image of an infant wouldn't have the same accuracy as that of an older kid because of how the face changes over the years. All babies have big, round eyes, chubby cheeks. Enormous foreheads. Toothless grins. There's nothing distinguishable about them. They all look the same to me. So who's to say what a baby's face would look like in twenty years?

And it doesn't matter anyway because scanning the missing children, not one bears a resemblance to me.

I push the laptop away. I reach into my bag and for the first time show the photograph to Liam. He asks who it is and I say, "Just some guy," though I feel in my gut that there's more to it than that. Because of some primal instinct to be close to this man, to know who he is. I tell Liam where I found the photograph, hidden in the cubbyhole behind the closet mirror.

"You think he's your father?" he asks, both a question and a statement. I shrug. He takes the photograph into his hands, holds it closely to his eyes, examining it before he slips the photograph back into my hands. My hands still shake, the tremor that for all these days won't go away. The room goes quiet, all except for the steady beat of rain against the window. It's a drizzle only, not a complete washout, though the day outside is ugly and gray. The morning's beautiful sunrise has been clouded over now; it's long gone. The melody of rain on glass is calming. I find myself soothed by it, tuning out everything else but that sound, wanting to sing along with it somehow, like a song's refrain.

And then it happens again. My eyelids close. They do it against my will. My head slumps forward, my neck no longer able to hold it up. It lasts a second. Only a second.

For one blissful second, I am asleep.

But then a jolt of electricity tears through me and my head snaps to. I'm awake.

"Jessie," I hear. I see Liam's hand fall to my knee. I turn to face him, his blue eyes so well-meaning. I'm overcome with a sense of belonging that I've rarely known before, only ever with Mom.

He touches my hair and for a single moment, something inside me feels warm.

He urges me to lie on his sofa. He offers up a pillow and a blanket, but I say no thanks. That I'm all right. "Jessie," he argues, but I say it again. I'm all right, though we both know that's not true.

I excuse myself, pushing my body from the sofa as if I weigh three hundred pounds. In the bathroom I splash cold water on my face. I stare at my reflection in the mirror. My skin has a grayish-green tint to it. I look sick, like I'm dying. My eyes sink into their sockets, deep bags formed beneath each. I press a finger to them, watching as they sink and then swell. Sink and then swell. My lips are dry, chapped around the edges, blistered, my cheeks concave.

I count the days on my fingertips. The days since I've been asleep.

The longest anyone has gone without a drop of sleep is eleven days.

I stare at my own sunken reflection, not able to make sense of what I see, but knowing that by this time tomorrow, I will be dead.

EDEN

September 23, 1997
Egg Harbor

I TRIED NOT TO let the desperation get the best of me, too afraid of what I might do if it did. I tried hard to keep busy, taking on extra shifts at the hospital, working overtime because being at home, alone, threw me easily off balance and I didn't like the feeling of being off balance, of being desperate, of feeling like I was losing control.

My home, Aaron's and my utopian cottage, quickly became a dystopia to me, a place where everything was undesirable and sad, and where I was in a constant state of dysphoria; I couldn't stand to be there and so I took to keeping myself out of the home all day, every day, doing everything imaginable to avoid the pine floors and whitewashed walls, the glorious tree swing that had once deceived me into believing this place was home.

I spent ten hours a day reading through patient files, trying to decipher what they were to be billed for and entering it into the hospital's system. It was meaningless and mundane, and yet a wonderful way to waste time. I took odd jobs on occasion, answering ads for a temporary cleaning lady or a dog walker or a driver to take a sweet elderly woman for dialysis treatments, keeping her company for the four hours it took to eliminate waste from her blood three times each week. It kept me busy and more than anything, I needed to be busy.

Time passed.

Last week I came home to find a separation agreement in a manila envelope, set beside the front door. In it, Aaron left me the house and all of our assets, taking from me only the debt, as much as he could anyway, the credit cards that were in both of our names.

Even in divorce he was protecting me.

I signed the paperwork post-haste, knowing that the sooner I did, the sooner the divorce was complete, I could ask for donor sperm without Aaron's consent.

In the meantime, I did everything I could to keep busy, knowing it would take months, nearly six of them, until the divorce was finalized.

Could I wait that long for a baby?

Oh, how I would try.

But as they say, the road to hell is paved with good intentions.

Because the minute the well ran dry and I found myself with nothing better to do, I drove by the quaint dance studio on Church Street and sat on the park bench, watching the little ballerinas come and go, and it was different now because I hadn't been there in months, since springtime, but everything was still the same. The bigger girls scurried out of the studio first, followed by their mothers, who carried coffee and talked.

And then, just when I'd begun to think that was it, the end of the procession, there came little Olivia with her short legs lagging behind, waylaid by things like heavy doors and sidewalk cracks, struggling to keep up. Her hair had been cut short, no longer in a bun but pinned to the sides of her head with barrettes. She was still easily distracted, that I'd come to learn, sidetracked by things like birds and bugs and today a leaf, bright red on the white concrete, the first indication of fall.

She paused to poke and prod at it as if it were alive, examining the redness of the leaf, the shape of its lobes, while the others gravitated away at their own pace so that the distance between them grew exponentially, and this time, Olivia's mother was too caught up in her conversation that she didn't see her daughter on her haunches, examining the leaf with the concentration and single-mindedness of a microbiologist. The woman's feet hit the street and she crossed the intersection, unaware of the fact that she and her child were now separated by a highway, the very same highway that once took a little girl's life when her mother was also not watching.

Some women were not meant to be mothers.

And some who were, some who would make the very best mothers, were refused the right.

It didn't seem fair.

Oh, what a good mother I would be, if only the universe would let me.

Suddenly Olivia's eyes peered up from the fallen leaf and, at seeing that she was alone, she began to cry. It was a process that went by degrees, a feeling of excitement first at finding the leaf, followed by frustration that there was no one around to show the leaf to, before sadness crept in, a great heartache that the others had left without her, leading to panic. Sheer panic. Olivia gasped first, choking unexpectedly on her own saliva, and then she began to cry, quiet tears, choked-up tears, while her little knees shook beneath their shiny white tights.

I'd be remiss to say that a series of thoughts didn't move swiftly through my mind.

How would I hide her?

Where would we go?

What would I call her? Because surely if she was a missing child, she couldn't parade around town as Olivia still. She'd have to be something else.

I leaned forward from the bench to lift the leaf from the concrete and asked if she ever collected leaves and pressed them between the pages of a heavy book. The sound of my voice, the sight of her leaf in my hand, gave her pause. Her eyes rose from the earth and landed on my smile, and for a moment there was a cessation of tears as I extended the leaf toward her and she took it from me with a shaky hand.

I rationalized in my mind that it would be Aaron's fault if I took the child—not mine, no, not ever mine—because that was the name of the game these days: blame.

If only he had shown up at the fertility clinic...

If only he hadn't walked out of my life...

He and I still would have a chance at our own child.

I wouldn't have had to take one that wasn't mine.

"Why are you crying?" I asked, though of course I knew the reason why. I remained seated, not wanting to scare her by standing tall and towering over her small frame. Outside, the temperatures were dropping again, fall drawing near. Soon the tourists would leave. On her arms there were goose bumps as loose strands of dishwater hair clung to the puddles of tears.

"Where's Mommy?" she asked, eyes searching the street. But only I heard it in the distance: the sound of girls' laughter over the sound of the wind. Olivia didn't hear.

Through the trees I could barely make out the red sleeve of a cardigan, the pink of a tutu, a length of brown hair.

"You lost your mommy?" I asked and, extending my own hand to hers, said, "Would you like for me to help you find her? Would you like for me to help you find your mother?

"It's okay," I said when she hesitated. "I won't hurt you."

It would be a lie to say she took my hand with ease, that she didn't stare at it for a minute, overthinking, some disquisition about not talking to strangers coursing through her mind.

But then she did take my hand, slipping it inside. It was a great shock to my system to feel this small, soft hand within mine, and it was all I could do not to squeeze tight with instinct, knowing that might make her scream. I didn't want Olivia to scream. I didn't want to scare her, but more so, I didn't want to draw attention to ourselves. For all intents and purposes, this was how it should be. I was hers and she was mine.

And then I began to lead her in the opposite direction of where her mother had disappeared. The direction of my car.

Olivia stopped, peering the other way over her shoulder—even a young girl could remember which way her mother had last been walking—but I said to her not to worry, that if we took the car we might find her mother more quickly than if we walked.

I pointed to my car in the distance. "It's right there," I said.

She thought about this a moment, standing frozen on the pavement, hemming and hawing, eyes moving back and forth from me to the car. A band of clouds had rolled in, blocking the earth from the sun, and as it did, the wind picked up its speed, chasing the warm day away. Outside, the temperature dropped by as many as five degrees and the day turned gray.

Fall was coming; fall was here.

"Well, that's okay," I said then, letting go of her hand. "If you don't want to find your mother, we don't need to," and it was reverse psychology, of course, making her believe that if she didn't get in the car with me, I might just leave her behind.

I didn't want to scare her, and yet there was no other way.

I was only doing what I needed to do.

I reasoned that we would only drive to the next town and then stop for ice cream. That I'd have her just long enough to teach her mother a lesson. Then I'd return her. Certainly I wasn't planning to *steal* the child, because that's not the type of person that I am. A kidnapper and a thief. I only wanted to borrow her for a while, like a library book on loan. To satisfy my craving for the time.

I had taken no more than two steps away when I heard Olivia's tiny feet scurrying quickly on the concrete, running after me. It worked.

Her hand reached up, and she grabbed a hold of mine, squeezing tightly, careful not to let go. I smiled at her and she smiled back, the tears evaporating quickly from her cheeks.

"Your mother must be here somewhere," I said then, and we walked that way, hand in hand, for a good ten feet or more. We moved slowly—at Olivia's pace, though I wanted to tug on her hand and run—and still, it took twenty seconds or less to traverse those ten feet. But in those twenty seconds I convinced myself that in some minute, negligible way, we looked alike, Olivia and me, though in reality we didn't. We looked nothing alike.

I wondered if, once she and I were sitting across from one another at a local diner, eating strawberry sundaes with whipped cream on top, I'd ever be able to return her to her mother.

And then a new thought crossed my mind. I could drive farther south, south of Sturgeon Bay, south of Sheboygan, south of Milwaukee. We could live somewhere else, far away from here, where people might believe that we were mother and child.

They would have no reason not to believe.

I'd rename her. I'd call her something other than Olivia.

And in time, she'd come to think of it as her given name.

"I don't have a booster seat," I said as we approached the car, "but that's okay for now. The seat belt will do just fine." And as we closed in on the car I extended a hand toward the handle, reaching out to open the back door for Olivia to climb through. "It will only be a short drive after all," I promised her. "I'm sure your mother is here somewhere."

In a single moment, I thought this through. I made a plan and it went like this. Once Olivia was in the car I would speed off the opposite way, far from town, away from her mother, not stopping until we'd passed Sturgeon Bay. There I would stop only to buy Olivia ice cream, something to soothe her, to make her not be scared, to quiet her certain tears. Ice cream and a stuffed bear or a toy from a gas station store, something she could clutch to her chest to make her feel safe. We'd drive all night, as far as we could go. Far away from here.

And that's when I heard it.

Olivia's name screamed urgently, emphatically through the cold air.

It was a high-pitched screech, whiny like a whistle. A distressed sound. What followed were the footsteps of a stampede, thousands of wildebeests running down the street. That's what it sounded like anyway, and as I peered up, hand still six inches away from the door, I saw Olivia's mother and her herd hurrying toward me, eight ladies with seven little ballerinas in tow, shouting commands.

"Olivia, come here right now.

"What do you think you're doing?

"Get your hands off my child!"

My hands grew slick. My heart beat quickly, more quickly than it was already beating. Under my arms there was wetness. Sweat. My head suddenly hurt. My brain thought quickly to manufacture a lie, as one of the ladies pointed at me and said, "I've seen you around here before," and I ransacked my mind for words, any words, but the words wouldn't come. My mind was holding them captive, detaining my words from me, though what it did do was measure the distance—computing the distance from the ladies to me, the distance from me to the car—doing the math, figuring it out, whether I could get Olivia inside the car before her mother and the other ladies reached us.

I *could*, I decided. But there needed to be no hesitation.

I needed to go.

Go!

I needed to go *now*.

But my feet wouldn't work properly, and my hand, slick with sweat, let go of Olivia's hand and suddenly she was running in the wrong direction, running toward her mother and away from me and away from the car.

"Who in the hell do you think you are?" Olivia's mother asked pointedly as she gathered Olivia into her arms and hoisted her to her chest. "What did you think you were doing with my child?"

And though I was completely tongue-tied, it was Olivia who did the speaking for me, who struggled in her mother's arms to be set free and there, once her feet were firmly planted back on the concrete while twirling her red leaf in her hand, she said, "You forgot me, Mommy."

And with that she took six tiny steps away from her mother's reach and extended her leaf to me. A parting gift.

I took it in my hand. "She was helping me find Mommy," Olivia crooned, smiling a toothless grin, but still, I could muster no words.

And then Olivia's mother changed tack, and her tone softened. The lines of her face disappeared and instead of reprimanding me or calling the police, as one of the ladies in the backdrop suggested she do, she thanked me. *She thanked me.* She thanked me for helping Olivia. Her cheeks turned red and her eyes filled with tears, and in that moment she believed were it not for me, she may have lost her child.

"You should keep a better eye on your daughter," I threatened, my voice and hands shaking like the leaves in the trees, clinging to their branches for dear life.

EDEN

May 11, 2016
Chicago

I sit on the front stoop, hands pressed between my knees to curb their shaking. I stare expectantly down the street, searching for that first glimmer of yellow to come bobbing along, the school bus, with Jessie on it. I check the time on my watch, knowing down to the minute what time the school bus arrives, but not having the tenacity to wait another three, because if I have to wait much longer I might get cold feet.

I need to get this over and done with. I need for this to be through.

I've combed and curled my hair. I lathered blush onto my cheeks for color, not so that I'll look nice, but so that I look alive, my current pallid tone far more synonymous with death and dying than with vigor. If I look healthy and robust, then maybe Jessie won't be as concerned. I wear a nice shirt. I plaster a smile to my face, one that sours the longer I wait.

I practice the words I'll soon say, saying them aloud so that I can get control of my cadence and rhythm, so that my voice doesn't shake the way it often does when I'm scared. Truth be told, I am scared, yes. I'm absolutely terrified. Though I won't dare say that to Jessie; for Jessie's sake, I'll put on a brave face.

The braking of the school bus sounds to me like the screech of a barn owl. I watch as Jessie clambers down the massive steps on the heels of her classmates, eyes lost on the ground as they often are these days. Her backpack is heavy; she slumps forward to counter the weight of it and I force back tears, knowing that my days of watching Jessie emerge from the school bus are coming quickly to an end.

I smile and she knows, the moment she arrives, that something is wrong.

"What's happened?" she asks, staring at me with the deadpan expression of a teenage girl, one that hides a legion of feelings behind that single blank stare. Sadness, confusion, fear. Her eyes—oh, how blue they are! Even to this day, they shake me to the core—are poker-faced. But not for long.

As I take her in, I realize that though she's wise beyond her years, she's still a child. A child who will be an orphan soon. I pat at the step beside me and tell her to sit down, cursing myself for trying too hard to look nice. I forget in that moment everything that I'd planned to say—all the wise old adages on life and death that I prepared to quote—and say outright to her instead, "Jessie, I'm dying," my voice flat and even, just barely above a whisper, trying desperately to stay calm for her sake. "I'm going to die," I say as that inexpressive demeanor cracks before me and tears rush to Jessie's blue eyes, flooding them instantly, a flash flood of tears.

I stare at her stoically, trying not to cry as Jessie breaks down before me. But it's hard to do. Jessie rushes into me, throwing her arms around my shoulders and neck. She pulls me in tightly as I purr into her ear, "Now, now. Don't cry. Everything will be all right," enveloping her in my arms, patting her back, stroking her hair.

"I'm not scared," I tell her, lying through my teeth because these are the words she needs to hear. "Sooner or later we all die, Jessie. It's only a matter of time. And this is mine."

To say I'm not heartsick would be a lie. To say I don't feel ashamed would be too.

Because after everything I did to make Jessie a part of my world, I'm leaving her alone to fend for herself, and for this, I feel guilty as sin.

JESSIE

I'M LYING IN BED when I hear a noise from outside. It makes me jump suddenly, makes me spring inches from the mattress and into the air.

What I expect to see when I look outside is a garbage can lid getting hurled to the ground, one of those galvanized steel ones clanging to the concrete. Because that's the sound I hear, the din of metal on concrete, and I imagine a colony of hulking rats climbing on shoulders to scale the garbage can, working together to carry off whatever's inside.

But instead when I peel the shade back and gaze out, I see nothing.

The moon, the stars are nowhere to be seen tonight. It's pitch-black outside.

For hours on end I find myself staring into the black nothingness that is Ms. Geissler's home. My body shakes from the cold, though as always I sweat. And I think that I have a fever, because that's the way it feels to me. Icy cold on the inside, but sweating through layers of clothes, my skin damp with sweat.

My clothes stick to me as my teeth chatter. I'm not sure I have it in me to survive another night. I wonder what a panic attack feels like, a breakdown. I think that's what's happening to me.

My eyes adjust to the darkness, making out shapes. The blackened windows, the balcony suspended three stories in the air on stilts, the flat roofline, the porch, the sliding glass door.

As I stare, I watch a squirrel leap from the branches of an oak tree and onto the rooftop. It vanishes into the eaves of the rooftop, as voices speak to me through the floor register again. *Peripheral cooling*, they say this time, and *mottling of the skin*, their voices weak and watered down, far away from here. But I can't be bothered this time to run and throw myself down over the metal grate because I know they won't hear me if I do. Even if I scream at them through the vent, they won't reply because they never do. Because they're only in my mind.

I hear the sound of footsteps too, quiet, restrained footsteps that slink up through the floor register and into the room with me. A giggle.

Shh, someone says, voice suppressed. *Let her sleep.*

I can't turn away from the window. Like bugs drawn to a light at night, I can't bring myself to look away. The window is the color of ebony, of charcoal. It's jet-black, the window shade motionless, completely inert.

I take in the rectangular shape of the glass itself—narrow and tall—the stagnancy of the shade. There is no one there. Behind the window and the shade, the room is empty and dark.

Until it's not.

Because, at three in the morning, the light flicks on.

There's an immediacy to it, a sudden unexpectedness. So much so that I almost fall from the edge of the bed. It happens all at once. A lamp turns on and the shades go up at the same time. The room becomes flooded with light.

For the first time I have a clear view of the room inside. What I see is a bedroom of sorts. An attic room, one space divvied up by three windows. Like a triptych, a painting where three canvas panels come together to create one scene.

In the first, a bed's headboard is pressed up against a wall paneled with a dated oak that stretches from floor to ceiling. The bed is unmade, a marshmallow-white comforter pulled down a foot from the head of the bed, pillows lay flat. There is a lamp on beside the mattress that lobs the soft yellow light across the room.

In the second canvas is the foot of the bed and the bottom two vertical columns of a four-poster bed frame. There is a wooden door on the back wall that leads to a hall. Or a closet. It's closed, so I don't know where it goes. A random cord dangles from the ceiling, belonging to seemingly nothing. At some point in its life, it might have been a fan or a light.

In the third canvas is the man.

Which makes me clutch a hand to my mouth, to keep myself from screaming.

He's leaned up against the window, the very same window where someone has been standing behind the shade watching me. His back is turned to me, as he sits on a ledge, pressing his back to the glass. He's dressed in brown, all of it, everything I can see, blending into the walls. Camouflage, a disguise. His hair is brown, pruned close to his head. I can't see his face or his eyes.

I stare at him for minutes, unmoving, he and I both frozen in place.

And then he rises. And as he does, I see that he is tall. He stretches in place, hands above his head, back arched. His stride is long and decisive. He crosses the room in three easy steps—what might take me eight or ten—all with his back in my direction, as if he knows I'm watching him. As if he knows, and he's toying with me. Playing a game of peekaboo. Of blind man's bluff.

His hands hang limply by his sides. I set my own hands on the window glass, as if reaching for the man on the other side of it.

I can feel it beneath my skin, something I can't quite put my finger on. Something about this man strikes a chord with me. His stature, his posture, the color of his hair. I've seen him before. Like Michelangelo's statue of David. You'd know it by David's carriage even if you never saw his face. He stands with his hand on his hips, left knee bent just a bit. His head is pitched to the right, looking at something off in the distance, something only he can see. Not me.

As my eyes fall to his right arm, I notice a watch on his wrist. A watch on his right wrist, which means to me that he, like the man in the photograph, is left-handed. I think of the man standing there in Mom's photograph in the saggy blue jeans. An afterthought to the lake and the boat and the trees. An addendum tucked neatly away in parenthesis. Almost forgotten, but not quite. I race to my bag and withdraw the photograph, holding it to the window so that I can see.

The stature is the same. Not just similar, but the same.

He's the man from Mom's photograph.

And then he turns, wheeling toward the window, quickly, in an instant. My hand slips unintentionally from my mouth as a scream slips out. I hold my breath, taking in his trim beard and his sun-tanned skin, knowing I've seen him before. I don't blink and I don't breathe. Because I know this man. It isn't just a hunch. Because there on his forearm is the very same scar, harder to see from the distance, but undeniably there. A six-inch gash, one that stretches clear from his wrist to beneath the cuff of a shirt, the skin around it puckered and pink.

And only then do I remember that the man in the photograph also had a scar.

As did the man at the garden. The one who sat reading Mom's obituary and looking sad.

The scar is the smoking gun. The one I was looking for. The one I couldn't see.

They're not two men who I've been searching for, but rather one man. And though it feels unimaginable, impossible, outrageous and far-fetched, I know it's true.

This man is my father.

He knows that I am here. He knows that I am here and he's come for me.

Because why else would he be there?

Now that I see them, his eyes are like hazelnuts, small and dark. He stares at me. Like me, he doesn't blink.

And then he steps from the window and reaches for the lamp. It turns off and then on again. A distress signal. An SOS. Morse code. Three short, three long, three short flashes of light. Save me.

He's speaking to me. Communicating.

I rise from the bed, sitting on the edge of it. I force my feet into a pair of gym shoes. The shoes resist. My feet have been sweating. They're tacky and they don't slip easily on. The laces of my shoes remain untied, trailing me as I go down the treacherous steps. I race out the front door, leaving it open wide, and across the dew-covered lawn.

At first I don't think. I just go.

Blades of grass reach out to tickle my legs as I cross the yard. The grass is long, in need of a trim, and my legs are bare, wearing only a pair of shorts. The air is nippy and brisk, but still, somehow, I sweat. It comes streaming down my hairline, gathering like swimming pools beneath my arms.

And then, ten or twenty feet from the carriage home, I start to question myself. What am I doing?

Suddenly I'm scared.

Three times I stop to get my bearings, looking around, in front of me and behind. Listening. A tree reaches out for me, brushes my arm, its leaves like the gentle caress of a human hand. I jerk back, startled and afraid.

It's dark outside. So dark that I can't see what's three feet before my eyes. I don't know what's there, if anything's there. My heart pounds inside me. "Is anyone there?" I call out, but no one replies.

Above me, I'm keenly aware that the blaze of light from the third-floor bedroom has gone dark. The house is black, no light anywhere. I think about going back, about turning around and going home. Of crawling onto the bed, of hiding beneath the sheets where I'll be safely on base.

But then I come to a spot that's halfway to the greystone and halfway back. I'm stuck in the middle, and the thought of going back seems as ominous as moving forward, especially since I left the door open wide. By now, who knows who's let themselves inside.

I hear scavengers in the distance. Raccoons, crows, rats. A creature scampers away from me on the lawn. Ringed tail. Masked face. Footprints like human hands. And I imagine a contorted human crawling by on all fours, releasing a guttural growl at me. Running away.

I make my way along the brick paver patio and toward the front door. There I climb the steps to the front door. Nearly ten of them, each tread precariously thin. At the top I pause to catch my breath. I breathe in, holding the air in my lungs. Absorbing it. Letting it fill my cells and bob through my bloodstream like a buoy at sea.

Two sidelights flank the solid mahogany door. I see my bedraggled reflection in each as I stand with my hand on my heart, gasping for air. My hair stands every which way; my skin is a bloodless white, deathly pale. There are purple bags beneath my eyes.

I knock on the door. It's a knock that's uncertain at first, but one that becomes more certain with each second that passes by. Once, twice, three times I knock. There's no reply.

Before I know it, I've knocked twenty-three times, each knock progressively louder, so that by number twenty-three, the knock is a pound. I raise my arm again but before I can bang once more, the porch light switches on. It startles me, the abruptness of it. Though after all this time, it's anything but abrupt.

Suddenly I'm no longer trapped in a black hole but instead doused with a bright white light that makes me go momentarily blind. For a whole six seconds after the front door opens, I see nothing. Just blotches, spots, dots. "Who's there?" I ask, voice still breathless, knowing it can be one of two people standing in the doorframe: the man in the attic window or Ms. Geissler.

"It's three in the morning, Jessie," she says to me. Her words are tired and annoyed. It's Ms. Geissler, who, unlike me, had apparently been sleeping, spared from a night of insomnia, unlike me.

My eyes focus to see her wrapping a red cotton robe around herself, tying the belt into a bow and patting down her hair. "What's the problem, dear?" she asks, her eyebrows scrunched up. "Is everything all right?"

"He's here," I say quickly, taking two small steps toward Ms. Geissler, bridging the gap from her to me. She takes a step in retreat.

"Who's here?" she asks. And I say, "Him. A man. Upstairs."

And it's the blankness of her expression that gets me upset, that makes me snap. That and my overwhelming fatigue, my persistent irritability thanks to a lack of sleep. "You know who I mean. You know exactly who I mean," I say roughly because I know he's here, in her home. She has to know that he's here. She has to *know* him, because why else would he be here? "The man in the window upstairs. The one who's been watching me. He's here."

She presses a hand to her heart. Gasps, "There's a man here? In my home?"

Her face goes white. She makes an offhand effort to peer over her shoulder and into the vacuous foyer as I take another step forward, one that gets my toes just inside her home. But only my toes. She resists, grasping the door hard and putting a foot behind it. She nearly shuts the door in my face. I lose balance, stumbling back onto the concrete stoop.

"I saw him in the window," I tell her, pointing at the staircase behind her. "Upstairs. A man in the third-story window," I say, and at this she relaxes visibly and smiles. She shakes her head and tells me that there's no one in the third-story bedroom, her voice so sure that for a second I believe it. She says again that no one's been in that room for months. Not since the squirrel incident, and then I think she's going to rehash it for me, the whole story about the squirrels inhabiting the third floor. I know now that it isn't true because there were never squirrels in that room but rather a man, my father, who she's been hiding from me all these days.

"The attic ladder," she tells me this time instead, "it's a pulldown thing," at which, like a mime, she grabs for an imaginary string over her left shoulder and pulls. "Broken for a couple of months. Wouldn't you know it," she says, "the exterminator managed to break the darn thing. I just haven't gotten around to getting it fixed."

"But I saw him," I insist, and she says quite simply, "You must be mistaken. There's no one there. Because how would anyone get up there, Jessie, without a ladder?"

It seems so sensible, the way that she says it. And for a fraction of a second, I doubt myself as she hoped I would do. But then his image returns to me—him standing there in the window, looking out at me—and I know that she's lying. That she's keeping him from me. Hiding him from the world just as Mom has always done.

"Let me in," I insist, pushing the door against the weight of her, and she says to me, "Now, now, Jessie. You had a bad dream, that's all," but of course this can't be true.

"You were dreaming there was a man in the room," she says to me. She reaches out a hand to mine but I pull briskly away. "Just a bad dream, that's all. It will all be clearer come morning."

"I know what I saw," I tell her, voice cracking. But her face is suddenly so pacific, so kind, and she asks if I'd like for her to walk me back to the carriage home so I don't have to go alone. It's dark out, she says. Hard to navigate the way. "But not to worry," she tells me. "I know this yard like the back of my hand," and she reaches for my arm to lead the way home. She winks at me and says, "And besides, I have a flashlight." And there it is, in the pocket of her robe. She flicks it on as if this conversation is over, as if she's put my worries to rest and now I can go home, feeling assured that there's no man in this home. No man watching me.

But I yank my arm away. "Why are you hiding him from me?" I ask. My voice becomes elevated, high-pitched, defensive. "Why don't you want me to see him? Why don't you want me to know that he's there?"

And then I let slip the one thought that's put down roots in the back of my mind, that's replaced all logical thought.

"Why are you keeping my father from me?" I scream.

Her face falls flat and she goes white, even whiter than she was before. She shakes her head, presses a hand to her mouth but says nothing. Nothing at first, before she carefully breathes out, treading lightly, "You're quite sure you saw a man in there?"

My heart nearly sings in relief. She believes me. *She believes me.*

I nod vigorously.

"Perhaps you're right then. Perhaps someone is there," she says with concern as she draws back the door and lets me in. "Why don't you go see," she suggests.

I think of my father, so close within reach. I soar past Ms. Geissler on the staircase, taking the steps two at a time up to the second floor. There I stand beneath that little hatch that leads up to the third floor. I listen for footsteps at first, hearing nothing, but remembering that I've stood here before and heard something.

He was here that night. Standing above me. Was he trying to contact me, to get my attention? To let me know that he was here?

I reach for the cord and give it a tug. The ladder unfurls before me, unfolding into makeshift steps. Two of the steps are split. Another is missing, just as Ms. Geissler said.

She warns me, "The steps, Jessie. They're not safe," though I go anyway, clutching the hand railing, which is unstable at best. "Bring the flashlight with you," she says, attempting to hand it to me. But I don't take it.

"There's a light," I tell her. "I saw the light. I don't need a flashlight," but she tells me to take it anyway, as she gives it a shake. I take it only to appease her, tucking it under the crook of an arm.

I begin to climb. I move slowly, walking though I want to run. The fourth step gives on me, splintering, and I shriek.

"Jessie!" Ms. Geissler yells, asking if I'm okay.

"I'm fine, I'm fine," I say, gripping the railing harder and pulling myself up and over the broken step.

Ms. Geissler makes no attempt to follow, but stands instead at the bottom of the stairs. She crosses her arms against her chest, watching as I go. She tells me to be careful. She tells me to go slow.

I reach the top step and hoist myself into the attic. The room is murky. Out the open windows, the sun is lost somewhere beneath the horizon. It's still nighttime, and yet there's a flush to the sky. Morning will be here soon.

I barely make out a lamp, the same lamp that for the past few nights radiated light. One of those old Tiffany-style lamps, with the stained-glass shade. But when I go to turn it on, nothing happens. The lamp is dead, the lightbulb burned out. I turn the knob around and around but still nothing happens. All I hear is the idle click that mimics my heartbeat.

I orbit the room, looking for him. I trip over things that I can't see. I hold my breath and listen, but I hear nothing. "Hello?" I ask, more begging than inquisitive.

"Come out so I can see you," I whisper to the man. My father. I tell him I know that he's here. That I want to see him, to meet him. That I've been waiting my whole life. I take small steps around the room, using my hands as a guide. My heartbeat pounds in my ear as I hold my breath, listening for breath, for footsteps, for him. A game of Marco Polo.

"Marco," I chant aloud to myself, but there's no reply.

I reach for the flashlight Ms. Geissler gave me. I turn it on. It casts a meager glow around the room, not much but enough. The light bounces on the wall from the tremor of my hands.

What I find is a wall of cardboard bankers boxes—dozens of them—with holes chewed out. Rodent droppings and old building supplies. Gallons of paint, boards of hardwood, boxes of screws and nails.

A makeshift nest—clumps of twigs and leaves—is nestled into the corner of the attic, and on it, there's some hairless and fetal-looking thing that looks like it's just climbed out of its mother's womb. A mother squirrel stands over her baby, scowling at me.

What I don't find is a four-poster bed. A white comforter. A cord dangling from the ceiling. A man. None of those things are here. It's just a ratty and dilapidated attic inhabited by squirrels, just as Ms. Geissler has said.

I feel like I can't breathe. The pain in my chest is immense, in my arm, my jaw, my abdomen. The room is empty, though as sure as I live and breathe, I saw a man here.

I stand looking out the window and toward the carriage home. I don't know how long I stand there, staring, thinking that maybe he will appear. That somehow we'll have swapped places. But he never appears.

I make my way back down the steps, where Ms. Geissler stands waiting for me. On her face is a complacent look. An *I told you so* look.

"Find what you were looking for?" she asks, though I can't speak. A lump forms in my throat, but I will not cry. I cannot cry.

"I told you, Jessie," she gloats, and I know then that she did this only to humor me. "There is no man there. Squirrels. Only squirrels." And then she thrusts the ladder back up so that the squirrels can't take over the rest of her home.

She shows me the door, but before closing it on me, she first asks, "Did you ever think, Jessie, that you're only seeing what you want to see? You need help." She all but pushes me out of her house and slams the door behind me. I hear the sound of a lock clicking shut.

The porch light goes off, and once again I am submerged in darkness.

I set myself down on the top porch step, feeling exhausted. My body aches from the lack of sleep, from ten nights of my mind depriving me of sleep. It's an insidious way to die, I think, from lack of sleep because there is nothing gory about it, no blood, no guts, and yet the effects are just as gruesome. I know because I'm living it.

As the sun begins to rise on the eleventh day, it's only a matter of time until I die.

This is what it feels like knowing you're about to die.

This is what Mom must have felt like knowing she would die.

I sit on the stoop and talk to myself, blathering about what's happening to me, hoping to make sense of it, but striking out. I can't make sense of it. I count to ten to make sure I can still do it, losing track at number six. I cry, a proper cry, shoulders heaving, the first in a long time. My heart, my head, every-thing hurts. I fold over sideways on the porch step, rolling up into the fetal position, pulling my knees into my chest, won-dering if this is where I'll die.

All at once I look up and have no clue where I am.

By now the sun is just barely beginning to rise. It turns the world from black to gray. One by one people appear on the street before me. Joggers, early-morning commuters.

As a hint of daylight fills the sky, I suddenly catch a glimpse of something on the other side of the street. It's a man in jeans and a jacket, bustling down the street with his hands in the pockets of his pants. His chin is tucked into the coat to keep warm, and there's a hat on his head, an orange baseball cap, and for this reason I know that it's him.

But how did he get here? How did he slip out of Ms. Geissler's home without me seeing him?

And that's when the answer comes to me. The balcony. The one that leads from street level up to the third floor.

He climbed down the balcony before I had a chance to go up the stairs, sneaking out as I cut across Ms. Geissler's lawn. That's when the light in the window went black. It went black because he'd already left. As I examined the attic with a flashlight, he was at ground level, looking in through the windows, watching me.

I rise quickly, calling for him, waving my hands to get his attention. I fall down the porch steps, all six or eight or ten of them. "Excuse me!" I scream, but if he sees, if he hears, he doesn't look and he doesn't wave back. He doesn't slow down. He never stops moving. He's in a hurry. He has somewhere to be.

I run as fast as my legs will carry me, which isn't fast.

The twitch in my eye has gone from one eye to two, so that they both spasm and I can't get them to stop. My hands shake. My arms ache, my legs ache, my back aches and, as I move across the street, not looking either way before I cross, a passing car nearly runs into me. The driver slams on their brakes to keep from hitting me.

I stand there in the street, three inches before the hood of the car, staring at the panicked driver, myself unfazed. Because I don't have it in me to be scared. The driver shoots me a dirty look. When I don't move, she douses the window with windshield wiper fluid, splashing me as she hoped to do. She screams out the window at me, and only then do I go.

By the time I turn away from the car, the man has advanced a quarter of a block or more. He's harder to see than he was before, farther away. Every now and then I see the orange cap bobbing and weaving down the street, but then it gets blocked by a low-hanging tree limb and I can't see him.

I panic; I've lost him.

But then again it returns, and I follow along.

I listen for the sound of footsteps, and though I'm a half a block away, I hear them. They're tenacious and quick, and for this reason, I know that they're his. I follow, having only the drum of footsteps to guide me, the drum of footsteps, steady like a beating heart.

But then, as I round the corner and pick up the pace, I hear something else too. They're words, breathed into my ear. *Earth to Jessie*, I hear, and I spin suddenly on my heels, glaring at a man who follows from behind. He's dressed in a suit and tie, an overcoat draped over him, smoking a cigarette. In the other hand, a coffee cup.

"What are you looking at?" he grills, tossing the cigarette to the ground. He grinds it into the concrete with the toe of a shoe and immediately reaches into his breast pocket for another. I turn away, saying nothing.

And then another noise comes. It's so soft, so subtle, hardly more than a whoosh of air against my ear, as I come to a red light and stop. *Psst*, says the noise, like the buzzing of a mosquito in my ear. I'm at a street corner, my eyes peeled to the walk signal, waiting for my turn to cross, hoping it was soon before I lose track of the orange cap. The street is congested, early-morning rush hour dissecting me from it.

Psst. Hey you, I hear, *hey, Jessie,* and I jump, my eyes turning away from the street to see who it is and who's calling me. The man with his cigarette is gone now, around the corner and out of sight, leaving a wake of smoke trailing behind. Behind me stands a corner coffee shop, the first floor of a three-story light-colored brick building. There are people milling around outside, just a small handful of them, though their bodies are turned away from me.

Jessie, I hear again, and I snap to attention. Who said that? Who's calling me?

There's a sudden chill in the air. I shiver. I pull my sweatshirt tighter around me, eyeing the people outside the coffee shop and taking them all in. But there's no one here that I know.

I turn away but still can't shake the feeling that someone is following. That someone is watching me. It's a gut feeling and there, at the fringes of my awareness, I feel it. Eyes on me though they're outside my field of view, burning a hole in my back.

On the other side of the intersection I pause, looking backward one last time, because I just can't shake that sense of being watched. And then I hear it again.

Psst. Hey. Hey, Jessie, and I turn suddenly, a spinning toy top on its tip. I almost lose balance; I almost fall to the ground. The world spins on its axis and I don't know what to blame for it, the lack of sleep or grief.

A man and woman walk behind me now, holding hands. Midthirties, pushing forty. They look slick and sophisticated, she taller than him in high heel boots, though they're both pinched and slim. "Did you call me?" I ask, but they exchange a look and tell me no. They part ways, slipping around me, one on either side. Once they pass, they rejoin hands, looking into each other's eyes before gazing over their shoulders at me. They laugh. I hear words giggled between them. *Lunatic* and *crazy*. They're talking about me.

And then there's a hand on my back. A warm hand that touches my bare skin from behind. It caresses me as every single hair on my arms and legs goes erect and I can't help myself. I scream. I jerk away, spinning around to find no one there. There's no one standing on the sidewalk behind me, though I hear it again. I feel it again. Lips pressed to my ear, whispering, *Earth to Jessie.*

I shake my head, willing it away, telling myself that it's nothing. That it's only the wind. I look up, coming to, realizing that I've lost track of the man I am sure now is my father. He's gone. I listen for the sound of his footsteps, searching the horizon for the orange baseball cap. I start to panic—eyes desperately lurching this way and that, hoping to see that pinprick of orange way off in the distance. I stagger down the street like a drunk. I can no longer hold my body upright because it's begun to collapse on me. I try running but I can't run, and so it's a shamble at best, feet dragging.

A hand latches onto my arm, a voice asks if I'm all right. I peer down at the hand on my arm, seeing a spindly hand, a bony hand. Rivers of blue veins roll across it. There's dirt wedged beneath the fingernails, lining the edges of the nail bed, and that's how I know. I know this hand; I'd know this hand anywhere. This is Mom's hand.

My eyes shoot up, taking in the woman draped all in white. She looks nothing like Mom. And yet, she says, "Jessie."

I'm so taken aback that I don't have it in me to respond. She stands before me, a halo of sunlight bearing down on her. She wears a wispy white blouse that billows in the early-morning breeze, the top button undone so I catch a hint of the pale skin beneath. On her bottom half is a skirt, a long one, stretching clear to her feet so that I can't be certain they're there. She looks fragile, delicate and, as she draws her hands through her hair, strands come with it. Clumps of hair fall from her scalp just like that, getting trapped between her thin fingers. Through the thin, floaty blouse I catch sight of her breasts. The breasts flat, nipples gone. Serrated suture marks criss-crossing her chest, the way Mom's used to be.

"Mom," I say. As impossible as it sounds, this woman standing before me is Mom.

"Mom," I beg this time, trembling as I reach for her, wanting nothing more than to draw her close, to wrap my arms around her shoulders and pull her in tight. I'm crying now, tears falling freely from my eyes. "Mom!" I plead, but before me she pulls suddenly back, sharply back, her eyebrows pleated. Her mouth drops open and she asks, "Do you need me to call someone for you? An ambulance, maybe?" as she stands a good three feet away and retreats a step for every step that I draw near. I grab for her again, but she tugs her arms out of reach from mine, setting them behind her back.

"I'm not your mom," she states. And it's so assertive, so firm, it gives me pause.

My eyes calibrate the image I see, the woman with the red hair and green eyes dressed in all white. Except that her hair is intact and what I saw as suture marks are instead lace.

It's not Mom.

I drop my hands to my sides, as she asks again if I need help, if there's someone she can call for me. I bark out *no*, though all at once I realize that I have no idea where I am, that the streets and the buildings are unrecognizable to me. That I've never seen them in my whole life.

Where am I?

How did I get here?

A siren wails off in the distance.

A car door squeaks open and then slams closed.

People push past me on the sidewalk, in a hurry to get here or there as the woman disappears into the crowds.

I cup my hands around my mouth, screaming up and down the street for my father.

And then, when I think all hope is lost, I see him. Out of the corner of my eye, somewhere in my peripheral vision, I catch a glimpse of orange as it slips behind the glass door of an apartment building on the other side of the street. I go to it, tugging on the door handle to follow him in, but find the door locked.

I press my face to the glass, staring inside. The lobby of the building is near empty. It's dated and retro with 1970s linoleum tile, the kind that seeps with asbestos. Where are we? Does he live here? Does he know someone who lives here? The tile is partly covered with some sort of commercial carpeting, bland and gray, to disguise the ugly tile. A postal worker separates mail into a million bins and though I knock on the glass for him to let me in, he ignores me. Either he can't hear or he doesn't care. He just goes about sorting the mail as if I'm not here, as if he can't see me, as if I'm invisible.

And I wonder then if I am invisible, if I am already dead.

I tug again on the tempered glass door. The hollow metal frame rattles in place. I smash the heel of my hand against the glass to no avail.

I begin to make my way around the building, in search of another way in. A freight entrance, maybe. But before I've gone twenty feet, a tenant comes tearing out of the building, eyes set on an incoming bus. I race back to the door, managing to slip in a hand in time to prevent it from latching. I sail inside. Behind me, the door closes tight.

My eyes look to the left just as a flash of orange disappears behind a door. A black-and-white sign beside it reads Stairs, the steps themselves explicated by a zigzag line. He's going upstairs. I follow along, racing toward the stairwell and after him.

I press hard on the steel door's push bar, making my way into the stairwell. I run, scaling the steps two at a time, clinging to the banister with a sweaty hand, pulling myself up the concrete stairs. The air is stuffy, suffocating, hard to breathe. There's a notable lack of oxygen in here. It's unventilated; there's no access to fresh air. I choke on nothing and it takes a moment to regain my composure, to stop myself from choking on the musty air.

There are sixteen floors in the building. Above me, I hear footsteps as they climb upward at a better clip than me. He's going too fast. I can't catch up. I call to him, but if he hears, he doesn't let up.

Somewhere between the eighth and ninth floors, my feet slip on the edge of the step, on some sort of tactile paving, yellow, rubbery lumps that are meant to have the opposite effect, to prevent people from falling. But not me. Rather my body keeps going, the momentum of the run thrusting me forward at a blistering pace. But, thanks to the tactile paving, my feet slow down, two things which are mutually exclusive because I can't stop and go at the same time. And so instead I trip, feet skidding beneath me. My body jerks, my hand latching on to the banister to keep me upright. Pain radiates down my arm, into my hands, seeping into the muscles of my rib cage, my neck, my back. But I keep going. He is right there, within reach. I can't lose him this time.

I scurry up yet another flight of stairs. I keep running, up the steps. Though before I know it, we've reached the top floor. The highest floor in the entire building, the sixteenth floor. The end of the line, I think at first, but not quite. Because he's still climbing. Because there's still one more flight of stairs, different from all the rest. More industrial, more heavy-duty. Not meant for everyday pedestrian use. It's more of an elaborate stepladder than stairs. But I scale it nonetheless, ten feet behind him. Beside it, a sign reads Roof Access.

There's a hatch at the top, a single slab of aluminum with a hinged lid. He pushes through it and I follow, mounting the last few steps of the stepladder and breaking free onto the rooftop of the apartment building.

At the top, the hatch door closes all on its own behind me. The wind forces it shut, the sound of it slamming closed, startling me.

I reach for the handle to tug it open again, finding it suddenly locked.

I'm trapped on the building's rooftop.

The city surrounds me. A panorama. With arms outstretched, I can't help but spin, taking it all in. Enjoying the view, knowing fully well this may be the last thing my eyes ever see.

The buildings and skyscrapers rise up like dominos around me and I stand on my own domino, waiting for my turn to fall. The lake is bluer than I've ever seen, a luminous blue that makes the blue of the sky inferior. An underling. Sunlight reflects off the glass of the buildings so that the whole world is suddenly aglow.

I circulate the building, looking for him, for my father.

Now that we're here, he's somehow disappeared. He's hiding from me. I call to him, but he doesn't reply. "Hello!" I scream. "I know you're up here!"

The roof itself is filled with all sorts of miscellany. An industrial cooling system. Exhaust vents. Access panels to this and that. It makes it hard to see. I search among various parts of the cooling system, looking for him. They're big, boxy things that make noise from time to time, like the whirring of a fan inside. I hold my breath. I refuse to breathe. Breathing makes noise and I don't want to make noise. I only want to listen.

A hand strokes me again, whispering into my ear, *Earth to Jessie.*

I pull back, drawing sharply away from the strange caress.

To the west end of the building, there's a fire escape, one that runs from ground level clear to the top, a thing so basic, so rudimentary, it terrifies me. It's little more than a metallic swimming pool ladder, four treads that lift you from the rooftop to the other side of the building.

That's where my father stands. On the fire escape. Now that the hatch is closed, the only way out of here, aside from a free fall, is the fire escape.

I go there, legs shaking. I call to him, voice more subdued now that I see him. Now that I've found him. Now that he's in reach. He's climbed over the roof wall, a three-foot thing, and onto the fire escape.

My hand reaches out for the ladder's handrail and I grab a hold of it and pull myself up. My hands are dripping and slippery. I go up one tread. It gives on me and I fall back down to the ground. I start again. One step and then two, watching on in horror as my father begins his descent without me, jogging down the steps at a steady clip, unfazed by the great height.

"Stop, please," I beg, hearing the anguish in my voice. "Please, don't go."

As I near the top, there's a moment of calm that comes and goes so quickly I almost don't notice it. For one split second the world is still. I'm at peace. The sun moves higher and higher into the sky, yellow-orange glaring at me through the buildings, making me peaceful and warm. My hands rise beside me as a bird goes soaring by. As if my hands are wings, I think in that moment what it would be like to fly.

And then it comes rushing back to me.

I'm hopelessly alone. Everything hurts. I can no longer think straight; I can no longer see straight; I can no longer speak. I don't know who I am anymore. If I am anyone.

And I know in that moment for certain: I am no one.

I think what it would feel like to fall. The weightlessness of the plunge, of gravity taking over, of relinquishing control. Giving up, surrendering to the universe.

There's a flicker of movement beneath me. A flash of brown, and I know that if I wait any longer, it will be too late. The decision will no longer be mine. I cry out one more time. And then I go, legs convulsing as I swing one leg over the edge of the building and onto the fire escape on the other side. I have to force myself to do it. It takes everything I have. All that's on the other side is a measly shelf, an overhang, that hovers seventeen floors above land.

I make my way toward him, but he's moving far too fast for me. And I'm scared, looking down where, beneath me, the earth tilts and sways. I'm overcome with vertigo. I feel nauseous; I feel like I could be sick. The steps of the fire escape are perforated to prevent snow and ice from forming, which does nothing for me now. I can see straight through them to the street beneath my feet. People like ants walk up and down the street, minding their own business, paying no attention to me. Cabs like matchbooks soar past.

The steps beneath me are corroded and weak. A handful are missing. In some spots, the fire escape pulls away from the building's masonry, bolts no longer holding tight. I take the steps two at a time, though they clatter each time my feet hit, the entire fire escape bucking beneath me. I have to take long strides over the missing steps.

I make it down only half a flight of steps before my knees give.

As they do, I lurch forward, staggering. I fall down the second half flight of stairs. The railing at the end is corroded, as much of the fire escape is. It's the red-orange of rust. As my body goes hurtling into it, the spindles give and I slip straight through, with nothing there to prevent my fall.

As I tumble off the side of the fire escape, my head swims.

I take one final look at the great distance to the ground, the distance I'll soon fall.

All at once, I'm falling. My legs follow the rest of me, feet making a last-ditch effort to cling to something, trying in vain to tether themselves to the steel of the fire escape. I try to grab it with a hand, but it slips straight through time and again, as I soar along beside it, unable to grab hold.

My arms and legs kick. They do the doggy paddle as I soar downward. I flail and kick, my body splayed as air rushes from beneath me, wrapping my hair around my face. I can see nearly nothing. Not that there's much to see anyway, other than the blue of the sky as I fall. There's no air resistance. The air does nothing to slow me down. My hands make a meek attempt to protect my head, some sort of Pavlovian response, as I thrust my feet downward, knowing my only chance of survival hinges on landing feetfirst. It doesn't work. I can't get them down. Another fire escape landing soars past but I can't get to it in time.

My insides scuttle to my center from the speed, from the velocity of the fall. A fall that feels like forever. Like I am forever falling. My face molded in fear.

I open my mouth to scream, but nothing comes out.

EDEN

October 3, 1997
Egg Harbor

IT'S BECOME AN ITCH that I can't reach. A hunger that no amount of food can satiate. A drought that a thousand rainfalls can't fix.

That unquenchable need to be a mother.

I think about it morning, noon and night.

At night I lie awake not sleeping, wondering how I will ever be a mother.

I don't know that I have it in me to wait until Aaron's and my divorce is complete.

There is adoption, of course, but as a single mother going through divorce proceedings and carrying an exorbitant amount of debt, I hardly think I'm a suitable candidate for adoption.

And so I must find another way.

I go to work early and I leave late, spending those extra few minutes staring at the babies through the nursery room glass. On my lunch break I eat quickly so that I have time to wander down to the labor and delivery unit and salivate over the newborns while the nursery room nurses tend to their every need, the bottles and clean diapers and the endless rocks in the rocking chairs.

I don't want to feel the way I do.

I'm not a bad person, not by any means, and yet it's an addiction to me. A disease. I'm unable to abstain from thinking about babies, from wanting a baby, from craving a baby as one does gambling or cocaine.

I've lost control of my own behavior. I don't know what I'm capable of, what I might do, and that in itself terrifies me. Once I was very rule abiding; I always did as I was told.

But now my neurotransmitters are in disrepair and quite simply, I'm not the person I used to be. That Eden is gone, replaced with someone I scarcely recognize anymore, someone I don't know.

October 7, 1997
Egg Harbor

Something happened today.

I had eaten my lunch—roast beef on rye from the hospital's cafeteria—sitting all alone at one of the smaller round tables, nibbling quickly, quietly and staring out the window at the visitors and outpatients who came and went through the revolving front doors, realizing how utterly alone I felt as the other tables spilled over with groups of four, five, six, all involved in conversations that didn't have a thing to do with me. Oh, how I felt so alone. When I was through eating, I set my tray beside the trash can and then went to visit the babies in the nursery.

A drug addict needing her fix.

As I stood there, peering through glass at the newborns sound asleep in their knitted blankets with their knitted hats, one little one in particular caught my eye, the name in the bassinet reading Jade Cutter. It was the name that caught my attention, not necessarily the baby herself, though she was perfect in every way, from the roundness of her head to the redness of her cheeks. But more so, it was the slip of pink paper in the bassinet that caught my eye, the one that listed her name, date and time of birth, pediatrician, and the names of her parents.

Joseph and Miranda Cutter.

Joe and Miranda.

They'd had their baby girl. They'd had their baby girl and they didn't tell me.

She was swaddled in a pink cotton blanket, eyes closed, mouth parted as she breathed in her sleep. A single hand had forced its way from the blanket, but Jade seemed unmindful of this, unlike other infants—I'd come to learn from my time spent observing them in the nursery—whose limbs needed to be controlled so that they could sleep. There was dark hair, a mound of it, that sneaked out from the edges of the pink hat and, though they were shut tight, I had to imagine her eyes too were dark like Joe's, though these, of course, were things that often changed over time.

And in that moment little Jade's eyes parted and she gazed at me, it seemed, and I was stricken with a sudden, purposeful, persistent need to hold her in my arms.

I stepped into the nursery, greeting the ladies there by name. There were two of them, one older and one younger, both of whom I knew fairly well. How many months had I been stopping by, telling the tale of how I was working hard to earn my degree so I could be one of them, nursery room nurses who tended to newborn babies? How many times had they let me into the nursery, allowing me to watch as they changed diapers and swaddled with the expertise of someone who'd done it a million times? How many times had they let me stroke an infant's cheek in his or her sleep, never once needing to remind me to wash my hands because I always remembered?

But not this time.

"You'll need to stay in the hall, Eden," the older of the two nurses said, a woman by the name of Kathy, and I felt a stabbing sensation in the chest as she pointed to the floor, to an imaginary line that dissected the nursery from the hallway tiles.

That's the line where I was to remain behind.

"But, Kathy," I attempted to argue, but she held up her hands and told me that there had been complaints that they'd been too lax of late, and hospital officials were cracking down on security protocols, and I wondered now if the babies were fitted with tiny security devices on their wee wrists or ankles to keep someone from walking out the front door with them. Someone like me.

"But it's just me," I reassured her, holding up my badge, reminding her that *I work here.*

Except that by that time, she'd turned her back to me and was attending to an infant who'd begun to fuss; she wouldn't let me in, and I could feel my hands begin to shake in withdrawal. There was a tightness in my chest and my head suddenly hurt. For a minute or two, I couldn't breathe. My heart was palpitating, strong, irregular beats that left me lightheaded, though neither of the nurses seemed to notice; no one noticed but me.

And then Joe was there coming to my rescue, as he appeared at the nursery to come lay claim to his baby girl.

"Joe!" I said too loudly, thrilled to see him, knowing that he was my key to that baby. Joe would get Jade out of the nursery; Joe would let me hold and coddle baby Jade as I needed to do.

He said hello to me, and what a nice surprise to see me, and at this, I felt a smile spread widely across my lips. My heartbeat slowed; the tension in my head and neck began to ease.

"Miranda called you to tell you the news?" he asked, but I said no, that I was working, that I had just come to visit the babies in the nursery when I saw baby Jade.

"Congratulations!" I said, offering an awkward embrace. Joe was not a man I knew well, and what I did know came from Miranda's own complaints about him. How he was a jerk, a lousy father. But I couldn't let this deter me now.

"How is Miranda?" I asked, and Joe replied as expected: Miranda was tired, Miranda wanted nothing but to sleep and already I imagined her, sore over her infant's need to eat.

Kathy glided the rolling bassinet out the nursery door to Joe's waiting hands, and when I made an attempt to follow, to accompany Joe to Miranda's room where I would sit on the corner armchair with Jade in my arms as I'd once done with Carter, he said to me, "Another time, Eden? My parents are here," meaning that they already had company, that Joe's mother and father were here to see baby Jade.

That I wasn't welcome in the hospital room with Joe's mother and father because as everyone knows, three's a crowd.

"Just for a minute?" I pleaded, staring at Joe, who looked worse for wear in that moment, tired and jaded. I could see it in his eyes: four children was too much.

I could help him.

I could take a single one off his hands.

Just one child.

"Just to offer my congratulations to Miranda and then I'll go?" I begged—and even I could hear the desperation in my voice—but Joe shook his head, and I felt like a child then, like a five-year-old child who'd just been told no.

Joe said that he'd pass my message along to Miranda and then he turned to go without me. He walked quickly on purpose, faster than my legs could go, and I felt the dismissal a thousandfold then. I was being brushed off, given the cold shoulder as if I carried a stigma on my sleeve.

The stigma of infertility, the stigma of miscarriage, the stigma of a woman whose husband was in the process of divorcing her.

I blinked and Joe was gone, disappeared down the hall and around the corner where I couldn't see him anymore, and immediately the headache returned, the palpitations, the sweat. The hospital walls began closing in on me as in a room nearby a lady, deep in the throes of labor, screamed, and instead of feeling sympathy for her, I felt a surge of jealousy and spite.

Oh, how I wanted to be the one screaming in the throes of labor pain! How I wanted to feel a baby inside me, wedging itself headfirst to get out. How I wanted to feel that baby press between my legs, to feel it crown as doctors and nurses gathered around telling me to push. *Push!*

My feet crept toward her room with instinct, setting my hand on the doorknob and turning it, opening it just a sliver so that I could see in. There was far too much happening inside the room for anyone to hear the door squeak. I stood in the doorway, inching a foot back so no one would see. A Peeping Tom. The door wasn't open and yet it was ajar, not quite closed tight, and through the crack I saw her laid out on her back, gasping from pain. I saw her gather handfuls of blanket in her hands and squeeze, pushing to get that baby out. I heard her scream, this throaty, guttural scream, crude and uninhibited as a nurse on either side told her to push.

"Push!" Her husband stroked her sweaty hair, brushing it out of her eyes. Between her legs was a shock of black and there I stared, wondering just where exactly she ended and the baby began as she pushed again, holding her breath—as I, in turn, held mine, parting my legs ever so and pushing too—bearing down, and this time, as she pushed, a baby came spilling out of her insides, covered in mucous, and the room was filled with a sudden rapturous bliss.

The door slammed shut in my face.

Someone had seen me.

I ran away, out of labor and delivery.

I was due back at my desk in just a moment. Soon the other women in billing would wonder where I had gone, and why I wasn't yet back from lunch. They would tell our manager. I would be given a scolding.

But I couldn't go back to billing at that moment.

I needed to get away.

I got behind the wheel of my car and I drove and drove.

I drove to the chophouse, needing to see Aaron, desperate suddenly to see him, for him to hold me in his arms, to stroke my hair and tell me everything would be all right. If I'm being honest, I was scared of the person I was, scared of the person I'd become. I was quite terrified, if Aaron didn't put a stop to it, of what I might do. My thoughts were scattered, sown like seeds in my mind, and there was no telling which ideas would bloom, the sensible ones like going home and putting myself to bed, or the misguided ones where I return to the hospital and force myself into Joe and Miranda's room, screaming like a lunatic, demanding that they give me their child.

I left the car parked haphazardly across parallel lines on the street outside, nearly a block from the chophouse. Parking in town was never easy to come by. I stepped from the car, my ankle giving on me as it sunk deep into a crater on the street. I shook it off, kept moving, feeling the ligaments beneath my shoes begin to ache and swell.

It had begun to rain outside, the sky darkening. The restaurants, the gift shops, the galleries that lined the street radiated light. They beamed from the inside out, while outside people scattered like roaches in daylight, hiding under canopies and slipping inside stores, seeking shelter, huddled in throngs beneath ample-size golf umbrellas, clutching one another, laughing.

But not me.

I made my way to the chophouse alone, fully intent on going inside. On speaking to Aaron. On begging him to help me, on pleading with him to take me back. I was desperate. What else could I do? The rain came pouring down, permeating my skin, so that I could feel it inside my bones. I hurried past people tucked warmly, drily beneath their umbrellas, no one offering to share. The rib of a passing umbrella poked me in the shoulder, but no apology came thereafter, as if it was my fault, as if it was my shoulder's fault for getting in the way of this man's umbrella.

I closed in on the chophouse, smelling that scent that always followed Aaron home and into bed with us, that coiled around us while we slept. Grease, Worcestershire sauce, the flesh of meat.

But before stepping inside, I caught a fleck of Aaron through the restaurant window, seeing his face through the small partition that separates the kitchen from the dining room. A flyspeck only, but in that flyspeck, there was a lightness about him, a nimbleness, a radiance to his skin. Rain streaked down the window, but I peered past it, watching as a smile danced on the edges of Aaron's face. In the very same fleck some other man made a wisecrack, I could only assume, because then Aaron was laughing, *laughing!*, the edges of his lips reaching upward to the sky like he hadn't done in years. Aaron was laughing and it was beautiful to see, an openmouthed laugh, nothing curbed or restrained about it, and I saw in Aaron's eyes a felicity that I hadn't seen in quite some time. Never did he press his hand to his mouth to hide the smile, but rather chuckled with all of his might.

Aaron was happy. Aaron had found his happy place.

Unlike me, his heart had healed and he was no longer broken. He was whole.

Oh, how I wanted to be there beside him, laughing too.

But I couldn't bring myself to do it, to shatter what had already been fixed. I'd ruin him, that I knew, if I stepped foot into the chophouse, as I imagined the laughter drawing to a sudden close if I walked in, that lovely smile vaporizing from his face at the sight of me.

And so instead, when a hostess poked her head outside and asked if I'd like to take a peek at the menu, I shook my head, scurrying the other way like all the other roaches, seeking shelter indoors from the rain.

It was an upscale restaurant where I went, fine dining with a bar attached, the kind where one might have a glass of wine while waiting for their table to be set. This hostess offered a table, but I strutted straight past her and to the bar—sopping wet, leaving a trail of rainwater behind me as I walked. I climbed onto one of the tall stools and ordered a chardonnay to drink. A chardonnay! The glass came to me full to the rim, a generous pour at the hand of a bartender with cavernous dimples and sparkling blue eyes, a man who must have been six years younger than me, barely old enough to be serving alcohol at an upscale establishment. And yet here he was, and in the moment I felt suddenly old, much older than my twenty-nine years, but that didn't matter. That was the least of my concerns.

With the wine he also brought a dish towel, which I used to towel dry the ends of my hair.

The first sip of wine tasted like battery acid to me.

It choked me on the way down, burning the lining of my esophagus so that the bartender raised an eyebrow at me and asked if I was all right. I pressed a hand to my mouth, nodding, but I wasn't sure that I was all right. The wine settled in the pit of my stomach, and the feeling was a mix of repulsion and nausea, along with a warmth and prickling that I quite liked.

And so I had another sip, wanting the warmth and prickling to have its way with me, to help me forget about Aaron and the miscarriage, all those wasted months trying unavailingly to create a baby.

How stupid I'd been in believing that with Dr. Landry's help we could outsmart nature. Aaron and I were infertile; that was the nature of the beast. That couldn't be changed.

The universe was laughing at me for my arrogance and my vanity.

I took another sip of wine and this time, I didn't choke.

I thought of my baby, of my unborn baby. Of my dead baby. I wondered what she would have looked like had she had a chance to grow full-term. Would she have looked like Aaron, with dark hair and light eyes, or would she have looked like me?

Would she have been a she, or would she have been a he? I still think about her all the time.

Had she been a girl, I would have named her Sadie.

I raised my glass to my lips and swallowed a mouthful, wondering if she ever crossed Aaron's mind.

Wondering if I ever crossed Aaron's mind.

By the second glass, the wine was no longer battery acid to me. It quenched that *hunger*, that *thirst*, like nothing else in the world was able to do. It spilled through my veins, anesthetizing my arms and legs, dulling my senses. I hadn't had a drop to drink in quite some time and so it didn't take much for the room to start to blur at the edges, for the stool to feel insecure beneath my seat.

With every sip thereafter I became a more youthful version of myself, someone more energetic, someone more carefree.

With every sip I became blissfully forgetful, forgetting at once that I was a soon-to-be divorcée, a woman who would never have a baby.

It was a quiet night, a Tuesday night, and so the bartender happily filled his free time speaking to me—about what, I hardly remember anymore—and, after that second glass of chardonnay was poured, I plucked a credit card from my purse, one that wouldn't be denied, and the bartender started a tab for me, telling me his name was Josh.

"You have a beautiful smile," he said to me, and I blushed, grinning, and he pointed at it and said, "Yup, that's the one," while smiling his own beautiful smile. For whatever reason I dug a tube of lipstick from my purse, a light shade of pink, and applied it to my lips, leaving light pink prints around the rim of my wineglass that he filled each time with a bountiful pour.

I unbuttoned the top button of my blouse, leaning farther over the bar, fully aware of just how pathetic it was, me, a lonely, depressed woman hitting on a bartender in a near-abandoned bar.

I had become a cliché.

"What's your name?" he asked, setting a bowl of nuts before me, a single finger brushing against my skin as he did, and I told him that it was Eden. He equated it to the garden of Eden, in other words, *paradise*, and I smiled and said I'd never heard that before, though of course I had, from each and every one of the lowlifes who came before Aaron when they were trying to pick me up in bars far less classy than this.

"What are you doing here all by yourself, Eden?" he asked while swirling a dishrag in circles before me.

I shrugged my shoulders and said that I didn't know.

What was I doing here?

I reached for my glass and downed the last few drops. At once it was refilled, and I downed that too, scarcely able to recall what came next.

Only bits and pieces stayed with me until morning, a montage of what may have occurred. Sliding from the barstool with the third glass of wine. Laughing at myself as strange hands helped me to my feet, refreshing my glass. A face far too close to mine. The deep groove of dimples. Words whispered in my ear.

"Wait for me," he said.

Standing on the street corner in the dark autumn night, I leaned against a streetlamp that didn't give off an ounce of light. Getting absorbed by blackness until even I wasn't sure if I was still there. It was raining still, a fine mist in the air, one which seemed to levitate and not fall.

And then suddenly there were lips on my neck, hands kneading my skin, though who they belonged to, I couldn't see. It was far too dark to see, but it didn't matter to me. I knew only that my extremities were numb from the alcohol, and it was cathartic to me, strange hands wandering along the landscape of my skin, exploring the valleys and hills with a certain vehemence I'd never felt before. A body pressed against mine, pinning me to the streetlamp, whispering breathless words into the lobe of an ear.

"Where's your car? I'll drive."

I heard the sound of an engine gunning, the stars coming at me at a dizzying speed before the world turned black again, and then the scratch of facial hair on my cheek, a hand groping at my chest with the impatience of a sixteen-year-old boy. A hasty man pawed at me, tearing at my blouse. What buttons remained clung to the fabric by strings, as he pushed me into the back seat of the car, moving with the deftness and agility of someone who knew what they were doing, of someone who had a history of strange women in the back seats of cars.

I felt the force of my skirt getting thrust clear up to my rib cage. The scratch of a fingernail as he tore at my panties, pushing them aside. The sound of a moan, my own forced moan tolling through the airless space because, even with the continuous thrust of his hips into me, I felt nothing and I wanted more than anything to feel something, to feel *any-thing*, because feeling something was far better than feeling nothing, and in that moment all I felt was nothing. Nothing that mattered anyway.

Instead, hot breath on the lobe of my ear. Handfuls of hair being clenched between hands, tugged consciously or unconsciously, I didn't know. Reggae music on a car stereo.

He panted out a name in rhythm, "Anna, Anna." Did he think that that was my name, Anna, or was there another woman in his life, a woman named Anna, and he was only pretending that I was her? I replied with "Yes, yes!" deciding that I would be his Anna if that's who he wanted me to be. A seat belt buckle drilled a hole into the small of my back, plastic plunging itself into me with every thrust of his hips, leaving its mark, though still I felt nothing, nothing at all, not until finally a spasm tore through him like a lightning strike and he collapsed against me, and then there was the weight of him, no longer supported by his own hands.

The weight of him. That I felt.

And then weightlessness.

A car door opened and closed and then there was silence.

He was gone.

I woke up in the morning in the back seat of my car, parked at the far edge of a public playground parking lot, beneath the shadow of a tree, my skirt still thrust clear up to my rib cage, the rest of me exposed, hidden only by the dewdrops that had settled on the windows overnight.

JESSIE

MY HEART BEATS INSIDE me like a cheetah. I'm screaming.

"*Psst.* Hey you, hey, Jessie."

There's a hand at my shoulder, rattling me. It's gentle, but insistent. I jerk away from the hand, arms flailing. I'm no longer falling.

A mouth presses closely to my ear, speaks in a breathy voice. A stage whisper. "Earth to Jessie," she says, and it's a numbing voice. A hypnotic voice. The perfect opiate.

I imagine where I am. On the grass. Body in bits on the ground, bleeding and broken, hardly able to move. In the distance, the sound of an ambulance's wailing siren as my father walks away from the scene unscathed.

The voice says *it's okay, it's okay*, three times or more while stroking my hair. I can't open my eyes. And yet I see her, a woman hunched over me on the lawn, while others crowd around her. She's gawking, her eyes fixated on the most gruesome parts of my battered body. A leg that bends backward, organs that protrude from the skin.

I know the voice. I've heard it before. But I can't place it.

I'm swimming beneath water. Sounds are muffled above my head. The dropping of a needle onto an old vintage vinyl record. Voices talking. A measured, high-pitched ping. Ping, and then nothing. Ping, and then nothing. Ping, ping. Voices in the background. Talking. Saying things like *morphine* and *slipper socks* and *ice chips*.

When I go to open my eyes, they're sealed shut. Taped down. Impossible to open.

My hands rise and I'm surprised to find that I can still move them, my arms and hands. That they're not broken after all. Not shattered into a million pieces across the concrete.

I press the heels of my hands against my eyes and rub hard, wiping the crusty discharge. Inside, my heart pounds hard. A song begins to play. Quietly. Background music. It's a song I know well because it's Mom's favorite song.

When I finally get my eyelids to lift, all I see is yellow. A blinding yellow light.

And that's when I know that I'm dead. That's the first clue.

The yellow light charges my eyes. It stuns and overpowers them, making them close again because I can't stand to keep them open; it hurts too much. I blink repeatedly, trying to adapt to the light. To orient myself, to find a reference point, to figure out where I am.

The second clue that I have that I'm dead is Mom. Because Mom is also dead. And yet, as I open my eyes, she's here, sitting five or six feet from me. She sits upright, on some sort of reclining armchair with castors on its feet, her gaunt legs propped on the chair's footrest. She's dressed in a roomy gown that slips carelessly from a shoulder, the hair on her head merely fuzz, as it was the last time I laid eyes on her alive. Which is why I know this is some sort of afterlife we're stuck in. Mom and me.

The room around me is blue. Blue walls. Blue sheets. A comforting, pastel shade of blue. I'm not on the lawn after all. I'm not outside, lying in the shadow of the building from which I fell. Rather I'm in a room, on a bed.

A woman stands beside Mom, lathering lotion onto her arms and hands, massaging the purplish, blotchy skin. I know who she is because I've seen her before, at the hospital before Mom died. She was Mom's nurse, one of them anyway. A woman named Carrie who was more religious than any about applying lotion to Mom's hands and feet, about turning her so she didn't get bedsores. Even when I begged for them to leave her alone so Mom could sleep.

She looks over at me and says, "Well, it's about time," and that's when I know that we're all dead. Mom, the nurse and me. They've just been waiting for me to arrive.

I know how Mom and I died, but I wonder, how did she?

"That stuff knocked you out cold," says the woman who squats on her haunches beside me, a second nurse. Her hand rests on my shoulder, the very same hand that only moments ago rattled me, mouth purring into my ear, *Psst. Hey you, hey, Jessie. Earth to Jessie.*

"What stuff?" I ask, feeling dazed and confused. Behind me, from a record player, Gladys Knight sings to me. There's the greatest sense that I'm still falling, though I'm well aware that it didn't hurt when I hit the ground. That when I crash-landed into the concrete beside the apartment building, I felt nothing. I don't even remember it happening. I must've been dead by then, I decide. A heart attack, a broken neck.

The room whirls around me. I push myself up so I sit, perpendicular, no longer lying down on a bed. There's a puddle of blankets on the floor, a pillow beneath my head. The second woman rises from the ground beside me and pulls the strings of a window shade so that they rise. I've seen her before. She's the same woman who kept me company the night before Mom died, and now she too is dead like me. How can that be?

How can we all be dead?

More blinding yellow infiltrates the room, making it hard to see much of anything clearly. But Mom. I see Mom. My eyes go back to Mom. To Mom sitting there. Mom, in the flesh. No longer listless. No longer bed bound. She looks sleepy still, her eyes glazed over, and yet on her face, a smile. "How about some ice chips, Miss Eden?" Nurse Carrie asks, offering a single piece of ice from the end of a spoon.

"The clonazepam," I hear, and it takes a minute to realize the nurse is talking to me, that I asked a question and she's answering it for me. "The stuff doc gave you to sleep. He'll be happy to hear it worked. You needed a good night's sleep. You were dreaming," she says. "Calling out, kicking in your sleep. Must've been one hell of a dream."

And as I finally start to get my bearings, I realize where I am. I'm in Mom's hospital room. Mom. Who sits six feet from me, upright, sucking on a cube of ice. Not six feet under, but six feet from me. No longer ashes, but now whole.

The clonazepam. The melatonin. That I remember. My own bloody, inflamed eyes. The doctor, concerned, offering something to help me sleep. Watching a newsmagazine show on the TV, a story about identity theft, while waiting for the pills to kick in, the nurse tucking me into bed, telling me about her daughter, dead in a car accident at the age of three.

The purple swimsuit, her daughter collecting shells from the sea. That I remember.

By the time I woke up Mom was dead, except that she wasn't dead.

It was all a dream.

My eyes adapt. The light becomes less painful, less blinding.

And that's when I see a man in the room too, and I know straightaway that it's the man from the dream. And I wonder if I'm still dreaming. If this is like the purgatory of dreams and I'm trapped somewhere between sleep and awake, having to atone for my sins before I can fully wake up. His back is to me as it's almost always been because he's there on a chair before Mom. He sits, though I see it in the body posture, the carriage, and I know that it's him. I'm not chasing him anymore because now he's here.

Ping, I hear then. Ping. And I turn to watch the movement of lines across Mom's EKG, the spikes and dips of her heartbeat.

"Dad," I breathe, my voice gravelly and hoarse. My heart throbs. Because after chasing him for all those days and nights, after spending my entire life trying to find him, he's here.

He's been here all along, waiting for me to wake up.

Except that as the man turns to me, I see that he's different. His face is not the face from my dreams. There's no facial hair anywhere, and his eyes are a grayish-green like sage. They're not brown. His hair is streaked with gray and there are lines across his face, forehead lines mostly, deeply set. His arms are blotched with pale pink scars.

It dawns on me then, slowly. Of course he's different from the man in my dream. Because in real life I never saw his face. I only caught a glimpse of the back of him when I was a girl, before Mom snatched the photograph from my hand.

Before we read a book, before we ate ice cream. Now I remember. I never saw that photograph again until it returned to me in a dream.

There's a book on his lap.

He leans forward, gathering Mom's hands into his. Hers are limp. He strokes her cheek, and I see in his eyes the look that he has for her. A look of adoration, a look of love. It makes me feel embarrassed, watching them. This moment of intimacy. It's not for me to see.

In all my life, no one has ever looked at me that way. I doubt anyone ever will.

His smile is deferential, kind. "No, Jessie," he says as he lets go of Mom's hands and turns back to me. "I'm not your father," he tells me, and at first I'm speechless because if not my father, then who? My eyes well with tears—wanting, *needing* him to be my father—as I sputter, "There was a photograph Mom had of you. I remember seeing it a long time ago. She took it away, she hid it, but it stayed with me. It was a picture of my father. It was *you*. You have to be him," I say, and he leaves her side to come to me.

He sits down beside me on the bed, a gap spread between us. He pats my hand, tells me his name is Aaron. "I knew your mother a long time ago," he explains. "We were married. She was my wife," but then he pauses, his own eyes red, and gathers himself. He won't cry in front of me. "I don't have any children, Jessie," he says, as if that should make it clear, but it only makes me more confused. More angry and more confused. Because how could he be Mom's husband but not my father? Didn't he want me?

My tone is more scathing, more exasperated than I mean for it to be. "Then why are you here?" I ask, and I see the anguish in his eyes, the grief. I pull my hand from his, seeing then that he doesn't have a wedding band. He's not married and I wonder if, after he and Mom were married, he ever was. He divorced Mom, he left her, I think, and there's a groundless anger that swells up inside me.

This man hurt Mom.

"I loved your mother very much," he says, as if he can read my mind. But then he rethinks and alters it a bit. "I *love* your mother very much," he says, before holding up the book from his lap. "Eden," he tells me, "your mother, she sent this to me," and I look at it, a brown leather book with a stitched edge, and in his other hand a note, written in Mom's handwriting on a piece of stationery. Stationery with her own name engraved along the edge. "It's her journal," he explains, though in all my life, I never once knew Mom kept a journal.

He hands the note to me. I skim Mom's words. In them, she tells him she's dying. She says that she wants him to have this journal so that he can finally have closure, so he can finally understand.

The last line reads, *With love, Eden.*

"Understand what?" I ask. And there it is again, that exasperation.

But his tone is compassionate and warm, his eyes soft. He rubs at his forehead, confesses, "There were some loose ends, Jessie," he says. "Some unfinished business between your mother and me." He asks, "What did Eden tell you about your father?" and I shake my head and admit, "Nothing. She never told me a thing about him."

He passes the book to me, the journal. He says that he thinks I should read it, that it would help me understand.

"Everything she did," he tells me, voice cracking, "she did for you. You should know that."

And then he rises to his feet to leave, but not before first confessing, "I wanted to be a father, Jessie. I would have loved to be a father. I would have loved to be *your* father. But sometimes life doesn't go as planned."

I don't know what he means by that. But I grip the journal in my hand; I press it to my heart, knowing I'll soon understand.

He says that he'll give Mom and me a few minutes. And then he leaves the room.

My eyes turn to Mom's. They're unfocused and disoriented, the top lid puffed up. She sees me but doesn't see me all at the same time. I wave; she waves back. But not right away, as if there's a broadcast delay. Her lips are a length of string, pilled and thin. They're dry, chapped, some sort of gunk collecting around the edges, which no one bothers to wipe. Her skin is a washed-out shade of gray blotched with purple and blue. A lack of oxygen. Poor circulation flow.

And yet she's there. Sitting upright. Waving.

"You're alive," I breathe as I go to her one last time.

The nurse leads the way as we drift into the hall. I take one look over my shoulder as we go, saying to her quietly, in a whisper, "It's a miracle." Because I don't want Mom to know how close she came to dying. "She's better. She's all better. Just like that. Overnight, and she's better," I say, a smile as wide as the Grand Canyon on my face. And suddenly nothing else matters. All that matters is Mom. I clutch the nurse's hand, wanting to celebrate the moment, to savor it. Relief consumes me, seeing that Mom has her strength back, some of it anyway. That she can sit up, that she can swallow. I'm thinking of next steps already. We'll begin chemo again. Maybe there is some clinical trial that Mom can participate in, some new medicine we can give a try.

"Oh, Jessie," the nurse says as we watch a family pass by in the hallway, flowers and balloons tethered to their hands. Her face drops. It gets overpowered with empathy, and for a minute or two she's speechless. The only smile she has to offer is a comforting one. Not a happy one. Not a celebratory one like mine.

It's a sympathy smile.

"Jessie," she says as she ushers me to a nearby bench and we sit, just across the hall from Mom's room so we can still see inside. "Your mother," she says, hesitating. "She doesn't have much time left."

"But—" I argue, thinking of Mom, sitting there in the room in a chair. Mom, more energetic than I've seen for weeks. Mom, making what looks to me like a speedy recovery. There's a spark to her eye, just a dot of light that wasn't there the last time I looked, days ago when she last opened her eyes. She'd been comatose for days like that; she couldn't swallow, she couldn't eat. The doctor said it wouldn't be long. And now here she is. Clearly he was wrong. Through the doorway I see Mom reach a hand out to nurse Carrie, rub at her throat. She can't speak. But she's asking for more ice chips, for a drink. "Look at her. See for yourself. She looks *fine*."

"She looks better. But the cancer. The cancer is still there. This happens, Jessie. A death rally, we call it. She will relapse, honey, and likely soon. Maybe hours, maybe days. There's no way to know for sure, but her body is still deteriorating. The cancer isn't cured. It's metastasized to the lungs, the bones. It's getting worse."

Which I know. Of course I know. I've heard this all before, many times. But looking at Mom now, it can't be true. It's like she's had this surge of brain power and awareness. Like she's come back from the dead.

And then I understand.

Terminal lucidity. As imminent a sign of death as any. The final blessing I'd been hoping for. Five more lucid moments with Mom. That's all I asked for. And here they are.

The nurse graciously turns off the machine as it flatlines. I wonder if she always does that, if her hand shoots there automatically the moment a patient dies so their beloved family members don't have to hear the damn thing scream. The ping from my dream has finally gone silent.

Mom's doctor presses the end of his stethoscope to her chest and we all look to him for guidance, for him to tell us she's dead, though we already know that she is. Her body lies peacefully on the bed, skin going white, blood draining from it. Already she's colder and more synthetic feeling than she was before. Her hands and toes unclench; her body goes lax. The doctor speaks. "Time of death," he says, "Two forty-two."

And with it comes great relief.

Mom's battle with cancer is done.

Mom's death rally lasted a total of three hours and fourteen minutes. For some of it she sat up with me in the chair, while Aaron watched from the corner of the room. He thought he should leave, that Mom and I should have this time together, but I asked him to stay. I did most of the talking. Mom could talk once she warmed up to it, but talking didn't come with ease.

I spent the time trying not to cry. But then, when I couldn't hold it in any longer, I sobbed, gulping down air and choking on it. Because there were things that needed to be said and I didn't have much time left. If I didn't say them, I'd regret it forever, for the rest of my life. "I don't know who I am without you," I confessed. "I'm no one without you." And though

I didn't say it aloud, I thought to myself that I'm vapor without Mom around. I'm nothing. A nonentity. A rock, a clock, a can of baked beans.

Mom stroked my hand as she did the day she told me she was dying. Caressed my fingers one at a time, and forced a smile that was as sad as mine.

"You're *you*," she said. "The one and only Jessie Sloane," as she stroked my arm with an anemic hand, the white flesh darkened here and there with bruise-like marks.

I squeezed into the same chair beside her, as if I was still a little girl. I don't know how we fit, but somehow we did. We sat like that for a while. As we did, one of my earliest memories returned to me, one of the few that hadn't been lost to time. In it, I'm about five years old. It's the middle of the night when Mom comes to me in my room. I'm sound asleep when she kneels on the floor beside my bed, whispering into an ear, *Jessie, honey. Wake up.*

And I do.

She helps me get dressed. Not fully dressed, but instead we slip a sweater over my nightgown, a pair of leggings beneath its hem. Socks and shoes. I follow her out the front door and into the blackness of night, asking at least a gazillion times where we're going, though all she ever says is *You'll see.* We walk hand and hand down the street.

There's a rare giddiness about Mom in that moment. A frivolity. She isn't restrained as she often is, but instead is playful and bright. We only walk as far as the home next door, but for me it seems an incredible adventure, some sort of magical, midnight escapade. We have to walk to the far side of the Hendersons' home where the gate is, cutting through their lawn as we go. Mom stands on tiptoes—her feet, I realize only then, are bare—to unlatch the gate, pushing it slowly open so it doesn't squeak.

Where are we going? I ask, and she says, *You'll see.*

We creep through the grass to a tree at the center of the backyard. A tall tree, sky-high, as high as my five-year-old eyes can see. Though it's too dark to see, I'm pretty sure the crown of the tree stretches clear into the clouds. There's a swing hanging there from one of the tree's branches, just a slab of wood with a thick rope that's looped through holes on each side. Mom tells me to hop on and at first I resist, thinking we can't possibly ride on the Hendersons' tree swing without asking. But Mom's face is radiant, her smile wide.

She sits down on the wood herself, pats the thighs of her pants. She tells me again to hop on, only this time she means on her lap. And I do.

I scramble awkwardly on, Mom hitching an arm around my stomach to help hoist me up. I sit on her lap, leaning back and into her as she gets set to launch us from the ground. Mom holds onto the rope with a single hand, the other folded around my belly. She walks backward as far as her bare feet can reach and then all at once, she lifts her feet from the earth and, just like that, we fly.

"Do you remember," I asked, snuggled there beside her on the hospital chair, "the time we broke into the Hendersons' backyard and snuck a ride on their tree swing?"

For as long as I live, I'll never forget the smile that bloomed on her face right then. She closed her eyes, reveling in the moment. The memory of the two of us nestled together on that tree swing. "It was the best night of my life," I said.

Shortly after the memory left, Mom got tired. The nurses and I helped her back to bed. Minutes later, Mom fell asleep.

She drifted back into some sort of minimally conscious state and passed away two hours later with me there at her side.

It's only after the funeral director comes to collect Mom's body that I finally rise from the chair. The room is remarkably quiet. No music playing, no familiar sound of the EKG.

The only sounds I hear now come from down the hall where other people lie dying.

Before he leaves, Aaron asks if I'll be all right and I tell him that I will. "I may not be your father," he says, "but it would mean the world to me if I could be your friend," and I tell him that I'd like that very much. He goes, and after he does, I see the nurse has already begun to strip the sheets from Mom's bed. Soon another patient will be here, another family surrounding them, watching as they die.

"Where are you going to go?" she asks, and I shrug and say stupidly, "Coffee," because nothing else comes to mind.

Beyond that, I have no idea where to go, what to do with my life.

But there's a part of me that thinks I can figure this out in time.

I try to reconstruct the dream. As I move down the bright, buzzing hospital halls, I try to piece it back together. But dreams have a way of fading fast, the mind a habit of deleting nonessential things. It's as if there's a fifty-piece puzzle before me and I'm missing all but five pieces. I've lost forty-five and only some of them connect. I remember only squirrels. Hot dogs. A hippopotamus. But I don't know what any of it means.

It's only as I cut through the hospital lobby, passing by the cafeteria, that I'm struck with the sudden sense that something is missing. Something that makes it harder to breathe. I come to a sudden stop and as I do, a body plows into me from behind, making my bag drop to the ground, contents spilling across the hospital floor. Mom's stuff—her lotion, her Chap-Stick, her journal—as well as mine. My driver's license, my credit card, dollar bills.

"My fault, my fault," I hear as I turn to see a man scramble to the ground to pick up my stuff. "I didn't see you. I wasn't looking where I was going," he admits as he rises to his feet and holds out the bag for me, my things shoved indelicately back in.

As he does I catch a look at his face for the very first time, and only then do I remember. I gasp. It's him. "Liam," I breathe, taking in that shaggy brown hair and the blue gum-ball eyes, knowing with certainty that he was there in my dream with me. There's the vaguest recollection of sitting on a sofa beside him, of his hand stroking my hair. It's a thought that makes me blush as I take a step closer to him. And though I don't know him, there's the greatest sense that I do. That we're already friends. "Liam," I say again.

But his face only clouds over in confusion. He shakes his head, stares vacantly at me like I'm mistaken. He looks tired. Stubble has all but taken over his face, and his hair stands on end. His bloodshot eyes are even bloodier than they were before, rivers of red running through the white. He shakes his head. "Jackson," he says. "Jack." And I find that I'm thrown completely off, feeling out of sorts because he's not Liam. Of course he's not Liam. Because Liam was only a dream. This man is a different man completely, though our late-night confessions over coffee were real. That was real, I remind myself, finding it suddenly impossible to remember what's real and what's not.

"I'm sorry," I stammer. "I thought," and I feel silly all of a sudden. "I should go," I say, taking the bag abruptly from his hands, excusing myself, trying to sidestep him and leave. But he doesn't let me leave. Instead he steps in front of me, reaches out his hand and says, "You never told me your name," and for a second there's the sense that he doesn't want me to leave. That he wants me to stay.

His handshake is warm and firm. He holds on a second longer than he needs to.

I reply, "Jessie," knowing for the first time in a long while that I am. I am Jessie Sloane.

"You're leaving, Jessie?" he asks, and I say, "No reason to stick around here any longer."

I don't have to tell him that Mom is dead, because he already knows. He can see it in my eyes. "Your brother?" I ask, thinking of the motorcycle accident. His brother flying head-first into a utility pole. "Is he going to be all right?" For a moment Jack—Jackson—is silent, but then he says, "Bit the dust last night," and my heart breaks for the both of us.

But there's also a sense of relief because, though we lost the war, the battle is finally through.

"Where are you going?" he asks, and I tell him I'm not sure. Anywhere. That I just have to get out of here, and he says he knows what I mean. His family waits upstairs in his brother's hospital room for the funeral home to arrive, to carry the body away. That's the last thing he needs to see. That's what he tells me. He shuffles from foot to foot, looking antsy and strung out, desperately in need of a good night's sleep.

I ask him if he wants to go for coffee, and together we leave.

That night, at home alone, I find the courage to open the journal. I caress its cover for a good fifteen minutes first, scared to death of what I might find inside. Maybe my father. Maybe not.

I sit on the sofa in Mom's and my home in Albany Park. Because for now it's not yet on the market, though I know that soon it will be. I carefully pull the cover back. A flattened leaf slips from its inside and onto my lap—red, with edges that fold up slightly at their edges—as does a photograph, which falls facedown on my thighs. There's a name etched on the back. *Aaron.* I know what the picture is before I ever look. The photograph I found as a child. The one Mom hid away in this journal so that I couldn't find it again.

My heart breaks at the familiar sight of Mom's handwriting.

My eyes wade through the pages, tears blurring my vision. Making it hard to take in the words. But I do anyway, curled into a ball on the sofa, beneath a blanket Mom and I once shared, listening to her favorite records over and over again on repeat.

Aaron showed me the house today, it reads. *I'm in love with it already—a cornflower blue cottage perched on a forty-five-foot cliff that overlooks the bay. Pine floors and whitewashed walls. A screened-in porch. A long wooden staircase that leads down to the dock at the water's edge where the Realtor promised majestic sunsets and fleets of sailboats floating by...*

EDEN

November 10, 1997
Egg Harbor

WHEN I AWOKE THIS morning there was the most unpleasant sense in my stomach, as if I'd swallowed some sort of gastric acid in the middle of the night and there it sat, lost somewhere between my throat and my intestines, not sure which way to go. Up or down. There was an awful taste in my mouth, as if I'd drunk a vat of vinegar before bed, and when I hurried for a glass of water to wash it down, I wound up hurling the water and everything else inside my stomach into the kitchen sink and then stood, clutching the countertop, tasting vomit, trying hard to catch my breath. There was saliva on my chin and tears in my eyes.

What did I eat last night?

Whatever it was, it wasn't much. I haven't eaten much for weeks, having subjected myself to a life of seclusion since my brush with that bartender in the back seat of my car. I haven't left the house other than for the bare necessities, for fear of running into him on the street. My home is my prison. I've been too ashamed to go outside.

Ashamed for a whole slew of reasons, my promiscuity only being one of them.

Overnight I had gone from being a respectable human being to a voyeur, a kidnapper, a misfit, a freak. The morning after my encounter with that bartender, I came home to find bruises on my neck from where he sucked my skin raw so that I couldn't leave the house until they healed, my skin returning to its usual shade of peach. Day and night I stared at those bruises, hating myself. What kind of person was I? What kind of person had I become?

I remembered the feeling of little Olivia's hand in mine.

Had that really happened, or was it only a dream?

Did I nearly steal another woman's child?

Two women's children?

The bartender had taken off with my purse too, snatched it right from the front seat while I lay in the back in a daze, leaving the car door unlatched, the interior lights on so that by morning the battery was completely drained. I walked the three miles home with a swollen ankle, clutching the plackets of my shirt together since the buttons had snapped clear off at his hasty hand. I spent the morning after on the telephone with various credit card companies, reporting the cards stolen, despising myself for getting into this situation in the first place, for letting myself be a floozy and a victim. I avowed to pay off my debt and cut the new cards the credit card company would no doubt send me to shreds.

I would never be a victim again.

I'd never trust anyone again.

I would never leave the house for fear I might try and pilfer someone else's child.

And so I've become a recluse, plunged into a state of depression where I go unshowered for days at a time, oftentimes not getting out of bed from morning until night. I eat only when I need to, when the hunger pangs are more than I can bear. I've lost my job, no doubt, though no one told me as much, but one can't expect to stay employed when they haven't gone to work for thirty-odd days. I'm drowning in debt, I assume, though I haven't found the energy to drag myself to the mailbox to retrieve the bills, but I'm certain I must be because just last night when I flipped a light switch on, nothing happened. I jiggled the toggle up and down and when that failed, tried another light switch.

It appeared the electricity had been shut off for nonpayment.

I went back to bed in the dark, planning to stay there for the rest of my life, which would be short as I swore off water and food too.

But then this morning the nausea wrenched me from bed, dragging me to the kitchen sink, where again and again I heaved, wondering what in the world was wrong with me.

And it was a slow dawning then, daylight arriving at its own sweet time, one shaft of light at a time.

For thirty-odd days I had lain in bed since my encounter in the back seat of the car, and in those thirty-odd days, my period—my ever-reliable period—hadn't come.

And now there was the nausea, the vomiting, and though every rational thought in my mind told me it wasn't true, it couldn't be true—after all, I was infertile; there was no way I could get pregnant of my own accord, without Dr. Landry's menagerie of drugs and devices—I knew instinctively that it was true.

I was pregnant.

To say I was happy would be a lie.

It wasn't that I didn't savor the thought for a second or two, that I didn't relish the idea of carrying a child, of birthing a child, of being a mother. There was no greater desire in the whole entire world for me. It's all I wanted; it's the only thing that mattered in my life.

But deep inside I knew this child would never come to fruition. A fetus it was, but a baby it would never be. It would be as it was the last time with the heartbeat that was there and then not there, the gallons of blood. I would lose this baby as I had the last, and it would be my purgatory, my punishment, being forced to endure weeks, maybe a month, of pregnancy, knowing as always that it would end with blood.

That trusty, reliable blood.

And so instead of being happy I stood there, back to the countertop, steeling myself for another miscarriage, to lose this baby like I had the last. Certainly the universe wouldn't let me keep this child. This, truly, was my penance, a gift that was given only to be taken away.

January 15, 1998
Egg Harbor

The joke is on me it seems, for I've made it through the first trimester without a single drop of blood.

The baby has survived thirteen weeks in my wasteland of a womb.

Only by necessity have I left the house, taking a job at a local inn where I clean rooms once the guests leave. There's nothing glamorous about it. Just stripping beds of sheets and washing endless mountains of laundry, scrubbing someone else's excrement off a toilet seat. The perk of the job, however, is that I essentially speak to no one, working alone in an uninhabited guest room or the laundry room, dealing only with dust spores and mildew, as opposed to the human race.

But the work itself is backbreaking. And those first thirteen weeks of the pregnancy were anything but fun and fancy-free. The morning sickness, the lethargy nearly got the best of me until the empty hotels beds were hard to resist—I envisioned myself sprawled out across them, wrapped up in one of the hotel's velour robes—but, for as much as I wanted to, I didn't give in to the whim.

Only second to a baby, I needed this job more than anything.

I haven't been to see Dr. Landry or another obstetrician, though there's a slight outgrowth to my midsection now, a bulge that makes my pants fit tightly so that I've taken to wearing sweatpants when I'm not stuffed into the uniform I wear for work, the polo shirt and the khaki pants, which I now leave unbuttoned so I don't flatten the baby.

The cottage is on the market again.

I can no longer afford to pay for it. I haven't been able to for months so that I'm in debt to the bank and the foreclosure threats have begun to arrive. The sign went in today, stuck there—forced into the nearly frozen ground—by the very same Realtor who sold us the home.

Oh, what she must think, looking at me now. How I've changed.

The Realtor didn't look the least bit different to me, but I was changed, hardly the same woman I was when we first met, less than two years ago.

After she left, I sat myself on the tree swing and swayed, moving back and forth through the nippy winter air. I did it until my fingers were numb and I could no longer feel the sturdy rope beneath my hands.

This was the closest my child would ever come to a ride on this swing.

The bay was empty now, not a boat anywhere, and snow

flurries fell on the dock, collecting like powdered sugar. There were birds in the trees, winter birds, cardinals and chicka-dees, but everyone else was gone, sunning themselves on one of those tropical islands where I only dreamed I might one day go.

The greenhouse door was frozen shut.

The flowers in the flower bed were dead.

I was still outside when I heard the doorbell ring, and thinking it was the Realtor—that she had an offer *already!*—I left my post to see.

But it was not the Realtor.

Aaron stood before me, his chestnut hair getting peppered with soft powdery snow. His eyes had a forlorn look about them, sad. He wore a coat, his hands set in the pockets of it, and as I pulled the door to, he offered a simple smile.

"Aaron," I said.

"Eden."

I couldn't bring myself to invite him inside, for the cottage was truly a mess, in a state of bedlam; I couldn't bring myself to show him what had become of our home. And so I stepped outside, onto the porch, my hair also getting peppered with snow. I pulled the door closed behind me. My feet were bare, covered only in socks, and against the concrete, they grew cold. Aaron, ever-obliging Aaron, ever-unselfish Aaron, ever-benevolent Aaron, shimmied at once out of his coat and wrapped it around my shoulders, saying to me, "You'll catch your death out here," and beneath the weight of his hands—which lingered there on my shoulders, gently liberating strands of hair that were trapped under the heavy coat, warm hands tucking them behind my ear, pausing there—I softened like a stick of butter left on the table too long.

We said nothing.

But I could see in his eyes that I had been wrong. That Aaron wasn't healed as I'd believed him to be the day I saw him through the chophouse windows. That he was only taped back together that day, a skimpy job at best, for the tape had come undone, it had lost its stick, and Aaron was once again broken, standing before me now, mere fragments of himself.

Oh, what have I done?

He hunched to my height, bending his knees ever so. He cupped his hands around my face—softly, delicately—as if those hands cradled an heirloom crystal vase, and I could see in Aaron's eyes that what he held was, to him, something fragile, something magical, something irreplaceable and beyond compare.

That, to him, I was irreplaceable and beyond compare as I'd always been.

That, in all these months apart, that hadn't changed for him.

His lips felt warm as he pressed them to mine, and there was nothing rushed about it, nothing presumptuous or brusque. "I want you back," he whispered into my ear.

"I need you back.

"I miss you, Eden.

"I am nothing," he said, "without you."

I am nothing.

Was it just my imagination, or did the baby inside me kick?

I stepped back from Aaron, tugging on the ends of my sweater to make sure that tiny bulge was concealed. Inside me the baby—not Aaron's baby, but the baby of some man I would never know—knew how to squint its eyes and to suck its thumb. Each day it grew bigger, arms and legs lengthening, organs and cells unfolding in my womb. It would come to be a person one day, a person perhaps with cavernous dimples and sparkling blue eyes, but never would I resent this child for the choices that I made.

Be careful what you wish for, the saying goes, but never would I harbor a grudge for all that I lost to have this baby. All that I will lose.

It might just come true.

I would have done anything for a baby. This I know without a shred of doubt.

The lump in my throat was nearly impossible to speak past. Something inside my larynx had swollen to two times its size and my eyes burned with tears. As they began to fall, Aaron wiped them from my cheeks with the pad of a thumb and again pressed his lips to mine, saying that everything was okay, that everything would be fine. He held me close, stroking my hair, pressing my hands between his to keep them warm.

"Can I come home?" he asked.

And I thought what it would do to him if I told him about the baby.

It would take those broken pieces of Aaron that remained and sliver them completely. It would pulverize them so that all that was left of Aaron would be ashes and dust.

"Yes," I said, feigning a smile, forcing the word past that knot. "Yes."

Aaron's knees nearly collapsed from the relief of it. He kissed me again, this time with passion and zest, then reached his hand toward the doorknob to let us both inside.

But I stopped him.

"Not yet," I said. "The house is a mess," I said. "Complete bedlam. Let me clean it first," I told him, and though Aaron tried to shoo it off, to tell me it didn't matter, that we'd clean it together, I said no.

That I wanted it to be just right.

That I wanted it to be perfect for him.

That *I* wanted to be perfect for him.

And at this he relented, and an agreement was made.

The following morning he would return with all of his belongings, and we'd start over with a clean slate. We'd be Aaron and Eden again. Just us. Just Aaron and Eden.

He kissed me goodbye—lips lingering on mine for what only I knew would be the last time—and then he was gone, his car pulling out backward down the long, winding drive, disappearing through dark tree bark. The leaves of the trees were gone, as soon I would be.

Life is full of regrets and this is only one of them.

It didn't take long to pack a bag.

By the time it was dark outside, I was heading south, south of Sturgeon Bay, south of Sheboygan, south of Milwaukee. Soon I would be living far away from here. My baby and me.

Dear Aaron,

I had a dream last night. In it, I was being chased. I ran in slapdash circles all night long, sweating and panicked as people tend to do in dreams, and for the longest time I couldn't see the angry face of the man who was chasing me. It wasn't until later, when I finally awoke, delirious and frightened, that I realized it was you, which puzzled me a great deal because after all of the grief and the heartbreak I've put you through, you have never been anything but selfless toward me. Compassionate and kind.

You, of all people, would never hurt me.

I remembered the way it is with dreams sometimes, how they have a habit of being less literal and more metaphoric, and I thought that sometimes with dreams like this, it's not about who's chasing you, but what you're running from.

I've spent the last twenty years running from the past, Aaron, from all the horrible things I put you through. And now I'm dying of cancer. I'm going to die. But I can't stand the idea of leaving this world without explaining things to you first so that you'll understand. It's only right that you have the closure you deserve. Every single day for the past twenty years I thought about calling you, asking you to meet. But I knew I'd never be able to verbalize all that I was feeling, that I could never put it into intelligible words, nor could I bear the thought of looking you in the eye and admitting what I'd done. And so for now, my journal will have to suffice.

I have a child, Aaron, a daughter, named Jessie, who means everything to me—and more. A mistake is what some might call it, but to me, she's perfection. Jessie has spent her entire life searching for her father. It should have been you.

With love,
Eden

★ ★ ★ ★ ★

acknowledgments

First and foremost, thank you to my smart, savvy and thoughtful editor, Erika Imranyi, for always having faith in me and my books, and for helping take my rough drafts and transform them into something that shines. I'm so proud of the work we do together and know with confidence that my novels are far better after you've left your mark on them.

Thank you to my wonderful and always encouraging friend and literary agent, Rachael Dillon Fried, for having my back, for knowing just what to say when I'm in need of reassurance and for always seeing the positive in everything I do.

Thank you to everyone at Sanford Greenburger Associates, Harper Collins and Park Row Books, including my publicity team of Emer Flounders and Shara Alexander; Reka Rubin for sharing my novels with the world; Erin Craig and Sean Kapitain for another gorgeous cover design; the copy editors, proofreaders, sales and marketing teams, and all those who play a role in getting my story into the hands of readers. I couldn't do what I do without any of you. I'm forever grateful for your diligence, enthusiasm and support.

To my wonderful friends who do not (I promise!) provide the inspiration for my less savory characters, but always supply an abundance of encouragement throughout the process, thank you! To the booksellers, librarians, book bloggers and the media who read and recommend my novels to your customers, patrons and fans, you are amazing! And to my readers worldwide, you're the reason I keep writing.

Lastly, thank you to my parents, Lee and Ellen; my sisters, Michelle and Sara; the entire Kubica, Kyrychenko, Shemanek and Kahlenberg families; to my husband, Pete, and our children, Addison and Aidan; and to Holly, who kept me company while I wrote—there will always be a spot for you by my side.

Read on for a special excerpt from Local Woman Missing, *Mary Kubica's newest riveting thriller that shows how some people will stop at nothing to keep the truth buried.*

PROLOGUE

11 YEARS BEFORE

THERE'S A SMUDGE OF lipstick on the collar of his shirt. She sees it. She says nothing about it. Instead, she stands there, bobbing the crying baby up and down like the needle of a sewing machine piercing fabric. She listens to his lame lies, his same, dispassionate *Sorry I'm late, but*s he reels off almost every night. He must have an arsenal of them amassed, and he uses them in rotation: a bottleneck on the expressway, a coworker with car trouble, getting stuck on the phone with some apoplectic policyholder whose house fire wasn't covered because of insufficient documentation of the damage. The more specific he is, the more sure she is of his betrayal. Still, she says nothing. If she presses him on it, he gets mad. He turns it around on her. *Are you calling me a liar?* For this reason, she lets it go. And also because it would be a double standard for her to make a big deal of the lipstick.

"It's fine," she says, taking her eyes off the lipstick.

They eat dinner together. They watch some TV.

Later that night, she puts the baby to bed, feeding her at the last minute so that she won't wake hungry while she's gone.

She tells him she's going for a run. "Now?" he asks. It's after ten o'clock when she steps from the bedroom in running clothes and shoes.

"Why not?" she asks.

He stares at her too long, his expression unclear. "When people do dumb shit like this, they always wind up dead."

She's not sure what to make of his words, whether he means running alone late at night or cheating on one's husband. She convinces herself it's the first one.

She swallows. Her saliva is thick. She's been anticipating this all day. Her mind is made up. "When else do you expect me to go?"

All day long, she's home alone with their baby. She has no time to herself.

He shrugs. "Suit yourself." He rises from the sofa and stretches. He's going to bed.

She goes out the front door, leaving it unlocked so she doesn't have to carry keys. She runs only the first block so that if he's watching out the bedroom window, he sees.

At the corner, she stops and sends a text: On my way.

The reply: See you there.

She deletes the conversation from her phone. Is she as transparent as her husband? Is what she's doing as obvious as the lipstick on his shirt? She doesn't think so. Her husband is hotblooded. If he had any idea she was sneaking out to hook up with some guy in his parked car on 4th Avenue, where the street dead-ends a hundred feet from the last house, he'd have beaten her to within an inch of her life by now.

She walks along the street. The night is quiet. It's the only time of day she looks forward to, lost in the anticipation of some guy she hardly knows indulging her for a while, making her feel good.

He isn't the first man she's cheated on her husband with. He won't be the last.

After the baby was born, she tried to quit, to be faithful, but it wasn't worth the effort.

This guy says his name is Sam. She's not sure she believes it. She's been seeing him off and on for months, whenever he or she gets the urge. She met him when she was pregnant of all things. To some guys, it's a turn-on. He made her feel sexy, despite the extra weight, which is far more than she could say for her husband.

Like her, Sam is married. And he isn't the only guy she's been seeing on the side.

The few times they've been together, "Sam" takes his ring off and leaves it on the dashboard, as if that somehow mitigates what he's doing. She doesn't do the same. She isn't one for feeling guilty. She's made herself believe that it's her husband's fault she does what she does. Turnabout is fair play.

The sky is full of stars. She stares at them awhile, finding Venus. The night is cold and her arms are covered with goose bumps. She's thinking about his car, how warm it will be once she gets inside it.

She's looking up at the stars when she hears something coming at her from behind. She spins around, eyes searching the street but coming up empty in the darkness. She chalks it up to some wild animal rummaging through trash, but she doesn't know. She turns back, goes back to walking, picking up her pace. She's not one to get scared, but she starts thinking of what-ifs. What if her husband is on to her, what if he is following her, what if he *knows*?

She tells herself he doesn't know. He couldn't know. She's a very good liar; she's learned how to silence her tells.

But what if the wife knows?

She isn't sure what "Sam" tells his wife when he leaves. They don't talk about things like that. They don't talk much at all except for a few preliminary words to kick things off.

Don't you look pretty.

I've been waiting for this all day.

They're not in love. No one is leaving their spouse anytime soon. It's nothing like that. For her, it's a form of escapism, release, revenge.

Another noise comes. She turns and looks again—truly scared this time—but finds nothing. She's jittery. She can't shake the feeling of eyes on her.

She starts to jog, but soon trips over an untied shoe. She's uncoordinated and nervous, wanting to be in the car with him, and not alone on the street. The street is dark, far too dark for her liking.

She senses movement out of the corner of her eye. Is something there? Is *someone* there? She asks, "Who's there?"

The night is quiet. No one speaks.

She tries to distract herself with thoughts of him, of his warm, gentle hands on her.

She bends over to tie the shoe. Another noise comes from behind. This time when she looks, car lights surface on the horizon, going way too fast. There's no time to hide.

Copyright © 2021 by Mary Kubica

Don't miss the other riveting thrillers by *New York Times* bestselling author

MARY KUBICA

  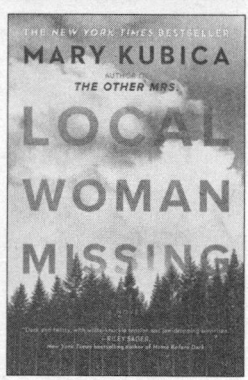

Available now.

Connect with us at:

BookClubbish.com/Newsletter

Instagram.com/BookClubbish

Twitter.com/BookClubbish

Facebook.com/BookClubbish

PARK
ROW
BOOKS

ParkRowBooks.com
BookClubbish.com

PRMK0775TR